Memories of a Ghost

by

Joe DeRouen

Small Things Press

Visit Joe's website at www.JoeDeRouen.com

First Printing: May 2015

ISBN 978-0-692-38886-0

Cover by Renée Barratt, TheCoverCounts.com

Author photo by Sunny Skaggs, SunnySkaggsPhotography.com

FIRST EDITION

Printed in the USA

✳ ✳ ✳

Small Things Press | www.SmallThingsPress.com

For my sister Rebecca Jones, and her husband Jeff

Acknowledgements

I'd like to thank everyone who contributed to helping make this novel happen, including Andee and Fletcher DeRouen, Cheri Romero DeRouen, Michelle Salrin Merritt, Rebecca Jones, Mackenize Reedybacon, Burgundy Wisrock, all the folks in my Small Things Street Team, everyone involved in NaNoWriMo, my writing friends in Book Review Depot and Author's Cave, my Facebook friends, Jonathan Carroll, Tim Powers, James P. Blaylock, and Richard Matheson.

Special thanks also go to Lisa Lauenberg, Tasha Derouen, my editor Robin Raven, my cover artist Renée Barratt, my photographer Sunny Skaggs, and my beta readers, Bruce Diamond, Zeecé Lugo, and Colin "The Barbarian" Rutherford.

Memories of a Ghost

Chapter 1

"Claire, I said your baby's going to be okay," echoed a far off voice, but she could barely comprehend the words. "I found the heartbeat. You were lucky this time. Your baby's fine." She shook her head, still not understanding.

Her eyes hurt, burned like they were wrapped in sandpaper. She blinked against the light, shading her eyes with her hand, focusing on an angelic face surrounded by beautiful blonde curls that stared back at her. The face slowly swam into focus, but she saw only confusion in the deep green eyes that bore into her own.

"Claire," said a voice, but the lips of the woman in front of her didn't move, "I know you don't want to listen to me, but we've known each other for over half our lives, and I think I've earned the right to speak my mind. And besides that, I'm your doctor, and it's my *job* to make sure you have a happy, healthy baby, and that's not going to happen unless you take care of yourself. Okay?"

Where was the voice coming from? She blinked, wrinkling her nose, comprehension slowly dawning as the woman in front of her did the same things she was doing. She was staring into a mirror, on the wall across from her. Turning away from her own reflection, the world came at her in a rush.

She found herself in what looked like a hospital room, stark, sterile, and white, smelling of antiseptics. She was lying propped up against a pillow, her shirt hiked up around her stomach. The mirror she'd been staring into hung from a wall covered in diplomas and certificates, and she was surrounded by computer monitors and various pieces of machinery. Her stomach felt funny, and a quick glance down the length of her body found a hand holding an electronic probe pressed tight against her belly.

The hand, she saw, sported neatly manicured nails and connected to an arm poking out of a long white sleeve. Her eyes followed the arm up to a torso, and the torso spread out to the body of curvy brunette with soft brown eyes and a smile that could light up a room. The woman wore a lab coat and carried a stethoscope around her neck, and the badge over her pocket identified her as Dr. Greenwald.

"Claire," said the woman, moving the probe away from her stomach, "talk to me."

Claire. That was the third time the woman had called her that. That wasn't her name, was it? She suddenly realized that she didn't know what her name was. In fact, she didn't know anything.

Her heart beat staccato against her ribs. "Dr. Greenwald..." she managed to stutter, her mouth struggling to form words, "I don't know who..."

The woman cut her off. "What's with this *Dr. Greenwald* crap?" she shouted, a wave of hurt flickering over her face. "Claire, I'm trying to help you. He's going to kill you, or your baby. And then how would you feel, knowing you could have done something to prevent it? How would I feel, knowing my best friend in the whole world...that she...that I..." She hiccuped into her hand, falling silent.

She started to respond, but whatever she might have said was drowned out by the shrill whine of a police siren. Her head pounded in beat to the noise, and white spots danced before her eyes. Without thinking, she pulled her shirt down over the sticky gelatinous substance that covered her stomach, swung her legs over the side of the table, and stumbled to her feet.

The office swam in her vision, and her knees buckled. She lurched backward into the table, nearly losing her footing. Her legs felt like lead weights, and she had to concentrate to put one foot in front of another. She kicked off her shoes—strappy, black high-heeled things—and managed to gain her balance.

"What are you doing?" Greenwald asked, alarm in her voice. She grabbed Claire's arm. "You can't just leave."

But she had to. She had to get out of there. The siren, closer now, mixed with another, and then one more, until all three pierced through her skull like hot needles. It was almost deafening, and it was all she could do not to scream. She pulled hard against the doctor, but Greenwald wouldn't let go. With a strength that surprised her, she pushed the woman away. Her arms wind-milled through the air and she stumbled backward, tripping over her own feet to land flat on her back across the linoleum-tiled floor.

She scrabbled to her feet, bolting from the office. Darting past an elderly nurse and through two double-doors, she burst into a room containing half a dozen women in various states of pregnancy. They all turned as one from the television mounted on the wall, ignoring Dr. Phil to stare at her. Their eyes were mirrors to a soul she wasn't even certain she possessed.

A hand wrapped around her wrist and she spun to meet her attacker, instinctively bringing a knee up into his stomach. It was someone else in a lab coat—a blond man no older than forty—and he doubled over in pain, falling motionless to the floor as she brought both her fists down into the back of his neck.

Dr. Greenwald stood in the doorway, her face a mix of fear and confusion. "My God, Claire," she said, her hand flying to her mouth. She held a red leather purse in her other hand, clutching it protectively against her chest. "What did you do?"

She stared down at the man lying unconscious at her feet. She had no idea. And then the sirens stopped. Just like that, the sirens stopped, and all was quiet again. The world around her seemed to calm, to stabilize, if only for a moment.

She knew she couldn't stay here, knew that if she did, she'd have to admit that she wasn't this Claire person, and, inexplicably, that thought terrified her. She didn't feel like a Claire, or anything else for that matter. She felt nothing but fear.

Greenwald slowly moved toward her, like a timid mouse approaching a sleeping lion. She reached out a careful hand while two nurses moved behind her, kneeling to tend to their fallen colleague.

"Claire," said the doctor, "I just want to help. Let's go back to my office and talk."

And then there were strong arms encircling her from behind, pinning her hands to her sides. She felt a sharp surge of adrenaline flood her system. Before she even knew what she was doing, she was moving. She stomped down hard with the heel of her foot, crunching unsuspecting toes beneath. Her attacker howled in pain and let go.

Her arms free, she spun on her assailant, a towering, beefy man clad in a blue smock. She drove her hand into his nose, feeling it snap beneath her strike. Blood exploded from his face as she swept his legs out from under him, watching in fascination as he flopped like a dead fish to the floor.

Greenwald was moving toward her, but she was already pushing out through the glass doors that marked the exit to the building. From the outside, she could see that it was a free-standing clinic of some sort, surrounded by offices of various shapes and sizes on all sides. There was another doctor's office next to it and, down the road, a grocery store and some other small businesses. Perhaps half a dozen houses stood across the intersecting street, hidden behind a grove of silver maple trees. She took all of this in, trying to get her bearings.

Spinning from the building into the cool, crisp morning air, she sprinted past a startled couple getting out of a tiny blue minivan, past a dentist's office and a Salvation Army building, and out onto the street, the rough pavement stinging her stocking feet. And then she saw the source of the sirens that had so alarmed her earlier.

Three police cars, an ambulance, and a fire truck blocked access on both sides of the four-lane road, surrounded by onlookers gaping at the collision that had apparently happened just minutes earlier.

A pink-haired, teenage girl sat crying on the curb, a fireplug of a policeman hovering nervously nearby, taking her statement. Less than ten yards away stood the object of the girl's distress. A white Ford Taurus sat askew across two lanes of traffic. Its grill and hood were covered in bright red blood, like a paint job only half-finished and still sticky wet. Bits of hair and shattered bone flecked the tires and the pavement, creating a grisly mosaic of colors.

"It was a silver sports car, one of those expensive ones. A BMW or a Jaguar or something," the girl said, wiping her eyes. "It pulled out in front of me and hit him and just kept going. I didn't know! I ran right over his b-b-body."

A trio of paramedics huddled around something just a few feet in front of the vehicle. Forgetting her panic, fascinated by the scene unfolding before her, Claire sidled past the onlookers. A man lay sprawled across the road, his eyes rolled back in what was left of his head. He was covered in welts and bruises from past traumas. Bits and pieces of him were missing, spread out across the road for all to see.

Mesmerized, she began pushing through the crowd. As she approached, one of the paramedics rose from the ground, calling something to the fireplug cop across the street. The other paramedics followed the first EMT's lead, and together they removed a large, black tarp from the ambulance and methodically unfolded it over the dead man.

A blond-haired man in a red rugby shirt and tan slacks pushed through the crowd, flashing a badge as one of the policemen tried to challenge him. He knelt beside the paramedics, exchanged a few words, then excused himself and walked over to the fireplug cop and the teenager.

Claire slowly disengaged herself from the crowd and walked to the side of the street. Thirteenth Street, the sign said, just past the corner at Persimmon, where she'd come from.

She watched a tall, pale man dressed in a dark suit accompanied by a smaller man in an apron slip through a pair of giant oaks on the other side of the street. They resembled a caricature of the magicians Penn and Teller, if Penn were a little taller and broader, and Teller even shorter. They whispered back and forth, casting sidelong glances at the tarp-covered body lying in the middle of the street, but their words stopped and their expressions changed the moment their eyes connected with hers.

It felt as if someone had walked over her grave. Panicking, she pushed past a pair of Goth girls and a red-haired boy, sprinting away from the scene, brown and red leaves crunching beneath her feet. A dozen yards later, she turned away from Thirteenth and veered down a side street, disappearing through a copse of trees.

Chapter 2

Out of sight of the two strange men, she still couldn't stop running. Her agitation turned to blind panic as she ripped past a weeping willow into someone's front yard, then took off down the sidewalk in a mad dash to find cover.

Narrowly avoiding a huge, green Suburban as it backed out of its driveway, she walked straight through a rose bush, ignoring the painful stabs of thorns ripping and tearing at her legs, and ran blindly into suburbia. She ran past dogs, fences, even a startled mailman, not stopping until she could no longer catch her breath, until exhaustion brought her to her knees in a spasm of tremors and vomiting.

Brushing her fingers through her hair, trying to rid herself of the sweat cascading down her face, she took stock of her surroundings; there were two sets of slides, a jungle gym, five wooden benches, and a long row of canvas swings hanging from a freshly-painted metal frame. She was in a park and, judging by the color of the leaves, it must be early fall.

The sweet smell of gardenias and honeysuckle filled her nose, and she suddenly realized how thirsty she was. Searching the landscape, she spied a water fountain across from the swings, standing next to a dilapidated set of restrooms and a dying oak tree.

Forcing herself to trudge across the grass, she almost collapsed as the ice cold water spurted from the fountain into her grateful mouth. Taking gulp after greedy gulp into her stomach, she drank until she could drink no more, and then promptly threw everything up. She dropped to her knees, retching. Tears clouding her vision, she watched as whatever she'd had for lunch pooled in the grass before her.

Struggling to her feet, she pushed through the door to the men's bathroom and stumbled to one of the sinks. Splashing her face with cold water, she tried to calm her pounding heart. Backing away from the sink, her eyes found the huge, tarnished mirror that took up most of the wall, and a stranger stared back at her.

Her short, blonde hair formed curls on either side of her head to frame her face, setting off her emerald green eyes. She had high cheek-bones, and would probably have been considered attractive if not for the black eye and swollen lip. She wore a blue sweater with pink ruffles on the sleeves and a pair of too-tight blue jeans. Both were covered in vomit.

The doctor said she was pregnant. If that were true, she mustn't be too far along. Her stomach was flat, and she had the body of a runner. She stood maybe five foot six or seven, and probably didn't weigh more than one thirty, one thirty-five, tops. She had a hard time gauging her age, but she guessed late twenties to early thirties.

If only she had a name to go with the image.

Searching the pockets of her jeans for identification, she came up empty. And then she remembered the purse that Dr. Greenwald had been carrying. It must have been hers, and she'd left it behind. Stupid! She was without money, without an identity, and without any idea how to find out who in the hell she was.

Claire. She rolled the name around her tongue, tasted it, digested it, and it still didn't feel right, but she had to think of herself as some-thing. So Claire it was, at least until she came up with something better.

What was her last name? She was willing to think of herself as Claire, at least for now, but she needed something else to go with it. Claire Smith? Claire Jones? Claire Huxtable? How about the red-haired girl on that old HBO series *Six Feet Under*, Claire Fisher? Hey, at least she remembered watching television. That was something.

She wasn't sure how long she stood there, staring at herself in the mirror, but eventually she noticed a watch on her wrist. It was fifteen minutes until two. The timepiece sported a huge Mickey Mouse head and used his little gloved hands to tell the time. She slipped the watch from her wrist, flipped it over, and studied the back, hoping for an inscription. But that would have been too easy. It was completely blank save for some scratches in the metal where someone had used a screwdriver to pry the back off the battery compartment.

The act of fastening the watch back around her wrist brought the realization that she wore both an engagement and a wedding ring. The wedding ring, also without an inscription, was a simple, unornamented gold band, while the engagement ring sported a full-carat diamond with a princess cut setting. So she was married. If she could find out where she lived, maybe her husband could help her regain her memory.

She slipped out of the bathroom and took a few sips of water from the fountain, this time able to hold it down. Her stomach grumbled. She knew she'd need to eat soon but, without money, the chance of finding a meal seemed alarmingly slim.

A Family Dollar store, a car wash, and a Casey's General Store gas station lay perhaps a dozen yards away, on the other side of the road where the park met the pavement. Maybe she could steal a candy bar or some beef jerky there, or dig through the garbage for scraps. And then, once her appetite had been sated, go about solving the mystery of who she was and how she'd lost her memory.

"Excuse me," echoed a voice from behind her, "but could y'all help me? I seem to be lost, and I know my wife and kids must be awfully worried."

Claire spun around and came within a hair's breadth of driving her fingers into the man's throat. There had been no one there seconds earlier, she was sure of it. But he seemed harmless. Maybe he'd been behind the tree, or she just hadn't noticed him.

His skin, a dark shade of mocha, looked almost like coffee with just the hint of cream. His jowly face quivered as he studied her in return, kind brown eyes searching her own. He stood maybe six feet tall, was pudgy around the edges, and, save for a few patches of graying hair and a huge, bushy moustache, was almost completely bald. Wearing a pair of yellow Bermuda shorts and a short-sleeved t-shirt that showed a MasterCard logo and exclaimed "The Master is in Charge," he was dressed completely at odds with the season, yet inexplicably didn't look the least bit cold. A pair of leather sandals completed the ensemble.

"Who are you?" she whispered, letting her hands fall to the side.

"You'll talk to me?" he asked, genuinely surprised. "It's been ages...I mean, they usually just ignore me. Treat me like a hobo or something worse. I miss my family."

"But who are you?" she repeated, watching his eyes.

"Yes, you're right. Where are my manners? James Cross, ma'am, but you can call me Jimmy. Just here from Chicago visiting my wife's kin, but I seem to have lost my way. And you are...?" He let the question hang there, waiting for her response.

She waited a heartbeat before answering. "I'm...Claire. Claire...Fisher," she added, taking the name of the character from the old HBO series. It would have to do for now.

"Pleased to meet you, Miz Fisher," he said, holding out his hand. When she started to take it, he stepped back and shoved both hands into his pockets. His eyes looked sad.

Taking the lead, she dropped down on one of the many benches littering the park and patted the green metal beside her, inviting him to join her. He surprised her by shaking his head slowly and taking a few more steps back.

"Not in much of a mood for sitting," he said, shrugging, "but you go ahead and take a load off, I don't mind."

She stared up at him, finally shrugging her shoulders in return. "So where's your wife and kids?"

"Wish I knew. It's funny. Last thing I remember, I was leaving the house to run an errand and then, wham, here I am. Been wandering around here for hours, but I can't seem to find no one to help me. Like I said, pretty much everyone has ignored me. I mean, everyone except for you."

They were interrupted by the appearance of an older woman, maybe in her early forties, jogging past them with her Great Dane. Seemingly just as oblivious to the cold as Jimmy, she was dressed in a tight pair of spandex running shorts and black jogging bra, and a blue water bottle hung from a loop around her waist. She paused for a moment to shake her head in their direction before continuing down the path, her eyes glued to the beaten earth before her.

"See what I mean?" Cross said slowly, his eyes following the jogger and her dog as they disappeared from view. "They just ignore me. Usually don't even look. Not my fault I'm lost, and not my fault I'm black."

That brought her thoughts back to the dead man in the street. Had she known him, or maybe even witnessed the accident? Maybe that would explain her amnesia, but it didn't make sense. Why would she walk into the Doctor's office after watching the man get run over and *then* suffer a mental breakdown a few minutes later? It didn't add up.

"Illinois hasn't always been friendly to the black man, I'll tell you that," he continued, working up a head of steam, "but Arkansas' a lot worse, and we've only been here for three days."

They were in Arkansas? She knew that the state capital of Arkansas was Little Rock. She also knew that Wal-Mart was headquartered in Bentonville, and that Bethel Transportation, a huge shipping business that specialized in imports and exports, operated out of Fayetteville, but, beyond that, her knowledge of the state seemed nonexistent.

She wished she hadn't been so quick to run away from the clinic. At least Dr. Greenwald knew her, could maybe even help her. If only she hadn't left her purse. Identification not-withstanding, she was hungry, and you couldn't get food without money.

"Miz Fisher, are you listening to me?" said Jimmy Cross, hovering over her. "You look a million miles away. I told you, I really need to find my family. Can't you find it in your heart to help me?"

He was practically in her face now. She didn't know this man, and didn't like him being so close. She moved to push him away, but he jumped back as if he'd been bitten by a snake.

"Look, Jimmy, I'll help you if I can, all right? But right now, I'm having some problems of my own. I'm starving, for one thing, and I'm lost, and I'm flat broke. So give me a break, okay?"

He cocked his head to one side, considering something. "I think…yeah, it's probably still there. Couldn't have gone anywhere, now that I think of it."

"What's probably still there?"

"Right over there," he pointed past her, to the base of a towering red maple tree. Its looming branches spread out toward the sky like fingers reaching for the sun. "About a yard to the right of that tree, maybe a foot or two down. An old mason jar filled with coins. Saw a couple of kids bury it there earlier today, maybe an hour or two ago. And right now, it seems like you need it more than they do."

How long had this guy been hanging around the park? She shook her head, and then dropped to her knees beside the great maple. Using her hands, she began to dig.

Chapter 3

Mr. Kingfisher stood at the top of the stairs leading down into the dark basement, assessing the damage. The radiator had been completely ripped from its foundation, and both the chair and the cellar door were in splinters, not to mention that poor Mr. Fuller lay in a pool of blood at the bottom of the steps. The radiator could be fixed, that was for certain, and the door and the chair could be replaced, but he wasn't sure what they could do about Mr. Fuller's neck.

They'd been together for years. He really would be sorry to see Fuller go, though he secretly suspected that they were probably better off without him. After all, it was on his watch that Connor West had escaped.

Mr. Fuller was only the fifth associate they had lost in all their years of playing the game, and he'd only been with them since the late eighties. All in all, they'd had a good run. They'd eventually find someone to take Mr. Fuller's place, just as Mr. Fuller had replaced Mr. Houseman before him, and Mr. Houseman had replaced Mr. Fulbright before that.

He walked down the stairs, long legs carefully stepping over Mr. Fuller's body. The damage was much worse up close. Mr. Fuller's nose had been broken, and a wild spray of blood stained the basement's cement walls and floor.

Kingfisher still wasn't sure how West had managed to get close enough to Mr. Fuller to break his nose, let alone his neck. They had grossly underestimated the man, and that mistake had cost them dearly.

West was dead and, with him, his secrets. He was, after all, the last of his line. But what was done could be undone.

Their employer, however, saw things differently. The man had been on the verge of hysteria before Kingfisher had managed to calm him down. In fact, come to think of it, things might end up being easier this way. Now that the mortal coil had been shed and was no longer a factor, they could use other, more convincing methods to extract the information that Mr. Lazarus so sorely desired.

Mr. Quarry crept down the stairs and into the light, nudging him from his reverie. He carried a toolbox in his left hand and traced the staircase banister with his right. The man was short and unassuming, and didn't talk much, but he was a fount of arcane knowledge. He definitely brought his share to this game they were playing.

"Mr. Quarry," he greeted, with a curt nod of his head. "Are we ready?"

"That we are, Mr. Kingfisher," Quarry answered. His eyes shifted to the body on the ground. "We've quite a mess, haven't we?"

"Indeed, but I have complete faith in your ability to set things right again."

"Indeed," echoed the smaller man, sitting the toolbox to one side and tightening his apron. "I'll certainly do my best."

Quarry dropped to his knees and began rifling through the toolbox. He withdrew a handful of black candles, a matchbook, a length of chalk, and a small bottle of salt. Mr. Kingfisher knew he didn't need a copy of the incantation; he'd long ago committed all of the words to memory.

Kingfisher watched as his partner rolled Mr. Fuller over onto his side, used the chalk to draw a pentagram on the floor, and then rolled the dead man on top of the pentagram. After making certain that the corpse's arms, legs, and head echoed the five points of the star, he surrounded the entire thing with a thick circle of salt. Finally, he adorned each of the star's five points with one of the candles, lighting each in turn, starting with the northern-most point and working left to right.

"There," Mr. Quarry said, clapping his hands against his apron in a small cloud of chalk dust. "The preparations are complete. Are you ready, Mr. Kingfisher?"

"No time like the present, Mr. Quarry," smiled Kingfisher, exposing a row of bright, white teeth which, he was proud to say, were still his own. "Point position?"

"Absolutely," Mr. Quarry returned the smile. His teeth, in contrast, were not so bright, but that only made sense with his diet. Still, Mr. Kingfisher would have to find a way to tactfully mention to the man that he might consider brushing and flossing more often. After all, they mustn't scare off the clientele.

Kingfisher watched as Mr. Quarry sat cross-legged at the northernmost point of the pentagram, next to the fallen Mr. Fuller's head. He seated himself at the south end, ready for his partner to begin the calling. Thoughts of what they had done mere hours earlier in this basement filled his head as Mr. Quarry chanted arcane phrases in Latin.

A hovering ball of light winked into existence, floating above the middle of the hastily-drawn pentagram, slowly spreading out to take on the visage of Mr. Fuller. The man looked confused and scared, his eyes the size of saucers. The ghost looked first at Mr. Quarry and then at Mr. Kingfisher before finally speaking.

"You can see me now, right? You can hear me?" he gestured helplessly at his bent and broken body lying before him. "I'm dead, and West's gone. Did you see what he did to me?"

"Obviously," Kingfisher smiled, clucking his tongue. "We hadn't thought you twisted your neck like that all by yourself."

The ghost winced and probably would have blanched had he been anything more than non-corporeal mist. But he wasn't, so instead he stuttered an apology and then reminded Mr. Kingfisher that he was, in fact, dead, and had probably suffered enough for his lapse in judgment in turning his back on their prisoner.

"That's all well and good," Mr. Kingfisher replied sternly, for he was never one to brook excuses, "but how did it happen in the first place? Did he have help?"

"I don't think so," admitted the ghost. "I went to change the radio, and the next thing I knew, he was behind me with that chain. And then I was here," he gestured with his arms, "and he was going through my pockets and unlocking the handcuffs. He broke through the cellar door, and that was the last I saw of him."

Mr. Kingfisher sat patiently through the dead man's explanation, growing ever most frustrated with their former colleague's ability to follow simple instructions. He had told the man time after time not to listen to the radio. It only served to offer Connor West a distraction and made their job all the more difficult.

"Look, I'm sorry, okay?" the phantom said, fear in his voice. "I know, you said no radio. I just got bored, that's all, with you two," he gestured at Mr. Quarry, who sat silently with his eyes closed at the point of the pentagram, "off God knows where, and..."

"As you should well know," Mr. Kingfisher interrupted, giving him a half-bow, "God has very little to do with it. You're certainly not going to heaven, after all, though I should also think you're not quite ready for hell either."

"What's going to happen to me?" the ghost whispered, his eyes flickering toward the top of the stairs. "I've tried to leave, but I'm stuck here. I can't get any further than the cellar door."

"Oh, don't worry. Soon enough, you'll leave this room."

"But how? Can you put me back inside my body?"

"Hardly," Kingfisher said. He rose to his feet and withdrew a paper-wrapped drinking straw from one of his pockets. He began to unwrap it. "You're dead. But you will be with us, Mr. Fuller."

"What's that supposed to mean?" the apparition pleaded, backing away. The heel of one foot brushed the line of salt and sparked, and a cry of pain spilled from his non-existent lips. "Hey, I can't get out of here. What are you doing?"

Mr. Kingfisher stepped forward, almost but not quite breaking the chalk outline. He crumpled the paper wrapper in his hand and dropped it to the cement floor, then slid the straw between his lips and began to suck.

"What are you doing?" the ghost repeated, as, quite against his will, he began to move toward the edge of the circle. He turned to Mr. Quarry. "For the love of God, what's he doing to me?"

Mr. Quarry remained silent, eyes still closed, though the hint of a smile played across his lips.

"I've already told you," Mr. Kingfisher said, between sucks, "that it really has nothing to do with God."

His appetite was raging now. He nodded in satisfaction as Mr. Quarry's eyes opened and he swept his hand over the chalk and through the salt, breaking both barriers in an instant. The ghost formerly known as Mr. Fuller screamed helplessly as he was sucked into the straw, swirling and swimming in a brief lightshow that would have put even the best Fourth of July fireworks celebration to shame. And then he was gone, Mr. Kingfisher's hunger sated. For now.

Letting the straw fall from his lips, he politely raised his hand to his mouth before allowing himself to burp. The spirit had been fresh, and it had been more than a week since his last meal. All he wanted to do now was lie down and let the food digest, but there was still work to do.

He watched as Mr. Quarry, now on his knees, withdrew a worn leather satchel from his toolbox. His partner opened the bag to reveal two rows of gleaming bright surgical instruments. He carefully removed a number three scalpel, measured Mr. Fuller's finger, made a clean slice, and popped it into his mouth.

Mr. Kingfisher had dined, and now it was time for his partner to do the same, but oh how Kingfisher hated the wet work. "Mr. Quarry, I think I'll leave you alone with your meal," he intoned, half-bowing as he walked toward the stairs, "that is, if you don't mind. I have other business to attend to."

"Absolutely, Mr. Kingfisher," said Mr. Quarry, his eyes rolling back in his head as he feasted.

Mr. Kingfisher turned without another word and headed up the stairs. The day was still young and there was much to do. Still, he thought, pulling a small stoppered vial containing the soul of a stillborn baby from his inner pocket, there's always time for a little dessert.

Chapter 4

Somewhere in southern rural Missouri, the ground rumbled. A 200-year old oak tree collapsed to the ground, sending crows and cardinals racing into the sky and squirrels and rabbits running for cover. Red foxes scurried deeper into the forest, and deer ran toward where the woods thinned out to meet the highway.

A passing semi-trailer hauling gasoline, whose driver was confounded by the sight of a dozen white-tailed bucks and does flooding into traffic, swerved to avoid hitting the deer, and instead slammed headlong into a minivan containing a vacationing couple with their two-year-old twin daughters, killing them instantly. The semi jack-knifed over the van and careened into the side of a hill, exploding in a rain of metal and gas.

Fueled by the gasoline, the fire spread quickly. The explosion instantly incinerated half of the trailers in the park on the north side of the road while simultaneously setting ablaze the trees leading into the woods to the south. A thick, black smoke rolled across the highway, covering everything in its path, choking out the few animals remaining in the wild and the trailer park refugees who sought escape from their burning homes.

Beneath the forest floor, something had rolled over in its sleep. Even dreaming, it relished the destruction it caused in the world above. But a thought nagged at it, tugged at it, and it couldn't seem to be able to get back to sleep again. Its eyes fluttered open, but quickly closed of their own accord. It didn't want to wake up, but something jostled it, prodded it, and it felt hungry. It had slept a very long time, and now it yearned to stretch and feel the wind at its back once again.

Long ago, when the world above it was all forest, it had roamed the Earth as a man. He had lived. He had loved and hated, hungered and fed, lived and died and then lived again. But that was so very long ago. While he had been powerful when he was alive, he had only grown in power upon his death, and, for a time, had ruled the lands from as far as the eye could see. But he had made mistakes, careless lapses in judgment that his enemies had used to usurp his control and defeat him.

They had buried him far from his homeland, a shame that he'd carried with him ever since. He still remembered the curse; not until the living and the dead both walked the land as equals would he be freed from the earthly prison to which he still found himself bound. Finally that had happened, at least for an instant, and it had been enough to stir him from his long and dreary slumber. But would it be enough to allow him to break free of his centuries-long prison and once again roam the world above?

He pushed tentatively against the rocks and dirt surrounding him, marveling as he felt the debris that had been his prison for so long fall way. He pushed again, harder, and felt his crypt give, and the spirit was soaring up through the dead branches and rocks and sediment that had surrounded him in his grave. And there it was; the sun, the glorious sun, beating down upon his fleshless body, filling his void with a raging furnace of heat.

But the criteria of the curse hadn't entirely been met. He still wasn't whole. Indeed, the dead and the living had both walked the Earth together, but only for the briefest of moments. The curse had been set aside long enough to stir him from his endless slumber, perhaps, but not enough to give him back his body, or even most of his power. For that, he sensed, he would need to seek out whatever had caused the rift between those who had hot blood flowing through their veins and those that did not, and make the tear permanent.

Closing his eyes, he allowed himself to drift upon the breeze that circled down and through the trees. Floating into the sky like a feather on the wind, he spun into the air, enjoying the freedom so long denied him. He couldn't go far, for he was still anchored to the earth that had held him for so long, but it was enough. Like a wolf that's caught the scent of a hare on the wind, he had the trail. And he could follow it, though not without a host.

He called out to one of the few animals still lurking in the burning forest; an old wolf recently separated from his pack. *Brother wolf,* he called, *come to me and together we will feast on the innards of man. Together we will take any female that catches our fancy, and together we will rule the great forest that lies beyond this one, feasting on the world and the very stars that hang in the sky.*

The wolf came, of course. Who could deny him? He moved into the predator's body, snapping his teeth at the smoke, enjoying the stinging bite of it in his nostrils and the sheer animal power of his ferocious jaw. And then he was running through the forest, moving like lightning on all fours, speeding south and away from the flames, toward the one who had managed to splinter the threshold between the living and the dead just long enough for him to break free.

Muscles rippled beneath his wiry frame, and he howled with sheer pleasure. A coyote darted from his path, and a mother groundhog and her babies hurled themselves into their hole. He paid them no mind, for his hunger was focused on something much more important than dinner. The world would soon be his again, and he was going to enjoy every last second of it.

Chapter 5

Her fingernails stung with dirt and bits of rock and wood buried underneath, and her hands were scratched and bleeding, but Claire kept digging, and, by the third hole, she had found the jar. It had proven to be closer to the tree than Cross said, and the metal lid of the jar was rusted shut. It looked like it had been buried a lot longer than just a few hours ago.

Cross had been precious little help during the digging expedition, always standing just out of reach, never offering his aid, as she tore into the dirt and grass at the base of the tree. But she was famished, and would be damned if she'd let a little thing like broken fingernails or a rusted jar lid get in the way of downing a few Snickers bars and an ice-cold Coke.

"How much is there?" he asked, moving closer. "I'd love a soda pop and a bag of chips, if there's enough left over."

Her fingers were so raw and slick with blood that she couldn't get a good grip on the jar. In frustration she threw it against the tree, watching with a certain satisfaction as the container exploded in a mixture of glass and silver. A big handful of coins, all half-dollars, tumbled to the brown grass that surrounded the tree.

"Whoa, girl," Cross chuckled, his laugh throaty and infectious as he watched her gather up the coins. "You don't mess around, do you?"

"Not when there's money involved," she grinned, counting the coins.

There were 26 half-dollars, for a total of 13 dollars. It wouldn't buy them much, but at least they'd eat.

Something was strange about the money. She checked the dates, and not one of them was newer than 1967. Eight of the half-dollars depicted Ben Franklin, the kind that were minted before Kennedy's assassination in 1963; the others were Kennedy half-dollars, and four of them were pre-1967 when they still made them from silver.

"Jimmy, this is weird," she said, looking up at the old black man, "these are all vintage coins, probably worth more than their face value. Why would anyone bury these?"

He cocked his head again, then shrugged and said, "But you can still spend them, right?" There was something about his eyes, a wild look that set her nerves on edge.

"As far as I know," she said, returning the shrug. "Let's go find out." She started across the grass to the parking lot, beyond which lay Olive Street and the Family Dollar store.

"I think I'll stay here," he said, backing away, "in case Dot and the kids show up. But bring me a soda and some chips?"

"Sure thing, Jimmy," she called over her shoulder. "I'll be right back."

When had it gotten so dark? She glanced at her watch, and Mickey Mouse told her it was nearly seven. But that couldn't be right! Had she really spent that many hours talking to Jimmy and digging up the jar? The last time she'd checked, it had been a little before two.

Shaking her head, she crossed the street and pushed through the doors of the Dollar General. The sign on the door had said, "No shirt, no shoes, no service," and so the first thing she did was to slip into the back of the store to try on shoes. She found a pair of neon green trainers that seemed to fit her, and they were only a dollar. Not the most attractive footwear in the world, but they'd do until something better came along.

She gathered up two bottles of Coke, which were two for a dollar, two bags of chips, also two for a dollar, and two giant Snickers bars (a dollar each,) for a total of five dollars. With tax, her total came to five dollars and forty-five cents. She hated to spend the half-dollars, but at least she got to keep all but one of the Franklins.

The clerk, until now not meeting her eyes, looked up at her when she passed him the money to pay for her purchases. "Hey, these are old," he said, then looked like he instantly regretted it. "I mean, they'll still spend…"

"Don't worry about it," she said, snatching up the food. "But if some little kids from across the street show up demanding their money, don't say I didn't warn you."

She turned around and walked through the doors into the now-cool night air, leaving the clerk to wonder just what in the hell she was talking about. Let him wonder. She was tired of doing all the wondering. At least he knew who he was.

"Claire!" yelled a voice from across the parking lot, nearly making her drop the bags of chips.

She tensed, turning to find the source of the voice, surprised to see Dr. Greenwald sprinting across the asphalt. Gone was the lab coat, replaced by a skirt and a casual pink top, and her hair was no longer piled atop her head in a bun, instead tied back in a ponytail.

Her instincts told her to run, but something made her hold back. Maybe they were friends, after all. She forced her feet to remain planted to the ground while she let the doctor catch up to her.

"Claire," she cried, sweeping her into an embrace. "My God, Claire, I've been looking everywhere for you." Greenwald began sobbing, soaking the shoulder of Claire's blouse with her tears.

"It's all right," Claire whispered, unsure of what else to say. She maneuvered her purchases into one arm, and stroked the woman's long, black hair with her fingers. "Shh, it's all right." And then a thought struck her: "Am I in trouble?"

Greenwald backed away, her glasses smeared with tears. Her make-up had run, and she looked a mess. Her eyes looked as hollow and as black as the night. "In trouble? Oh! You mean for what you did to Dick and Jerry. No, you're not in trouble. They were too embarrassed to press charges, though it'll be a while before they'll look at you the same way again. They were just as freaked out as I was, and I think you broke Dick's nose. But where did you learn to do that? It wasn't that self-defense class we took in college, was it? If I remember right, you were more interested in the instructor than in learning to defend yourself from his advances." She shot her a little half-hearted grin.

"Look, I'm sorry about that." She returned the smile, feeling foolish for it. She didn't know this woman, wasn't privy to the history they apparently shared. "I just kind of...lost my head, for a moment."

The woman's concern seemed to move toward anger for an instant, but she pressed it down. "I've been looking for you all day, you know. I even called Pete. You weren't at home, weren't at the mall," another of those smiles, "and I didn't know what to think. If I hadn't stopped for gas...what are you doing over here?" Her eyes seemed to really take her in for the first time. "And what happened to you? Is that...what is that?"

"I threw up all over myself," she chuckled ruefully, trying to keep her feet planted firmly against the pavement in an effort not to bolt. "I guess being pregnant will do that to you."

"I guess." She looked doubtful. "Look, we should really get you to the hospital. I'm worried about you."

"No hospital," she demanded, her heart shifting into high gear, "but I'll let you take me home, if you want. But first there's a man I have to see about a Coke and some chips."

Her eyes scanned the park for Jimmy, but he was nowhere to be found. She crossed the street to look for him, against Greenwald's protests, but he had disappeared. She sat one of the bottles of Coke and a bag of Lay's Barbecue potato chips on the park bench.

"Okay, maybe not," she finally said, giving up. Puzzled and disorientated, she let Dr. Greenwald lead her back across the street and to the convenience store parking lot.

Greenwald clicked a button on her key ring and the lights to a silver and black Cadillac Escalade blinked on and off, and the locks disengaged. Claire followed the doctor to the SUV and climbed into the passenger's seat, enjoying the give of the dark gray leather seats beneath her. Her legs felt like she hadn't sat down for a very long time.

The doctor slipped into the driver's seat and started the car. She stared at Claire for what seemed like an eternity before speaking.

"Jeff's still out of town for that conference, isn't he?" she asked, turning over the car's engine. It roared to life, but Greenwald made no move to drive out onto the road.

Was Jeff her husband? "I think so," she finally answered. "I've been a little mixed up today, so I'm not really sure."

Greenwald waited a heartbeat and then continued. "I'm worried about you, Claire, and I don't want you to go home to an empty house, though I have to admit that's probably better than the alternative."

Her mouth made a silent 'o,' as if that was something she shouldn't have said. "At any rate, how about spending the night at my house? Tomorrow's my day off, so we can stay up late, watch a movie, girl talk, you know? I can call in an order to Red Curry and we can head over to my house, eat some Thai food, veg out in front of the television, and reconnect. We can even have your snacks," she indicated Claire's armful of junk food with the tip of her chin, "for dessert. What do you say? I feel really bad about what happened this morning, and I think we need to talk about it." Her words came out in a rush, almost as if she was afraid of being turned down.

But what alternatives did Claire have? "Sure," she said, drawing the word out, not meeting Greenwald's eyes, "I'd like that. My life's been a little…weird lately, and maybe you can help me fill in some of the missing pieces."

"I'll certainly try," Greenwald said, briefly touching Claire's hand. "Oh, I almost forgot!" She reached behind her, into the dark back seat, and pulled out a purse—the purse she'd be carrying in the lobby of the clinic—and Claire's shoes. "These are yours. I mean, these pumps can't really compare to your new green tennies," she said, scrunching up her nose as she smiled, "but I thought you might like to have them back anyway."

"You bet," Claire agreed, her pulse quickening at the thought of finally finding out who she was. She took her things from the doctor, the woman who was supposed to be her friend, and immediately began to look through her purse.

"The usual?" Greenwald asked, pulling a pink iPhone from her pocket. In response to Claire's blank look, she added: "From the restaurant, goofball."

"The usual," Claire said back to her, wondering what exactly her usual was. She suspected that she was about to find out, and, with the grumbling of her stomach reaching an all-time crescendo, hoped that she liked Thai food.

Claire searched frantically through her purse while Dr. Greenwald—no, Leesie, she corrected herself, staring at the back of a photo she'd found in her purse—retrieved their supper from inside the small restaurant. Someone, probably herself, had written "Claire and Leesie" on the back of a photo of the two of them that she'd found in her wallet. The photo looked at least ten years old, judging by the hairstyles and the fresh, young skin of the girls looking back at her.

It looked like it'd been taken at a party or maybe a school dance. Claire had braces in the photo, and wore a pink taffeta prom dress and a matching ribbon in her hair. She had her arm around Greenwald, and they were both aping for the camera. She yearned for the photo to bring back a memory—something, anything! But her brain wouldn't cooperate, and her mind remained blank.

She flipped through the rest of the photos. One was of her in a wedding dress beside a dark-haired man with hazel eyes (Jeff?) in a tuxedo. Another showed a young woman with strawberry-blonde hair and piercing blue eyes standing beside a snowman. She was dressed in a leather jacket and gloves, and her face wore a look of mock-surprise as she pointed up into the sky at the falling snow.

The door to the restaurant jingled and she looked up, watching Leesie as she exited the restaurant with a big, brown bag cradled in her arms. She turned to wave at an Asian man inside before heading toward the car.

Claire stared again at her driver's license, wondering about the woman pictured. Her name was Claire Fleming Summers, and her birthday was September the twenty-ninth. She stood five foot seven inches tall, had green eyes, and lived on North Mallard Lane. Beyond that, it told her precious little.

She slipped the wallet back into her purse just as Leesie opened the door. The doctor passed the bag to her, and she wordlessly accepted it, placing the hot container of food across her lap. It smelled great, and she wondered not for the first time what exactly she was getting ready to eat.

"Eshe said to tell you hello, said you and Jeff were in two nights ago," Leesie said, slipping the key into the ignition and turning over the motor. "You should have told me. We could have gone somewhere else, or hit a window."

What did she say to that? "You know I never get tired of Thai food, Leesie," she said, knowing the moment that it passed her lips how lame it sounded. "Besides, you seemed to have your heart set on it."

"You haven't called me that since college," Leesie said. "These days, it's always Elisabeth. But I've kinda missed it. Hey, do you want to stop by Red Box, or just see what's on TV tonight?"

She shrugged, not wanting to guess her taste in movies. For all she knew, she hated comedies but loved historical dramas. She didn't want to get into the fact that she couldn't remember a damn thing about her life, at least not yet.

"TV it is, then," sighed Leesie when she failed to answer, and they drove down Walnut Avenue in silence.

Claire found herself studying the landscape. None of it felt the least bit familiar. The town seemed small, but there was a fair amount of traffic up and down Walnut. She took in all of the businesses around her—Walgreens, Popeye's Chicken, Wal-Mart—but none of it rang a bell. Sure, she knew that Wal-Mart was a huge discount store chain, but couldn't remember ever stepping foot inside one.

They passed a cemetery on the left, and she was struck with the sheer amount of visitors she saw. She squinted against the lights of on-coming traffic and realized that they weren't visiting graves after all; they were just milling about, walking this way and that, some staring over the fence toward the road, the others seemingly oblivious to the world around them.

"Weird," mumbled Claire, transfixed by the scene unfolding before her. They were at a traffic light now, right across from the graveyard. She jumped in her seat as a handful of them turned to stare at her.

"What's weird?" asked Leesie, playing with the radio while waiting for the light to change.

A Colbie Caillat song filled the car, something about looking inside yourself when you need a light to guide you home, and Claire decided that she liked it.

"Those people," she said, gesturing across the road, "what're they doing?"

"What people?" Leesie asked, looking back in the direction Claire had pointed. "I don't see anyone."

Claire stared toward the cemetery. Her foot, previously tapping in time to the music, stopped moving. A deep chill traveled down her spine. Now they were crowded against the wrought iron fence that surrounded the graveyard, their arms sticking through the gaps in the metal, reaching out to her in seeming desperation, wanting to consume her.

"Go," she screamed, kicking at an imaginary gas pedal in the passenger's floorboard of the Escalade, "go, go, go!"

"What's wrong?"

"Just go!" Claire pleaded, her fist closing around the door handle, ready to bolt from the car.

"I can't, the light's not green!" Leesie snapped, staring at her like she was crazy. "Claire, what's going on?"

She was about to scream again, beg Leesie to just *drive*, but fell silent as her eyes turned back to the graveyard. It was deserted. Everyone was gone.

Chapter 6

Carthage, Illinois

The gates had closed for the evening at Moss Ridge Cemetery, but the graveyard still had plenty of traffic. The light of the moon, barely a crescent, illuminated the graveyard just enough to prevent Farris Hale from falling over a headstone and breaking his neck, but not enough to save him from stumbling into one of the half-dozen mausoleums that littered the cemetery and scraping his knuckles.

He tried to act nonchalant about it, to pretend that he'd somehow meant to bang his fist into the side of the crypt, but none of the other kids were having it.

"So hard up that you're hitting on the dead, eh, Farris?" laughed Caleb Morton, high school senior and resident jock in their little band of partiers.

"I've heard," added Susie Parker, in a stage whisper, "that he's been down here a few times before, on the off chance that he'll get to screw a ghost."

Walt chuckled derisively, high-fiving Caleb, while Jasmine just smirked. Ever since Susie had caught him hiding under the bleachers in junior high, she'd given him a wide berth. Though he'd only been doing what he'd come to do best—hiding from Brian Blackford—she'd accused him of trying to look up her skirt, and refused to believe otherwise. While he was pretty certain she'd never told anyone, he didn't want to give her reason to start now. He turned beet red and kept his mouth shut.

Farris should have been at home studying for his calculus test on Monday, but instead was here freezing his ass off, trudging through a cemetery in the middle of October. But when Sabrina Locke had invited him to their party, he knew it was an offer that he couldn't refuse—even if it meant putting up with Susie and her never-ending stream of insults and putdowns.

The ghost thing was, of course, a reference to *Small Things*, the fantasy novel that local author Shawn Spencer had written about Carthage. Quite a bit of the book had taken place in Moss Ridge, including one scene where the ex-FBI agent's dead wife rose from the grave to heal him from an otherwise life-ending wound. Farris had fallen in love with the book the moment he read it and had taken to exploring witchcraft and the supernatural, and Caleb and his friends had hounded him endlessly for it.

He didn't really care what any of them thought. All he cared about was Sabrina, the sixth member of their crew. He'd had a crush on her ever since he could remember, and she'd finally agreed to go out with him, tonight, provided it be a group date with her friends.

Truth was, he would have climbed the highest mountain, swam the deepest sea, just for the chance to buy her a slice at Ruskin's Pizzeria. If he had to spend time with her goofy friends in order to be with her, it was a small price to pay.

He, Sabrina, and Caleb had been the best of friends during grade school, but things changed when they entered junior high. Suddenly, they were popular, and he was not. Caleb played football and baseball, and Sabrina blossomed into the prettiest girl in school, while he spent most of his free time on the Web. They saw less and less of each other as the school term progressed, and he could no longer remember the last time they'd hung out or even talked for longer than a few minutes. Farris still missed them.

In terms of popularity, he was doubly damned before he even got out of diapers. He was named after a movie made years before he was born, and even then, because of a nurse's mistake, the name had ended up spelled differently. That just gave the other kids something more to make fun of, and most of them had taken full advantage of the opportunity.

"Kinda creepy out here at night," said Jasmine, teeth chattering, displaying her usual flair for stating the obvious.

But she was right; it was creepy, not to mention disrespectful. Most of the Friday night parties in Carthage took place at the lake, even during the winter months, but the cops had taken to patrolling so often that Caleb and his friends switched their party spot to the cemetery. As long as they weren't too loud, Caleb said, they could drink and smoke all they wanted with no one being the wiser.

Walt lowered the cooler he'd lugged through the gates to the ground, popped it open, and passed out Pirate Monkey homebrewed beers all around. It was his father's brand, and featured a one-eyed monkey dressed as a pirate on the label.

The pirate used to have a pipe until someone on the city council complained that the image promoted smoking. Rather than have his beer yanked from all the taverns in Hancock County, Walt's father altered the image and later sold an original case of the beer on eBay for five-hundred bucks.

Alcohol didn't exactly agree with Farris, but he screwed the cap off the long-necked brown bottle and took a tentative sip. The alcohol burned his throat, but at least this time he didn't spew it all over his shoes.

Caleb and Susie were already making out, rolling around the dirt in front of Tanner McGee's grave like a pair of dogs in heat. Jasmine and Walt had also paired off, walking through the rows of plots, counting off names of all the people that their families knew that were represented by the markers.

That left only him and Sabrina. Too tongue-tied to say anything, he just watched her. Her beautiful porcelain skin glowed in the moonlight, and her long, black hair glistened against the stars. She was the most beautiful girl he'd ever seen, and, if he wanted to let her know how he felt, it was now or never.

He started to say something but, to his surprise, she caught his eye, pressing her finger to her lips. She walked over to him and clanked her bottle against his in a toast. "To the start of another beautiful friendship," she said, standing on her toes to kiss his cheek, "and whatever else may come."

Farris felt like he might pass out. He was pretty far down the social ladder in school. In fact, the only reason Caleb had agreed to let him come tonight was that he offered to buy everyone's dinner beforehand. The meal had cost him over sixty dollars, but if that's what it took for Sabrina to notice him again, it was money well spent.

"You're beautiful," he said lamely, staring down into her deep green eyes.

She looked at him for a moment, seemed to come to a decision, and then leaned in close and whispered, "get ready to act scared."

He stared at her. What was she talking about? Sure, he was scared, but he was determined to push past the fear. She stared into his eyes, seemingly waiting for him to do something. And then he kissed her.

His whole body was alive with fire. It was magnificent! He'd imagined this moment a thousand—no, a million—times, but never in his imagination was it as good as this. He felt her tongue probe his, gently at first and then with more force, and he wrapped his lanky arms around her waist and pulled her closer.

The kiss seemed to last forever, and he noticed her lipstick tasted like cherries. But then she grew rigid, her arms fluttering at her sides. Something was wrong. Farris pulled back, staring. Her eyes were wide as saucers, and she looked even more pale than usual.

"Behind you," she said in a loud stage whisper. Rolling her eyes, she pointed at something just over his shoulder. "Oh God, Farris, oh no, behind you."

He whirled on his heels, coming face-to-face with an honest-to-God ghost. The thing was huge, maybe seven or eight feet tall, and shrouded with an eerie luminescent glow that outshone the moon. Wispy, tattered bits of chains and white rags hung from its neck, and weird protoplasmic goo dripped from its chin.

The ghost loomed over him, and his heart nearly exploded. He felt something warm and wet soak the front of his jeans, only later realizing that he must have pissed his pants. He worked his jaw to say something, anything, to warn the others, to protect Sabrina, but the words wouldn't come out.

And then Sabrina, his wonderful, beautiful Sabrina, was laughing. He turned to see her staring at him, giggling into her hands. He knew that she sometimes laughed when she was nervous, but soon everyone joined in, snorting, pointing at him and chanting his name. Caleb threw an empty beer bottle at him that just missed his nose by an inch.

Were they crazy? They had to get out of here, before the ghost killed them.

"Ouch!" yelled the ghost, pulling a sheet up over his head. It was Brian Blackford, town delinquent and Caleb's sometimes-running buddy. "Dude, you hit my shoulder. That hurt like a son of a bitch."

Farris felt something inside him break. It had all been a joke. Just one big, stupid joke. Even Sabrina, the love of his life, had been in on it. She'd tried to tell him, perhaps taking pity on him at the last second, but he hadn't understood. He felt the rush coming from his stomach, but it was too late to stop. Before he knew what he was doing, he was throwing up all over Brian Blackford's white Nikes. Beer and pizza stained the boy's shoes, and then Blackford was upon him, punching, kneeing him in the stomach.

"You little turd," he said, cracking a hard fist against the back of his head. "Do you know what these fucking shoes cost me? Do you have any idea, you stupid little piece of shit? Any idea at all?"

"Hey," Sabrina yelled, and, for the first time, Farris heard real fear in her voice, "it's not his fault. Get off of him."

"He was tonguing my girlfriend," Blackford shot back, kicking Farris in the balls, "so it sure as hell was his fault. What, are you telling me you liked it?"

Sabrina was dating Brian Blackford? Of course she was. How could Farris have ever thought she'd go for him? His groin ached with a white-hot pain and he thought his nose was broken, yet none of that compared with the sick, twisted-up way his stomach felt at the thought of Brian kissing Sabrina.

"No, Brian, of course not," she said quickly, her voice shaking. "You know it was just a prank. You're the one I'm going out with. But enough is enough. Let him up."

"She's right, man," Caleb said, walking toward them. "You don't want to do this. Up until now, nobody's done anything wrong. We all had a good laugh out of it. Now let's get out of here before someone calls the cops."

Farris was on his hands and knees, his face covered in blood, struggling to push himself to his feet. All he wanted was to get out of the graveyard and never show his face in school again, never see any of them ever again.

"Fuck that," Blackford said, stomping down on the back of his neck.

Farris felt his spine snap, and then he felt nothing. He heard Sabrina crying behind him, yelling at Brian to stop, and wondered what Brian was doing to him. He had no idea, because he couldn't see anything. And then his hearing went, and the whole world went silent and he thought no more.

Chapter 7

"I could lose my job if anyone finds out about this," Norman Broussard whispered. He couldn't afford to lose his job, but it's not like he could afford not to take the thousand greenbacks these guys were offering him, either. If they just made it quick, in and out, no one should be the wiser.

"We won't take up much of your time, Mr. Broussard," said the larger of the two men, seemingly reading his mind. "But my friend here simply must see his nephew."

"Yeah, yeah, I understand," he said, though he really didn't. These guys seriously creeped him out. They dressed and talked like twins, but they couldn't look less alike if they tried. And the little guy had the strangest smell about him, something both alien and familiar at the same time. He couldn't place it.

He'd been a security guard for six months, just something to pay the bills while he got his grades up and re-qualified for his scholarship. He really didn't need this shit. If he weren't behind on his rent and about to lose his apartment, he would have turned them down flat. His life was a mess, however, what with Amelia breaking up with him and school going down the toilet, so unfortunately he really did need the money.

"It's this way," he said, avoiding their eyes.

He led them through the employee's entrance, down a dark hallway with a chipped cement floor and walls that needed to be painted ten years ago, and into the morgue. The county morgue was rarely full but always had at least a few residents, and the dead bodies just out of sight in the long metal drawers never failed to set his nerves on edge.

"Okay, I think your guy's over here," he said, flipping through the intake chart. And there he was, the only resident of the night, John Doe number twelve. He walked across the room, found the drawer, and slid it open.

He started to unzip the black bag that held the earthly remains of Mr. Quarry's recently departed nephew, but a hand across his shoulder made him jump.

"That'll do," said Mr. Kingfisher, maneuvering himself between Norman and the body bag. "Wait outside now."

"Actually," he said, standing up a little straighter, "I really can't. You guys shouldn't even be back here. I could lose my job if anything happens. If I didn't need the money, I never would have…"

"And you'll get your money, Mr. Broussard," said Kingfisher, displaying a perfect row of bright, white teeth. "But we need to take the body." He turned from the man, picking up the corpse as if it were nothing more than a sack of oats, and threw it over his shoulder.

Mr. Quarry crossed the room, flashing Broussard a brief smile before holding out an envelope. "We always pay as promised," he said, thrusting the envelope into the security guard's outstretched palm.

Norman didn't know what to do, so he did the only thing he'd been trained to do—he drew his gun, carefully backing away from the two men.

"I really can't let you do this," he said, voice trembling. "I can't lose my job. The money will mean nothing then. I just can't do it. Now put the body back and get out of here, and we'll forget this whole thing ever happened."

Quarry looked toward Kingfisher, who gave him a near-imperceptible nod. And then Kingfisher was moving again, walking past Norman, to the door that lead through the hallway and out into the night beyond.

"Hey!" said Norman, a little louder than he'd intended. "Put the body down. I mean it. I will absolutely blow you guys away."

He cocked his little handgun. He'd never fired it anywhere except at the range, but he'd shoot these guys if he had to and answer for it later. He could hide the money and claim it had been a break-in, that he'd found them just as they were preparing to make their getaway with the body.

And then Quarry was upon him, wrenching the gun from his hand, taking his index finger with it. He cried out in pain, watching in disbelief as the short, stocky man pulled the bloody finger from the gun and wrapped his tongue around it, sucking it into his mouth.

"Oh, Christ," he screamed, his heart jack-hammering in his chest. "Oh, Christ! Oh, Christ! Oh, Christ! Take the fucking body, just fucking take it, I don't care!" He held his bleeding hand to his chest, stumbling backward. He bumped into the open drawer, slipped and fell, but before he could regain his footing Quarry was upon him, ripping at him, tearing into him with bare hands and razor-sharp teeth.

He watched in disbelief as Kingfisher carefully placed the body across the coroner's desk and withdrew a drinking straw and a small stoppered vial from his inner pocket. What *the fuck is that for,* he thought, just before Quarry's teeth found his neck and everything shifted to black.

Chapter 8

Claire was starving, but the food would have to wait a little while longer. With the smell of *Pad See Ewe* still in her nostrils, her stomach grumbled as she adjusted the water temperature for her shower. She needed to remove the day's adventure from her skin. Her clothes were already in the washing machine, though she had a feeling that, while the vomit might wash out, she'd be stuck with the blood.

What she'd seen at the cemetery still rattled her, but she managed to convince Leesie that it was just a case of low blood sugar. Who were all those people, and why had they been looking at her that way? She forced herself to forget about them, feeling the tension finally begin to leave her muscles as she stepped into the shower.

The steaming hot water felt wonderful against her skin, sluicing down over her breasts to plane off her stomach and pool at her feet. She reached through the steam to remove a bottle of shampoo from the wire rack that hung below the shower head, vigorously working it into her short, blonde hair. She rinsed the suds from her scalp, trading the shampoo for an avocado shower gel that she used to soap her entire body from neck to toe before spinning in a slow circle to rinse it all off again.

She wanted to stay in this huge tile and porcelain bathroom forever, but she knew she couldn't. Not only was her dinner awaiting her, but the rest of her life beckoned as well. She had to find out why she'd lost her memories, and what she needed to do to regain them. And, unfortunately, that meant admitting her amnesia to Leesie. She wasn't sure why she felt so hesitant to share her condition with the doctor, but she knew she couldn't put it off forever.

Still enjoying the heat of the shower, she closed her eyes and let her mind wander, searching for any errant memory, even a thread, that she might snatch, pull on, and unravel. But there was nothing. She remembered facts and ideas and concepts, things like how to ride a bicycle, check out a book at the library, or buy a lottery ticket, but she couldn't remember ever actually doing any of those things. It was so frustrating that she stomped her foot in response, sending a wave of pain up through her shin.

And then she remembered.

It was her fourth birthday, and the house was filled with red and green balloons, presents wrapped in all shades of paper, and laughter. All of her friends—four little boys and two girls, all dressed in costume—were gathered around the table, watching her. She took a deep breath, preparing to blow out the candles on her *Thundercats* birthday cake, but couldn't quite reach it. She edged forward, leaning across the table, when suddenly the chair she was standing on toppled over, sending her sprawling to the floor.

She landed badly, her leg buckling beneath her, and she felt something inside her knee snap. Someone, maybe her mother, ran over to her, scooping her up in her arms, asking if she was all right, but she couldn't stop crying.

Everyone was looking at her, and one of the children, a little boy dressed as a fireman, casually leaned over the table and blew out all four candles on her cake. There was no malice in his face; he was just doing what needed to be done, and the candles, quite simply, needed to be blown out. He was a fireman, after all, and that's what firemen did. She knew that, knew that he hadn't meant anything by it, but it still broke her heart.

Tears trailed down her cheeks and she clutched to the memory like a life preserver, but it left her as surely as the flames from the phantom candles. Wiping the tears away with the back of her hand, she turned off the water, stepped out of the shower, and picked up an oversized blue towel from atop the toilet tank.

She'd remembered something. Trivial as it was, she'd remembered a tiny fragment, a brief snapshot in time, of her former life. It was something, and it would have to be enough for now. She finished toweling off, wrapping herself in the huge terrycloth robe that Leesie had hung on the door for her. She could still smell the Thai food, and followed the scent out of the bathroom, down the hallway, and into the living room.

Leesie's house felt comfortable and inviting, and she almost felt at peace here. A huge, brown leather couch and matching loveseat dominated the room, surrounded by a large stone fireplace on one wall and a flat screen television on the other. The walls were painted a very light tan, an eye-catching contrast to the darkness of the furniture, and the hardwood floors were oak, further accentuating the organic look and feel of the living room. There were houseplants hanging from planters throughout the dwelling, giving the whole interior an almost forest-like atmosphere.

The wooden floor felt cool beneath her toes, and she paused by the window, studying the neighborhood. She watched as a white pickup truck drove slowly down the block, passing a blue Honda. The neighborhood beyond was beautiful and elegant, if a bit predictable, littered with huge brick houses that mostly looked alike and alternating weeping willows and maple trees every hundred yards.

She looked up into the sky, watching as a plane shot by overhead. The moon, a tiny silver crescent, was barely visible behind the approaching thunderclouds. She thought she saw a streak of lightning in the distance, but couldn't be sure. She hoped it would rain tonight. Perhaps the rain would wash away whatever morass of confusion surrounded her, washing away the amnesia, leaving something more recognizable beneath. It was a silly thought, she knew.

"Food's getting cold," Leesie's called out in a low, throaty chuckle from the next room over. "You act like you've never been here before."

"That's something we need to talk about," she muttered to herself, following the scent of the food into the dining room.

Claire sat down, enjoying the feel of the padded oak dining chair beneath her legs. The dining room was just as stately as the other rooms in the house, decorated with an understated flair that made her feel comfortable. A huge oil painting depicting tiny, colorful fish cavorting with little dancing heart people hung from the north wall, while built-in bookshelves boasting dozens of medical tomes interspersed with classic and current mysteries and thrillers filled the east.

"This is great," Claire said, between bites, as she wolfishly devoured the food. *Pad See Ewe* was, apparently, a spicy dish with chicken, egg noodles, and broccoli in a soy sauce. She enjoyed the heat of the dish, marveling at how the spices intermingled with the red pepper to make her sweat.

"Far better than candy bars and potato chips," Leesie said, smiling, "though chocolate does have its place." She'd chosen the Evil Jungle Prince, a garlicky dish with shrimp and bamboo shoots served over brown rice that looked every bit as delicious as the *Pad See Ewe*.

"You know," Claire said, working up her courage, "I have to tell you something."

Leesie's mouth was full, so she raised her eyebrows and motioned for Claire to continue.

"I don't know who I am." There, she'd said it. She felt herself tense up, preparing for the other woman's response.

"Honey, there are plenty of days when I don't know who I am, either. I mean, I'm thirty-two, single, and not likely to get together with anyone any time soon. And even if I did, it's not like my family would approve anyway, is it?" She said cryptically, archly raising an eyebrow. "Add to that the fact that I have a three-hundred-thousand dollar mortgage and don't really like any of the partners in my practice but am stuck with them because I can't afford to go it alone. So, yeah, there are some days when I don't know who I am, either, but what can you do?"

"No," said Claire, finishing off the last of her food, "that's not what I meant. Leesie, I really don't know who I am. The first thing I remember, other than bits and pieces of a birthday party when I was four, is waking up in your office today, on the examining table, scared out of my mind."

Leesie had just taken a swallow of her Diet Pepsi and, in a scene worthy of any sitcom, spewed it all over her shirt. "Oh, come on. You're not serious?"

"As a heart attack," Claire admitted, looking away. "That's why I...did what I did in your office. I was scared, terrified out of my mind. I just had to get away. I think it might have had something to do with that man that was run over today. Maybe I knew him."

"So you really don't remember anything?" Leesie asked, dabbing at her top with a white linen napkin. "If this is real, we need to get you to the hospital."

She rose from her chair, circled the table, and began examining Claire's head. "I'm looking for bumps or bruises," she explained when Claire jerked away. "If that bastard hit you hard enough to..."

"What bastard?" She whispered, her pulse quickening at the thought. Had someone done this to her?

"Jeff," said Leesie, pulling a chair to sit beside her. "Your husband."

"My husband hits me?"

"Well, you've never said as much, but I know he does. I mean, look in the mirror! You have a black eye, a busted lip. What kind of man does that to the woman he's supposed to love?"

"But how do you know he hits me," Claire asked, defending a man she couldn't even remember, "if I've never said anything? Maybe I'm just clumsy. Or maybe I got hurt taking that defense class you mentioned."

"Oh God, you're telling the truth, aren't you?" she said, putting her hand on Claire's knee. "We took that class over ten years ago, sweetie. You really don't remember anything?"

"Not a thing," Claire admitted, blinking. And then she couldn't hold back the tears. The day came out in a rush, the fear, the running, the panic, all of it, and she was sobbing into her best friend's shoulder, feeling helpless and completely alone.

"It's okay," Leesie said, holding her close. "Shh, it's okay. We'll work through this and, tomorrow, first thing, we'll visit the hospital and get you checked out. You don't have any contusions, and there's no sign of a concussion, but you never know."

"This really sucks, you know?" she said, the tears turning first to soft hiccups before finally subsiding. "But thank you for being my friend, even if I don't remember you."

"Anytime," Leesie whispered, stroking her hair, "always and forever."

Chapter 9

The next thing Farris knew, he was standing beside a weeping Sabrina, watching helplessly as Blackford kicked him repeatedly in the ribs. He swung a fist at the boy's chin but spun *through* him, tumbling through to the other side. His mouth fell open as he stared down at himself.

No, he corrected himself; it wasn't him, not any longer. It was just a body, a discarded shell that was of no more use to him now than Blackford himself was to the world at large. But as worthless as he was, Blackford was alive, while Farris knew without a doubt that he was dead.

And then he could hear again and the world came back in a rush. But everything was different; for one thing, he could see in the dark. The grave he was lying across belonged to Margaret Ruskin, first wife of Fred Ruskin, the guy who started the pizza chain. Both of them were rumored to be inspirations for two of the characters in *Small Things*, but Spencer had never confirmed that. According to the date on the headstone, which he could somehow read despite the light being all but non-existent, she had been dead for fifty years.

Everything around him seemed at once sharper and out of focus, almost as if he were viewing it through those cheap red and blue 3-D glasses you sometimes got with DVDs or magazines. While he could see the details on a tombstone in near-perfect darkness, he couldn't smell a thing. It was as if his nose was permanently stopped up. And then he realized it was because he wasn't breathing.

If you didn't have a body then you didn't need to breathe, and if you couldn't breathe you couldn't smell. It was simple physics, but it didn't make the thought of never again smelling his mom's fresh apple pie or Sabrina's lilac-scented perfume any more palatable.

"Stop it, Brian," Caleb pleaded, pulling the boy off Farris's body. "Enough already. Let him up."

"What the hell is wrong with you?" Sabrina shouted, hugging herself as she looked down at Farris's body. He could see the hairs on her perfect, alabaster arms stand at attention as she shivered in the cold night air. "He's no threat to you. Why can't you just stop? My God, he's bleeding!"

"Hey," Brian mumbled, looking like a hurt puppy, "you don't have to get all pissy about it."

Pissy? He was dead, and Brian was worried about Sabrina getting *pissy*?

"We'd better get out of here," shivered Walt, his face as white as a sheet. He was staring down at Farris's body. "He's not moving. I think he's dead."

"He's just being a baby," Blackford said, prodding the body with his foot. "Come on, baby, rise and shine."

"Dude," muttered Caleb, dropping to his knees to feel for a pulse, "he's not being a baby. Oh Jesus, Brian, you killed him."

Sabrina began to scream, and didn't stop again until Susie wrapped her hand around her mouth. "Christ, Sabrina, get a grip. If someone hears you and calls the cops, then we're all gonna go to jail. And I don't know about you, but I'm planning on going to college, and nobody's gonna take a girl charged with murder."

"She's right," Jasmine said, looking as though she were about to bolt. "We have to get out of here."

"I didn't...I didn't mean to..." Brian whispered, his face wrinkling up like he'd smelled a dead skunk. "I mean, it wasn't my fault..."

Wasn't his fault? If it wasn't his fault, whose fault was it? Was it Farris's fault, for having a neck that had snapped a little too easily when someone had freaking stomped on it? He kicked at Brian, growling in frustration as his leg passed through his killer.

"What was that noise?" Sabrina gasped, looking straight through him.

Had she heard him? Farris jumped up and down, screaming at the top of his lungs, "That big fuck killed me, but I'm not gone yet!"

"Just the wind, Sabrina," Caleb said, though he looked a little unsure. "Shit, it's cold out here."

The wind was picking up, and it looked like a storm might be brewing. Great, that's all he needed. Sleet and snow to cover up whatever evidence might tie Blackford to Farris's murder. But Caleb had probably been right. Whatever Sabrina had heard wasn't him, because none of them seemed able to hear him now. He stopped jumping and let his phantom arms fall uselessly to his sides.

"Okay, here's what we're going to do," Susie interjected, taking the lead. "We bury him, right here in the cemetery," she shined the flashlight a couple of plots to the right, letting it fall on a grave that didn't yet have a marker. "Right there. The earth is still fresh. It's perfect. Everyone will think he ran away, and they'll forget about him inside of a month. No one will ever know."

Was she nuts? Of course someone would know! His parents would look for him. They'd never believe he'd just run away. He was making straight A's in school and had a good shot at a scholarship to Western Illinois University after he graduated, so why would he run away from home?

"This is crazy," Sabrina sobbed, her eyes burning holes through her best friend. "You can't bury him there. You can't bury him anywhere! Susie, we killed him. Your stupid little joke killed him. You and Brian's macho temper. This won't just go away. It can't just go away. It just can't."

"It can if we let it," Susie countered, her face a mask of stony reserve. "Walt, you go grab the shovels out of the back of Caleb's car. Caleb, empty Farris's pockets and grab his keys. We'll hide his car out behind the dam. With any luck, it'll be days, maybe weeks, before anyone finds it. And by that time, his body will be worm food."

"Shovels?" Caleb raised his eyebrows, his face a mask of confusion. "But I don't have any shovels."

Susie grinned, and for the first time Farris saw something other than spite behind her pretty cheerleader eyes; he saw pure malice. "Oops. My bad."

"You see, Caleb," Brian smiled, wrapping his arm around Caleb's shoulder, "we haven't been entirely honest with you."

What the fuck was going on here?

"I know for a fact that the shovels are in your car," Susie said brightly, throwing him her best smile, "because I put them there. I have to confess that we sorta planned this. Been planning it ever since I caught him hiding under the bleachers in junior high, looking up my skirt."

That wasn't how it happened! Besides, he hadn't known Susie was a homicidal sociopath then, so who could blame him? And she did have killer legs.

"You...you," Sabrina stammered, her face flushed with anger, "you planned all this? You and Brian? What, have you been fucking him, too?"

"Kinda sorta," Susie smiled, fluttering her eyelashes. "Hey, a girl's gotta do what a girl's gotta do, right?"

Without warning, Sabrina slapped her full force across the face. Susie fell back, startled, into Caleb's waiting arms. "Listen, bitch. I don't care about that piece of crap," she screamed, pointing at Blackford, "but you two killed someone. You killed my friend. You killed Farris. Don't you get it? You killed Farris!"

Susie slowly rubbed her cheek, gently caressing the huge red welt that formed beneath her long, polished red fingernails. "You ever do that again," she smiled sweetly, "and you'll see just how much of a bitch I really am.

"Now Walt, be a dear and go and fetch those shovels, won't you? And, Caleb, Jasmine? You'll do exactly as we say, or you're going down for this. If you'll notice, Caleb, those are *your* boots that Brian's wearing," Brian waggled his right foot in the air to illustrate the point, "and Walt, your fingerprints are all over those beer bottles. Sabrina, of course, left her DNA in Farris's mouth after their little game of tonsil hockey, and Jasmine…if you don't do what I tell you to do, I'll rip your fucking heart out and let Brian eat it for lunch. Are we clear?"

Jasmine hung her head, slowly nodding. Everyone in school knew that Jasmine pretty much did anything that Susie told her to do, so why start thinking for herself now?

Hot tears trailed down Walt's face, but he did what he'd been told, stumbling through the graveyard to retrieve the shovels from Caleb's car. Caleb, for his part, just looked stunned. His face turned red for a moment and Farris imagined he smelled smoke burning as the gears in his jock brain furiously turned. In the end, though, he just nodded once, which Susie rewarded with a stroke of her hand.

"Caleb, you can't let them do this," Sabrina pleaded, her breathing rapid. "They killed him, and now they're going to…to dig up…"

"What can we do?" he retorted, hands balled up into fists. "If we say anything, she'll take us down with her."

"Smart boy," Susie purred, running her hand down his chest. "There might be some hope for you yet."

"You're all insane," Sabrina yelled, waving her arm through Farris's midsection. "You're going to get caught, you know that. You'll never get away with this."

"Wanna be next?" Brian smiled smugly, wrapping one of the rusty chains from his costume around his fist. "I care about you, Sabrina, I really do, but Susie's the shits. Ain't never lived life until you've driven down the blacktop doing eighty with your dick in her mouth. She taught me to see the world in a whole new way, and if she says the word, girlfriend or not, you're history."

"So how're you going to explain two bodies?" she answered defiantly, but Farris could see the fear in her eyes. No doubt they could see it, too. She finally looked away, dropping her gaze to her green tennis shoes, and he knew Susie had won.

"You're not much of an actress," Susie said to Sabrina. "I know you tried to warn him. That was stupid."

"What would you have done if he hadn't thrown up?" Sabrina asked, staring off into the distance. "Would you still have killed him?"

"Absolutely," Susie grinned, taking Brian's hand. "That was just serendipity. Brian was gonna pretend that Farris hit him. Either way, the geek was a goner."

"And why that grave, Susie?"

"Why do you think, dumbass? Because I'm smarter than you. It's insurance, in case you ever decide to talk."

"We got the shovels," Walt said, Jasmine by his side. Farris could see she'd been crying, and Walt had his fingers wound tightly around her hand. "I sure hope you know what you're doing."

"I guess we're gonna find out," Susie said sweetly, kicking at Farris's corpse. "Now let's get started. With any luck we'll be done in time for breakfast, and pancakes are on me."

Chapter 10

Nadine Pahari lay on her back atop the stripped-down bed, the pink sheets and matching flowery comforter lying in a heap across the room, one wrist manacled to the bedpost. She gazed at the posters on the wall, watching Johnny Depp and Matt Smith staring unblinkingly back at her.

Once upon a time, her room had been a place of respite, a safe haven from her parent's expectations and demands, but now it was her prison. Depp's eyes seemed to follow her wherever on the bed the two-foot length of chain attached to her wrist would allow her to move, and she desperately wanted to rip the poster from the wall and burn it.

Had she only been trapped in here two days? She wasn't sure anymore, but it felt like months.

The day had started innocently enough. She'd stayed home from school, feigning an upset stomach to get out of gym. Sure, it was a stupid thing to do, but she hadn't known the consequence would be quite so harsh.

If she hadn't answered the door, they might still be alive.

Her father, a surgeon at Mercy Hospital, and her mother, an optometrist at Wal-Mart, had raised her better than this. She'd been taught never to lie, and always, no matter what, to own up to her obligations. She had failed them miserably on both counts, and this room and whatever fate awaited her was her punishment.

She was on her period, something that had started a couple of years ago, three days before her eleventh birthday. The last time she had taken gym "on the rag," the other girls had teased her unmercifully.

Unclean Nadine, that's what they called her. She had been Unclean Nadine for over two years now, since just before the end of fifth grade. She had hoped that the next grade would let her start over, that the slate would be wiped clean, but it didn't work out that way.

It didn't matter that most of the other girls had long since hit puberty. She'd been the first, and the name stuck. Unclean Nadine. Even her former best friend, Caitlyn Myers, had joined the name calling.

Nadine's mother told her she was pretty. She had long, black hair, with light brown eyes and skin to match, but she didn't feel pretty. She was the only Indian in her class, which automatically separated her from the other girls in school. It probably didn't help that she was more interested in comic books and video games than make-up and gossiping about boys.

She was an outcast, a social pariah, and the nickname made sure she stayed that way. Somehow, she'd do anything to hear those taunts right now.

It was just before noon when the doorbell rang and, thinking it was probably the mailman with another eBay package for her father, she answered it without first looking out the window. Another thing her parents, who'd moved here from New York when she was three, had always warned her about. Look outside before opening the door.

That had been her first mistake, one of many she would make that day. She found two strange men, one huge and one not much taller than she was, standing on her doorstep. They were both dressed in dark gray suits, and the little one carried an old-time medical bag. She should have slammed the door right then, slammed it and called the police. But she had been more intrigued than she'd been scared.

Because they were dressed alike, and because they wore suits, at first she thought they might be Mormons or Seventh Day Adventists dropping by to give her family the usual spiel. It wouldn't have been the first time, and she always enjoyed talking about Hinduism with them, telling them about Vishnu and the other Gods of her religion, frustrating their attempts to convert her to Christianity.

They weren't here on a religious mission, the big one told her. Their names were Mr. Kingfisher and Mr. Quarry, and they would require the use of her house for an indeterminable amount of time, thank you very much.

She did slam the door then, but it was too late. The giant, Kingfisher, caught the door with his hand and pushed through, and the little one tackled her, driving her to the ground before she could reach the telephone. She thought they were going to rape her, kill her, but they didn't do anything of the sort. What they did was much, much worse.

Mr. Kingfisher said she might be useful.

They wasted no time, however, dispatching her mother, who came home at half-past noon to check on Nadine. The little man, Quarry, was on her before she was even halfway through the door, dragging her inside, bending her arm behind her back and pinning her against the wall.

Nadine screamed, screamed long and loud, but no one heard her, no one came running to her rescue, no one called the police. Kingfisher silenced her with a massive hand over her mouth, and she was forced to watch as, using the various scalpels, ratchets, and other tools she didn't recognize, the smaller man dissected her mother alive, cutting her into little pieces, eating each before moving on to prepare the rest.

Dr. Raaka Pahari was dead long before he was finished.

After Quarry had dined, Kingfisher removed a wrapped plastic straw from his jacket. He carefully removed the paper from the straw before sticking it into his mouth and inhaling deeply through the hole. And then, curiously, he was done with it, dropping both the straw and the paper into the kitchen trashcan.

That's when they dragged Nadine, sobbing and shaking, into the bedroom. Kingfisher bound her to the bed while the smaller man removed her phone from its charger and used masking tape to affix a small, square mirror to her window. The mirror faced outward, into her yard, and he drew a strange-looking little squiggle on the back.

Her father had, she imagined, suffered a similar fate to that of her mother, though thankfully she hadn't been forced to watch. Bound to her bed, locked in her room, she heard his screams, heard him begging for them to stop, pleading with them to spare his daughter. Finally, he fell silent, and she knew it was over.

His words still echoed in her brain. That night, after she'd finally fallen asleep, she dreamed that she had been the one to eat her father. She dreamt that Kingfisher had lifted her into an impossibly-huge highchair, tied a bib around her neck, and that Quarry had scrambled on top of the kitchen table to feed her little fried bites of her father from a Porky Pig fork she'd eaten with as a kid.

She woke up screaming, and didn't stop until Kingfisher had come into the room. He held her close, touched her cheek, and gently kissed the tears from her eyes, all the while his hand stroking her long, black hair.

If she were good, he promised, she might stay alive, but her parents were gone and never coming back, and that was just something she'd have to accept. It wasn't anything personal, he said, just business.

She broke down, crying into the man's shoulder, all the while thinking about the pocket knife hidden under her bed, imagining shoving it through his eye and into his brain.

Nadine couldn't reach the knife. She'd tried over a dozen times, maybe twice that, and all she had to show for her work was a dull, aching pain in her shoulder and an injured wrist where the manacle had dug into her skin and nearly rubbed it raw.

She also couldn't move the bed. It was far too heavy, fate's way of paying her back for choosing the wrought iron monstrosity she had picked from the catalogue when they first moved to this house three summers ago.

So she let Kingfisher hold her, comfort her, and kiss away her tears. Steeling herself to his touch, she vowed to herself that if she ever got hold of the knife, she wouldn't hesitate to use it.

That had been two nights ago, she was pretty sure of it, and she'd been stuck in this damn room ever since. After staring at those posters for three days she hated Depp and Smith and didn't think she'd ever be able to watch *Pirates of the Caribbean* or *Dr. Who* reruns ever again. She hated them, hated the normalcy and innocence they stood for, but not as much as she hated herself for letting all of this happen, for staying home from school and opening the door to the two strangers in the matching dark gray suits.

Kingfisher occasionally brought her meals, consisting mostly of scraps from the kitchen, but rarely spoke to her after that first night, and she hadn't even seen his diminutive partner since he murdered her mother.

She had to beg to go to the bathroom, and more often than not her screams would go unheeded and she'd be forced to relieve herself in a plastic bucket the giant had left for just that purpose.

And it was because she had so little contact with the men that she was surprised when, just a few hours after the sun went down, Kingfisher came to her room. Without a word, he removed one end of the manacle from the bedpost, took the chain in his hand, and beckoned for her to follow.

"Where are we going?" she asked, nearly hyperventilating. Were they going to eat her, the same way they had eaten her parents?

"To the basement," he answered, shushing her with a huge finger to his lips.

"You said you'd let me go. When are you going to let me go?"

"What I said was that if you were good, you might live."

"Why are you doing this?" Nadine's dark brown eyes filled with tears. "What did...what did my mom and dad do to deserve this?"

"Not a thing," Mr. Kingfisher said, pulling her along behind him. "Sometimes bad things happen. The why's and how's are not your concern. Now be quiet. Mr. Quarry is working."

The smell of mold and mildew filled her nostrils as she clambered down the stairs. Compared to the dim moonlight the window to her bedroom let in, the basement was ablaze with light. It hurt her eyes, and she had to blink to allow herself to adjust to the glow.

The first thing she saw when her eyes adjusted to the brightness was Mr. Quarry sitting cross-legged upon the cold basement floor, drawing arcane little symbols on the eyelids of a corpse with a jagged piece of charcoal.

Retching, she bolted from the giant, got two stairs up before she felt herself yanked violently back with the chain. Stumbling, she turned, teetering on the stairs before falling into the railing, catching herself, scraping her arms across the wood. She yelped in pain, a long splinter piercing the palm of her hand.

"Be still, child," growled the giant, pulling her close. "I told you, Mr. Quarry is working. We'll get to you soon enough."

"And there we have it," Quarry said, painting a perfect upside-down star on the dead man's stomach.

Mr. Kingfisher surveyed the body. It was in terrible shape, he said, but it would have to do. She forced herself to follow his gaze, to look at the dead man, feeling a wave of relief wash over her when she realized it wasn't her father.

She stared, fascinated. The man was Caucasian and sported a tattoo that she couldn't quite make out on his left shoulder, something with letters. There wasn't much left of his face, but he looked like he had once been handsome in a rugged sort of way. He had collar-length dark red hair, though she couldn't tell if he was naturally a redhead or whether his hair had been stained by the blood.

He was naked, and his penis, the first one she had ever seen in person, looking surprisingly shriveled and tiny, like a frightened, miniature groundhog trying to escape its shadow.

Her mother and father's killer had drawn all over the body, marking up the palms of his hands, his belly, his forehead, and the bottom of his feet with squiggly little symbols she neither recognized nor understood.

The harsh trilling of the phone, the old phone the giant had plugged into the jack in the kitchen that very first night, rang from upstairs, interrupting her study of the dead man. She turned, grateful for the distraction, to stare up the staircase.

Kingfisher sighed, dragging her across the basement, fastening her chain to a water pipe. She wished he hadn't, because she didn't want to be alone with Mr. Quarry. She found a fixed point on the wall and stared hard at it, doing anything she could to avoid the little man's eyes.

She needn't have bothered. He ignored her entirely, anointing the body with various oils from a myriad of bottles he removed from his bag.

"It was, as you might have imagined, our Mr. Lazarus," said Kingfisher a short time later, walking back down the stairs, "phoning to check on our progress."

Quarry clucked his tongue against his teeth, saying nothing.

"So, then, Mr. Quarry, are we ready for the blood?"

"Indeed," said Quarry, eyes turning toward Nadine.

Blood? Oh God, they were talking about her!

Kingfisher crossed the room in three big steps, removed her chain from the water pipe, and led her to the body.

"Please don't do this," she begged, pulling frantically against the chain. "I'll do anything. Please, don't kill me!"

"If you hold still," said Quarry, for the first time speaking to her, "this won't even hurt. Here, I can use your hand."

He touched her and his hands felt simultaneously cold and dry, like a snake slithering over her skin. He was deceptively strong and had no trouble turning her hand over against her will, palm facing the ceiling. With the other hand he removed a pair of tweezers from his bag and deftly removed the splinter, a long, ugly bit of weathered wood, letting it drop harmlessly to the floor.

"Now that wasn't so bad, was it?" Kingfisher asked, laying a hand on her shoulder.

She was about to reply when Quarry, his hand still around her wrist, shoved a sharp needle into the incision the splinter had left in her palm. The needle was connected by a rubber tube to a shunt of some sort, and she watched in horror as her blood traveled quickly through the rubber to spill out the end of the shunt.

Her hand felt like it was on fire. She screamed, struggling against his grip, but he wouldn't let go. Instead, he moved her from one place to the other, in a counter-clockwise motion, allowing the metal shunt to drip blood across the body, covering the areas he had marked earlier with charcoal.

He yanked the shunt from her skin and pushed her away, sending her sprawling across the cement floor. She tripped, braced herself for the fall, landing hands-first on the dirty basement floor, bringing up dust. Both palms felt raw, and her right hand, the one Quarry had cut, left bloody prints wherever it touched the rough cement.

"What…why did you do that to me?" she sobbed, rocking back and forth, knees pulled up to her chest. "Please, just let me go."

"Tomorrow," Kingfisher said, gently pulling Nadine to her feet. "After tomorrow, you'll never have to deal with poor Mr. Quarry or myself ever again."

She stared at the giant, wondering what tomorrow might bring. Whether death or her escape, she wasn't sure that she really cared anymore.

At least with death, she would forget all that she'd seen and heard since the two strangers had broken into her home and taken over her life. If she lived, she'd have to deal with not only the loss of her parents but also the memories of what had been done to them. She didn't know which was worse.

Chapter 11

Claire found herself in a graveyard. The sky was rolling with thunderclouds and the air was so thick with moisture that it almost hurt to breathe. She was eleven years old and had snuck out of the house for the first time in her life. She was dressed in cowboy print pajamas and wearing moccasins, trying desperately to be brave.

Johnny, her best friend since Kindergarten, had been jazzing her for weeks about sneaking down to the old cemetery. They all knew, or at least suspected they knew, what Claire's father could do, and Johnny had dared her to see if she could follow in his footsteps. She, in turn, had dared him to come with her, and he'd readily agreed.

Only Johnny wasn't here. He had sworn on a stack of bibles that he'd meet her here at midnight, but it was nearly twelve-thirty and he still hadn't shown up. Her clothes were damp with the pervasive summer humidity, and she wanted nothing more at that moment than for her dad to find her, take her home, and ground her for a week. Even if she missed *Quantum Leap* and all of the *Thundercats* reruns after school, it would be worth it just to be at home in bed and safe in her room.

She'd wait another fifteen minutes, and that was it. She set the alarm on the new watch she'd gotten for her birthday for twelve forty-five. If Johnny didn't show up by then, well, screw him. She'd shown up, that was for sure, and if he didn't believe her, she might have to punch him in the nose.

She surveyed the cemetery, for the first time taking in all the headstones and crypts that littered the landscape. Even in the dim light given off by the half-moon overhead, she could see that there was a rich history here just waiting to be explored. Some of the dates went all the way back to the late 1800's, but the ones that really creeped her out were the stones with only a single date. Babies.

That brought her thoughts back to Johnny. She knew that his mother had given birth to a stillborn little girl years before either of them was born. She wondered for a moment if the baby's grave was somewhere out here, immediately feeling guilty.

And then her watch alarm went off, and that's when all hell broke loose. She'd forgotten about the alarm and jumped back in shock as its incessant beeping shrieked through the night. That's when she first saw them. There were dozens of people roaming about the cemetery, looking at headstones and chattering to each other.

In that moment every single one of them turned to face her, their eyes locked onto hers. They began to advance toward her, arms outstretched, murmuring. She wanted to scream, but her lips wouldn't work. Her heart beat fast against her rib cage, and she almost peed her pants. She lurched backward, falling over a low marble marker, landing hard. Pain shot through her shoulder, and she felt tears welling up in her eyes.

They were all over her in an instant, grabbing at her hair and clothes, needing to be with her, to consume her. Only none of them actually touched her. Their hands went through her, but, each time they did, she learned a little more about them. The knowledge just appeared full-blown in her head and wouldn't go away no matter how fervently she prayed for it to stop.

Daniel, who'd been having an affair with his wife's sister, died in an explosion at the plant; he wondered if Mary's husband, his brother-in-law, ever found out the child she was carrying wasn't his.

Little ten-year-old Ellie had been raped and murdered by her father, a disturbed and violent man who had blamed the attack on the retarded Negro boy across the street. The town had lynched the boy, and her father had gotten away with his crime.

Robert, who, at age ninety-five, had died in his sleep; Charlene, a teenager who'd driven drunk the night of her prom; and Fergus Smiley, a military man who'd survived the Civil War only to slip and break his neck hanging Christmas decorations. All these and more assaulted Claire's mind, overrunning her psyche.

And then Johnny was there, grabbing her by the armpits, pulling her through the cemetery, over the tombstones, and out the huge iron gate that separated this place of death and despair from the rest of the town, and from the living.

She rolled onto her stomach and threw up. Johnny patted her on the back, telling her that it was going to be all right, and finally she climbed shakily to her feet.

"I'm sorry," he whispered, leading her across the road to her bicycle. "I just had to find out, had to see if any of it was real."

"So what did you see?" she spat, jerking away from him. She started crying again but turned away, tears streaking down her cheeks. She wiped her eyes with the back of her sleeve before turning defiantly toward him, demanding that he answer the question.

"I saw enough," he finally said. "I didn't see them, if that's what you're asking. I couldn't see them, but I know they were there. I know they're real. I saw your reaction. It's real. Everything they ever said about your dad is real. And you, too."

Johnny, her bicycle, the cemetery, all of it whirled away in a soupy mist as some unseen force began to shake her, repeating her name over and over again. She wanted to fight, to run away, but then finally, mercifully…

…she was awake, and Leesie sat in bed beside her, her face full with concern.

"Are you all right?" she whispered, her hand on Claire's stomach. "I heard you scream out in your sleep. It took forever to wake you up."

Claire felt her pillow; it was soaked with tears. The dream, already slipping away, had seemed so real. A childhood friend, a cruel prank, a bond forever broken.

"I'm okay," she finally answered, draping her hand across Leesie's. "I'm glad you came."

"What were you dreaming about?" Leesie asked.

"No clue," she said, reaching for the last tenuous threads of her subconscious but falling short. Had it been about Jimmy Cross, the man she'd met at the park? There was something there for a minute, just out of reach, but then it was gone. Try as she might, she couldn't dredge it back up again.

She thought back to last night. They'd watched television and talked until just past two in the morning, devouring a huge tub of Ben and Jerry's Chunky Monkey ice cream between them, getting to know each other all over again. Just girl talk, Leesie had said, but it had been more than that. It was obvious that Leesie cared a great deal for her, and she wanted more than anything to be able to remember those feelings and return them in kind. More than anything, she wanted her life back.

She'd learned a lot from their talk. She knew that she was a successful illustrator of children's books and had a sister currently living in Dallas, but there was still so much she didn't know. Leesie told her that they'd first met in eighth grade, when Claire's family moved to Arkansas from Texas, and had both graduated with honors from Rogers High School. But she couldn't tell her what books she read, what boys she had crushes on, or if she'd always wanted to be an illustrator or if had just been something she'd fallen into.

They poured through Leesie's photo albums and their high school yearbook, and more answers came forth through Claire's questions, however she still had little idea what kind of person she'd actually been before all this started. Why would she marry a man who abused her? And whatever happened to Ian, the boy Leesie said she'd dated throughout their senior year of high school and well into college?

Still full of questions but exhausted, she finally allowed Leesie to lead her to the spare bedroom-cum-office where she'd be spending the night, but not before promising her friend that she'd let her take her to the hospital in the morning. She'd barely managed to get undressed and pull on the pajamas that Leesie had loaned her before falling asleep on the daybed.

"Scoot over," Leesie finally said, wedging herself into the tiny bed. "It's just a little past three, and I don't know about you but I'm still sleepy. It'll be just like high school, minus getting drunk, talking about boys, and making fun of Missy Sanchez."

Claire grinned sleepily, wishing she could remember anything at all about high school. She rolled over to make room for her friend before finally letting her eyelids drift shut. Within seconds she was asleep again, and, mercifully, stayed that way until morning.

Chapter 12

Farris watched from beside Sabrina as Caleb, Walt, and Brian dug his grave. Susie sat astride the beer cooler, her little black skirt hiked up past her knees, while Jasmine hovered uselessly between the two girls like a fluttering butterfly. No one but Susie had spoken for the last ten minutes, and that was only to give instructions where to dig. Apparently, she'd been planning this for a long time.

"Farris," Sabrina whispered to his corpse, tears trailing down her cheeks, "I'm so, so sorry. I didn't want to do this. They said it'd be good for a laugh, and then that would be it. Oh God, I never meant for you to get hurt."

He reached out for her, watching helplessly as his hand passed through her cheek. Brian had made it painfully obvious that he was more than ready to kill her. All Susie had to do was give the word, and Sabrina Locke would join him in his makeshift grave. He'd wanted them to be together since fourth grade, but this wasn't exactly what he'd had in mind.

"Just stay put, Sabrina," he whispered, pretending that she could hear him, "and do whatever they say. I'm toast, but you don't have to be. Whatever you do, just don't forget me. Don't forget me, because I'm never going to forget you."

"I did like you, you know," she whispered, her teeth chattering. "Remember when we were lab partners in biology, in junior high? You were so funny, and so smart. And I knew you liked me, knew you had a crush on me. But everyone made fun of you, and…I was just too weak, too scared, and too…too fucking afraid of not being popular, of every-one making fun of me, to say anything."

Farris stood there with his mouth open. If he still had a heart, he knew it would be racing a mile a minute. She liked him. She actually liked him. Too bad her boyfriend had to go and murder him before he had the chance to find that out. As happy as he was at the revelation, the being dead thing kind of took the wind out of his sails. He was sev-enteen and had never slept with a girl, much less kissed one, and now he never would. Being dead definitely put a damper on one's social life.

"Almost there, guys," Susie said happily, breaking the silence. "In a minute you're gonna hit a concrete lining. You'll have to lift it out of the grave and set it aside. Be careful not to crack it, and don't cut your-self. We're gonna bury our boy beneath it, where he'll be all nice and cozy."

"Concrete?" Walt asked. "Why's there concrete in a grave?"

"To protect the coffin from moisture, dummy," Susie said. "Most graves have 'em, even though they're rarely mentioned in movies or books. Guess it's not a convenient plot point, but in this case it'll serve us just fine."

Farris heard one of the shovels clank against something hard. That must be Susie's concrete liner. He walked toward his killer, peering down into the grave as Brian and Caleb wedged their fingers around the cement and hauled it out of the hole. Walt helped them, and to-gether they lowered it to the ground beside his body.

In just a few minutes, his corpse was going to be tossed unceremo-niously into that deep, dark hole and sealed forever. But what would happen to him, to the ghost him? Would he be forever cursed to haunt the graveyard, or would he be free to follow Susie home and do his dead level best to somehow turn her life into a living hell? If it had to be one or the other, he hoped with everything in him that it was the latter.

"I think I just hit the coffin," Brian said, digging again, "But something's funny. I think…it's all broken, like…oh, Jesus, oh fuck, oh fuck!"

A hand burst through the dirt, grabbing Brian by the wrist, pulling the teenager kicking and screaming into the open grave.

"Thanks for the help," said a gravelly voice from inside the pit, "I've been trying to get out of there since this morning. Coffin wasn't a problem, but that concrete was a real bear."

Jasmine was screaming, clutching at Sabrina, while Walt and Caleb threw aside their shovels to crab walk frantically away from the grave.

Wailing now, Jasmine sobbed into Sabrina's shoulder while she sat unmoving beside Farris's body, slowly rocking back and forth, her eyes fixed on the open grave.

Susie just stared, eyes wide and face turned ashen, watching as a human form clawed and crawled over Brian's kicking legs, pulling itself from the earth and out of the grave.

"And you," he said, pointing an accusing finger at Susie, "you actually thought you were going to get away with it? You killed poor Farris over there," he gestured at the spot where Farris's ghost stood, "before he'd even had the chance to really live. What's wrong with you kids today anyway? No respect for human life.

"Now, you, young lady," he said, pointing at Sabrina, "I'm disappointed with."

Farris heard a sharp snap as the man knelt down into the grave and twisted Brian's neck. The teenager's legs spasmed once, twice, and then stopped moving. The killer pulled himself over the dead boy's body and out into the graveyard.

The man's curly, gray hair was matted to his head and caked with mud, and worms crawled in and out of his flaring nostrils. His complexion was waxy, probably from the embalming, and he was dressed in a nice blue suit and black wingtip shoes. The suit was soiled with dirt and mud, and ripped in several places, but the shoes seemed to have survived the climb out of the grave with only minor scuffing.

"This isn't happening. This isn't happening," Susie repeated over and over, staring at the walking corpse in shock.

Tears filled her eyes, mascara streaking down her cheeks. She stumbled slowly backward, tripping over the cooler of beer. Bottles of Pirate Monkey rolled everywhere, some falling into the open grave while others cracked against Margaret Ruskin's headstone, spilling their contents to soak into the cold cemetery dirt.

"Of course it's happening," the man said, lumbering across the grass. "Shit like this happens all the time, Susie, at least these days. And you'll be pleased to know that Farris, who's standing over there," he gestured toward Farris's ghost, "is watching every minute of it."

The zombie could see him! "Please don't hurt Sabrina," he screamed, jumping up and down, waving his arms in front of his face. "I'll do whatever you want, but please don't hurt Sabrina."

"Wouldn't dream of it, kid," he said with a wink, shuffling toward the blonde sociopath with the killer legs.

"You…you killed him," she whispered, pointing at the open grave. "Oh my God, you killed him. You…what are you?"

"I kinda, sorta killed him," the zombie muttered in a sing-song voice, imitating Susie, "and you might want to think about getting out of here, before I do the same thing to you."

But Susie was already up and running, dancing around the edge of the grave, moving toward the cemetery gates.

"Sorry," said Sabrina, standing between her and escape, "but it's not gonna happen."

She punched the cheerleader hard in the mouth, breaking teeth and bloodying her own knuckles. Susie dropped like a rock, still as the cold night air that threatened to suffocate the graveyard around them.

Farris wanted to cheer. He had no clue what was going on here, but at least his death wasn't going to go unavenged.

Jasmine whimpered to herself while Walt and Caleb just stared at the zombie in wide-eyed disbelief, slowly backing away from the open grave and the dead man who stood before it.

Sabrina, however, stood her ground, chin defiantly thrust into the air. She wasn't going anywhere, and he loved her all the more for it.

Caleb and Walt finally broke into a run, following Jasmine as she ran screaming from the graveyard. They clambered into Caleb's car, gunned the engine, and spun out of sight.

"So, Daddy," Sabrina said to the Zombie, arms crossed in front of her, teeth chattering from the cold, "it's not that I'm not happy to see you, but would you please tell me what in the hell is going on here, and why you're not dead like you're supposed to be?"

Chapter 13

The zombie was Sabrina's *father?* So that's why he looked familiar. He knew that Gabriel Locke had died three weeks ago, but hadn't made the connection to the dead man he saw in front of him. He seemed to remember that Sabrina had an older half-brother or half-sister out there somewhere, from her father's previous marriage, but other than that knew precious little about her family.

Apparently, Sabrina's mother had been the guy's second wife, and Farris knew that they'd split up and he'd remarried again just before his death. Old Gabriel certainly got around. He wondered if this whole rising from the dead thing was a common occurrence for the Locke family. Then again, nothing had been common about this night.

"So let me get this straight," Sabrina said, crouching on the ground near her dead father. "Farris is here, but we can't see him?"

"That's about the size of it," Gabriel answered, loosening his tie. "He's standing right over there," he pointed at Farris, "staring at you like some lovesick puppy."

If Farris weren't already dead, he would have wanted to die, and if he still had skin, it would have turned a deep shade of red. As it was, all he wanted was a voice. He longed to tell Sabrina how proud he was of her for standing up for him when it mattered the most, and not letting Susie get away with her crime.

"Hi Farris," she said, waving in his general direction. "I'm really, really sorry I got you into this whole mess. If I'd known how messed up Susie was…"

"Tell her I forgive her," Farris said, enunciating as if he were addressing someone hard of hearing, "and that…"

"You can tell her yourself," Gabriel interrupted, reaching out to lay a mottled hand across Corpse Farris's chest. "Now hold on, son, this is really gonna hurt."

One moment he was standing beside Sabrina, staring down at his body, and the next he simply wasn't. It was as if someone had turned off the lights and the sound all at once, and he was floating alone in an empty vacuum.

And then he was back in his body again. He drew in a huge breath and screamed. His muscles were contracting, cramping, and he writhed around on the ground in the most terrible pain he'd ever experienced in his life. It felt like all of his nerves were firing at once, sending angry little pulses of energy from the tips of his toes to shoot out the top of his head.

He tried to talk, but the only thing that escaped his lips was a sputtering, guttural gasp of pain. His teeth gnashed down hard on his tongue, blood filling his mouth to drain back into his throat and sinuses. He choked, wheezing and hacking up bloody phlegm, trying to catch his breath.

"Jesus," said Sabrina, rolling him on his side and rubbing his back. "What did you do to him, Dad?"

"Am…I alive?" Farris finally managed to choke out. Talking hurt like hell, but nothing could compare to the excruciating stab of pain that started at the back of his neck and shot straight through his chest.

"You're a helluva lot closer to being alive than I am, kid, but you're still dead."

"Then…how?" he whispered, trying to wrap his mind around all the events that had unfolded in the last few hours. "And why do I hurt so much? And how are *you* alive?"

"I wish I knew the answer to that one myself," he said, thumping himself on the chest. "It's not supposed to work like this. When I died, I certainly never expected to wake up again. That coffin was a nightmare getting out of, and I don't relish going back anytime soon.

"Farris, I put your spirit back in your body and everything's pretty much working again. What I couldn't do for myself, I can do for you. You'll have some problems, to be sure, but you'll age just like anyone would, you'll heal, though slower than most, and you'll have a certain affinity for brains."

"Dad!" Sabrina said, before he could react. She rolled her eyes. "Farris, he's only kidding. At least about the zombie stuff."

"You...you," Farris stammered, losing it, "*knew* about him, what he could do? Knew that I was a ghost?"

"I've always known he had certain abilities," she admitted, "things he could do that were pretty much unexplainable, at least to me. It apparently runs in the family. But when he died, I thought he was dead for good. I'm still reeling from that one. Hell, I think I'm actually in shock as we speak.

"As for you, I had no idea. If I had, I probably never would have gotten into the whole biology class thing." A deep blush spread across her cheeks and she looked away, but Farris could see she was smiling.

"But this," he said, waving his arms to encompass his body, "is incredible. I mean, I was dead, and now I'm not."

"Farris, I took a life back there so I could give you back yours," Gabriel interjected, laying a hand on the teenager's shoulder. "Not something I'm proud of, but, under the circumstances, it seemed like a fair trade."

"From my perspective, I have absolutely no problem at all with it," Farris said, his legs like spaghetti as he climbed to his feet. He still felt a little shaky, but at least he could stand now.

"Your body is healing, and inside of twenty-four hours you should be back to the way you were before that kid broke your neck. But I'm not as strong as I was before I died, and it takes a certain...mojo, to do what I did. If I die again before you're healed, I'm not altogether sure you won't follow suit."

"So," said Farris, stretching out the word, "this whole undead thing might only be temporary?"

"Kid, you don't know the half of it. But if I can get to where I need to go, it might not even be an issue. You have a car, right?"

"If you can call it that," Farris grimaced, thinking about his clunky 2003 Buick Le Sabre. The car was purple and had over a hundred-thousand miles on the odometer, but at least it ran.

"Wait a minute Dad," said Sabrina, moving closer, "where are you going? I mean, where can you go? You're supposed to be dead."

"Doesn't matter," he growled, "because if this thing doesn't get fixed, and fixed soon, there won't be anyone around to remember me anyway. And I doubt that I'm the only one who rolled over in his grave today."

"What're you talking about?"

"South," he said cryptically, ignoring the question. "Farris and I are going south. Or maybe it's west, I'm not entirely sure yet."

"Me?" Farris interjected, surprised. He owed the man his life, but what about his family? For that matter, what about school? "I can't go. My mom and dad will go nuts."

"But you're the man with the car, Farris," the Zombie said, smiling, "and after being locked in a coffin for three weeks, I could certainly use the company. Besides, Sabrina's friends," he shot his daughter a re-criminating look, "are probably already at the police station, giving their spin on what just happened. If we don't get out of here now, there are going to be an awful lot of questions, especially once Susie here wakes up."

"Well, I'm going," said Sabrina, for the first time daring to touch her father's arm. There were tears in her eyes as she pulled him into an awkward embrace. "I've already lost you once, and I'm not going to go through that again."

"I'd say no," the Zombie whispered, stroking his daughter's long, dark hair, "but I know you'd just end up following me anyway."

"Damn straight."

"You know, on second thought," said Farris, thinking about Sabrina, "maybe I will come along, after all. Like you said, I'm the man with the car. And after what you did for me, how could I possibly refuse?"

Chapter 14

It was just before ten in the morning when Claire and Leesie arrived at the Mercy Medical Center, a large, sprawling complex just a few minutes from Leesie's two-story colonial in the Champion Estates development. When morning came she tried to beg off, but Leesie wouldn't hear it.

She was beginning to regret ever agreeing to visit the hospital in the first place. Dr. Frazee, a gruff, fifty-something neurologist, was insistent on doing a battery of tests, while Dr. Sturdivant, a red-headed psychiatrist who couldn't be more than a day or two over thirty, wanted to treat her with drugs and therapy.

Physically, there was nothing wrong with her. The CT scan results were normal, as was her blood work. They'd done a CBC and a TOX panel, and tested for drugs, but everything came back normal. Her reflexes were fine, her vision 20/20, and she exhibited no symptoms of having recently suffered any sort of physical trauma short of the black eye and the fat lip. After spending half the day sending her from one lab to another, Frazee apologized to them and begrudgingly handed her off to Dr. Sturdivant.

Sturdivant's tentative diagnosis was PTSD—Post Traumatic Stress Disorder—though of course she had no idea what sort of stress might cause her to lose her memory in the middle of a pregnancy exam. There had been one scary moment, according to Leesie, when they couldn't find the baby's heartbeat. They had found it a moment later, she quickly reassured Claire, and the baby couldn't be healthier. Had the fear of losing her baby pushed her so far over the edge that she'd forgotten who she was? Claire didn't think so, and Sturdivant seemed to agree.

At first Dr. Sturdivant didn't want to see Claire with Leesie present, but finally relented. Everyone knew more about her than she currently knew about herself, after all, so there was no real sense of confidentially to breach.

They sat in Sturdivant's inner office, the psychiatrist in a beautiful black leather chair, Claire and Leesie on a matching couch. A sturdy-looking steel-and-glass coffee table separated them, and they were surrounded by a collection of antique ceramic and metal face masks hanging from the walls. The masks seemed to mock her, setting her nerves on edge.

One in particular, a brass monstrosity that depicted the goat-god Pan, nearly made her forget the promise she'd made to Leesie and abandon the hospital altogether. She fought down the panic, and, after a few minutes, felt her heartbeat return to normal.

"PTSD can rear its ugly head in many different ways, from many different causes," Sturdivant said, shifting in her seat. She sipped on a steaming cup of coffee, pausing to blow away the steam.

Sturdivant was a little over five feet tall and maybe a hundred pounds soaking wet. Her long, red hair and a manic glint in her emerald green eyes, however, made her resemble one of the wild wee folk of Ireland, a thought that made Claire giggle silently to herself as they talked about her condition.

"Like what?" Leesie finally asked, prompting Sturdivant to continue.

"A long-forgotten memory that suddenly resurfaces," explained the psychiatrist, "perhaps triggered by something that reminded you of an event that you'd blocked out from your past. It could be something as simple as a smell, or a sound, or even one thought that led to another that reminded you of the initial trauma."

"Annie," Leesie said, using the psychiatrist's first name, "how likely is it that her amnesia was caused by the PTSD?"

"While I have to admit that a memory loss like this is very rare in cases dealing with post-traumatic stress," she said, brushing an errant lock of crimson hair back from her eyes, "it's still my best guess. Of course, it's hard to diagnose anything in one session."

"But assuming any of this is true," interrupted Claire, growing frustrated with all the back and forth, "how do I deal with it? How long will it take to get my memory back?"

"You may remember everything tomorrow, or it may take months," Sturdivant said, giving her a half-smile. "There's just no way I can give you a definitive timeline. What I can do, however, is work with you, get you on some medication, and help you face this head on as quickly as possible."

"What kind of medication?" she said, suddenly wary. The thought of medicine made her nervous, though she had no idea why.

"First, we'll treat the PTSD and see what happens. I'd like to start you on twenty-five milligrams of Zoloft, ramp up to fifty, and then reevaluate in three or four weeks and see where we are then. The medication is perfectly safe for your baby," she smiled, apparently taking Claire's sudden unease as concern about the little body growing inside of her, "and I'll be working with you at least a couple times a week so we can figure out what caused all this and get you back to leading a full and productive life."

"She doesn't normally see patients for therapy," Leesie added, "but she's going to make an exception for you."

I don't need any favors, she wanted to say, struggling to prevent the words from passing her lips. They were doing their best to help her. Still, she felt like a rat in a maze, except that, instead of cheese, the prize awaiting her was some awful, half-buried memory that she'd apparently forgotten.

"That's great," she finally said, between gritted teeth. "How soon can we start?"

"How about Monday? I think I have an opening at," she paused, flipping through a black leather book, "three fifteen in the afternoon. Will that work for you?"

"As far as I know," she said. If she had any other pressing engagements, she certainly wasn't aware of them.

"Great," Sturdivant replied as she wrote out Claire's prescriptions. She ripped two pages from the pad and passed them to Claire.

The first was for a Zoloft starter kit. According to the instructions, she'd take twenty-five milligrams of the drug each day for seven days before switching to fifty milligrams. There were no refills on the scrip, presumably because she'd get a regular prescription once she finished the starter pills.

The second was for something called Buspirone. The prescription was for 90 five milligram pills. She was supposed to take them as needed, up to three times a day. She looked at the doctor, raising her eyebrows.

"You mentioned you've been having nightmares," Dr. Sturdivant explained. "This should help you sleep, and will take the edge off the anxiety that the Zoloft might cause for the first few weeks as your brain chemistry adjusts itself. Those are safe for your first trimester, and after that, if you still need help sleeping, we'll put you on something else.

"And now, I want you to go home. Familiar surroundings may spontaneously trigger memories. I know that might seem scary to you right now, because it's so unknown, but you need to give it a try. Look through old photos. Let yourself remember."

Claire thanked her, and, with Leesie, left the office and followed the corridor to the main thoroughfare through the hospital. She felt guardedly optimistic. Maybe her life wasn't a total wreck, after all. If the medicine worked, she might even be able to pick up the pieces and start connecting the fragments she'd managed to remember with everything Leesie had told her.

They walked to the in-hospital pharmacy, a subsidiary of Wal-Mart, and dropped off her prescriptions. She had a frightening couple of minutes when she couldn't find her insurance card, but finally located it tucked into her wallet behind her Visa. The whole event left her feeling stupid and depressed, one more ride on the emotional rollercoaster she'd boarded yesterday at Leesie's office.

They'd just sat down on a wooden bench, one of many interspersed throughout the hospital, when Leesie received a page.

"I need to get this one, hon," she smiled, putting away the pager and pulling a tiny red cell phone from her purse, "it's the clinic. But I'll be back before your scrip is filled."

She stood up, dialed her phone, and walked off toward the lobby.

Upon Leesie's insistence, she'd called MedaLab this morning, where her husband was employed, and asked when he'd be getting back from the conference. His secretary, a beleaguered-sounding woman with a New Jersey accent, said that his plane was expected in at six o'clock this evening.

With everything Leesie had told her about him, she wasn't sure she wanted to be there when Jeff got home, but she knew that she needed to be. If she were going to remember anything, she needed to immerse herself in the life that she'd apparently led for the last four years, and she needed to find out what, if anything, her husband might have had to do with her amnesia.

Leesie didn't want her to go home, but her mind was made up. She had a map to Leesie's house and a telephone number, if she needed it, and she'd obviously learned to fight somewhere. If push came to shove and Jeff was as bad as Leesie said he was, she definitely wouldn't let the man hurt her.

"Have you seen my mommy?" said a young voice from behind her. Startled, she spun around, surprised to see a brown-haired, blue-eyed boy no older than six or seven dressed in a blue Batman costume. He carried a Jack-o-lantern pail in one hand, and the mask to the costume in the other.

"What's your name?" she asked gently. His cheeks were red and she could see that he'd been crying.

"Lucas," he whispered, his eyes darting back and forth between her and the hallway, "I can't find my mommy anywhere."

"What's your last name, Lucas?" she gently prodded, reaching out for him. She let her hand fall to her side as he backed away.

She patted the bench beside her, but he made no move to take the seat. He did, however, inch a little bit closer, and she decided that was good enough for now.

"Foster," he finally said, answering her question. "My name is Lucas Foster, and I live at 484 Hudson Street in Rogers, Arkansas, and I can't find my mommy. I've looked everywhere for her and my brother, and...and..."

He started to sniffle, tears welling up in his larger-than-life little boy eyes. He looked genuinely scared. What kind of mother would let her son wander away from her in a big hospital like this, she wondered, but mentally checked herself. What was important now was finding the boy's mother; recriminations could wait until later.

"It's okay, Lucas," she whispered, wanting more than anything in the world to take him into her arms and dry his tears. But he still seemed skittish, so she decided it best to keep her distance. "We'll find your mommy, I promise. What's her name? I'm sure we can have the pharmacist page her or call her cell phone."

"Cell phone?" he gave her a funny look, like what she'd said was the strangest thing he'd ever heard. "She was just here a minute ago. Sam and me, we were just gonna go to one last house. We were walking with a bunch of other kids. One of them rang the doorbell and then something happened, and then Mommy and Sam were gone."

"One last house?" she repeated, staring at him. "You mean trick-or-treating? When was this?"

According to Leesie it was early October, which meant Halloween was at least two weeks away. She felt her heart skip a beat. How long had this little boy been lost?

"Just a little while ago," he said, shaking his pail at her like the answer to her question should have been obvious. "See? We got Snickers bars. And not the little ones, the regular size ones like you get at the store!"

"My favorite, too," she said, marveling at how quickly kids could change gears. But if she were going to help him, they needed to get back to the matter at hand. "What did you say your mommy's name was?"

"My mommy's name is Sherry Foster," he said, his voice trembling. His face fell as he was reminded of his missing mother. "And my dad's name is Mark Foster, only he doesn't live with us anymore. My mom has to be around here somewhere, right?"

"I've told him," intoned another voice, gruff and scratchy, "that his mom ain't nowhere around here. He's been looking for her for a long time. Besides, if she were here, they'd a found each other by now, don't you think?"

Claire looked up to find a huge mountain of a man staring down at her. He was dressed in threadbare thrift store clothing and wore once-white tennis shoes now stained a yellowish-brown. He was almost bald, save for a thin smattering of greasy black hair that covered the back half of his skull. The man looked to be nearly blind in one pale green eye and rheumy in the other.

She knew that looks could be deceiving, but she definitely didn't want this guy hanging around Lucas.

"Go away, mister," said Lucas, surprising her. "My mommy won't like you making fun of me."

"Look, kid," he said, reaching out to ruffle the boy's hair, "I ain't making fun of you. I've been here a long time, and your momma ain't here. Just accept it and move on. She ain't here, ain't never been here, and she sure as hell ain't looking for you."

"What an awful thing to say!" Claire said, her voice rising as she clambered to her feet. "He's lost and scared, and he just wants—"

"Ma'am," the pharmacist called to her, his voice echoing as if from a great distance, "I said, your prescriptions are ready."

"Just a minute," said Claire, wheeling around to face him through the Plexiglas enclosure that protected him from the outside world. "Can't you see I'm in the middle of something?"

She turned back to Lucas and, where there had just been him and the gruff old man a moment before, now dozens of people in every manner of dress roamed the halls. One man, missing half his leg, shuffled down the hallway on crutches, while an old woman did wheelies around him in her wheel chair. Some were dressed in hospital gowns, others in street clothes, and a few weren't even dressed at all.

She blinked several times, shaking her head violently. This couldn't be happening. She reached for Lucas's shoulder but missed, sprawling against the bench, cracking her knee against the dark, polished wood. She rubbed it, looking around in dismay. Everyone was gone. Lucas, the old man, all of them, they were all gone. It was just her and the pharmacist.

"Ma'am, are you okay?" he asked, coming out of his cubicle. "Do you need me to call someone? You don't look so good."

"I'm okay," she answered, knowing full well that she wasn't. She was having hallucinations, talking to people who weren't even there.

She was so far from okay that it wasn't even funny, but the worst of it was that she still had absolutely no idea what "okay" might even be for her. Was she schizophrenic? The thought that she might never truly know what was wrong with her chilled her to the bone.

"Okay, sorry about that," said Leesie, rounding the corner. "Are you ready…what's wrong? Claire, you're shaking. What happened?"

"I'm okay," she said, repeating the lie she'd told the pharmacist. "It's been a long day already, and I just want to go home."

Chapter 15

Nadine tried to sleep, but the acrid odor of urine kept her tossing and turning. It seemed like days since Mr. Kingfisher had been in to change her bucket, though she knew it had probably only been two or three hours. She had long ago given up asking to go to the bathroom and now peed in the bucket like it was second nature.

This certainly gave new meaning to the nickname "Unclean Nadine."

She read in a book once that human beings, if properly motivated, were only a step away from becoming animals. She had no doubt that it was true, and wouldn't be surprised if, sooner or later, she found herself eating off the floor and howling at the moon.

Her hand still hurt from where they'd stuck her with the needle. Mr. Kingfisher had bandaged her palm with gauze and tape he'd found in the bathroom, but she thought it was getting infected. The bleeding seemed to have stopped, but it throbbed every time she touched something or rolled over.

Today was Saturday, she was almost certain of it. She wouldn't be missed in school until Monday, if even then. Certainly none of her classmates would miss her, though hopefully one of the teachers would. But if they called and no one answered, what could they do? They'd just assume that she was sick and that would be the end of it.

She decided to face facts. No one was going to show up and get her out of this situation. Her parents were dead, and nobody knew what had happened. If she were going to survive this, she would have to take care of herself.

Having long given up on the knife under her bed, she finally realized that she had other options. Her bed stood against the west wall of the room, four or five feet from the window. She knew she couldn't reach it by herself—she'd spent half of last night trying—but with a little help, she might at least be able to snag the mirror they'd taped to her window.

Her captors seemed to be spending most of their time in the basement, so she didn't think they'd hear it if she broke the mirror. And if they did, would she be any worse off than she already was?

She had been in the same clothes forever, and her bra was killing her. She had ignored the pain, using it as a focus to keep from going completely insane. But now she reached up under her shirt, behind her back, and undid the clasp. The garment slipped from her breasts, falling loose.

The bra slipped easily through her left sleeve and over her injured hand, but she couldn't get it past the chain on her right. The window was to her left, on the other side of the bed from where the chain attached to the bedpost, which meant she would have to use nearly all of the two-foot length of the chain just to perch herself on that side of the bed. She needed to somehow get the bra off of the chain and into her other hand.

She gnawed at the strap with her teeth, tearing and gnashing, slowly wearing through the fabric. Twenty minutes later, her jaw hurting and gums numb, she bit through the last thread of elastic and fabric, the bra falling free from the chain. Victory!

Heart beating fast, she rolled over on her stomach and sat on the other side of the bed, her right arm stretched out behind her. She'd never been more thankful for being born left-handed.

Nadine let one end of the bra fall to the floor, flicking her wrist mid-drop, snapping it at the mirror. She was still more than a foot short. She tried again, with the same results. Frustrated, she considered just throwing the bra at the mirror, but there was no guarantee that the mirror would even fall, much less shatter, and even if it did she might not be able to reach one of the shards.

Her new tennis shoes, the green pair she'd gotten from the mall just a few days ago, sat on the floor beside the foot of the bed, lime-colored laces calling out to her.

Changing her tack, she tied a sling into one end of the bra, hoping she could catch one of the shoes in its elastic. Rolling back the way she'd come, she flattened out on her belly, stretching the chain as far as it would reach. Her fingertips just cleared the edge of the bed.

Breathing slowly, seeing the shoes in her mind's eye, she closed her eyes and lowered the loop she'd created in the bra over the edge of the bed. No luck. She tried again, and again, muscles aching, screaming for her to give up, but she wouldn't listen.

Finally, she caught something. She took a deep breath and tried to slow the beating of her heart. Slowly, she pulled the bra, slowly, slowly, the toe of one of her shoes just visible past the foot of the bed. And then it dropped, landing beyond her sight.

Her eyes welled up with tears. She'd been so close, but the loop just couldn't hold the weight of the shoe.

She rolled onto her side. Her arms felt like little rubber bands, stretched to their limits. Like the bra, she just wasn't strong enough to get through this on her own. She was trapped and, sooner or later, now that they no longer needed her, Mr. Quarry would slither into her room and eat her like a snake downing a fat gerbil.

Flinging the bra from her fist in a sudden burst of anger, she was at first annoyed when it failed to go anywhere. She looked down, realizing the clasp had gotten caught on her blouse. The clasp! Instantly she went to work, untying the loop, reworking the male end of the clasps, all three of them, into little hooks.

Vishnu, Shiva, Buddha, even Jesus, if you're listening, let this work!

She snagged the tennis shoe on the third try, and it only took three attempts after that to leverage it up and over the foot of the bed.

Her breathing ragged, her pulse racing, she snatched the treasure and scooted to the head of the bed, greedily working at the laces. They came out easily, adding another thirty-six inches to the length of her bra. She tied them together, knotting the shoe lace through the female side of the clasp, tugging both ends of her prize to make sure it was secure. The knot held true.

Her fingers were sore and cramped, and so she tied the shoe lace end of the makeshift grappling hook to her pointer finger. The anchor cost her three inches in length, but better that that allowing the string to slip out of her hands and losing the bra.

She rolled over on her stomach, coming up to perch on the far side of the bed. Flicking the bra out from her hand, she still fell short of her target. Reeling the material back in, she stretched as far as the chain would allow, feeling the metal dig deep into her aching wrist. She leaned away from the chain, grunting as she felt the cuts from last night rubbed raw once more. And then she snapped her arm, stretching out her fingers, releasing the bra in one fluid motion.

This time, the grappling hook reached its mark. The three little bra clasps perched precariously on the edge of the mirror, creating Nadine's imagined bridge to freedom. Her breath caught in her throat, knowing one wrong move could send the mirror tumbling permanently out of reach.

Sending out a silent prayer to any god who might be listening, she yanked back on the bra, feeling the tape come loose, sending the mirror somersaulting to the floor. Miraculously it did not break, instead landing on its back atop the rug halfway between her bed and the closet.

The mirror had landed on top of the bra strap, the clasps still caught on the edge. She slowly reeled in the mirror, every little bump in the carpet an obstacle to avoid. But she needn't have worried. The bra itself acted as a sledge, pulling the mirror along in much the same way ancient Egyptians had used logs and shims to move heavy stones.

Soon the mirror was in her hands, her heart beating so fast that she could feel it in her ears. She rolled onto her back and untied the shoelace from her finger, shoving the whole thing behind the bed and under the mattress.

Nadine looked at herself in the mirror, the first time she'd seen her reflection since yesterday morning. Her face looked pale and wan, and the mascara she'd put on while her mother was at work had run. Her hair was greasy and tangled, and she had bags under her eyes.

But she was alive. Whatever else had happened, she was still alive. And she would do whatever it took to stay that way.

Nadine slipped the mirror between the bed and the flat sheet, using the weight of her body to softly crack it without alerting any would-be eavesdroppers. Carefully removing her handiwork, she was pleased to see several dagger-like slivers of glass amidst the tiny crystals and silvery dust that remained of Mr. Kingfisher's mirror.

She thought briefly of the squiggle on the back, wondering what its purpose had been, but quickly dismissed it. It didn't matter. What mattered is that now she had a weapon, something she could use to win her freedom. She slid one of the glass daggers into her jeans pocket, leaving the rest hidden under the sheet.

Nadine would choose her attack carefully, striking at the time when opportunity best presented itself. And then no one would ever hurt her again.

Chapter 16

The sun was beginning to set as the huge gray wolf finally emerged from the hills. He sat back on his haunches, panting, exhausted. He had run nonstop all day, halting only to hunt rabbits and squirrels and to drink from whatever ponds and streams he could find. Stretching out across the rocks, he let his muscles relax for a moment before climbing to his feet and creeping carefully down the cliff.

He found himself in a field behind an enormous building. It was something called a Wal-Mart, one of the birds told him, a sprawling marketplace where men traded their wares. He slunk lower to the ground, on guard now for anyone who might see him. But humans were blind and rarely saw what they weren't looking for, so he hardly needed bother.

The wolf crept around the side of the marketplace, sniffing the wind. There were men and women everywhere, many different races, in various states of health. There were fat ones, thin ones, old ones, and young ones, all equally slow but also equally cunning. He would have to tread carefully if he wanted to survive this dangerous encounter with the humans.

Across the field of stone, he saw it: a huge brown and white dog, standing tall and proud in the back of a gigantic metal carriage. The dog sniffed the air, perhaps sensing the wolf's presence. It paced back and forth in the bed of the carriage, whining softly, sneaking glances at the marketplace for signs of its master.

The dog was a close cousin, but, in the end, it was no wolf. The wolf had no master save the Great Spirit, who would have been out of the carriage in an instant had their places been reversed. The wolf whispered softly into the wind, singing promises of running and hunting, fish and raccoons, calling its cousin to him. And eventually, as the Great Spirit had known it would, the dog came.

But, still, the canine was cautious. It followed the wolf behind the marketplace, sniffing carefully, warily, never once turning its back. Its wariness showed the wolf great respect, and for that the great gray hunter was proud. The dog was no enemy. He yearned suddenly to run back to the mountains, bidding the dog to follow him, and, together, they would hunt squirrels and frolic in the sun.

But, alas, that was not to be, for that was not what the Great Spirit wanted. He shot the dog one last, wistful glance, and then crept slowly forward to press his nose to the canine. He felt a great and powerful presence float from his body, through his blood, and out from his coat, leaving him weak and confused and wondering why he had traveled so far from his home. The wolf growled at the dog standing before him, nipped at its leg, and then slowly backed away. He turned and ran up the hill, thinking only of the forest, never once looking back.

✳ ✳ ✳

The dog trotted out from behind the Wal-Mart, thinking that today was a very good day. He sniffed the air, surveying the land around him. It had been here dozens of times before but, somehow, this time was different. The air smelled sharp and crisp, and his senses were on edge; there was a crow there, strutting through the grass island and eating bits of fallen popcorn. And another dog, a female, inside a car just about thirty yards from his master's truck. She was in heat but, sadly, he didn't have time to give her his seed.

The Great Spirit had entered him and required him to do things, things that he didn't understand. He would have no time for bitches, for playing catch, or for rolling in the sun, at least not until he had carried the spirit where it needed to go.

He turned away from the scent of the female and hopped into the back of the truck, where he'd been before he'd heard brother wolf's call. And not a moment too soon, for here came his master.

"Hey, Butchie," called the gruff old man, reaching out to scratch him behind the ears, "good boy, good coon dog. Sorry I took so long. But I got you some 'Ol Roy, feed you up just fine as soon as we get home, and then we'll play us some catch. That's a boy, good dog."

His master's touch had always been comforting, but not today. No, today he just wanted the old man to climb into the truck and drive. On any other day, he'd drop to the ground, roll onto his back, and let his master rub his belly. But it was all he could do to resist the urge to rip the man's throat out.

His master much have sensed this, for he yanked back his hand and stared at the dog. "Are you okay, boy?" he asked, concern and confusion dancing in his eyes. "You're not acting like yourself."

He sniffed the old man's fingers, tentatively licking his mottled, liver-spotted hand. He'd play the game for now, if that was the only way to get the man to climb into the truck and start driving. He rolled onto his back, showing his belly for the old man to rub.

"That's a boy," crowed his master, stroking his fur. "Just hungry, aren't you Butchie? There, there, good dog. We'll be home soon enough, and maybe after you've had your dinner and a walk I'll get out the Frisbee. What do you think about that, Butchie? There you go, that's a boy, that's a good boy."

As soon as the truck was on the highway, the dog began to howl at the barely-visible moon. He enjoyed the cool night air rushing past his jowls, invigorating him. Just a little while longer, he told himself, and he would be home. And then he would do the Great Spirit's bidding. Together they would hunt the night, taking whatever they wanted.

Yes, today was a very good day.

Chapter 17

The American Airlines flight from St. Louis to Northwest Arkansas was nearly full and, after several delays that resulted in the plane getting a late start, the mood on the 747 was growing sour. The passengers were upset with losing an extra hour in their already busy lives, and the crew was irritated at having to deal with angry passengers. The situation fed on itself, and it wasn't getting any better.

Jeff Summers, however, sat in business-class, sipping scotch and feeling happier and more at peace than he had in years. He'd just closed a deal that would mean that his company's new product, a mouthwash that took the place not only of other mouthwash products but also of toothpaste, would receive prime aisle placement in Wal-Marts all over the country. After floundering in his new position for the first few months of the year, he was finally coming into his own and making his mark in the company. Flight delays notwithstanding, it had been a great day.

His thoughts turned to his wife. He regretted the argument they'd had before he left, regretted hitting her more than anything. He and Claire had been married nearly six years and it had been good, at first, but when she'd suffered the miscarriage, things had taken a turn for the worse. Everyone had been so nice to her, so understanding, so comforting. They didn't seem to understand that he was hurting, too.

It had taken them so long to get pregnant. Three years and over twenty thousand dollars in fertility treatments later, and a miscarriage was all they had to show for their efforts. His sperm had a motility problem, the doctors said. "Lazy sperm," they'd called it. For whatever reason, his sperm refused to get the job done. He'd taken medicine and they'd tried in vitro fertilization, but nothing worked.

Finally, just as they'd all but given up, she'd gotten pregnant, only to lose the baby a month later. That's when the hitting started. He just needed for her to feel some of the pain that he was feeling. Oh, sure, she'd lost a baby, too, but the baby had been a boy—his heir—and what good was working your ass off flying all over the country selling mouthwash if you didn't have someone to pass everything down to after you were gone? He with the most toys wins, but what do you do with those toys when it's time to shuffle off this mortal coil? He needed someone to bond with, someone to mold; he needed a son, and finally, with any luck, she was about to give him one.

It had been just like he'd told her. Once they'd given up on fertilization treatments and just went back to having sex, she'd gotten pregnant again. With the pressure off, his guys had finally gotten the job done. If she could just hang on to this one, things were bound to get better between them.

Their relationship had never been what you'd call passionate. Claire was like an old shoe; she was comfortable. And, sure, every once in a while he felt the need to try on a different pair, as he'd done last night with that red-headed Pfizer account exec at the hotel, but he always came home to his familiar pair of slippers. His wife was the one he'd chosen to spend the rest of his life with, and that's what marriage was all about.

"Sir," said Bethany, the knockout stewardess who'd flirted with him when he'd boarded the plane. She slowed the beverage cart to a stop beside his seat, brushing her hand against his shoulder and smiling coyly. "If you need anything, anything at all, you just let me know, okay?"

He returned the smile, trading his empty glass for another scotch. At six foot two with wavy black hair and the charm of an old time silver-screen movie star, he'd always been blessed with the ability to get whatever woman he wanted, and Bethany would be no exception if he decided to follow up on the playful banter. But he didn't intend for it to go that far. He did love his wife, and while joining the mile high club was tempting, he didn't feel comfortable having his adventures too close to home.

"Just the scotch for now," he winked, leaving his options open, "but I'll definitely let you know if anything comes up later." The double-entendre always got them. Watch the master at work.

"Anytime," she smiled, moving on down the aisle.

"Excuse me," said his seat mate, returning from the bathroom. He maneuvered past his knees, careful not to hit Jeff with his cane. "Quite a line back there. Still think they should install a business-class bathroom. Would save the walking."

Jeff nodded noncommittally, pulling in his knees to give the other passenger room to maneuver around him. As comfortable as business-class was, there was still only so much space on any given plane. Jeff held the man's walking stick for him as he lowered himself into his seat.

His seat mate's name was Jack Bethel, of Bethel Transportation, Shipping, and Import. He had prematurely graying hair and walked with a pronounced limp, a result of, Jeff had found out in a conversation earlier, a rare and progressive form of bone cancer that had taken part of his femur and left him with a partial prosthetic.

"Just missed the drink cart," Jeff said, raising his already-half-empty scotch in toast, "but I'm sure she'll be back around later."

"Not much of a drinker," Bethel shrugged, his bony shoulders rising up and down like a crippled Ichabod Crane.

Jeff wished he could say the same. He'd tried to get off the juice more than once, but then something would happen and he'd find himself falling off the wagon again. After a while, it just didn't seem worth it. Alcohol and women, those were his vices; it could always be worse. At least he didn't smoke or do drugs.

"The cancer," he continued, though Jeff was only half-listening. "Pain pills don't mix well with alcohol."

"I'll be sure to recommend you for some of our trials," Jeff responded, recalling the promise he'd made earlier in the flight.

MedaLab, the company he worked for, was working on several cutting-edge treatments for bone cancer. If he could get Bethel in on one of the groups, it would certainly score him some points. It was always useful to make contacts like Bethel, contacts he could use later if he decided to jump ship and go to work for another company. And if the man felt like he owed him something, well, so much the better.

"I'd appreciate that," Bethel said, smiling, though the smile seemed forced to Jeff, "though I'm scheduled to start a new trial any day now. We'll see how that goes first. But now, if you'll excuse me, I've got a call to make."

Jeff stared at the man, watching as he unattached the sky phone from the back of the seat in front of him but didn't dial. Surely he didn't expect Jeff to get up and wander around the plane while he made his call.

But apparently he did. Bethel made a little shooing gesture, effectively dismissing him, before turning toward the window. His shoulders hunched, he cradled the phone between both hands as he waited for Jeff to leave. Unbelievable.

Jeff got out of his seat, deciding to play nice and give the man his privacy. He resented the imposition, but, if he acquiesced and went along with it, he might be able to use the relationship to his advantage later. He was just a business manager now, in charge of selling to Wal-Mart, but he intended to move up the ladder sooner rather than later, and Jack Bethel could help him do it.

Bethany, who'd just finished serving drinks and was finally sans cart, ran her hand coquettishly through her hair as she caught his eye. She smiled and turned abruptly away, slinking slowly down the aisle toward the bathroom, pausing only once to give him a sultry gaze over her shoulder.

Well, why the hell not? Bethel might be on the phone for a while, and he had to occupy himself somehow. He'd always wondered what privileges and benefits might come with membership in the mile high club, and suspected he was about to find out.

Chapter 18

Claire stood in front of a red brick house on North Mallard Lane, the one that her driver's license said was hers, trying to find the courage to go inside. She walked the length of the front yard again, noting how the small silver maple tree supplied shade for one of the two outer bedrooms while at the same time providing a focal point for the landscaping that surrounded it. It was a beautiful house, but it was what lay inside that terrified her.

After they'd left the hospital, Leesie had driven her to the clinic to pick up the baby blue Toyota Prius that Leesie said belonged to Claire. After that she'd followed Leesie to the house, just six or seven blocks away from the park on Olive Street where she'd spent most of yesterday afternoon.

Leesie had wanted to stay, but Claire insisted that she cross this particular threshold by herself. Besides, Jeff was due home in just a few hours, and if the animosity that existed between her husband and her best friend was anything like what she'd sensed from talking to Leesie, it was probably best that her first interaction with Jeff take place alone.

First? She was supposed to have been married to the guy for the last six years. She sighed. Maybe Dr. Frazee had been right and she should have checked herself into the hospital. She still had the sense, however, that there was more to her amnesia than just being freaked out by her baby's heartbeat, and if that was the case she'd be better served out in the real world trying to put the pieces of the puzzle together rather than locked in some psychiatric hospital for the mentally forgotten.

Okay, she told herself, *enough dawdling*. It was time to go into the house. She walked to the door, took the key ring from her purse, and plunged the key into the keyhole. She turned it slowly, listening to the hollow click as the lock disengaged from the tumblers.

Swinging the door open she almost expected to see herself on the other side, wondering who this strange doppelganger was breaking into her home, but of course the house was empty.

She walked into the foyer, and half a dozen full-color illustrations of whimsical scenes from imaginary worlds hanging on the wall to the right immediately caught her eye. In one, a kind-looking cow held the hand of a little boy as they walked down a cobblestone road. In another, a huge, purple dinosaur with incredibly sad eyes cowered in the corner of a child's bedroom, doing its best to hide from a tiny field mouse that threatened it with a big club more than three times its size.

The drawings, she imagined, must be from the children's books that she illustrated. She stared at them, fascinated. Even after Leesie told her what she did for a living, she'd never imagined that she had such talent. The work was beautiful, and captured an innocence that she couldn't quite believe had come from her. She could have stood there for hours, admiring the work, but instead made herself push further into the house, following the yellow and tan tile into the living room.

The smell of garlic immediately assailed her nostrils, and she realized that she'd smelled it earlier, in the entryway, but had been too preoccupied to notice. She wove herself through the spacious living room, moving past bookshelves filled to bursting with all manner of books and Blu-ray discs, past a massive widescreen television that took up most of one wall, past a matching yellow suede couch and loveseat, and into the kitchen, a roomy space near the back of the house filled with stainless steel appliances and an island work area that rested in the center.

She followed the smell past the pots and pans that hung from hooks above the island to its source; a green and white ceramic crock pot sitting on the counter, plugged into the wall and turned on low. She hurriedly unplugged the crock pot before lifting the lid to peer inside. It was a pot roast, or what was left of one. The atmosphere inside the crock pot had completely dried out, causing the meat as well as the vegetables surrounding it to dehydrate, leaving nothing more than a charred mess.

Shaking her head, she placed the lid back on the crock pot and set about exploring the kitchen. Other than a file box of recipes she found in one of the drawers on the island and an address book filled with names that she did not recognize, she didn't find much to help her. Suddenly famished, she scrounged a bag of Sun Chips from the pantry and a bottle of water from the refrigerator before retreating back into the living room to sort through the mail she'd picked up from the mailbox before coming inside.

Dropping herself onto the loveseat, she scanned the mail; a bill from Cox Cable; another bill from Sprint, which she recognized as being for the cell phone she carried in her purse; a *Lucky* magazine; a *Time* magazine; a catalog from Outdoor World; a Citibank Visa bill; and a hand-addressed letter to her from Melissa Fleming, the younger sister Leesie had told her about.

Aside from the letter and the *Lucky*, everything was addressed to Jeff Summers, the man who was supposed to be her husband. So she sat those aside, along with the magazine, and ripped into the letter from her sister. A pair of photographs fell out, along with a handwritten note:

Dear Claire,

Hope all is going well with your new project. Just got moved and wanted to share my new Dallas address and phone number. I still have the same Gmail email.

Enclosed photos are from last summer. Sorry it's taken me so
long to send copies. Busy, busy, busy!

Love you,

Mel

An address and phone number were carefully printed at the bottom
of the letter. The first photo showed Claire and a young woman with
long, strawberry blonde hair, presumably her sister, clowning around in
a living room she didn't recognize. Claire had her sister in a headlock,
and both women were grinning like fools, mugging for the camera.

She flipped over the photo; "Claire 1, Mel zip, Chicago, but I'll get
you next time" her sister had written on the back. She loved the girl already.

The other photo showed a very different Claire. She and Jeff stood
side by side, hands clasped, staring into the camera. They were both
smiling but her smile looked tense, almost forced, as if she wished she
could be anywhere but there in that room. Her free hand hung limply
at her side, while his held an open can of Budweiser.

The back of this photo said simply, "Claire and Jeff, Chicago." She
let the picture slip from her fingers to flutter gently to the floor. Apparently, everyone knew that she was unhappy in her marriage but her.
Of course this made perfect sense, since she didn't know anything at all
about her life. She felt an incredible sorrow sweep over her, and it was
all she could do to force herself off the loveseat to continue her search.

Traversing down the hallway that lead to the back of the house re-
vealed a perfectly-kept bedroom, a nursery-in-progress, an art studio,
and an office. It was the office that interested her, because it housed a
computer, and where there were computers, there were records.

The office, she assumed, belonged to Jeff. Built-in bookshelves
lined one wall, containing high school and college trophies for football,
baseball, and swimming. An antique Winchester Lever Action rifle

hung above the shelves, and the huge head of an eight-point buck hung above that. A gun cabinet filled another wall, loaded with more rifles, shotguns, and pistols.

She walked to the computer desk and sat down on the leather office chair, staring at the PC that stood atop it. The computer had been left on, thank God, so she didn't have to worry about a login password. She scanned the desktop, seeing the usual Internet Explorer, Outlook, and Microsoft Office icons, along with links to such programs as the Google Chrome browser, Golden Palace Poker, ACDSee graphic file viewer, and WinZip, a program that compressed files to allow for maximum storage space on a hard drive.

The phone rang just as she was opening Microsoft Word, startling her. She snatched it up out of instinct, quickly wishing that she hadn't. She held the phone to her ear, listening, not trusting herself to speak.

"Claire?" said a man's voice on the line, "Claire, are you there? I'm calling from the plane, and the connection's not so good."

"It's me," she finally answered, banging the desk in frustration. The caller ID identified the caller as 'American Airlines Sky Phone,' and so she assumed it was Jeff. She did not want to have this conversation right now, but couldn't see a way out of it.

"Listen, I'm going to be late. The plane was delayed, so I won't be getting in until eight fifteen."

She had no response for that.

"Claire?" Jeff asked, clearly frustrated. "Look, I'm sorry about Wednesday night, okay? But can we just let it go? Start over tonight, when I get home?"

"I think I'd like that," she said slowly, though she supposed she'd already 'started over' without him. "I think I'd like that a lot."

"Great," he said, but something in his voice told her that he was almost disappointed with her answer. "So will eight fifteen work for you, or do I need to make other arrangements?"

What an odd question. "Sure, I'm fine with it if you are."

"Okay, I gotta go. Love you."

"I love you, too," she made herself say into the phone, wondering whether or not it was true. She pressed the off button without waiting for him to say goodbye, and then went back to browsing Word files.

Mostly the files were business correspondence, reports about mouthwash sales, and, curiously enough, erotica. She wondered if Jeff had written them. One told the story of a man home sick from work who ended up having three-way sex with a girl scout and her mother, and another was about a young boy getting seduced by his aunt. Gross, but nothing that shed any light on how or why she'd lost her memory.

Claire clicked open Internet Explorer, and the browser loaded the front page of the Wall Street Journal website. She searched though the saved bookmarks, but couldn't find much of interest save a link to a "barely legal" pay site on the Web. So her husband was seriously into porn. If that was the least of her concerns, she was probably doing okay. At least she hadn't found any links to sites that gave detailed instruction on how to induce amnesia in your wife in three easy steps.

Frustrated, she pushed back from the desk and rose to her feet. According to her Mickey Mouse watch it was five in the afternoon, which meant that Jeff would be getting home in less than four hours. The thought of meeting a husband at the door that she couldn't remember terrified her, and not for the first time that afternoon she second guessed her decision to not allow Leesie to stay with her.

Her studio contained an easel in one corner, a drawing table in another, and an antique writing desk wedged between the two. A khaki-colored futon adorned the opposite wall, littered with half a dozen pillows of various shapes, colors, and sizes. An old teddy bear sat in the middle of it all, looking up at her with feigned disinterest. She smiled and picked up the bear, hoping it might spark a memory. Nothing.

A painting of tiny, colorful fish flying through the sky alongside a half a dozen heart people caught her eye, and she immediately recognized it as a twin to the one at Leesie's house. She assumed the work was hers, making the fact that Leesie had adorned her wall with another painting in the series all the more special.

More of her artwork filled the walls, but these were blown-up covers of finished books. The cover for *A Smile is Worth a Thousand Jelly-beans* showed a little girl greedily hoarding candy beneath her bed, while *Fletcher's New Frog* boasted a little boy wearing a baseball cap carrying a blue frog on his shoulder. The amphibian sported a mischievous smile, as if it and the boy shared a secret that only the two of them knew. There were seven or eight others, containing everything from beautiful-ly-illustrated polka dot dinosaurs to cavorting elephants to soldier mice carrying exaggerated guns made from chewing gum and Popsicle sticks.

There was another one leaning against the futon, not yet hung on the wall. Maybe it was new. It was titled *The Lonely Platypire*, and showed a purple platypus wearing a red and black Dracula cape and sporting little fangs standing in a playground. The little creature looked forlorn as he watched a pig, a duck, and a lizard playing without him. Claire guessed a Platypire must be some sort of vampire platypus.

She stared at the artwork, still amazed that she could create covers like that. The easel displayed a half-finished oil painting of a little blonde girl in pigtails and curls chasing a pink and yellow striped bunny up a set of stairs.

The desk, as it turned out, was a rollaway and contained a laptop computer inside the top drawer. She hit the power button. Her pulse quickened in anticipation at the thought of browsing through forgotten memories, but her hopes were dashed when, after it had powered up, the computer beeped and asked her for a password.

She tried her birthday, her driver's license number, her middle name, and every other bit of information she could glean from her purse, all to no avail. Her maiden name didn't work, either, nor did her husband's name, Leesie's name, or her sister's name; the dialog box spurned her at every turn, insistently beeping for the right keyword to unlock an imagined treasure trove of information hidden just inches beneath her fingertips.

Frustrated, Claire slammed her fist against the desk and immediately felt something furry rub itself against her ankle in response. She jumped back, startled, surprised to see a long-haired, white cat winding itself around her feet.

Corduroy, the cat Leesie had told her about, the feline companion she'd apparently had since college. She reached down to stroke the cat's pretty fur, but jumped back in pain as the animal hissed and sank its teeth into her hand. She cursed as the white ball of fur and fangs shot out of the studio and straight down the hallway.

"Here kitty, kitty, kitty," she called lamely, following the cat through the house.

Shit, she couldn't believe it. So flustered had she been when she'd entered the house that she left the door wide open. Claire watched helplessly as the cat darted out the door and into the darkening afternoon. She chased after him, which only served to make the cat run faster.

"Corduroy, come back," she called, holding her wounded hand to her stomach as she followed his trail.

But the cat was having none of it. Instead he kept running, pausing only to hiss over his shoulder before darting straight into the path of a red Honda Civic. The car tried to swerve but the front tire caught him head on, sending his sleek, white body careening crazily into the curb.

Claire ran screaming down the driveway, watching in horror as the cat spasmed and twitched in pain. A long, red gash marred his head, and his fur was matted with blood. He mewed pitifully into the air, clawing at some unseen foe inches from his face. And then he fell silent, breathing shallow and labored.

The car screeched to a halt, and a visibly shaken woman in her late fifties stumbled out of the car.

"I'm so sorry," she gushed, trembling, "it just darted out in front of me. I didn't even see him until it was too late." Tears streamed down her wrinkled face, and she gripped the side of her open door for support. "Lord, I'm so sorry."

Claire knelt beside the dying cat, stroking its blood-stained fur. She didn't even remember the little guy, but would have given anything if she could take back what just happened.

"Should we take him to the vet?" said the driver, a hint of anguished hope in her voice. "I'll pay for it, of course. Anything."

She ignored the woman's words and continued to stroke the cat. It looked up at her suddenly, its fading eyes sparking with the light of life. It tentatively moved its neck, snaking out a wet, sandpaper tongue to lick her hand. The cat mewed once again, long and quizzically, and then stood straight up, bounded into her arms, and began to purr.

"Oh my lord," said the gray-haired old woman, shaking her head, "it's a miracle. I could have sworn I hit him. I know I did, but I guess it wasn't as bad as it looked."

Claire knew it, too, but they both must have been wrong. The cat nuzzled her throat, his purring vibrating loudly in her ears. She looked down at his head, and the gash had disappeared. The blood, however, still covered his fur, though the cat looked as sleek and healthy as any she'd ever seen.

The driver of the Honda was moving her lips, saying something, but Claire had no idea what. She may have forgotten a lot of things, but she knew that cats didn't spontaneously heal themselves. And, unlike the little boy she'd seen in the hospital, the one who had disappeared without a trace, the red blood staining Corduroy's snow white fur was incontrovertible proof that the animal had actually been hit. She hadn't imagined this; it was all too real.

The cool October air chilled her, but it wasn't the temperature that caused a shiver to creep up her spine. The amnesia still needed to be puzzled out, but for the first time she sensed that was the least of her problems. Something strange was happening, something unnatural, and, like it or not, she was right in the middle of it, and she had no clue how to ever set things right again.

Chapter 19

Dark clouds circled through the sky, the moon barely visible behind them. The leaves had all fallen from the trees, and winter was on the horizon. Claire wondered whether it would snow, and if she even liked cold weather.

Claire pulled into the parking lot in front of Olive Street Park and turned off the car. She had sensed something strange about Jimmy Cross; the way he dressed and talked, not to mention his knowledge of the glass jar. She hadn't been able to put her finger on it then, but now, after what had happened at the hospital and with Corduroy, she was starting to get a few ideas.

Holding a plastic bag she'd gotten from the Casey's General Store, she let herself out of the Prius and crossed the park to the bench where she and Jimmy had spent yesterday afternoon talking. Of course, he wasn't there. Maybe she was wrong about all of this, but she had to find out for sure.

She reached into the bag and pulled out a bag of Frito-Lay BBQ potato chips and a twenty-ounce bottle of Coke Classic, sitting both on the bench.

"Yo, Jimmy," she said out loud, "I brought you some snacks. You must be hungry, as long as you've been waiting out here."

"What do you mean?" said a voice from behind her; it was Jimmy. "I haven't been here that long, Miz Fisher. Just a few hours, that's all."

She held her breath and slowly turned around.

It was Jimmy, still dressed in the Bermuda shorts and t-shirt that he'd been wearing yesterday. It had to be nearly freezing, but he wasn't even cold.

"So you remember me?" she asked, reaching for his arm.

He jerked away, tempering the rejection with a smile. "Remember you? I just saw you, what, ten minutes ago? You went across the street to get us some food, then you were gonna help me look for my family."

"Jimmy, that was over twenty-four hours ago."

"Don't kid a kidder, Miz Fisher," Jimmy said, chuckling, but she sensed apprehension beneath his laughter.

"Jimmy, do you remember what I was wearing last time you saw me?"

She'd rummaged through her closet and came up with an entirely different wardrobe before driving to the park; a pink cashmere sweater, gray slacks, and a pair of brown suede boots.

"Hey, you're wearing something different. How'd that happen?"

"That's because I went home and changed, Jimmy."

"But that's not possible," he stammered. "You weren't gone that long."

"I was, Jimmy. I also showered, ate, and slept."

"So how is this possible?" he challenged her, angry now. "Are you saying I'm nuts?"

"No," she said quietly, "you're not nuts, though I'm beginning to think I might be. But I'm going to say it anyway. Jimmy Cross, you're not real."

"What," he said, laughing, "you think you imagined me?"

"That's what I thought at first," she admitted, "but I looked on the Internet and…"

"Internet?" he interrupted. "What's that?"

"Just look at this," she said, holding up a printout of a Google search she'd done some thirty minutes earlier on Jeff's computer.

"But...but...that's impossible," he sputtered, backing away from her. "Where did you get that?"

"I already told you, I found it on the Internet. The Internet is a worldwide network of computers all connected together. You can access any of the computers through any of the others, effectively making the sharing of information instantaneous." It wasn't a perfect explanation, but it was good enough.

Google had led her to the website for the *Arkansas Democrat Gazette*, a daily newspaper covering Northwest Arkansas, and from there she had searched the archives for any references to someone named Jimmy or James Cross. A chill went up her spine as she recalled the story the search had returned.

"And...something you got from that...that thing, it says I'm dead?" he asked, his eyes begging her to lie. But she couldn't. The poor man had suffered enough already.

"I'm so sorry," she said, reaching out to touch his shoulder. Her fingers passed through his arm. "But you must have known. After all this time, you must have had a clue."

"Yeah, I suspect I did," he finally admitted, staring at his arm, "but I keep forgetting. It...it wasn't something I wanted to remember, I guess, and after a while I just convinced myself that it never happened."

"But you do remember the accident?"

"I do, but...it was no accident. How long ago was it, again?"

"Almost forty years ago," she whispered. "Do you want to tell me about it?"

"Lord...forty years? But yes...yes, Miz Fisher, I expect that I do."

"Call me Claire," she smiled, finally allowing herself to sit on the bench. Her legs were shaking and her pulse was drumming in her ears, but she needed to hear Jimmy's tale.

"I hope you like stories, Claire, because this one's a doozy."

* * *

It was the shank of the summer, when the sun is so hot and the air so humid that it's all you can do just to suck in oxygen. The green grass had turned a sort of scorched brown, and the trees had grown extra leaves just to replace the ones that had shriveled up and burnt off. The sky was so parched that it refused to rain, and the ground practically turned to dust beneath your feet. That's how hot it was that summer, and that's why what happened played out the way that it did.

Jimmy Cross, his wife Dot, and their twelve-year-old twin daughters Sheila and Sarah were three days into their week-long vacation when the air conditioner at Dot's parent's house stopped working. They'd driven the eight hours from Chicago to Rogers so their little girls, turning thirteen at the end of the month, could celebrate their birthday with their grandparents. But there wasn't gonna be no celebrating if everyone was hot and miserable.

Dot's daddy called the man at Hammermill's Heating and Air, but when he'd given his address, they told him that everyone's AC was broken that summer, and it was gonna be at least a week before they could get anyone out to the house.

Had it been a white man calling, they'd have been out there that afternoon and had it fixed in time for supper.

But they weren't white, and they weren't never gonna be white. Jimmy came from a long line of factory workers and, before that, farm workers and, before that, slaves, and he always swore he'd do better for his family. And he did, too.

Jimmy was the first in his family to not only finish high school but also to graduate from college. He'd always had a way with numbers, and had used that talent to earn a master's degree in mathematics at

Western Illinois University. After he graduated, he ended up getting a job teaching math at PS 122, one of the high schools in Chicago, where he'd remained ever since.

He made enough to support his family and put a little away each month for his daughters' education, which was just fine by him. He also got to help the children, teaching them to look at numbers in a whole new way, occasionally keeping them interested long enough to graduate.

Jimmy had an attractive, loving wife who supported him in everything he did, two beautiful daughters that worshiped the ground he walked on, and a job he enjoyed. If he'd been thinking straight, if he hadn't been half out of his mind from the heat, hadn't drunk one too many Budweiser beers on the in-laws porch, and hadn't been so hell-bent to prove a point that was obvious to begin with, he'd never have done it.

Instead of toughing out the summer, maybe running down to Sears and buying a few extra fans, he got in an argument with his wife and in-laws. Exactly what they argued about wasn't important, only that it ended with Jimmy swearing up and down that they were made to wait out the heat simply because they were black, and that his daughters weren't going to suffer for something they had absolutely no control over.

Against Dot's protests, he marched out of the house, got into their new blue station wagon, and tore out of the driveway, determined to give Hammermill's Heating and Air a piece of his mind. He swore to himself that he wasn't going to leave until he got some satisfaction, but he never even made it to the service shop.

Rogers was a small town, a flyspeck on the map, but if you've only ever driven there a handful of times before, you might get lost. And that's exactly what Jimmy did. One wrong turn ended in another, and another, and before he knew it, it was getting dark and he was out in the middle of nowhere. He'd given up on finding Hammermill's by then, but any attempt to retrace his route and find his way home only served to disorient him further.

He was down to less than an eighth of a tank of gas and had absolutely no idea where he was. Still, he waited until the road, which had turned from pavement to gravel a good fifteen miles back, changed to dirt before he finally decided to stop and ask directions. The houses were sparse here, maybe one every half a mile or so, and finally he just chose one at random.

It did cross his mind that a black man might not exactly be welcome out in the boonies of Arkansas at dusk, but, not exactly having any other options, he walked up the porch steps of the ramshackle two-story farmhouse and rang the doorbell.

"Hello?" he called out after a while, but no one came to the door.

There was an old red Chevy pick-up parked in the driveway, so someone must be home. He rang the doorbell again, and then, when still no one answered, he finally tried the door. It was unlocked. If he could just get in and use the phone to call Dot's father for directions, he reasoned, it wouldn't hurt anybody. He could even leave a note and a couple dollars as payment.

He waited a few more minutes before slipping through the door in search of a telephone. The place was decorated in early American hillbilly, littered with broken and stained chairs, a couch missing two of its three cushions, empty beer cans, and at least a month's worth of newspapers piled up in the corner. It smelled like a pig sty, and it was even hotter in here than it was outside. He began to wonder if anyone really lived here at all.

His unvoiced question was answered by the squeak of a loose floorboard from upstairs, followed by a loud curse and muffled voices. And then there were footsteps echoing down the stairs, coming closer.

"Hello?" he called out, his pulse racing. Suddenly this didn't seem like such a good idea. "Look, I need to use the phone and the door was open. I hope that's okay. I just need to make a local call, and I don't mind paying."

"What you doing in my house, boy?" said a voice from the top of the stairs.

Jimmy stood stock still as the owner of the voice walked down the steps. A teenager, no older than sixteen or seventeen, ambled lazily into view. The kid had long, brown hair that hung down past the middle of his back, and was dressed in a pair of threadbare jeans and a sleeveless white t-shirt. He had a cigarette hanging out of the side of his mouth, and he carried a bottle of beer in one hand and a shotgun in the other.

"Look, I don't want any trouble," Jimmy said, holding up his hands. He couldn't look away from the shotgun. "I just need to use the phone."

"And that gives you the right to break into my house?" the teenager asked, reaching the bottom of the stairs. He was quickly joined by two other boys and a girl, none of them older than eighteen. "You weren't trying to rob me, now were you, boy?"

"No, son, I just need to use the phone," he said, slowly moving back toward the door. "If that's a problem, I'll just mosey on out of here."

"Hear that, Slim?" said one of the other boys, a dark-haired kid with a pock-marked face. "This here nigger thinks he can just 'mosey on out of here.'"

His cheeks burned at the slur and he took a deep breath, fighting down anger.

Slim and the other boy snickered, but were quickly silenced by a stern glare from the girl, a thin, blonde thing who looked like she might snap in half if she were caught outside in a strong wind.

"Ya'll don't hafta make fun of the coon," she said sweetly, as if the term was an endearment, "he don't know what he's doin'. They jus' get like that, these coons, so used to rifling through people's trash cans and the like, can't hardly keep them out if they wanta get in."

"Mirabelle's right," snickered the third boy, younger than the rest but just as hard looking, "ain't his fault he come rootin' around our roost."

"Mira might be right," said Slim, racking his shotgun and bringing it level with Jimmy's chest, "but if you let one varmint in, more will surely follow."

Jimmy's face turned red and it took everything he had not to knock the son-of-a-bitch on his ass. Instead he wrapped his hand around the doorknob, slowly turning it, easing the door open.

"I don't want any trouble," he repeated, snaking a foot around the edge of the door. "I'm leaving now."

"You're not going nowhere, nigger," Slim smiled, pulling the trigger.

Jimmy dived through the door just as buckshot exploded from the boy's shotgun, peppering the wall where he'd been standing with little bits of metal.

They were trying to kill him! He slammed the door, dove from the porch, and ran for the car. He heard one of the men scream something just as he reached the station wagon, so he dropped to a crouch on the far side of the car. Slim's shotgun barked and the front windshield exploded in a rain of glass and buckshot, raining down all over Jimmy's head and shoulders.

A sharp pain shot across his chest and for a moment he thought he's been shot, but there were no holes in his shirt, and no blood. He crawled into the car, gunned the engine, and shot out of the driveway. Another round of ammunition destroyed his back window, sending glass fragments everywhere.

His chest hurt like crazy and a dull, aching pain spread down his left arm. Sweat poured from his brow, and he prayed to the Lord Almighty to let him live long enough to apologize to his wife. He slammed his foot against the pedal, scattering dust and bits of rock everywhere as the tires spun beneath the car. Finally gaining traction, the station wagon lurched forward and peeled down the road in a frantic roar.

But it wasn't over yet. Slim and his buddies had managed to crank up the ancient Chevy he'd seen parked in front of their house and were pulling out of the driveway. Another shot of pain wracked his chest, and he had to gasp for breath. The back of his head hurt. He ran his fingers through his hair, bringing back blood. Buckshot or glass, something had gone into the back of his head and he was bleeding like a stuck pig.

He pushed the car to its limit, racing from seventy to eighty and finally to ninety miles an hour. He screamed past cows and pigs and one surprised old man on a bicycle and still they followed. Everything went black for a second, and when he opened his eyes again he was careening toward the ditch.

He jerked the steering wheel to the right, sending a mist of dirt spraying into the air. The car wobbled and for a second he thought it might flip, but he managed to correct the turn, straightening the car. And then he felt the tires hitting gravel and knew he was finally off that God awful dirt road.

The houses were closer together now, the farms slowly being replaced by backyard swing sets and trampolines the further he went. He was getting closer to town. He risked a glance in the rearview mirror and saw that Slim and his gang had given up the chase. Turning his eyes toward the road again, he started to recognize some of the landmarks. There was that old water treatment plant he's passed earlier. He was going to make it!

He thanked God for giving him another chance, and promised to get down on his knees and beg Dot and her parents to forgive him for being such a stupid, old fool. And then another bolt of agony shot through his chest, nearly doubling him over. He turned the steering wheel and suddenly the car was spinning through the air, and the ground was where the sky should have been.

The last thing he remembered was thinking of Sheila and Sarah, wishing he'd paused to tell them how much he loved them before storming out of the house. He pictured their beautiful brown eyes and their shared smile that could melt an iceberg. For an instant, miraculously, his chest no longer hurt and the stultifying Arkansas heat felt suddenly cool. And then everything went dark, and he thought no more.

✳ ✳ ✳

"And that's pretty much the whole story," Jimmy whispered, looking down at his shoes. "The next thing I knew, I was wandering around this damned park looking for my family."

Claire felt hot tears running down her cheeks. The newspaper article she'd downloaded had only mentioned the accident. Surely someone had seen something. But no, the bastards had gotten away with it. She crumpled the paper into a ball and shoved it into her purse.

She and Jimmy were alike, in a way. They'd both lost their memories, though he'd lost his life as well. She wondered for a moment which was worse; never being able to go back to the ones you loved or not remembering how or why you loved them. She decided it was worse for him, because he knew what he had lost.

"I'm sorry, Jimmy," she finally said. Her arms fluttered uselessly at her sides. She felt the need to touch him, to comfort him somehow, but knew the act of doing so would only make more obvious everything he'd lost.

He slowly raised a hand to her cheek, brushing away her tears. It felt as though a gentle breeze were tickling her skin, or perhaps more like a butterfly slowly fluttering past her face. She smiled and his hand fell away, and together they sat on the bench beside where they'd first met just a little over twenty-four hours ago.

"In all my time here," he said, looking into her eyes, "you're the only one that's ever been able to see me. Why is that?"

"I wish I knew," she whispered. "You've told me your story, and now it's time for me to tell you mine. Though there's not much to it, I'm afraid."

"Nonsense, girl," he chuckled, laying a feathery hand upon her knee. "Surely you have people that love you, friends, a husband, children...?"

"All of those except for the kids," she confessed, "but that's the thing, Jimmy. It doesn't do me a whole hell of a lot of good if I can't remember them."

So she told him her story, about waking up in the clinic and not knowing who she was, about Leesie and Jeff, about Corduroy, about the strange connection she sensed to the man who had died on Thirteenth Street, and that she was in fact Claire Summers and not Claire Fisher, as she'd originally claimed. She told him everything she knew, which really wasn't much of anything, but it still felt good to get it off her chest.

"So you saw them in the hospital too, huh?" he finally said when she was finished, referring to the ghosts. "Lucas and the old man."

"I think so," she admitted, and the more she thought about it the more she was convinced that it was true. "And in the graveyard, too, on the way to Leesie's house."

"And that thing about the cat, that's some weird shit."

"No more weird than standing around a park talking to a dead man," she said, laughing, taking in the absurdity of the whole situation.

"Yeah, there is that," he nodded, looking thoughtful. "You know, when I was a boy, I remember talk about those that had something called 'the shine.' My Grandmomma's momma, for one. She was supposed to be able to see the dead. Grandmomma always believed it, but my old man, he always said it was a bunch of hooey. I agreed with him, too. Until now."

"So I have 'the shine'?" she smiled. "Great, it sounds like a venereal disease."

He colored slightly, but let it pass. The values and social mores of his time were certainly not those of Claire's. "Have you tried going back to the clinic?"

"What do you mean?" she asked. Leesie had told her that the baby was fine, and she wasn't due to have another appointment for six weeks.

"Well," he said, tapping his finger to his temple, "if you saw the kid in the hospital, and you can see me, who's to say you can't see him?"

She finally understood what he was getting at. "I hadn't thought about that, but you're right. If his spirit is still where he died and if I can talk to him…"

"Then maybe you can see if there really is a connection and, if there is, you can get some answers," he finished for her, smiling. "See? Being dead don't dull the brain that much, leastways once it gets working right again."

"You're a genius, Jimmy," she beamed, but immediately sobered. "But how do I help you? I wouldn't begin to know where to find your family, and I'm not sure what I would, or could, say to them if I did."

"Don't worry about that," he said, looking down at his shoes again. "Dot's probably dead by now, and the twins…lord, they'd be in their fifties, older than I was when…when I died. More than likely married with kids and grandkids of their own. I just wish I knew how things turned out for them, and that I'd gotten the chance to say goodbye."

Claire had a thought. She might not be able to help him say goodbye but, using the Internet, perhaps she could at least find out what had happened to his daughters. She glanced at her watch; it was a quarter until nine. She'd forgotten how quickly the day had passed with Jimmy yesterday afternoon, and Jeff was due home any time now.

"Jimmy, I've got to go," she said in a rush, springing up from the bench, "but I'll be back. Will you promise me you'll wait for me?"

He gave a low, throaty chuckle. "Now where would I go, Miz Fisher?" he said, using the alias she'd originally given him before she knew her real name. "Of course I'll be here. Been here for the last forty years, I suspect one more day can't hurt."

Chapter 20

No one wanted to stop their car for a dead man. They'd learned that lesson the hard way. After two long hours of walking alongside Interstate 44 with their thumbs out, they were still only about ten miles outside of Mount Vernon, Illinois, the little town where Farris's purple Le Sabre had dropped its engine block.

Gabriel had kept them driving all night, going this way and that, before finally deciding that they needed to be going in the opposite direction, toward Missouri. They were shivering from the snow falling overhead but no one even slowed down, much less offered them a ride.

Gabriel's decaying face probably wasn't helping matters. While Farris had almost completely recovered from his wounds, including his broken neck, the man who had brought him back to life still looked dead. Sabrina had applied a liberal amount of make-up around his eyes and lips, but some things you just couldn't hide.

It had been less than twenty-four hours since Farris had died, and things still weren't going his way. With nowhere else to go and no way to get their car repaired until morning, they'd been forced to spend the night at a flea-bag motel sandwiched between a steel plant and an all-night strip club. The following morning had been even worse, as they waited for the tow truck to haul in their car and then waited again for the mechanic to pronounce the vehicle a lost cause.

Farris cursed himself for not paying better attention to his car. They had a little over fifty dollars between them, which wouldn't even come close to paying for the repairs. The mechanic told them that they'd be better off finding a new car and offered to buy the old one for scrap.

After paying the tow charge, the sale of the car had added exactly one hundred and twelve dollars to their stash. If the bus ran out here they'd have been set, but of course it didn't. It was probably for the best, anyway, since bus drivers more than likely weren't much on turning this way and that any time Gabriel got one of his feelings.

They marched alongside the road in silence, teeth chattering and thumbs stuck out awaiting a ride, when, finally, Sabrina spoke.

"'South' or 'west' doesn't tell us much, Dad," she complained, rolling her eyes at Farris. "I mean, Oklahoma, Arkansas, Louisiana, Mississippi, Alabama, Tennessee, Texas—any of those would be doable, but compass directions don't leave us much to go on."

"It's either Arkansas or Oklahoma," Gabriel said, closing his eyes and rocking back and forth in place. "I'm pretty sure of it."

The zombie had been periodically performing the trick ever since they left Carthage. He wouldn't tell them why they had to "go south" or "go east," only that the world was in serious trouble if they didn't.

"Okay, Dad," she said, walking on ahead of them, "we'll keep going west."

Farris cast a sideways glance at her, wishing they could have spent this much time together when he was alive. The girl had seemed in shock at first, seeing her dead father return from the grave, but had at least recovered to the point where she felt comfortable needling him about the whole directional thing.

Inexplicably, however, she seemed to grow quiet around Farris, and wouldn't look him in the eye. His post-death relationship with her seemed alarmingly similar to the one they'd shared before he died. He didn't like it but didn't have any idea what to do about it.

A jet black eighteen wheeler covered in flames pulled off the road a few yards in front of them, the driver leaning out the window and beckoning them forward. The rig hauled a huge platform filled with brand new cars of all sizes and shapes, more than likely heading for a dealership.

"Ya'll need a ride?" called the man, tipping his rebel flag adorned baseball cap in their direction.

"We do," said Sabrina, elbowing past her father "We're heading toward Arkansas. Can you give us a lift?"

"I can take you as far as Joplin," he offered, eyes on Sabrina.

They could see the man more clearly as they approached the cab. He was in his late forties or early fifties, had a full beard and moustache, and looked as though he hadn't slept in days. As if to illustrate the point, he shook a pill from a bottle of No Doze and popped it into his mouth, washing it down with Mountain Dew.

Gabriel took the front seat while Farris and Sabrina made themselves comfortable in a brand new candy apple red Ford Fusion near the back of the rack. Ray, their host, had offered to let Sabrina ride in front, but Gabriel had taken the seat for himself, no doubt out of fear for his daughter's virtue. If Ray had noticed anything strange about Gabriel, he was polite enough not to mention it.

"God, I hope Dad knows what he's doing," Sabrina said, once the truck began to move. "I'm just seriously freaked out here."

"That makes two of us," said Farris, studying her face in the rear-view mirror. He had climbed into the driver's seat, while she had slipped quietly into the back. "Sabrina, can I ask you something?"

"I guess so," she said, shrugging. There was an edge to her voice.

"Did I do something wrong?"

"What are you talking about?"

"You haven't said more than two words to me since last night," he explained, feeling his cheeks grow flushed. "I mean, I know I'm dead and all. I guess that freaks you out too, huh?"

"It's not that," she whispered into the darkness of the car, "or I guess it is that, but not the way you think. I'm the one who did something wrong, not you."

"What do you mean?" he asked, leaning across the seat.

"Don't you get it? You're dead, Farris. Dead. And I'm responsible. I swear, I never meant for any of that to happen, and I'd take it all back if I could, and I'd make you whole again. But I can't."

"And I'm not asking you to," he said, reaching through the gap between the seats to touch her shoulder.

She jerked away, eyes glistening with tears. "Well, maybe you should," she sobbed, cradling her head in her hands. "How can you forgive me so easily? God, I was such a bitch to ever go along with any of that. I knew it was wrong. I knew it, but I let Susie and Brian talk me into it. And now you're dead, and I'm to blame."

"We all make mistakes," he said, climbing to his knees so he could swivel around to face her. "I mean, I'm alive, or at least as close to alive as a dead teenager can get. And, according to your father, we're about to embark on this great adventure to keep the world from being ripped asunder. Do you know how long I've waited for something like this to happen to me? Granted, I didn't see myself dead, but still."

"I never meant for us to stop being friends, you know. I missed you. It was just something stupid that happened, and by the time I realized it, we'd both made new friends, and it seemed like it was too late to do anything about it."

"It's never too late," he whispered, "and I'm not going to let a little thing like a seriously bad lapse in judgment get in the way of what could be the start of another beautiful friendship."

"You're a real goofball, you know that?" she said into her hands, looking at him from between her fingers.

"So I've been told," he said, again laying a hand on her shoulder. This time, she didn't pull away.

"What's it like, this whole being dead thing?"

"So far, it's not much different than being alive," Farris admitted, "and the company's a hell of a lot better."

"Come here," she whispered, gesturing with her forefinger. "I've never made out with a dead guy before, and there's a bit of a Goth chick hiding somewhere inside me that seriously wants to give it a try."

She patted the soft leather beside her, and he clambered through the gap and into the back seat. His heart raced as her arms encircled his neck, pulling him closer. She leaned into him, brushing her lips softly against his, moaning under her breath as their kiss grew longer. The moonlight made her eyes glisten like diamonds, and her lipstick still tasted like cherries, only sweeter.

"Wow," he said, simply, as they finally came up for air, "that was even better than the first time."

"Much better," she agreed, kissing him again, "because, this time, it's for real."

Chapter 21

Pete Snow looked at his watch. It was just before eight o'clock in the evening, and he was officially off duty, but he'd heard the call on his radio and decided to swing by to check out the situation. A body being stolen from the county morgue was bad enough, but the fact that whoever had done it had murdered a security guard and replaced the missing body with Broussard's showed a cool calculation that really set his Spidey sense to tingling.

Broussard's body has been mutilated almost beyond recognition. His right hand index finger was missing, as was part of his chest, arms, and neck. The wounds were serrated and looked almost like the bite marks of a wild animal, though Snow had never seen an animal that could pick up a corpse and stuff it into a metal drawer.

If Amelia Ruiz, a college student and an intern at the morgue, hadn't insisted on a thorough search of the lab after Broussard didn't show for his shift, it might've taken them days to realize what had happened.

Ruiz had been involved with Broussard until two weeks ago when, according to the girl, she caught him in bed with an old girlfriend. She was pissed off, no doubt about it, but his gut told him that she wasn't responsible for his murder.

Danny Sandidge, Snow's old partner, was in charge of the crime scene. Snow, however, was the ranking officer. He could take over the investigation, but he didn't want to give Danny any more reason to hate him than he already had. He'd bide his time and wait until Captain Wedesky called him or showed up to make everything official.

"Seriously, Pete, we got this," Sandidge growled. "You're not looking for another promotion already, are you?"

Snow stood just under six feet tall and weighed one seventy-five to Sandidge's two fifty and change, but still towered over his former partner. He often wondered how Sandidge had passed the department physical, but figured he'd been grandfathered in.

The two were a study in contrasts: in addition to the differences in body types, Snow had blonde hair just a shade past his ears—as long as the department would allow—while Danny's graying hair was cut to within a quarter inch all around. When they'd first been partners they'd earned the nickname "the odd couple," and the name had stuck until Snow became a detective.

Snow passed the exam on his first try while Danny had failed it four times before giving up, and he knew it had left a sour taste in the older man's mouth. Jealousy was a bitter pill to swallow, and that jealousy had slowly turned to resentment and finally into outright hate.

That had been two years ago, but he knew that Danny was still sore over it. They'd been tight before the exams, but he could count the times on one hand his former mentor had spoken to him afterward. Danny had seen him through the bad times, had even been there when his wife left him and he'd gone on a week-long drinking binge, but couldn't seem to handle the good.

"I'm not trying to step on your toes, Danny," Snow said, hands held out in mock surrender, "just heard the call on my radio, that's all, and thought maybe you could use a hand. Besides, that's my John Doe that was stolen."

He'd caught the case yesterday morning, on the way to Wal-Mart Corporate to interview a witness in an embezzlement case. He had also made plans with his ex-wife, to take her to Johnny Carino's for their twice-a-month lunch date. He hated to cancel, but she ended up calling it off before he even had the chance.

This wasn't your standard involuntary vehicular manslaughter case. The victim had been dehydrated, half-starved, and beat to within a quarter-inch of his life before being struck by the vehicle. He was certain the man had been held prisoner, perhaps somewhere nearby, but a thorough search of all the houses in a two-mile radius of the accident hadn't turned up anything remotely suspicious.

He shook his head. It had definitely been a weird day, and Claire's disappearance hadn't made things easier. Elisabeth, thankfully, had called him this afternoon to let him know Claire was safe. That was one thing off his mind. He'd spent a good hour looking for his ex's best friend before having to go back to the crime scene.

And if his day hadn't been strange enough, Snow was almost certain he had seen the dead man's face before.

They'd tried to fingerprint their John Doe, but there wasn't much left to work with; the tips of his fingers had been ground down to almost nothing. Dental records might help identify him, but that would take weeks.

The dead man had two sets of tattoos: nine small skulls on the back of his neck and the letters "RLTW" written in script on his left shoulder. Separately the tattoos weren't unique enough to provide a lead, but together they just might hold the key to his identity. There existed an FBI database of tattoos and other identifying marks, and if the dead man had ever been in prison, his tats should be there.

Though he served in the Navy, Snow knew that RLTW was an acronym for the Army Rangers motto, "Rangers Lead the Way," which probably meant the man had served in the military. Whoever could get the drop on a ranger deserved at least a grudging measure of respect.

The first step toward finding the dead man's abductors was identifying the victim, which had been made considerably more difficult by the disappearance of the body. Snow spent all night looking through mug shots from the last three years, but the deceased's face wasn't in any of the books.

He knew he'd figure it out sooner or later. The man's identity kept gnawing at him, a name almost on the tip of his tongue before flitting away again like a manic butterfly on speed.

When he heard the John Doe had been stolen, there was no way he wasn't going to involve himself in the case. They'd made no headway whatsoever on tracking down the car that had struck the victim, so he had to approach the case from another angle.

"Knew you couldn't keep your hand out of the cookie jar," Sandidge said, rolling his eyes at one of the other cops. "Tell you what? Why don't you go on home and we'll call you when we find something."

"He's just bored, Danny," said the other policeman, trying to break the tension. Jon Sharkey, a veteran both Pete and Danny were friendly with. "He'd rather be back on the beat with us than investigating meth labs and purse snatches, eh, Pete?"

"Ain't that the truth," Snow muttered, though it wasn't true. He loved his job, couldn't get enough of it. Comparing his career as a beat cop to being a detective was like taking a bite of hamburger before downing a filet mignon. It just didn't measure up, but he sure as hell wasn't going to say that while Danny was within earshot

His cell phone rang, and he excused himself to answer it. Caller ID told him it was the Captain, and in less than two minutes the case was officially assigned to his workload. It was going to be a long night.

Chapter 22

Jeff was already home by the time Claire pulled into the driveway and maneuvered her car into the garage. He was sitting on a lawn chair, just inside where the garage met the laundry room, waiting for her. She smiled and waved, felt her stomach drop when he glared and wouldn't wave back.

"Where the hell were you?" he said under his breath, leaping out of the chair as soon as she opened the door to her Prius.

"I'm sorry," she said immediately, tripping over the words, "I just had to run to the store." She climbed out of the car, keeping the door between her and her husband.

"I had to take a taxi home," roared Jeff, and she could smell alcohol on his breath. "Cost me forty fucking dollars!"

"I'm sorry," she repeated, finally understanding from their conversation earlier that he'd meant for her to pick him up. "I thought you had your car."

"Claire, you knew my car was in the shop," he said, as if talking to a small child. His nostrils flared as he stepped another foot closer. "What's so important that you couldn't show up at the goddamned airport? And why aren't you wearing any makeup? I'm gone for four days, and I come home to find you looking like shit. What's wrong with you?"

"The baby," she lied, touching her stomach. "I haven't been feeling well for the last couple of days. I just…I've been forgetting things, and today my stomach started hurting, and…"

His face immediately softened. "The baby? Is he all right?"

He? According to Leesie, they didn't yet know the sex of the baby. "The baby's fine. I just need more rest, the doctor said."

"Then what are you doing out here?" he said gently, taking her arm and bumping the car door closed with his hip. "Let's get you inside. We can order out for pizza, take it easy tonight. You know I don't want anything to happen to the baby."

"I know," she lied again, letting him guide her into the house, hoping with all her heart that everything Leesie had told her about her husband was wrong.

"Just put up your feet and relax," he said, "and I'll order us that pizza."

She slunk down into the big couch in the living room, grateful for the chance to get off her feet. She really was tired, and, she realized as her stomach grumbled, hungry as well. She stretched out on the long leather couch and tried to relax, watching Jeff's retreating figure as he left the room to order the pizza.

Corduroy surprised her by appearing from under the loveseat and leaping into her lap. All purrs and starfish paws, he was a very different kitty than the suspicious tom she first encountered this afternoon. She slowly stroked his fluffy white fur, giggling softly as he dragged a sandpapery tongue across her knuckles.

She let the cat cuddle against her chest as she surveyed the rest of the room. The room was laid out in a sort of modern contemporary design, all soft earth tones and reproductions of famous artwork hanging from the walls. She wondered if it were she or Jeff that had influenced the design of the living area.

A black and white wedding portrait hung above the widescreen television, the photo capturing a seemingly-candid scene of Jeff feeding her wedding cake. He was dressed in a sharp black tux and she in a long, elegant white wedding dress. They both looked happy and in love, totally unlike the picture she'd gotten of their marriage in the last two days.

She felt like a fraud, an imposter who'd stolen the life of Claire Summers and was trying to make sense of the facts and insinuations she found herself presented with. It was as if she were a pod person, stuck in a life that wasn't really hers. She stroked Corduroy's fur, nuzzling closer to the cat as she tried not to cry.

And then Jeff was there, yanking the cat off of her by the scruff of his neck. "I told you, stay off of her," he scolded the cat, shooing him out of the room.

"What did you do that for?" she asked, already missing the cat's warm breath against her neck.

"It's not good for the baby," Jeff answered, anger in his voice. "If you've been letting that damned cat lie around on you all day, maybe that's why you haven't been feeling well. I told you, we should just get rid of that thing, give it away or have it put to sleep."

Get rid of Corduroy? Leesie said she'd had the cat since college. She couldn't imagine giving him away, and would certainly never put a healthy animal to sleep. She flashed back to the car accident earlier today, and imagined Jeff would have been thrilled if the cat had stayed dead.

"It's all right," she finally said, turning her eyes away from him, "I won't let him on me again."

"Good girl," he said, the ire draining from his voice almost as quickly as it had appeared. Moving her feet to sit beside her, he placed them on his lap and began to stroke her skin. "Pizza will be here in twenty or thirty minutes. We'll eat, watch a little TV, and then turn in early. Sound like a plan?"

"Sounds like a plan," she agreed, wishing she and Corduroy were at Leesie's house, or anywhere else in the world instead of here with her husband.

But she kept her silence, pretending to relax with her feet on Jeff's lap until the doorbell rang. Jeff got up to answer the door, returning with a huge pizza. The pie, an extra-large thin-crust with pepperoni, sausage, and extra cheese, smelled heavenly, but she had lost her appetite.

✳ ✳ ✳

Something was happening. Gabriel Locke could feel it, and it made his teeth itch. His son was in serious trouble, and if he didn't get there soon the whole world would surely follow suit.

"So what do you do for a living?" asked Ray Davies, the truck driver who had picked them up outside of Rolla.

The man smelled like he hadn't bathed in days, which was a good thing because it probably meant that he couldn't smell the stench emanating from Gabriel's embalmed body. Rotting flesh was a buzz kill.

"I'm in construction," he finally said, because it had once been true, "but I've been out of work for a while, so me and the kids are going to try our luck south."

"You'll do well in Missouri, then," the trucker said, pronouncing it 'Missouruh,' his eyes on the road as he sipped coffee from a huge Love's thermos. "I don't know if you heard, but they had an earthquake outside of Bolivar yesterday. The quake itself didn't do a lot of damage, but a big rig carrying a tanker of gasoline jackknifed on the road and caught fire. Burned half a forest, took out eight houses. Killed thirty-seven people before they managed to put it out. Huge mess, but I bet you'd find work there."

"Do you know what time the earthquake hit?" he asked, already certain he knew the answer. He had awoken in his coffin at precisely twelve fifteen, according to the glow-in-the-dark watch he'd been buried with.

"Around noon," said Ray, blinking his lights at another rig he recognized. "You been living in a cave or something?"

"Or something," he agreed, knowing there had to be a connection.

"Some weird shit," the trucker continued, "and not just in Missouri, either. In Texas, where I'm from, an entire freakin' cemetery flooded. Saw it on CNN, there were bodies everywhere. A church imploded and killed a bunch of people in Tennessee. Found out it'd been built on an old Indian burial ground. And in Chickasha, Oklahoma, an old SUV containing a couple of kids that went missing a few years back suddenly floated up out of the river, proud as you please. The paper said the kids were perfectly preserved. Definitely some weird shit, and everything happened almost exactly at the same time."

And Arkansas was the epicenter of it all. Whatever had caused the earthquake in Missouri was big enough to cloud the whole mess, but he'd bet his life, if he still had it, that everything had originated to the south.

"Religious folk are saying it's all portents of the end of the world," Ray continued, shaking his head. "But I say, sometimes shit just happens. Don't you think?"

"Shit definitely happens, Ray," agreed Gabriel, wondering how much time they had left before whatever shit was released in Missouri hit the fan. Everything else was minor, but something powerful enough to cause that much damage was a force to be reckoned with.

"And when it rains, it pours," the trucker said, taking another sip of his coffee, "and sometime it's all you can do just to duck and cover and wait out the shit storm."

"Amen, brother," he nodded, lighting up the other half of the cigarette his benefactor had given him earlier. He let the smoke fill his dead lungs, still enjoying the nicotine rush after all these years. "But you don't know the half of it."

Chapter 23

Sabrina lay asleep, curled in the crook of Farris's arm, when it happened. They'd made out earlier in the back of one of the brand new Ford Fusions traveling atop the semi-trailer heading to Joplin, with her father and Ray, the truck driver, in the cab and none the wiser. It sounded like something from those old *Penthouse Forum* letters. Farris still couldn't believe it.

He was only seventeen years old and, being dead, would never really get any older. If someone had told him even yesterday that he could trade his life for even one hour of kissing Sabrina Locke, he would have done it in a heartbeat. But now that it had happened, he didn't want to die. He wanted more. He wanted to see the world, to experience life fully, and, more than anything, he wanted to explore the possibilities. He wanted to be alive again.

Would he and Sabrina stay together after this adventure? He hoped they would, wanted that more than anything, but he wasn't sure that she could truly love a dead man. Whatever happened, he desperately wanted to hang around long enough to see how it all turned out. He felt truly alive for the first time in his life, fully aware of the irony.

His fingers, he noticed, were turning blue. He shifted Sabrina's head to his lap, watching in fascination as the color returned to his digits. The funny thing was, he hadn't felt his arm falling to sleep. Still some effect of the spinal damage, no doubt. Gabriel assured him that he would heal, but it scared him that he hadn't even felt it.

Farris looked down at Sabrina's sleeping form, his heart full to bursting. He'd loved her since they were kids, and it had nearly broken his spirit when she abandoned him in middle school, but he knew that he'd abandoned her, too. He could have tried harder. He could have told her how he felt. He'd cheated himself, a far worse crime than anyone else could have ever perpetrated against him.

Those were the thoughts that filled Farris's head when the first bug hit the windshield. Another soon followed, and then another, their little bug bodies exploding as they hit the glass. But something was wrong. One of the bugs, a grasshopper, turned to dust the moment it touched the wiper, and then a headless black bird swooped down from the skies, slapping with wings askew into the side mirror.

A great darkness, much darker than the late evening sky outside, fell abruptly around the semi. One by one, the stars overhead blinked away, and the lights from the other vehicles on the road vanished as dead insects and birds rained from the sky, covering everything in a blanket of death.

The truck veered first to the left, then to the right, rubber screaming against pavement, and then they were jackknifing across the road, Sabrina awake and screaming.

Farris could no longer see through the blackness that enveloped them. He felt the truck moving one way, the cars perched upon its back straining to move the other, and suddenly screeching metal gave way to chains snapping and harnesses popping, releasing their load to roll and tumble to the highway below.

The stench of burning plastic and metal, like an overheated vacuum cleaner, filled his nostrils. Something was on fire.

"Hold on," Farris screamed, pulling Sabrina close.

"What happened?" She yelled back, hands finding him in the darkness.

And then they were falling, their car sliding off the trailer, rolling into the road with eleven other Fords, all scattering across the pavement in a cacophony of screeching rubber and metal.

The sound of something hitting glass echoed from the right, a whooshing explosion to their left temporarily leaving Farris deaf. He pushed Sabrina underneath him, protecting her as best he could from the destruction.

He felt one of the other cars careen into theirs, hitting the front driver's side of the vehicle with a thunderous crack, sending it spinning away across the pavement. The Fusion rotated in lazy circles, once, twice, three times, before finally coming to a halt, shooting sparks into the air as it scraped against the railing that lined the shoulder of Interstate-44.

For a moment Farris still couldn't see, and then the darkness left them, falling away as quickly as it had descended. Death no longer rained from the skies, but it had wrought much damage. The devastation that surrounded them was incredible. Broken and burning vehicles littered the landscape, and not just the vehicles the truck had been carrying. A thick carpet of dead animals and insects paved the road in every direction, as if a black snow covered the landscape.

An overturned SUV straddled the median that separated the two parts of the highway, smoke pouring from its belly. A yellow Mustang stood three yards from them, one of the other Fusions from the truck lying upside down across the hood. He could already see that the driver was dead, crushed by the impact. The semi itself lay on its side across four lanes of traffic, like the discarded skin of a monstrous metallic snake.

"My God," Sabrina whispered, sitting up, taking in the carnage. Then: "Dad!"

Farris was up and moving, kicking at the door, but it wouldn't budge. One side of the Focus was caved in and ruined where one of the other cars had slammed into it, and neither of the doors would open.

The other side of their vehicle pressed tight against the safety railing that had finally stopped their runaway car, and the windows, which had miraculously survived intact, were electric and couldn't be rolled down without turning the ignition. They were trapped.

Sabrina crawled into the front seat, frantically trying both doors. They wouldn't budge. Leaning back into the passenger's seat, she covered her eyes with her arms, kicking out against the windshield. Not even a crack. She kicked it again, crying out in frustration when nothing happened.

"I can't lose him again," she sobbed, pounding the glass with her fists, blood staining the windshield as she scraped her knuckles against the rearview mirror.

"Let me try," Farris said, scrambling into the front of the car.

Instead of kicking the windshield, he concentrated his fury on the driver's side window, figuring that, because it was smaller, it might not be as sturdy. On his second kick the glass spider-webbed. It took two more kicks to break through, and then he was crawling out through the broken window, Sabrina behind him.

Farris counted at least twenty cars and trucks littering the highway, not counting their own and the jackknifed semi. Chaos was everywhere; the few fortunate survivors tending to the injured, mothers holding dead children, husbands mourning the loss of their wives.

Orange flames illuminated the night sky, cars burning with abandon. Smoke rolled through the wreckage like a London fog, making it hard to see more than a few feet in any direction. Some of the walking wounded worked to extinguish the flames, beating at them with blankets and coats, but most just sat or laid at the side of the road, too stunned and broken to do anything else. Wails of anguish and pain echoed in the night, intertwined with the high-pitched squeal of crying babies and the prayers and curses of the injured and the dying.

They broke into a run, their footsteps crunching beneath them as they maneuvered past the broken cars and dying bodies that littered the Interstate highway. The semi's cab burst into flames, the blaze seeming to lick the stars that filled the sky above them.

"Daddy!" Sabrina shouted, running for the cab.

Ray, the driver, lay sprawled face first on the road in front of the cab. Blood surrounded his still form, and it didn't look like he was breathing.

"He's still in the cab," said Farris, seeing the unconscious face of Gabriel Locke staring back at him through the splintered and broken front windshield. "See what you can do for Ray, I'll get him out."

"Hurry," she pleaded, dropping to her knees beside the trucker.

She immediately felt for a pulse, shaking her head. "He's gone."

But Farris wasn't listening. The cab had finally come to rest on the driver's side, so the only way to access the interior was through the shattered windshield. Paying no attention to the fragments of glass that poked and tore at his skin, he squeezed himself inside. The cab was a shambles, the glove compartments open, their contents everywhere.

Farris pushed past the detritus, finally reaching Locke. The man hung limply from his seat belt, not moving, his arms dragging the ground.

"Gabriel, come on, we've got to get you out of here," he rasped, working the seat belt.

It was stuck. He pulled harder, but it wouldn't budge. The cab was already on fire, smoke nearly suffocating him, and he could smell gasoline from the truck's tanks. They didn't have long before this whole thing went up in a massive explosion.

"Farris, can you get him out?" It was Sabrina, and she sounded desperate.

"Working on it," he answered, his eyes scanning the debris at his knees. "Get away from the truck, before we all go up."

"I'm not going anywhere without you!"

Digging through the cab, he came across a black-handled pocket knife. He immediately started sawing at the belt, holding the material taut with one hand and cutting with the other.

And then it gave way and Locke tumbled to the ground. Farris half-pushed, half-rolled the man to the broken windshield, scurried over him and through the opening in the cab, finally pulling him out by the armpits just as the inside of the truck began to smoke. Within seconds flames were shooting through the broken windows, licking Farris's feet as he dragged Sabrina's father to safety.

"You shouldn't have done that," said Ray's voice, from behind him.

Farris dropped Locke to the ground, spun on his heels.

The trucker stood behind Sabrina, one arm around her throat and the other pointing at Farris. Half his face was gone, and one eye hung limply from its socket. Sabrina squirmed in his grasp and he tightened his grip, pulling her closer.

"Who are you?" he asked the trucker, his dead heart beating stacca-to against his ribs. "What are you?"

"Gabriel Locke needs to stay dead," Ray said, motioning to the man lying at Farris's feet, "There are forces at work here bigger than you, bigger than all of you."

"What…what do you want me to do?" Farris stuttered, his eyes moving from Ray's one good eye to Sabrina and back again.

He'd dropped the pocket knife in the truck. If only he'd brought it with him, maybe he'd have a chance to use it against Ray. His eyes scanned the area surrounding him, but he saw nothing that could be used as a weapon.

"Roll him back into the truck," the dead trucker rasped, "and let him burn. Once he's gone, I'll let her go."

"Farris, don't you dare!" Sabrina screamed, coughing, yelping in pain as Ray's arm pressed hard against her throat.

The air filled with the sounds of sirens. The Calvary was finally on their way, but he knew Sabrina would be long dead before they arrived if he didn't do something fast.

"Do it, Farris," whispered Locke, between the shrill warnings of the sirens. "Do what he says, and roll me toward the truck."

"All right," Farris said to both of them. Turning his back on the trucker, he started to push Locke back toward the flaming cab.

Sabrina struggled against Ray, but he was too strong for her. She went still in the trucker's arms, and Farris feared the worst.

"Take this," Locke whispered, passing him a small handgun. "Picked it up in Mount Vernon, thought we might need it."

Farris pretended to slip, dropped to his knees and palmed the gun. It felt light in his fingers, too light, but he didn't dare sneak a peek at the weapon. He rose to his feet, sliding the pistol under his shirt. And then he was moving again, pushing Sabrina's father closer to the waiting flames.

"He's too heavy," Farris complained, trying to stall for time. "I can't lift him."

"It's really simple, Farris," said the trucker. "Either he dies or Sabrina dies. It's your choice."

The sirens grew closer, but still not close enough. And there was no way he could shoot Ray without hurting or even killing Sabrina. Even if was an expert marksman the risk would be great, and he was about as far from being an expert as someone could get.

"Shoot, Farris," Locke whispered from the ground, "I promise you, Sabrina will be fine."

His heart in his throat, Farris pretended to trip over Locke's body. He fell forward, twisting, pulling the gun from his jeans, aiming for Ray's head.

He pulled the trigger, praying that his aim was true.

A long stream of water arced through the air, hitting the trucker square in the eye.

For a moment he just stared, looking incredulous, and then he started to scream. Letting go of Sabrina, Ray flung both hands at his face, clawing, moaning in agony, his skin puckering and burning beneath his fingers.

Farris was up and running, hurling past Locke and his daughter, squeezing the trigger over and over again, drenching Ray in water.

A blood curdling howl escaped Ray's lips and he ripped at his face, his chest, his body, tearing away huge swatches of skin, digging deep to the bone. And then the spark of life seemed to leave him, there one moment and gone the next, and he shook, spasmed, and fell to the cold, wet ground, finally, mercifully, dead for real.

Farris felt a rush of heat at his back and felt himself being pushed forward, thrown through the air by the concussion of the blast. The gasoline had finally reached the cabin, and the resulting combustion created an inferno that could no longer be contained. Flames shot everywhere, lighting the night sky like a fireworks display. Farris tucked his head, rolling with the force of the explosion, finally coming to a stop on the other side of Ray's body.

He rose to a crouch, shading his eyes against the flames, but the fire was so bright that he couldn't make out a thing.

"Sabrina!" he called at the top of his lungs, struggling against the heat, plodding toward the cab.

And then she was there, pulling him close, holding him, and saying his name over and over again. He locked his arms around her, the fear of losing her still bathing his body in adrenaline. He realized they were crying, both of them, and not just from the smoke.

"Kids, we still have a job to do," said Locke, standing behind his daughter. "We'd better get moving."

Locke had shielded Sabrina from the explosion, keeping his daughter safe. Farris felt a strong surge of affection for the old man.

At last the cavalry arrived, in the form of three fire trucks, four ambulances, and at least twice as many state trooper cruisers. They watched from the shadows as EMTs, cops, and firemen scurried onto the scene, running to the carnage that waited on the other side of the jackknifed truck, mourning the dead and triaging the living.

"A water gun filled with holy water?" Farris finally asked, slipping his hand into Sabrina's as they walked away from the burning semi-trailer.

"Close," said Locke, moving further into the shadows, "but no cigar."

"Then what?"

"Plain old tap water mixed with silica gel and sea salt. Demons hate sea salt almost as much as they hate silver and holy water. Won't kill them, but it sure hurts 'em bad, and the silica gel disrupts whatever mojo gets them inside of the bodies they inhabit if the possession is recent enough."

"So, Ray was a demon?" Sabrina asked in a hushed tone.

"Ray was just an ordinary man until he got mixed up with us. No, the demon didn't get inside Ray until he was already dead. Those bugs? Strong spirit magic, stronger than I've ever seen. Someone doesn't like us."

"And that someone doesn't want us to get where we're going, do they?" said Farris, more a statement than a question.

Locke answered him anyway. "As Ray said, there are forces at work here that are bigger than any of us. And they're scared. They got a taste of what it would be like if that gateway between life and death didn't exist, and they want it, want it real bad. But we're not gonna give it to them. And once he's safe, they're not gonna be able to take it."

"Once who's safe?" Farris asked, his hand tightening around Sabrina's. "What gateway?"

"My son," Locke answered, "Sabrina's brother. He's the gateway now, he's what they want to destroy, and if these bastards get to him before we do, they just might get their way."

Chapter 24

Butchie prowled slowly through the grass, sniffing the wind. A cold front was coming, and it was going to rain tonight. What he was hunting, however, was far more elusive than weather. He was stalking death itself. He had followed the trail halfway across town, through yards and across parks and highways, to this darkened road in the middle of the city.

The dog sniffed the pavement, smelling blood. This is where it had happened, where the man who stood astride the threshold between life and death crossed the same gateway he was supposed to guard. Butchie picked up the scent from the road and followed it back to the source.

Creeping through trees and bushes, he followed the smell to a big, brick house just a little way from the road. He circled the house three times, letting the smells and sounds wash over his senses. And there it was. The human whose blood he followed had been in the house. He could still smell the man's sweat in the grass beside the door that led into the dwelling. Butchie smelled something else there as well, something just beneath the sharp, acrid tang of blood and sweat: he smelled fear.

So entranced was he in deciphering the scents that they were almost upon him before he noticed their footsteps.

The dog scurried behind the house, crouching low in the bushes as he listened to the door squeak open. Two men carried a dead body between them, working to maneuver it out through the basement door. Behind them trailed a little girl in chains. He wanted to take them right then and there, but something told him to wait. The Great Spirit's hand guided him gently but firmly in the right direction.

He watched with a sharp eye as they ducked through the trees, walked out into the road, and laid the dead man down upon the very spot where he'd fallen.

The dog tilted his head. This was strange behavior. Why take the kill back to the spot where they'd brought him down? But it didn't matter. All that mattered was the Great Spirit, and heeding its commands. Part of Butchie knew that the Great Spirit would soon be leaving, and when that happened he'd have nowhere else to go.

A strange melancholy settled over him, like an old, wet blanket, and he felt almost sad. And then the men were moving again, kneeling beside the dead man, and he trotted cautiously closer to the edge of the road.

Someone was talking, but it wasn't either of the men or the little girl. It was an old woman, yanking a small, gray bitch on a leash behind her. He could sense the woman's fear, but also her anger. The bitch yipped, baring her fangs at the two men who stood in the middle of the road. Were they also after the Great Spirit's prize?

He immediately sprang into action, launching himself through the trees at full speed, intending to reach the corpse before they did. But something happened that stopped him dead in his tracks. The noises of the city grew quiet and the air went still as the moon turned a strange shade of orange. A droning hum filled the air, and the old woman halted in place, looking disorientated.

Butchie skidded to a stop, hunkering down beneath the safety of an old maple tree. Apprehension filled his belly as he watched the larger of the two men walk up to the old woman and snap her neck. He grew more ill at ease as the man picked up the snarling bitch and hurled her into one of the trees. She bounced against the trunk, rolled off a branch, and finally caught hold about halfway down, her leash wrapped around some branches. Her motionless body swayed back and forth, hanging by its scrawny neck. She howled once, a mournful cry of fear, and then fell silent.

Ignoring the female, Butchie crept closer, daringly reaching the edge of the road. One of the men, the small one, chanted something, and the body at his feet began to twitch, shuddering and gasping as if awakening from a long winter's sleep. And that's when Butchie knew what he had to do.

Chapter 25

Tonight, thankfully, the moon was waxing crescent, and so they could do most of their work in the dark. It wouldn't do to get caught at this late stage in the game, not when they were so close.

Kingfisher removed an elegant silver pocket watch from his jacket; it was just a few minutes before midnight. Normally he abhorred technology, but the watch was old enough that it didn't really bother him. He set it nightly against the monstrosity Mr. Quarry kept attached to his wrist, the wristwatch that connected every twelve hours with the atomic clock out of Boulder, Colorado. But that was good. Being off by even a millisecond could spell disaster. And so while he tolerated the simple technology inherent in his timepiece, he recognized his partner's for what it was—a necessary evil that the smaller man endured so that they could keep to their schedule.

"Ready, Mr. Quarry?" he asked, bending down to grasp the dead man's ankles. Mr. Quarry nodded, and together they lifted the nude body and carried it out into the night.

Mr. Kingfisher smelled rain on the wind, though it was probably still an hour or two away. Good. The ritual for putting West's spirit back in his body was much more complex than the spell for calling forth Mr. Fuller's ghost. It wouldn't do to have an errant raindrop wash away the blood that Mr. Quarry had used to bind the containing symbols to the man's body. No, that definitely wouldn't do at all.

They pushed through the copse of trees that separated the house from the road, the girl led by a chain behind them. Mr. Quarry silenced their march with a cough. It was his game now, and Kingfisher would follow his lead. He glanced at his watch. It was 11:58, just two minutes before midnight. They waited while a police car slowly drove down the road and then disappeared around the corner.

The wards they had set up would conceal this part of the road from view while also encouraging anyone who happened upon them to get the sudden and undeniable urge to walk or drive away as fast as they could. The spell, which relied on the moon, a certain demon, and more than a little of their host's precious blood, had to be performed precisely at midnight or it wouldn't work.

The mirrors they had placed throughout the house kept their retreat from being noticed by all but the most determined, and even then it was a simple task to subvert their attention. They'd used a variant of the trick earlier in the day when Detective Snow had shown up on their doorstep. The detective left confused and disorientated, but firmly convinced that he'd searched the house and found nothing. Convincing Snow to move along was a simple parlor trick compared to blanking out half a city block.

Together, along with the girl, they walked the remaining half a dozen yards into the street. 11:59 p.m. Lowering West's body to the concrete, they placed it in as near as an approximation of where he had fallen as they could without a photo. Mr. Kingfisher backed away from the body, while his partner dropped to his knees and placed one hand on the dead man's forehead.

"What are you doing?" interrupted a voice from across the street. An old woman with short, gray hair, probably in her late seventies or early eighties, stared at them from her porch. She had a leash wrapped around one hand, connected to a small slip of a poodle that yipped frantically into the darkness. "Oh my God, what did you do? And that girl! Oh, honey. Stay right there, I'm calling the police."

Mr. Kingfisher sighed as the woman turned to stalk back toward her house. He laid a hand across Mr. Quarry's shoulders, turning his eyes away from the woman to stare at his watch. Just fifteen more seconds. He dropped the girl's chain, knowing that when it struck midnight she wouldn't have the ability nor the wherewithal to run.

The poodle stared at them from across the street, baring its fangs, growling and barking. It tugged against its leash, struggling to get free, but then fell silent and stood stock still as it stared straight up at the moon.

Clouds stopped moving overhead, and the air grew still. All of the noises in the night, the crickets, the slow drone of traffic from the city surrounding them, faded and then fell away. In a seeming gesture of defiance, the stars twinkled in the sky one last time before stopping, caught on some otherworldly canvas like a single frame in a movie. They were in the midnight hour, safe from the prying eyes of anyone who might dare to venture toward their little stretch of road.

"What's happening?" the old woman called out, stumbling against the curb. "What did you do? I'm going to call the police."

Mr. Kingfisher removed his hand from his confidante's shoulder, stood up, and flexed his muscles, enjoying how the low light from the moon reflected blue across his skin. He didn't want to waste time dealing with the old woman, but it couldn't be avoided. If he did nothing then surely, when their hour was past, she'd turn around, march right back into her living room, and call the police. And they couldn't have that.

He strode across the street, grabbed the woman by the neck, and crushed her windpipe. He let her go, watching as she crumpled to the ground. He wouldn't have minded tasting her soul—the vintage ones had a certain, unique flavor—but there just wasn't time.

Almost as an afterthought, he picked up the angry poodle and launched it into the tall maple that crowded the woman's front yard. The surprised little dog yapped and growled as it flew through the air, tumbling through a group of branches before finally catching on one halfway down the tree. It scrabbled for purchase but its leash had gotten snared between two branches. It whined pitifully, whimpered, and then was no more.

"It had to be done, Mr. Quarry," he said, shrugging his huge shoulders as he took his position beside the corpse. "Otherwise we might have had to vacate the house early, and you know how inconvenient that would be."

"Very inconvenient," Quarry agreed, putting both hands at West's temples. "And are we ready now?"

"As ever," he responded, watching intently as Mr. Quarry's eyes rolled back in his head and he began to chant in a long-dead language that neither one of them truly understood.

Nothing happened at first, but then the body began to spasm, writhing on the road like a dying catfish. Blood poured from its fingertips, where Mr. Fuller had ground them down to fine nubbins, and its chest began to heave as the body sucked stale air into its dormant and shriveled lungs. Mr. West was waking up, and soon their employer would have all the information he needed.

Kingfisher retrieved the chain from the ground and pulled the trembling girl toward him. She was the final component in the ritual, the blood that would allow West's spirit back into his body, the vessel through which they would control the gateway.

He still hadn't decided whether or not Nadine Pahari would survive the night. Numerous times had he imagined tasting her soul, devouring her innocence, but she might have other uses that would ultimately prove more valuable to them. Only time would tell.

From out of nowhere, a huge brown and white coon dog flew through the air. The growling animal hit Mr. Kingfisher in the chest, knocking him off his feet, sending the girl tumbling to the ground. And then the dog's sharp teeth were around his wrist, ripping and tearing, shaking its head back and forth in a wild frenzy as it tore into his skin.

Mr. Quarry was upon the animal in a second, tearing it from Mr. Kingfisher's arm, twisting its head nearly from its shoulders. The dog shook once before rolling onto the road with a wet flop, dead.

"That was…most unexpected," Mr. Kingfisher said, taking his partner's hand, pulling himself to his feet. The dog should have been just as disoriented as the poodle and its master. How had it approached them, let alone attacked?

"Mr. Kingfisher," intoned the other man, "I think we might have a problem."

He looked over Mr. Quarry's shoulder. The symbols inscribed upon the dead man's body should have bound him to the circle they'd drawn on the street, but instead he was gone. They'd brought him back to life, and now Connor West, the one man that could control the gateway between the dead and the living, had vanished.

Chapter 26

Claire lay on the couch, soaked in sweat. She tossed and turned, her eyes briefly fluttering open. She whimpered, mumbling something about a dog, but then fell silent. Slowly her body relaxed, and once again she began to dream.

She was in the same graveyard as before, the one where Johnny had betrayed their friendship. She was older now, seventeen or eighteen, and it was the night of her prom. She should have been dancing with her friends, getting drunk on spiked punch, but instead she'd been stood up by her date.

It had taken all her courage to ask him to the prom, but at the last minute he'd feigned illness and begged off, claiming to have come down with the flu. Imagine her surprise, then, when, arriving at the school by herself, she'd seen him dancing to a Jewel song with another girl.

Embarrassed and angry, she ran from the gym, climbed into the old Honda Civic her father had given her for her birthday, and drove to the only place where she felt at peace: Moss Ridge cemetery.

The spirits no longer inspired fear in her. Instead, she found their presence oddly comforting. The dead, after all, weren't dangerous; it was life that brought you pain.

She stomped through the graveyard, kicking at gravestones, punching trees until her knuckles bled. She was finally going to get laid tonight, but now it was all fucked up. She'd even paid for a hotel room.

This was the worst night in her life, and there had been some pretty bad ones along the way. Damn it all to hell.

"Quit feeling sorry for yourself," said a soft voice behind her, echoing through the empty cemetery, "or you're going to wake the dead."

"Looks like I already have," she mumbled, recognizing the voice. "Sorry, Mags, but screw you. You don't know what I've been through tonight."

It was Margaret, a spirit she'd been talking to for almost as long as she could remember. She'd been murdered forty years ago, and was still tied to the Earth.

"You're right," she said, materializing before her, "I don't. But I do know that it's never a good idea to wake the dead."

"What are you talking about?" she growled, avoiding the spirit's eyes. Margaret had a way of making her feel tiny and insignificant. And tonight, especially tonight, she wasn't in any mood for one of the ghost's lectures. "You're awake, there's Huey over there, Marvin, and there's Robbie, over by the fence. The gang's all here."

"I meant them." She pointed to the ground, beneath where Claire now stood. "The ones still tied to their bodies, the one's that haven't walked the Earth since they were put into the ground. You wake them up, and there's going to be consequences. Didn't your father teach you anything?"

"We don't talk so much anymore," she said, looking away.

"You'd be wise to start," Margaret whispered, brushing a phantom hand against her cheek. "You've been given a great gift, but with that gift comes great responsibility. But you already know that."

"Yeah," sighed Claire, feeling the anger drain from her body, "I guess I do, but sometimes it's a little too easy to forget."

"That's why I'm here," the spirit said, smiling, "to help you remember. Always remember, Claire, always remember, remember, remember, remember…"

It was as if the ghost were a broken record, stuck in the same groove. She stared at Margaret, started to go to her, but then the ground began to shake and a hundred, thousand hands shot up from beneath the ground at once, grabbing her ankles, her legs, pulling her down, down into the ground, grabbing, touching, feeling, needing her, needing to possess her, to own her, to pull her under and...

She awoke with a gasp, her eyes snapping open to find Jeff looming over her. He was moving his hips rhythmically against hers, slamming his body into her over and over again in an attempt to get inside her. She opened her mouth to scream, but he clamped his hand down hard over her mouth and nothing came out. She could smell the sweet stench of alcohol leaking from his sweat.

"Get off of me," she managed to eke out, struggling under his grasp.

His hand moved to her throat, tightening around her windpipe, as he continued to thrust his half-hard dick at her.

"How does it feel, baby?" he whispered, speech slurring.

Stars swam in front of her eyes, and she felt perilously close to blacking out. "I said," she rasped, her throat on fire, "get the fuck off of me, you son of a bitch."

But he wouldn't listen. His hands tightened around her throat as his hips bucked, trying to shove his way into her like a rabid animal in heat. "Come for me, baby, come for me," he moaned, his eyes rolling back in his head. "You know you want to."

And then she was moving. She rolled her hips up, pushing him away from her. Snaking one arm between his hands, she thrust her palm straight into his nose, feeling the cartilage shatter. His head snapped back, startled, and she locked her legs around his left arm, grabbing his wrist and bending his elbow away from his body, bending it in a direction it was never meant to go.

His face awash in blood from his ruined nose, he screamed in pain and rage. And still she held on to the arm bar, putting all her weight into it, hyper extending the elbow nearly perpendicular to the rest of his body as she felt something pop.

"Jesus, Claire, Jesus Fucking Christ, let go!" he sobbed, dangling helplessly between the couch and the tile floor.

She finally released the hold, letting him fall the rest of the way to the floor. He pulled his ruined arm close to his chest, tears streaming down his cheeks as he scooted away from her. His penis was completely flaccid now, and he stared at her in shock.

Claire rose to her feet on shaky legs. She'd fallen asleep wearing the gray slacks she'd worn to the park, but now they were gone, thrown carelessly across the room along with her red cotton panties. Her legs hurt like hell and her stomach was clenched in knots. She threw up all over the couch before stumbling across the floor to retrieve her clothes.

"Jesus, Claire," Jeff repeated, clambering to his knees, "what the fuck is wrong with you?" His face was red, and he balled his one good hand into a fist.

"You were trying to rape me," she yelled, pulling on her panties. "I fell asleep, and you tried to rape me."

"Rape?" he said incredulously, circling her like a wolf. "We're married, Claire. I get to fuck you whenever I want to, remember? You never minded before."

"I do now," she said, pulling on her slacks, "You ever touch me again, you son of a bitch, and so help me God, I'll kill you."

"It's that cunt Elisabeth, isn't it?" he growled, his hand closing on one of the many empty beer bottles that littered the room. "She never could stand me. If you think I'm going to let this slide, you've got another think coming."

He advanced toward her, holding the beer bottle like a club. His broken arm hung limply by his side, but Claire knew that a dog was always most dangerous when wounded. He took another step forward, breathing hard and gnashing his teeth.

Fully awake now, she backed away, amazed at what she had done. Jeff had accused Leesie of somehow being responsible for teaching her to defend herself, but she knew her friend had done no such thing. Where had she learned to fight like that?

"You know that I settled for you, don't you?" he asked, waving the bottle at her. "I could have any woman I wanted. Hell, I had two this past weekend. I can fuck any woman I want, Claire, but I married you. You! And this is how you repay me?"

The arrogant prick. He admitted to cheating on her in one breath and then told her she should be grateful to him in the next. Amnesia or not, she knew that she didn't belong here. If being married to this monster was part of the package, she wasn't sure she ever wanted to regain her memory.

"I'm leaving," she said. "I'll get my stuff, and Corduroy, and then I'm out of here. Move out, burn down the house, I don't care, but I never want to see you again, and if I do, I'll break your other arm."

He threw the bottle in one quick motion, bouncing it off her skull. Stunned, she fell back against the loveseat, everything spinning in her vision as somewhere she heard the bottle shatter against the floor; and then he was upon, slapping her hard in the face, spitting at her, kicking her legs out from under her. He climbed atop her chest, straddling her, pinning her arms to her sides, digging his knees into her ribs. He reared back and hit her across the jaw with the back of his hand, splitting her lip open and spraying blood everywhere.

"You won't leave me, you stupid whore," he roared, rearing back for another slap, "you don't have the fucking guts!"

And then he was howling in pain, slapping at his back and shoulders as he tumbled to the floor. He tried to brace himself but landed on his broken arm, a bloodcurdling scream springing forth from his lips. He slammed face first into the tile, Corduroy on his back, the cat growling and hissing as it dug its claws in deep, shredding his skin. He shuddered once, spasmed, and then passed out. Bloody drool ran down his chin to pool on the floor beneath his open mouth.

"Good kitty," she mumbled, rubbing her jaw. She reached out to stroke the cat, who casually sprang from Jeff's ruined back to land in her lap. She nuzzled her face against his, and then she was crying, sobbing hysterically into the cat's long, white fur.

Her husband of six years had just tried to rape and kill her. Leesie had been right; the man was a monster, and it took everything she had not to pick up a shard from the broken beer bottle and slit his throat. How long had she put up with this?

She hugged the cat fiercely, knowing that he may have just saved her life. Corduroy purred and licked errant tears from her cheeks, bringing a smile to her lips. She rubbed her nose against the cat's long fur before shifting him from her lap to the back of the loveseat.

Pushing to her feet, she stumbled through the kitchen in search of a length of rope. She finally found a long nylon cord in the garage that looked strong enough to bind Jeff's hands. She carried the coil back into the living room, startled to see him struggling to his feet.

She kicked him hard in the face, feeling a surge of relief as he collapsed again to the floor. She carefully bound his hands and feet with the cord, trussing him up like a holiday goose.

When she was done she surveyed her efforts, pronounced them sound, and collapsed in a fit of giggles against the loveseat. Tears in her eyes, she didn't stop laughing until Corduroy, sniffing her bare feet, pounced on her lap and began to once again make starfish paws on her stomach.

Her ribs ached from laughing, and she wondered if she were going insane. She'd just survived attempted rape and nearly being murdered, and all she could do was laugh.

Shaking her head, she sat about gathering a few things she'd need for her trip; her laptop; the photo album she'd found in the bedroom; a few days' worth of clothing; and Corduroy's cat carrier, which she finally found in the garage. She didn't plan on being here when Jeff woke up, and the sooner she got out the better.

She searched the kitchen for cat food, coming up with an unopened bag of Eukanuba and a half a dozen cans of Iams Seafood Medley. These she threw into a plastic shopping bag from Wal-Mart, along with a toothbrush and other toiletries she thought she might need.

"Claire?" sobbed Jeff, looking up at her with pleading eyes. "Jesus, baby, untie me. I can't even feel my arm anymore, and I think I'm starting to go into shock. I'm sorry, we can work this out. You know I love you."

"Untie you so you can attack me again or hurt Corduroy?" she scoffed, hands on her hips. "No thanks. And I don't need love like yours."

"I have a *problem*," he said, stressing the word. "I drink too much. I know that. But we've had sex like that before, and you never broke my fucking arm."

"I was a different person then," she said, guiding Corduroy into his pet carrier.

"Remember when we first met? I was working with Elisabeth's brother, and he introduced us, thinking we'd make a good pair. And he was right! And now that we're having a baby, things can only get better."

So that's why Leesie sounded so remorseful when she'd first told her about Jeff. She thought it was her fault that the two of them had gotten together, but she couldn't have known the man that he'd become.

"If you ever come near me or my baby again," she said, for the first time feeling protective of the child she was carrying inside her, "I'll kill you."

"Brave words when I'm tied up on the floor," he spat, his demean-or instantly growing dark. "You let me up now and we'll forget this whole thing ever happened. But you'll never keep me away from my son. Never in a million fucking years. If I have to come after you…"

"You'll what? Rape me? Try to kill me? Been there, done that."

She took a step toward him, and, when he flinched, she knew she'd already won.

"Please baby, don't leave me," He pleaded, his swollen eyes looking up at her in fear.

"Goodbye, Jeff."

Walking through the kitchen and into the garage, she never once looked back. Placing Corduroy's pet taxi in the passenger's seat, she circled the car to shove the laptop and clothes into the trunk. Taking one last look at her house and the surrounding neighborhood, she wished that she could remember her previous life if only so she'd know what she was giving up.

She turned over the car's engine, her eyes drawn to the time flash-ing on the dashboard; it was almost one in the morning. She dug the cell phone out of her purse, intent on calling Leesie, but at the last mi-nute decided against it. It was late, and she didn't want to risk being re-buffed. Better to show up unannounced and see what happened. It was far more difficult to slam the door in someone's face than it was to hang up a phone, though she doubted that Leesie would do either.

Pulling out of the driveway, she paused for a moment as she clicked the garage door opener and watched it close on a life she couldn't remember. She shook her head at this strange turn of events, heading for Leesie's house just as the storm clouds that had been threatening the city since this morning began to unleash a torrent of rain and hail. She put out a steady hand to calm Corduroy and then switched on the Sirius satellite radio, quickly spinning the dial away from the preset Jazz station.

Do I really listen to that crap? She moved through several channels, finally settling on a station that played hard rock classics. She could definitely use a little Jimmi Hendrix in her life right now.

A trio of police cars roared past her, lights on and sirens wailing. She held her breath but, thank God, they kept on going, past the park where she'd met Jimmy Cross and toward the other side of town. She finally let herself exhale, listening to Corduroy purr as she stroked his fur through the bars of his plastic prison.

Chapter 27

Connor West shuffled through the street, rain splashing down all around him, lurching across the pavement like a wounded bear. Only he wasn't Connor West, not really. He had some of his memories, the ones that hadn't been destroyed during the man's death, but even those were filled with holes. Still, the Great Spirit drew upon them for knowledge of this new world through which he walked and of the language that its inhabitants spoke.

When he'd leapt into the gatekeeper's body, he hadn't expected to find it as hollow and as empty as a skin drum. He'd ridden the dog to the two shamans' hideaway, lurking outside as they prepared to perform their ceremony. He'd taken his chance the moment it had presented itself, claiming his prize and mastery over the very fabric of life and death.

Only the prize was gone, and all that remained was the shell of the man who had once wielded it. Worse still, he didn't seem to be able to leave. Try as he might, he was anchored within, trapped by the flesh of a dead man, still no closer to the eternal life that dangled like a fat rabbit just beyond his grasp.

He'd been dealt a heavy blow, but was far from defeated. Somewhere near was the gatekeeper's spirit, and this body would lead him to it. Once he'd consumed the spirit, all he'd dreamt of, everything he'd once had, would again be his. He who controlled the doorway between life and death, controlled the universe. All he had to do was turn the key.

The Great Spirit went still, listening. The ghost was so close he could almost taste it. The world around him was large, but his tracking abilities were legend. He would find the spirit, shove it back into this rotting body, and control it, using it to bring himself back to life.

And the heavens have mercy on anyone who might stand in his way.

Chapter 28

Lightning flickered across the horizon as Claire climbed out of the car, pet carrier in one hand and a bag of cat food and an overnight bag in another. The rain was coming down in buckets now, and she wished it could wash away her sins as easily as it sluiced across the sidewalk leading up to Leesie's house.

She'd almost killed a man tonight, using skills she'd acquired God only knows where. He had almost raped and tried to kill her, but that didn't make her actions any less horrific. She'd enjoyed watching him squirm, listening to him beg as she walked out the door. Breaking his arm and bloodying his nose had been self-defense, but there was no excuse for the rest.

Where had she learned to fight, and had she always been able to communicate with the dead? As much as she yearned to know the answers to these questions, a part of her was terrified to find out. Leesie had painted the picture of not only a warm and caring artist but a genuine friend, but what if that image was colored more by their shared past than by the person she was today?

Corduroy let out a pitiful meow and she realized that she'd been standing beside the car letting the rain soak them both. She pressed the remote lock on her key ring and walked the rest of the way to Leesie's door. Taking a deep breath, she steeled her nerves and rang the doorbell.

Leesie was dressed for bed but looked wide awake. "Jesus, Claire. Are you all right?" she said in a rush. "Oh my God, your face. Jeff did this to you, didn't he? That bastard!"

"I gave better than I got," Claire said, wiping her feet on the welcome mat. She stood straddling the doorway, neither inside nor out. "Do you mind if we spend the night?"

"We?" she asked, confusion crossing her face until she noticed the cat carrier. "Oh! You mean Corduroy. Of course! You know you're always welcome here, and so is your cat. Come on in."

Leesie pulled her through the door and into a long embrace, only letting go when Corduroy mewled in protest. Leesie gently kissed her tears away, and only then did she realize she'd been crying.

"Thank you," Claire said, looking away. "I mean it. I was afraid that you wouldn't…I mean, I have been an awfully lot of trouble."

"Sweetie," Leesie said, taking her hand in her own, "you're never trouble. Now come on, let's get you settled in and warmed up."

Leesie unpacked Corduroy's litter pan and cat food while Claire padded into the bathroom to take a quick shower. It seemed to take forever, but she finally cleaned Jeff's blood out of her hair and his scent from her body. The cuts and bruises on her face still stung, but she knew that, unlike her marriage, they'd eventually heal.

Pressing a hand to her stomach, she was disappointed when the baby didn't kick. She knew it was still far too early, but she wanted to connect to the life growing inside her. She needed to remember something more than graveyards. She felt as if she might float away, might cease to exist and just vanish from the beautiful tile bathroom, leaving nothing behind.

Claire shook her head. At this rate, she'd wind up in the loony bin for sure. She toweled off and then slipped on a pair of red silk pajamas she'd found in her closet at home. The pajamas felt nice against her skin, and she wished fervently that she could remember ever wearing them before tonight.

"Feeling better?" Leesie asked as she walked out into the living room. "Can I make you a nice cup of tea?"

"That'd be great," she said, following Leesie into the kitchen, "but you don't have to make it. I'm so sorry for getting you up." According to the clock on the wall, it was almost two in the morning.

"First of all, I wasn't asleep," Leesie said, pulling a china tea pot from one of the many cabinets that adorned her kitchen, "but even if I were, you're my best friend. Besties are there for each other. You've been there for me enough times in the past, so, please, don't worry about it."

"God, my life is so fucked up. Maybe I would have been better off letting Dr. Frazee admit me to the hospital, after all."

"Probably," she said, putting the water on to boil, "but you didn't, so we're going to make the best of it. And your life isn't all that fucked up, and now that you've finally gotten Jeff out of your life, it's only going to get better."

Claire sat down at the kitchen table. "I nearly killed him, you know."

She saw Leesie stiffen. "Jeff, you mean?"

"I fell asleep on the couch. When I woke up, he was on top of me. He was…trying to have sex with me. He had his hands around my throat. I didn't know what else to do," the words came out in a rush, "so I hit him, and then I broke his arm."

"He was having sex with you while you were asleep, and you broke his arm?"

"I said trying. He was drunk and couldn't get it up, lucky for me."

"So what happened next?"

"I had to get him off me. I twisted around and put his arm in a *Ju-jigatame*, this move where I lock my legs around his shoulder and hyper-extend the elbow, and it just snapped. And then I…why are you looking at me like that?"

"A *Jujigatame*," Leesie asked, her eyes wide, "what on earth is a *Jujigatame*, and how do you know all this stuff?"

"It's basically an arm bar, and I don't know how I know."

"Well, I'm glad that you did. That bastard could have really hurt you and the baby."

"There's more," Claire whispered, dreading what she had to say next. "Remember Jimmy Cross, the man I mentioned talking to at the park?"

"I remember you mentioning him," she said, "but what does he have to do with any of this?"

"Not much," said Claire, a nervous laugh escaping her lips, "seeing as he'd dead."

"But you just saw him yesterday. When did he die?"

"According to the newspaper article I downloaded from the Internet, he died in a car wreck on July 13, 1976."

"Okay," Leesie said, ignoring the shrill whistle of the tea pot, "but you just saw him yesterday, right? How is that possible?"

"I saw him today, too," Claire admitted, looking away. "Tried to touch him, and my hand went right through his shoulder. I also healed my cat from a life-threatening injury with just the touch of my hand."

"Claire…"

"Let me finish. It seems that not only can I talk to ghosts, but I can heal animals. But not people, apparently, since I can't seem to get rid of these bruises. And of course you've already seen my *Xena, Warrior Princess* act. Want to see what I can do for an encore?"

"Sure," she said, finally getting up to remove the tea pot from the stove. "Let's see the encore."

"The question was rhetorical," Claire smiled, feeling stupid. "But I can show you how a *Jujigatame* works, if you really want me to."

"Claire, have you already started taking the Zoloft? It's rare, but sometimes people can have bad reactions to SSRIs. Hallucinations are pretty damned uncommon, but I've heard of it happening before. I think we should take you to the emergency room."

"I knew you wouldn't believe me," she sulked, putting her head in her hands. "Hell, I barely believe it myself. Until I healed Corduroy, I thought I was nuts. But Jimmy's real, and so were the ghosts at the hospital."

"You saw ghosts at the hospital?"

"Only a few," Claire said weakly, "though I did see a bunch in the graveyard off Walnut Street."

Leesie poured them both a cup of tea. "Claire," she said, walking over to the butcher block and drawing out a filet knife, "you're the only person in the world I'd do this for. If you can see ghosts, and if you can heal things, heal me."

Before Claire could say or do anything, Leesie drew the knife across her forearm. A thin line of blood sprang up from her skin, trickling down her wrist to pool in the palm of her hand.

"I already said I couldn't heal people," Claire said, jumping out of her chair. "Why did you do that?"

"To illustrate a point, though in hindsight it seems pretty stupid," she admitted, staring blankly at her arm. "Shit, this hurts. Can you get me a bandage out of the guest bathroom? I'll be…"

She fell silent as Claire touched her arm, and together they watched as her skin healed itself. Flesh melted together and within seconds the only proof that the cut had ever been there was a tiny white scar and the blood covering her arm. A few seconds later the blood was still there but even the scar had disappeared.

"Okay," Claire said, feeling giddy, "I was wrong. I can heal people, just not me. This is really weird."

"Lady," said Leesie, leaning against the stove for support, "you don't know the half of it. Ghosts too, huh?"

"Uh-huh," she agreed, leading Leesie back to the table. She sat her down and then sat beside her, slowly sipping her tea. "So, do you believe me now?"

"Do I have a choice?" Leesie said, staring at her arm.

"Rhetorical question?" she asked, knowing that it was.

Leesie nodded. "So tell me about these ghosts, and start at the beginning. I knew I shouldn't have left you alone this afternoon. You always get into trouble without me."

"Tell me about it," she said with a sigh, and then told her everything she knew about Corduroy's accident and Jimmy's murder.

"That's some story," Leesie said, when she was done. "Claire, I'm a doctor. I believe what I can see, what I can prove. But this…if I hadn't watched my skin literally stitch itself together with my own two eyes, I'd be driving you to the psychiatric unit right now. But either I'm crazy, too, or you're telling the truth."

"At least as much of it as I know," Claire admitted, wishing she could remember something, anything, of her life before yesterday. Surely she didn't develop the ability to kick ass and heal people overnight, much less communicate with spirits.

"Well, at least you're in good company," said Leesie, gesturing toward the television. "Strange things have been happening all over today. Well, yesterday, actually. That's what I was doing when you rang the doorbell, watching CNN."

"What do you mean?"

"Freak earthquakes and a fire that took out half a town in Missouri, cemeteries collapsing in on themselves, and a homicide at a cemetery in some little town in Illinois. Some teenagers stole a body, killed their friend, and then blamed his death on the missing corpse, which police still haven't recovered. Two other kids are still missing."

"Sounds like its right up my alley," Claire said, moving into the living room in hopes of catching some of the news.

Anderson Cooper was there, standing at the gates of a cemetery. The graveyard looked oddly familiar to her, and with a start she realized it was the same one she'd seen in her dreams.

"...alleged homicide and kidnapping," he was saying, his steely blue eyes staring straight into the camera as snow drifted down from the sky to cover the gravestones behind him. "Farris Hale and Sabrina Locke, both juniors at Carthage High School, are still missing, as is the body of Gabriel Locke, Sabrina's father, who died after losing a long battle to lung cancer three weeks earlier.

"Sheriff Thomas Brady has taken four teenagers, also juniors at the local high school, into custody. Willard Cummings, the Hancock county district attorney, has not filed charges, stating that they are only needed for questioning at this time."

"But you can read between the lines," said Leesie, walking into the room. She picked up the remote and aimed it at the television. "It's obvious they did it. But this is depressing. Let's watch Cartoon Network or Skinamax or something."

"No," Claire shouted, stepping between Leesie and the television, "I want to see this. There's something about..."

"I'm sorry to interrupt, Anderson," said a woman's disembodied voice, identified by the words on the screen as belonging to CNN anchor Brooke Baldwin, "but we've just had breaking news in Bentonville, Arkansas. We're now taking you live to affiliate reporter Ronald Shaw, reporting from outside the county morgue. Ronald?"

"Thanks, Brooke. In Bentonville, Arkansas, home to retail giant Wal-Mart, reports are still coming in. For those that just joined us, Norman Broussard, 23, a night guard at the Benton county morgue, was found murdered this evening, his body reportedly mutilated almost beyond recognition. Amelia Ruiz, the intern who found his body, discovered the corpse when doing a routine search of the lab after Broussard didn't show up for his shift. The body of an unidentified man involved in a hit and run car accident yesterday morning—that body was missing, and Broussard had been left in its place.

"But here's where it gets really strange. Benton county resident, Eileen Travers, 84, a retired school teacher, was also found murdered along with her pet poodle at the intersection of Thirteenth and Persimmon in Rogers, which is right next door to Bentonville, where the unidentified car accident victim lost his life. Arcane symbols have reportedly been found drawn in chalk on the road, approximately where the accident happened."

"That's truly bizarre, Ronald," said Baldwin's voice, "especially with everything else that's happened in the last two days. Have they confirmed yet that Mrs. Travers' murder is related to the murder of Norman Broussard?"

"Not yet, Brooke," Shaw responded, shifting as the camera panned in closer, "but we'll keep you up to date as more information becomes available."

"Wow," said Leesie, the remote hanging limp in her hand as they watched CNN go to a commercial. "I didn't know about that one."

"The thing is," Claire said, looking away from the TV, "I think they're all related, to each other and to me."

"What are you talking about?"

"That graveyard," she said, "I've dreamt about it. I've been there before, I'm certain of it. And that guy being killed right outside the clinic, it's too much of a coincidence."

"At this point," Leesie admitted, "I'm too tired to tell what's real and what isn't. It's almost three. How about we go to bed and look at all this from a new perspective in the morning?"

"I'm exhausted," Claire agreed, wondering even as she said it just what in the hell she'd gotten involved in, "so I think I can live with that."

"Get a good night's sleep," Leesie said, kissing her on the cheek, "and things are bound to look better in the morning."

"They couldn't look any worse," Claire called over her shoulder as she walked up the stairs and toward the bedroom, hoping it was true.

Corduroy was there waiting for her. She flicked off the light and climbed into bed, snuggling up against the white tom. Thirty seconds after her head hit the pillow, she was asleep and dreaming.

Chapter 29

Mr. Kingfisher had never liked the weather. Like technology, it was too unpredictable. But this time, the rain actually benefited them. West had to be weak and would surely need to take shelter soon. He wouldn't be able to get very far before they found him.

Mr. Kingfisher hated driving almost as much as he hated the weather, and tended to delegate that task to Mr. Quarry. Tonight, however, his partner's talents were needed elsewhere, and so he found himself driving their perfectly maintained 1942 black Town and Country Woodie station wagon. Mr. Quarry sat hunched in the back seat, beside the terrified young girl they'd been forced to bring with them, rolling his bones and moving a bit of string connected by a safety pin to the tip of one of West's fingers over a map of Rogers they'd found in the house.

He hated to bring the girl, but there wasn't any other way. Because they had used her blood to reawaken West's body, the two were inexorably bound. West's finger would lead them to his body, but once they found him they would need the girl to control him.

"Turn right, Mr. Kingfisher," Quarry instructed from the back seat, his eyes never leaving the map, "and then immediately take a left. There, that's it."

Mr. Kingfisher turned the car. It was getting hard to see, and he feared the hail might damage the roof of the station wagon.

"We're getting closer, Mr. Kingfisher. Keep going straight, and then…wait, he's moving again."

Mr. Kingfisher pressed down hard on the brakes, causing the vehicle to fishtail as it skidded against the wet road. He turned into the slide, and the car slowly regained traction.

"Please, just let me out," Nadine pleaded, pulling against the chain that connected her wrist to the seat. "I won't tell anyone what happened, I promise."

A stern glance in the rearview mirror silenced the girl.

"Where do we go now?" Mr. Kingfisher snapped, immediately regretting his tone. Mr. Quarry didn't control the weather, nor did he control Nadine Pahari.

"Do forgive me, Mr. Quarry," he said, as he brought the car to a stop beside a convenience store, "this weather…it does things to me."

"Nothing to forgive, Mr. Kingfisher. Now turn right at the intersection, then left on Walnut Street. He's moving again."

The runes Mr. Quarry had inscribed in West's flesh would keep the man's spirit bound to the body they were even now tracking, and he would have to go to ground sometime. They would find him eventually and, once they did, would use the girl to control him. After they got him back to the house, they would do whatever was necessary to discover his secrets.

Mr. Lazarus would finally have what he needed and they could once and for all put this dreadful town behind them.

Chapter 30

Jeff Summers lay in a pool of his own blood and vomit, half-drunk and whimpering in pain. He couldn't believe what she'd done to him. He wriggled across the room on his stomach, crying out every time his broken arm brushed against the cold tile.

They'd had sex like that many times, and while she never really seemed to get into it, she'd never reacted like that. Once he got out of this mess, he would definitely enjoy teaching her and that dyke friend of hers a lesson.

Just a few more feet, he thought stubbornly, as he inched across the floor. One of their cordless phones was plugged into the outlet next to the end table. If he could pull the cord down with his teeth, the phone would fall to the ground and then he'd be able to dial it with his nose.

He was almost there—just a few more inches. There! He gingerly took the cord into his mouth, rolled his head back, and pulled at the phone cradle. He felt resistance at first and then the phone was teetering, rocking back and forth on the edge. Finally, it fell, landing square in the middle of his forehead. He scuttled away in pain, nearly losing it as he rolled over on his broken arm. He bit down so hard that he lacerated his tongue. His mouth filled with blood, and he started to gag.

It was all for nothing, because it was just the cradle. The cordless phone wasn't there. He screamed a litany of curses, wishing on all that was holy that Claire was here so he could put a bullet through her brain. But first he'd torture her, humiliate her just as she'd humiliated him. Maybe start by tying Elisabeth to a chair, slowly pulling her fingernails out. And he'd make Claire watch…

His fantasy was interrupted by a loud banging at the front door.

"Help," he screamed at the top of his lungs, "I'm trapped in here. Call the police. There's a key under the rock by the front door. Please, help me!"

The banging subsided and he heard the familiar sound of a key disengaging the tumblers inside the door. He couldn't see what was happening but heard the door swing open and the tap-tap-tap of someone walking across the tile.

"Please, for the love of God, help me," he pleaded, struggling against his bonds. "Mexicans, they broke in. There were three of them. Robbed me blind, broke my arm, and kidnapped my wife. Please, untie me." He didn't dare tell his rescuer the truth.

The footsteps grew closer, stopped, and then he felt someone grab his shoulder and wrench him around to roll over on his back.

A naked dead man stared down at him, the corpse's flaccid penis having turned a deep shade of gray. Half of his head was gone, and he could see brain matter beneath the broken bone. Matted blood and shredded bits of scalp clung to his long, red hair, and the tips of his fingers were missing. Jeff wanted to scream, but the man's ruined hand clamped down over his mouth.

Looking down at Jeff with bloodshot eyes, he shot him a lopsided smile. "Connor West," he slurred. His lips were gray, and Jeff could see that he was missing part of his tongue. "Where is he?"

The thing moved its hand so Jeff could talk.

"What…*are* you?" he whispered.

"Connor West," the thing repeated, but it didn't make sense. Was he looking for Connor West or was he Connor West? This must be a prank, someone in a costume that Claire had sent over to scare him.

"You're not real," he said, false bravado in his voice. "No one could have survived those injuries."

The dead man smiled, reached into his head and twisted, showering Jeff with a fine mist of blood and brains. Jeff screamed, and once again the man's hand clamped down tight over his mouth, smearing his lips with gray matter. His would-be rescuer pushed his face against Jeff's and repeated his question. "Where is Connor West?"

"Please don't hurt me," Jeff whimpered when the monster removed his hand. "Take whatever you want, just please don't hurt me."

And then the dead man thrust his fingers, what was left of them, at Jeff's skull, pressing tight against his right temple. He held them there for a moment. Jeff screamed in agony, his body seizing, but when the zombie finally removed his fingers Jeff was still alive and there didn't seem to be any blood.

"I have a …proposition," whispered the dead man, rolling the word around on his tongue as though he were sampling a new flavor of ice cream. "Claire hurt you. I can hurt her in return. Lead me to her, and together we can both get what we want and make the…little bitch suffer."

Where before the dead man had spoken like an Alzheimer's patient, he now used full sentences; it was as if he had pulled the words from Jeff's brain and were using them to communicate, like one of those universal translators from the old *Star Trek* show.

"Or, if you'd rather, I can make what she did to your arm seem like a paper cut. So what do you think, *Jeff Summers*?"

He hurled his name like an insult, and Jeff flinched.

What choice did he have? If she hadn't attacked him, hadn't chosen that moment to finally grow a spine, none of this would even be happening. Some small part of his brain knew the thought wasn't logical, that one event hadn't necessarily led to the other, but giving up Claire certainly beat dying.

"All right," he finally said, his voice trembling, "let's do it."

✳ ✳ ✳

Claire was dreaming again, only this time she knew she was dreaming. She stood just inside the gates of Moss Ridge Cemetery, the same ones she'd seen on CNN, holding her sister's hand. She knew she was there for her father's funeral, but she didn't know how he'd died. She felt hot tears streaming down her cheeks as Mel grasped her hand, and together they walked to their father's coffin.

"He wanted to see you," Mel whispered, a hint of recrimination in her voice. "You're all he talked about, but we couldn't find you."

"I'm sorry," she whispered, looking across the graveyard and into the sun. She stared hard without blinking, enjoying the pain as the sun's radiation burned into her retinas. It made her feel alive, something that she hadn't felt for a very long time.

She knew she was dreaming, but went through the motions anyway. It was almost as if she were an unwilling participant in a play with only herself as an audience. She stopped fighting it after a while, gave into it, and just went with the flow.

"I know," Mel said, pressing her head against Claire's shoulder. "I just…I needed you, too. That damned cancer. It ate away at him, ate him up until his body just couldn't take it anymore. We thought it was getting better for a while, and then two weeks ago things got really bad. In the end, he could barely stay awake, but he still asked for you."

Why was Mel telling her this? She felt bad enough already. But it was a fair trade, wasn't it? Her father had missed half her life, and she'd missed the end of his. At least she was here for his funeral.

"Let's just get through this," Claire whispered. "Once this is over, you can berate me all you want."

"I'm not trying to berate you," Mel snapped, "but you could have helped him, couldn't you?"

"Doesn't work like that, little sister," she said, pushing down an ugly retort. "Couldn't have helped him anymore than I could have helped you when you broke your arm, remember? As Dad used to say, 'it's a blessing and a curse.'"

"But you can talk to him after, right?"

"Yeah," she said, putting her arm around Mel's shoulder, "we can both talk to him afterward, and any other time I'm in town. Dad was a real prick sometimes, but I loved him, and I'm going to miss him, too."

Mel seemed like she wanted to say something, but instead she sighed and pulled Claire into a hug. "He loved you too, you know. And so do I. God, I can't even imagine what I'd do if I lost you both. Don't be such a stranger from now on, okay? Promise me that."

"I promise," she whispered into her sister's ear, knowing even as she said it that it was a lie. "Now come on, the minister's about to start his spiel."

Together they sat down in the uncomfortable metal chairs that littered the lumpy, fake grass rug that covered the ground and prepared to say goodbye to their father. They sat like that for a long time, well after the minister and the other mourners had left, just holding each other, sharing stories, and remembering their father. Finally, it was time to go.

And that's when their father's ghost woke up.

Claire awoke with a start, wild eyed and breathing heavy. She'd had a dream, something about Mel and her father, but she couldn't quite remember what it was. She grasped at it like an errant gossamer string, a scene in a graveyard somewhere, but it floated away as if it had never been.

She looked around the strange room and her eyes fell on the clock beside her bed. It was four in the morning, just an hour or so after she'd fallen asleep. Corduroy had been cuddled up next to her, but now the old tom was nowhere to be seen.

Unable to sleep, she got up to go to the bathroom but was met by Leesie on her way back to bed.

"Claire, are you all right?" Leesie asked, rubbing sleep from her eyes. "I heard you yell out in your sleep again, and then Corduroy raced into my room like his tail was on fire. Another bad dream?"

"I don't think so," she said, leaning against the wall, "but it could've been. I was dreaming about Mel, and my father, but it's gone now."

"Want to talk about it?" Leesie asked, gesturing for Claire to follow her into the master bedroom.

"I'm not sure what there is to talk about," she said, "but sure."

It was a beautiful room, airy and comfortable, decorated in earth tones. A huge king-sized bed filled one end of the room, balanced by a television and a massive dresser on the other. The floor was made of wood, and it felt cool beneath her bare toes.

She sat on the edge of the bed, looking up at Leesie.

"Not to make a habit of this," Leesie said, smiling, "but scoot over. I'm tired, and that damned cat of yours doesn't seem to want to let me get any sleep."

Claire patted the mattress beside her, feeling a strange rush in her stomach as Leesie started to crawl into bed. The baby? No, the baby was fine. This was something else, something new and confusing. She looked up into her best friend's face, not for the first time noticing the smooth contour of her jaw and the full, red lips that interacted to form a perfect smile. She really was beautiful.

Their eyes met and Leesie looked embarrassed, and, before she even realized what she was doing, Claire was reaching up, pulling her down, brushing Leesie's lips with her own to silence her protests. The kiss turned deeper, tongues and hurried breaths, until finally Leesie, red-faced and flushed, pulled away.

"Sweetie," she whispered, clutching Claire's hand. She brought it slowly to her lips and kissed her fingers. "I'm the lesbian here, remember? Not you. Are you sure you want this? Hell, I mean, you don't even remember what you want. I mean, I, me and you, we've never…"

Claire silenced her with another kiss. "Did anyone ever tell you," she breathed, nipping at her lips between kisses, "that you talk too much?"

"Only you," Leesie replied, moving her mouth to Claire's neck, "Every other time I open my mouth." She began trailing heated little kisses down Claire's throat, slowly slipping the red pajama top over her head to let it drop soundlessly to the floor.

Her tongue and teeth met Claire's hardening nipples, and it felt amazing. Claire arched her back, needing more, and then Leesie's hand was sliding between her legs, pushing her panties aside, and she realized with a surprise that the cotton material was soaking wet.

A low moan escaped her lips as Leesie's fingers moved expertly between her legs, rubbing, teasing, and finally, in a frenzy, thrusting in and out of her, bringing her to a sudden and explosive climax.

They lay together afterward, Leesie's head on her chest, stroking each other's hair and enjoying the afterglow of making love.

"That felt good," Claire finally whispered, her skin still electric.

Leesie giggled, and then said, "You think? See what you've been missing all these years?"

"It feels like I've been doing it all my life," she smiled, pulling herself from her lover's arms, "for whatever that's worth coming from an amnesiac."

"What're you—"

"Shh," she whispered, sliding down the bed.

She reached out to remove Leesie's panties, surprised to discover that she wasn't wearing any. She started by placing delicate little kisses on each knee, slowly moving up her thighs, before settling between her legs, her tongue effortlessly finding Leesie's clitoris and the soft wetness that lay beyond. With each flick of her tongue, she brought her best friend and newly-discovered lover closer to the edge.

"Oh my God, Claire," Leesie whispered, writhing beneath her expert touch, as she finally came to orgasm. "That was wonderful. Are you sure you've never done this before?"

She wanted to say no, but the trouble was she wasn't sure of anything. Instead of answering, she pulled Leesie closer, enjoying the sound and feel of her breath against Claire's skin.

"Remember any more about your dream?" Leesie asked sleepily, forming herself into the crook of Claire's arm.

"Actually, yeah, I think I do," she said, seeing the same cemetery they'd watched on the television in her mind. "My sister and I, we were at my father's funeral. He'd just died of lung cancer."

"Well, that's weird," Leesie yawned, her eyes half-lidded.

"How so?"

"Honey," she said, rolling over to face her, "your father's not dead. He's never had lung cancer, and he hasn't smoked since before we were out of high school. He and your mom are alive and well and living in Little Rock, where they've been for the last five or six years. They were up here for a visit just a few months ago."

Claire grew suddenly quiet, and the room began to swim. She remembered more of the dream now, how she and Mel had comforted each other, and how their father's spirit had risen from the grave to talk to them after everyone else had gone. How her father had finally told her how proud he was of her, something he'd done precious little of while she'd been alive.

Only it hadn't been *Claire's* father, not really, and her sister hadn't really been Mel. She just looked like Mel in the dream, because that's all her mind had to associate with the thought of a sister. She remembered the other dreams now as well. Johnny tricking her in the graveyard, and again in the cemetery with the ghost named Margaret, after she'd been stood up by her prom date.

"Claire, honey," Leesie said, alarm in her voice, "what's wrong? You're white as a ghost."

"Did I have a date to my senior prom?" she suddenly asked, half-afraid of hearing the answer.

"What're you talking about?"

"Just tell me," she said, grabbing her by the shoulders. "Did I have a date to the prom?"

"Of course you did," Leesie responded. "We both did. That was back when I was dating boys. It was a double date. I went with Tim Stewart, good Jewish boy that he was, and you went with Alex Rodriguez. You dated him through most of high school, but you guys broke up that summer. Claire, are you remembering something?"

She was remembering something, all right. She remembered that night at the prom, being stood up, only it hadn't been a boy that had ditched her for someone better, it'd been a girl. And she'd ended up going stag, not on a double-date with Leesie. She hadn't even known Leesie then and didn't know her now, not really, despite the carnal acts they'd just performed.

For all she didn't know, she now knew one thing to be undeniably true. Whoever she was, no matter how badly she wanted to believe otherwise, she wasn't Claire Summers.

Chapter 31

Claire Summers didn't know where she was or how long she'd been there, only that she couldn't move, couldn't see or hear anything, and couldn't feel her arms or legs. The last coherent thought she could remember was being absolutely terrified when Elisabeth couldn't find the baby's heartbeat. Everything after that was a blur, a random stream of consciousness interrupted by falling asleep for long periods of time and then waking up again in the same state as when she'd nodded off.

Several scenarios played out in her mind. What if she had suffered a stroke and now lay in a hospital bed somewhere, alive but unable to communicate with the outside world? Or perhaps she was dead, and this was limbo. She couldn't imagine that it was hell, even if she believed in the concept, because as confused and disorientated as she was, paradoxically she also felt safe and cared for.

A third option was that she'd been kidnapped and was being kept in a constant state of sedation by drugs. That might explain the safe feeling, and that she only seemed to come out of her stupor for small periods at a time. But she was hardly a worthy target for a kidnapper. Neither Jeff nor her parents were rich, and most of the money she'd made from her artwork was tied up in investments that, even if liquidated, would hardly make anyone wealthy.

She suddenly felt something, as if someone had rolled her over on her back. She squinted into the perpetual darkness that she'd come to call home but couldn't see a thing. She tried to speak, to cry out for help, but the words wouldn't come. Frustrated, she kicked out at whatever held her, whoever kept her captive, but her legs wouldn't move.

But why was she fighting? Suddenly, it all seemed so silly. She was warm and comfortable. She wasn't hungry, and she was safe. What else could she ask for? She wondered not for the first time how the baby was, and if he or she were in any danger, then decided it didn't really matter.

She felt herself drifting again, and then everything went black.

Chapter 32

Claire sat at the kitchen table in red pajamas, alone in the dark, drinking lukewarm Earl Grey tea and staring at her laptop computer. She hadn't been able to sleep, and desperately needed answers.

Bypassing the laptop's login had been easy enough, though she had no idea where she'd learned to do it. Commandeering Leesie's Mac, she instinctively searched Google for a program called "Offline NT Password and Registry Editor," downloaded it, burned it to a CD, and used the program to reset the laptop's password through the registry's Security Account Manager file.

She was disappointed by what she found. Even her emails didn't prove very illuminating. Apparently, she belonged to a Yahoo discussion group offering support for women with husband's who had fertility problems, and most of her inbox was filled with messages from that group. There was also an e-mail from Mel asking if she'd received the snail mail letter and photos, another from a teacher named Henry Martin wanting her to speak at some sort of art school function, a Viagra advertisement, a letter from someone in Nigeria offering her ten million dollars, and a note from her agent about a potential new client, but nothing much else of consequence.

Her Facebook and Twitter accounts provided even less illumination than her email, and were mostly used to promote the children's books she illustrated. She found a few messages in her mailbox from people that she supposed were Claire's friends, but nothing that gave her any information that she didn't already possess.

She was about to give up on the laptop when she found a program shortcut hidden inside an Excel folder. The folder was used to store information on the funds she made doing art for the children's books, but among the document files was an icon for an executable file labeled simply "MED." A medical history, perhaps?

Curious, she clicked the shortcut and was rewarded with a screen for a program called *My Electronic Diary*. The journal itself was encrypted, of course, and she had no better luck guessing that password than she did for the Laptop.

Letting her instincts guide her, she opened a command prompt, navigated to the MED directory, and accessed the encrypted diary file with a text editor. Most of the file was gobbledygook, but the encryption algorithm wasn't very good and so there were whole chunks of readable text interspersed throughout the file.

Still can't believe I did it, one such piece of text read, *but I'm so glad I did. Been planning it for weeks. J will never find out, and we'll finally...* Finally what? The rest of the text was completely unreadable.

She browsed further through the file, finally finding another section of unaltered text. *Met him at a comic book store, of all places. Had half a day before the convention, and wanted to pick up the latest issue of* Morning Glories *and a copy of the new* Go Girl *graphic novel I'd heard so much about. Didn't find the graphic novel, but...*

But what? She paged downward:

...so guilty afterwards, but during, it was magic. He actually seemed to want me, made me feel attractive for the first time in a very long time. More gobbledygook, and then, *finally give him what he wants, and I'll always have that night in Florida.*

The rest was completely unreadable.

She closed her eyes, thinking about what she'd just read, trying to remember. She caught a glimpse of a comic book store, stolen glances between a man and a woman, laughter, a touch, and a handful of Batman comics. She was remembering something. She fought to follow the thread, grabbing hold like a Pit Bull after a bone and refusing to let go.

Dinner at the Captain's Tavern, flirting over drinks, a stolen kiss in the parking lot, Florida humidity making their clothes damp, more kisses as they pushed through the door into the hotel room. Skin on skin, hands on her breasts, clothes carelessly strewn across the room and shoes kicked off at the foot of the bed. A quick glance at the mirror that hung over the hotel room dresser. A well-muscled, red-haired man kissing the long, slender neck of a woman with short, blonde hair and deep green eyes, pulling him toward the bed, ignoring the offer of a condom, guiding him inside her…

Claire's eyes opened. Maybe she was crazy after all, because there was no way that she could be anyone but who she seemed to be—Claire Fleming Summers, abused wife and illustrator of children's books. What had seemed almost possible just a few minutes ago in the bedroom now felt like the stuff of fantasy.

She had Claire Summers' face, her body, and, more than likely, even her fingerprints, so ergo she was, in fact, Claire Summers. Nothing else made sense. She still couldn't explain the talking to ghosts stuff, or the healing, but everything would come in time.

The dreams, she imagined, were just her mind's way of trying to make sense of a traumatic, life-altering situation. But this memory, the memory of the hotel room in Florida, and her indiscretion with a man who wasn't her husband, that was real.

She almost had herself convinced when the front door splintered open in a thunderous explosion of wood and metal, cracking straight down the middle. A foot clad in a steel-toed boot stepped through the opening, and hands worked to push the two halves of the door aside.

Claire was up in an instant, running, moving to the stairs that led up to the room where Leesie still slept. She chanced a quick look over her shoulder as she reached the door, and saw Jeff's bruised and bloody face peeking through like a caricature of that famous scene with Jack Nicholson in *The Shining*.

Another hand reached through the door, past Jeff, pushing through the frame to pull bits of splintered wood out of the way. Together they worked to gain entrance to Leesie's home, squeezing through the hole they had just made. She caught a glimpse of the other man's face just as he pushed the last remaining pieces of debris inside and a scream caught in her throat.

It was the dead man from the street, wearing a face that she knew intimately but still couldn't place. Something so familiar about his face…

She leapt up the stairs, taking them two at a time, almost slamming into Leesie as she traveled the same route downward. They met on the landing, arms akimbo and tangled as they jockeyed for position.

"Claire, I heard a noise. Are you okay?" Leesie half-whispered the question, sleep still in her eyes. She wore a white terrycloth robe, presumably with nothing beneath. "What was that noise?"

"Move," she whispered, surprising herself. "Back up the stairs."

"Honey," shouted Jeff's voice from the foyer, "I just want to talk. And we will, right after I slit that dyke's throat."

They were inside the house!

"Jeff?" Leesie asked, instantly awake. "Get out of here right now, or I'll call the police."

She started to push past Claire, who grabbed her by the shoulders, spun her around, and shoved her up the stairs.

"Claire, what're you doing?" Leesie demanded, fighting her at every step. "This is my house. He can't just—"

"He's not alone," Claire said in a low voice, as they reached the top of the stairs. "Do you have a gun in the house?"

"A gun? I do, but it's in my night stand, and the bullets are in a safe in my closet. Why did you let him in?"

"I didn't, he broke down the door. Okay, no time for the gun. That oak outside the guest room window, have you ever climbed it? Scratch that, stupid question. Of course you've never climbed it."

"Come on, baby," called Jeff, his sing-song voice echoing up the stairwell. "Don't make this difficult."

"I'm going to call Pete," Leesie whispered, pulling toward her bedroom.

This was the second time she had mentioned Pete, and she still didn't know who he was.

"There's no time for him to get here before they get to us, and we don't want to be trapped in a room with no way out. Do you have your cell?"

"Downstairs, charging on the kitchen counter," she responded, no longer resisting as Claire drug her through the hallway toward the guest room. "God, Claire, what's going on?"

"Go to my room and get the window open. If it's painted shut, break the glass. Do whatever you have to, go out the window and climb down the tree. I'll be there as soon as I can. If you don't see me within two minutes, tops, get the hell out of there and meet me at the park. Understood?"

"What about Corduroy?"

"He can take care of himself until we can get back here to get him. Hell, he can probably handle himself better than we can."

"Claire, I'm not going anywhere without—"

She grabbed the woman's shoulders, shaking her. "Go!" She pushed her through the door before spinning to face their attackers.

Jeff was the first to reach the top of the stairs, and she rewarded him with a spinning back kick that sent him careening into the dead man behind him, sending them both flailing to the landing below.

"Connor West," shouted the other man, pushing Jeff away from him.

Jeff rolled off the dead man, shaking his head and rubbing his jaw where she'd hit him. He spat a thick gob of blood against the wall, struggling to his feet. Still rubbing his chin, he reached into his pocket with his right hand and pulled out a handgun.

She wished she'd broken his right arm instead of his left.

The dead man struggled to his feet, pulling back a startled Jeff by the scruff of his neck and pushing past him to take the stairs.

Connor West. The name sent chills down her spine, but she didn't know why.

She turned, sprinting through the bedroom door, spinning to slam it shut behind her.

The window was open and she could see Leesie shimmying down the tree just outside the house. It was still raining, and she was already drenched. Her white robe clung to her like a blanket of dew on the first morning of spring.

She reached the window just as the door flew open, but she didn't wait for them to walk through. Instead, she dove out the second-story window and into the downpour, catching one of the giant oak's branches on the way down. She used her momentum to spin in the air, landing on the ground in a crouch. She reached the earth just before Leesie, who dropped from the tree seconds later.

Claire blinked her eyes, slowly shaking her head. She was sure she'd seen something out of the corner of her eye, just as she leapt through the window, but wasn't sure who or what it could have been. She pushed the question to the back of her mind, promising to revisit it later.

"Come on," she whispered, grabbing her friend by the wrist, "we need to get out of here."

"But where?" Leesie demanded, her eyes darting back and forth from Claire to the window. "I don't have my car keys. Where can we go?"

And then they were running, Claire pulling Leesie behind her, circling around to the front of the house. Her feet dug into the grass, mud oozing between her toes as she fought for traction.

Risking a look over her shoulder, she saw no signs of Jeff and his dead companion. Had they given up? More than likely they had watched them from the window and were even now running through the house for the front door. They had to move, and fast.

Claire's Prius beckoned from the driveway. She pulled the pajama top from her body, buttons popping, scattering into the night. Shielding her eyes with her free hand, she wrapped the shirt around her elbow, cracking the glass with one quick hit, sending spidery little cracks from the epicenter of the break outward.

Rain sluiced down over her bare breasts and her nipples grew instantly erect, reacting to the wind and the cold, but she didn't have time for modesty. She reared back, ignoring Leesie's muted protests, and drove her elbow into the window again, and again, until the glass finally exploded in a shower of slivers and shards.

And then she was someplace else.

Chapter 33

It was another window, in another time and place. Dressed from head to toe in black, she was nearly invisible in the shadowed neighborhood. Claire carried a briefcase in one hand, shifting it to the other as she dusted the glass from her jacket.

Reaching through the shattered window, she found the door handle and carefully opened the door. The sweet odor of mildew and rot assailed her nostrils, but she waved it off and continued inside.

She found herself in an old, abandoned tenement that was long ago left to ruin by one of the many slumlords that seemed to have popped up after the floods.

New Orleans hadn't always been like this. The city had once been beautiful, almost magical, before the deaths and the damage that hurricane Katrina had wrought. Parts of it still were (the French quarter, thank God, remained untouched) but much of the city would never recover, and the people trying to take advantage of the mess only made things worse. The whole ugly situation disgusted her.

Doing a quick survey of the building, she found nothing out of the ordinary. The building had once been a beautiful antebellum mansion, complete with surrounding gables and courtly wainscoting, but that was long ago.

In the ensuing years, the huge dwelling had been turned into a multi-family apartment. The building had been allowed to fall into a state of disrepair despite the families living there and finally, when the floods came and the tenants abandoned it for higher ground, it had become a ghost of what it once was.

She had researched the house before agreeing to take the job, methodically unearthing everything about its history that she could find. She knew about the secret passageway that led from the cellar to a drainage ditch approximately a quarter mile from here, and what time of day the light from the sun would blind anyone looking up at the third story window on the south side of the dwelling.

Claire even knew the work schedules of the few neighbors that still lived on Mariposa Lane, where the house was located. Most importantly, she knew the itinerary of the man who would show up tomorrow afternoon to inspect the property that he had just purchased, the old house that stood directly across the road from this one. Hector Mendoza, the man she had been hired to kill.

Mendoza, a one-time Columbian drug lord, had been living in the states since 1997, when he'd narrowly escaped a coup that had left his wife, children, and brother dead. He escaped to America, where he took his experience in drug trafficking and turned it into an empire of illegal gambling, prostitution, and child pornography. And now, using a zoning loophole, he intended to turn the property across the street into an X-rated studio and money-laundering shop.

Someone out there didn't like it, and had turned to her for help. The operation would net her a cool $350,000, which, when spread out among the various accounts she had in the Caymans, would bring her net worth to nearly four million. She turned down more jobs than she accepted these days, but jumped at the chance to take this one.

She was an assassin-for-hire, and she finally had the security to only take the jobs that piqued her interest. A former Army Ranger stationed in Afghanistan, she'd been dishonorably discharged six years ago after taking the fall for a black market ring she was only peripherally involved in. She managed to escape being court-martialed but, having no money and no real prospects, decided to turn the training and sniper skills the Army had given her to good use. After the first kill, everything had been easy.

Claire had gone freelance six years ago, setting up contact through the Internet. Those interested in her services knew how to find her (or at least how to find someone who could find her) and, if they paid enough and the project inspired her, she'd take the job. She'd done nine hits since she first set up shop, and this one would put her into double-digits.

Climbing the stairs to the third floor, Claire found the envelope beneath a loose floorboard. She slipped on a pair of throw-away latex gloves before fishing it out of the hole. In her line of work, you could never be too careful.

The envelope was crammed with 250 one-hundred dollar bills, totaling twenty-five thousand dollars. It also contained a small slip of paper that showed that $325,000 had been wired to her bank account. The paper included a series of numbers that she needed to confirm the transaction. She flipped open her disposable Tracfone, entered the number for the bank, and briefly spoke to the man who answered on the other end. She gave him the numbers and he confirmed the deposit and the amount.

She hung up the cell. All told, the process had taken less than thirty seconds. She dropped the phone to the floor and stomped down hard, shattering it into a dozen pieces, and then removed a Bic lighter from her jacket pocket and lit the slip of paper and the envelope on fire. She held the paper until the flames reached her fingertips, letting the flames singe her skin before finally dropping the burning wad to the floor and stomping it to ashes.

The twenty-five thousand in cash was just a precaution. After a botched job two years ago, she always demanded part of the money on site in cash. That way, she'd have immediate access to at least some of her considerable fortune should anything go wrong in the field. Twenty-five grand wasn't much, but it was amazing how much cooperation you could purchase with a few well-placed bribes.

It was just past four o'clock in the morning, and the target would be here at precisely three the following day. That meant she had eleven hours. She dropped to the ground, opened the briefcase, and began to reassemble the plastic 7.62 mm Springfield Armory M24 sniper rifle. The bolt-action rifle was military grade and made to perform. It could drop a target at over 600 yards, though tomorrow's target would be less than one-third that distance.

The briefcase also contained three bio-degradable plastic bags of water, a handful of MREs, a dozen comic books, and a fourth plastic bag to contain her urine and feces. Once she was in position, she dare not move for fear that someone might spot her. Once she'd chosen her position, she would move only enough to eat, drink, flip the pages of her comics, and relieve herself in the bag.

Removing the latex gloves, she stuffed them into her jacket pocket. She glanced at her watch. It had taken her less than three minutes to assemble the rifle. She positioned the weapon, lay down behind it, and tested the scope. Perfect. She could cover the entire street from her vantage point high in the house, and should have no trouble taking out the target when he appeared.

The scrape of a shoe against the wooden floor warned her of an intruder, and she rolled on her back, swinging the rifle out in front of her. The butt of the weapon connected with flesh, and the man, holding his stomach, doubled over in pain. He had short, brown hair, wore wire-rimmed black glasses, and was dressed in a navy blue suit. He carried a Taser in one hand, which she quickly kicked away into the darkness of the room.

"Sloppy, Mr. Fuller," echoed a voice from the shadows, "it appears we'll have to do your job for you."

She dropped to a crouch, eyes searching the shadows. Nothing. How had they gotten in here without her seeing them?

"Mr. Quarry," said the same voice, a little closer now. "Please subdue our charge."

From out of nowhere, a small man in a similarly-dark suit appeared. He was balding, and she could see he held a small hypodermic needle in one hand and a pair of handcuffs in the other. He jammed the needle toward her midsection but she rolled her hips, narrowly escaping the hit.

She grabbed his arm and used his own momentum and weight to throw him over her body, where he crashed into his recovering partner. Both men went down in a heap of flailing arms and legs. She turned to run, but was met by a third man—a giant of a man with short, dark hair who stood probably six foot ten and weighed at least two-eighty— also dressed in an identical dark suit.

It would have been almost comical if she weren't scared shitless. Together, the smallest of the trio along with the largest reminded her of a warped version of the magicians Penn and Teller. The one in the middle, the one she'd taken down first, didn't seem to fit with the other two.

Penn flashed a brilliant smile, showing off a set of beautiful white teeth. He held out his palms as if to show he was unarmed.

"It doesn't have to be this way. We have no reason to kill you. But one way or another, you are coming with us."

"Like hell," she snarled, reaching into the small of her back for the holster that held her Glock 22.

Withdrawing the gun in one smooth motion, she shoved the .40-caliber handgun into Penn's face and pulled the trigger. Click. Nothing happened. She pulled the trigger again, and again, with the same results.

The gun worked, she knew it did. She'd taken it apart, cleaned it, and reloaded it just last night, and again this morning. The gun had fifteen rounds in the magazine and one in the breech, but behaved as though it had never been loaded.

"It isn't good form," Penn said, reaching for the gun, "to draw a weapon on an unarmed man."

She let the gun fall to the floor and in one fluid motion feigned a turn and hit him with a spinning back fist. Her hand hurt like hell where she'd connected with his jaw, but the blow barely seemed to have registered.

A small trickle of blood ran from his lips. He smiled, lapping it up with the tip of his tongue.

And then the smaller man was upon her, wrestling her to the ground, and she felt herself go limp. He injected her with the hypodermic, and the other man, Mr. Fuller, pressed the Taser into her hip.

She bucked once, losing control of her muscles. Teller straddled her chest, his eyes wild and his mouth a maw of razors. He rolled her violently over, twisting her arms around her back, clicking the handcuffs into place.

Her vision was fading, and her body hurt like hell. She couldn't move, and the last thing she remembered was Mr. Fuller's wing tipped shoe kicking her hard in the face.

Chapter 34

She was falling through darkness, and then someone was shaking her shoulders. A voice echoed from far away, like wind blowing through a canyon. She thought she heard someone calling her name, except it wasn't her name, and it wasn't her shoulders they were shaking.

She opened her eyes, blinked, looked around. Gone was the house in New Orleans, the pair of television magicians with it. Claire was topless, standing beside a blue Toyota Prius, and Leesie was yelling something at her, shaking her shoulders.

"They're coming," Leesie whispered, gripping her hand. "Claire, we need to go. What's wrong with you?"

Shaking as many of the tiny slivers of glass as she could from her pajama top, Claire wrapped it around her exposed breasts and then slipped her hand through the broken window. She popped the lock, and the doors unlatched.

"Get in, scoot over, and keep your head down," Claire said.

She pulled the door open, pushed Leesie into the car, and slid in after her. Risking a glance across the yard, she saw Jeff and the dead man shambling across the lawn.

The corpse moved slowly and her husband, broken arm hanging limp from his shoulder, seemed to be keeping pace with it. That would give them a few extra seconds, maybe enough time to hotwire the car. If only she'd thought to grab the keys on their way out.

"Look in the glove compartment, under the seat, anywhere. I need something sharp, preferably a screwdriver."

Leesie opened the glove compartment, looked through it.

"Will this work?" she asked, handing over a five-inch instrument made of brass.

It looked like a leather punch but was actually a tool used to break glass in case of an emergency. The tip wasn't as sharp as a screwdriver, but it would probably work. Claire snatched the instrument and began to work on the steering column.

The plastic covering fell away and she reached under the column, found two wires, and quickly stripped them with her fingernails. She pressed the wires together, twisting, waiting for the tell-tale sign of the engine turning over, but nothing happened.

"Honey, I just want to talk," Jeff yelled through the wind, just a few yards from the car, "right before I tear your fucking head off and shit down your neck."

The street lights running down the block illuminated the pair, and she could see Jeff's gun, a .50-caliber Smith and Wesson, pointing out in front of him. She flashed back on the gun cabinet in his office, remembered seeing the weapon locked behind the safety glass.

"This isn't going to work," Claire whispered, letting go of the wires.

Visualizing the set of car keys safely tucked away in her purse in Leesie's guest room, she remembered the key to the Prius had a computer chip. She could get around that problem, but it would take considerably more time than they currently had.

"My car," Leesie suddenly whispered. "We can take the Escalade."

"That won't work. Key has a chip in it, can't start the car without the key. Doubt your Escalade is any different."

"I keep a spare key in a magnetic box, under the driver's side wheel well."

"And you're telling me this now?" Anger flashed through Claire.

"I didn't think about it before. I'm not used to running away from your husband in the middle of the night, okay?"

"Still, it's in the garage, isn't it? We can't get to it."

"Sure we can. Garage door's broken, has been for about a month. Kept meaning to get it fixed, but now I'm glad I didn't. We can open it from the outside."

Jeff and the dead man were almost upon them now. They were approaching from the passenger's side of the vehicle, and she could see Jeff's gun leveled at the window.

"Crawl over me, get out, run like hell. I'll hold them off. Roll down the back passenger's side window, back up, stop the car for ten seconds, and then get out of here." She leaned back in her seat and opened the door.

"I'm not leaving you here," Leesie protested, pushing between Claire and the steering wheel. "I'll run them down if I have to."

"Just do what I tell you to do," she snapped, moving into the passenger seat, "and we'll both live to argue about it later. Now go!"

Leesie hit the pavement running, her bare feet slapping against the wet driveway as she raced for the garage. Jeff turned, pointed the gun at Leesie, and fired.

He missed, but not by much. Claire watched helplessly as the bullet zinged past Leesie's head, burying itself into the brick mailbox just past the driveway. The woman dropped into a crouch, tucked her head down low, and scuttled across the driveway.

"You fuck!" screamed Claire, kicking open the passenger door with her legs.

And then she was moving, running, propelling herself at Jeff, who swung the gun toward her but didn't fire.

She leapt through the air, tackling him around the midsection, knocking him back into the walking dead man who shuffled behind him. They all went down in a heap, Claire using her momentum to roll clear of the pair and back to her feet. She started to sprint for the garage but fell hard to the pavement as a strong hand encircled her ankle.

It was the zombie. She twisted around, kicked him hard in the face, but he wouldn't let go. A streak of lighting illuminated the sky, exposing his ruined face and cracked skull. It was definitely the same man she'd seen lying dead in the middle of the road on Thirteenth Street two days ago.

"Conner West," said the dead man, keeping his grasp on her leg while Jeff disentangled himself from the dead man and stumbled to his feet. "Hold still, and this won't hurt much."

"You keep saying that name," she rasped, her eyes darting around her for anything she could use to escape. "Who the hell is Connor West?"

"We both are," replied the corpse, shambling to its feet. "At least until I kill you."

What did that mean? But then Jeff was on his feet, aiming the pistol at her head, and she realized she might never find out.

The roar of the Escalade caught their attention, and Claire used the distraction to snake her hands around Jeff's foot, twisting it hard. He yelped in pain, stumbled forward, firing the gun. The bullet exploded from the muzzle, hitting the dead man square in the chest.

The corpse bellowed in surprise, loosening its grip on her ankle, and that was all the opening she needed.

Twisting beneath his grasp, maneuvering onto her stomach, she pushed up with her arms and tucked her head tight to her chest and rolled. Planting her free leg into his abdomen, using his weight and the grip he had on her ankle, she pulled the dead man up and over her hips, sending him sprawling through the air to land with a sick crunch flat on his back on the pavement.

"You little bitch!" Jeff screamed, gun in hand, limping toward her.

She was on her feet in an instant, running, leaping through the open window of the Escalade, skidding into the back seat. Leesie slammed on the gas, tires squealing as the SUV peeled out of the driveway.

Two shots cracked behind them, the first going wide, the next taking out the back window, and then they were screeching down Leesie's street, down Penny Lane, and finally out of handgun range.

Turning the corner in a squeal of wet rubber on road, they nearly barreled into an ancient Town and Country Woodie station wagon heading in the opposite direction. Claire sat up, peered out the broken back window, and watched the car turn toward Leesie's house.

She was almost certain that the huge man who resembled Penn Gillette had been driving.

"Are you all right?" Leesie asked, voice shaking. "I heard the gunshot."

"Not a scratch," she assured her, leaning back into the seat.

She hadn't seen another car, so didn't think they needed to worry about being pursued by Jeff and his new friend. And even if it occurred to them to track down her keys and drive the Prius, she'd made such a mess of the wires that it would take them hours to put everything back together again.

"Okay, so where do we go?"

"Where we know they're not, which, for now, means my house." She held up her hand to stop Leesie's protests. "In and out, five minutes, tops. We need clothes, a gun, money, and then we need to get the hell out of Dodge until I can figure out what's going on."

"Pete's just across town. Maybe we should go there instead?"

"You've mentioned that name before. Who's Pete?"

"Pete's my ex-husband, and he's also a detective on the Rogers police force. He helped me look for you yesterday, and he can help us now."

"No cops," she warned, bile rising in her throat, "not even one you used to sleep with. Not until we have absolutely no other choice."

"Who *are* you?" Leesie asked, their eyes meeting in the rearview mirror.

"I wish I knew," she whispered, though she thought she might finally be starting to figure some of it out. If she was right, things between them would never again be the same.

Chapter 35

Thunder rolled in the distance and lighting flashed across the sky, illuminating the trees that surrounded the neighborhood. Jeff Summers stared after the retreating Escalade, imagining putting a bullet in the lesbian's head. Everything was her fault. If he could just get rid of Elisabeth, he'd have Claire—*his* Claire—back again.

Jeff stared at his rescuer. He looked dead many times over, and yet the gunshot, a bullet dead center in the chest, hadn't even fazed him. He wondered not for the first time what he'd gotten himself into. He shook his head, stumbling against the abandoned Prius, feeling nauseated.

His grip tightened on the gun, knuckles turning white. Suddenly he was throwing up, vomiting pizza and beer all over the ground in front of the car. Coughing and retching, he stared at his feet, watching helplessly as the downpour of rain washed away the bile. Something was wrong with him, something more than just a hangover and a runaway wife who had just kicked his ass.

Why was he doing this? He loved Claire, had loved her since the day they first met. He regretted every single thing he'd ever done to her, but didn't know how to make things right. One lie led to another, and then another, and after she'd lost the baby, things had gotten even worse. He began to cheat and then, feeling guilty about his indiscretions, blamed her. That's when the hitting began. He knew the booze didn't help, but he just couldn't quit drinking. He didn't want to hurt her. It just happened, and he felt powerless to stop it.

Head lights shone through the rain, interrupting his thoughts. An ancient black car rumbled down the road, heading toward them.

"Shoot them," ordered the dead man, speaking for the first time since Claire and Elisabeth escaped, "and then follow me inside." The living corpse loped toward the house, leaving Jeff alone.

He started to protest, but then Jeff knew what he must do. He shoved the gun into his left armpit, removed the old clip, and inserted a fresh clip into the gun before dropping to one knee and firing at the car. His first shot bounced harmlessly off the grill, the second embedding into the cement beneath the vehicle's tires.

The third shot hit the right driver's side tire, blowing it out.

Skidding across the macadam, the Chrysler swerved left, swiveled, finally finding purchase, coming right at him.

"Oh fuck," Jeff yelled, jumping clear just as the vehicle careened into the Prius in a crescendo of broken glass and scraping metal.

He watched as a huge man, nearly seven feet tall, rose out of the driver's side of the black vehicle, a much smaller man clambering from the back seat. Both were dressed in immaculately pressed dark suits, and the shorter of the two dangled something from the end of a cord.

Whatever it was that hung from the string swung in lazy, counter-clockwise circles, dancing hypnotically. It suddenly stopped and pointed toward the house.

Jeff stood up, aimed the gun at the taller of the two, and pulled the trigger. Click. Nothing. He pulled the trigger again, but it wouldn't fire. Hands shaking, he checked the safety, aimed, and fired again. Still nothing. The gun had a full clip. This didn't make any sense!

The big man smiled, and it was all he could do to tear his gaze away and run for the house. Heart racing and lungs aching, he ran down the driveway and through the broken door.

The men outside scared him every bit as much as the walking corpse. What was he even doing here, trapped between them? He felt the now-familiar nausea take hold and begin to turn his stomach sour and he nearly threw up again. He slumped against the door frame, catching his breath.

Risking a look out the door, he spied the men from the car walking up the driveway. They had someone else with them, a girl no older than twelve or thirteen. She was dressed in jeans and a yellow blouse, and looked like she was of Middle Eastern descent. The girl had a chain around her wrist, and the giant led her like a dog on a leash.

"Come this way," said a voice over his shoulder, "we can escape through the back door, and then we'll find Claire and this will all be over."

The dead man stood in the doorway that led from the living room to the kitchen, beckoning with broken and discolored fingers.

Jeff stared at him, eyes moving between the dead man and the front door. Death, no doubt, awaited him in one direction, while madness lay in the other, and while he wasn't sure which was which, he knew he couldn't abandon the little girl to the men outside.

He'd done enough wrong tonight, and there was no way he was going to add anything else to the list.

"Connor West," yelled a trembling voice from outside; the little girl. "Come out of the house."

What in the hell was going on? He risked a quick look around the edge of the door. They were no longer moving. The little girl stood stock still, her chain pulled taut by the hand of the giant. Her eyes were squinched shut, and she looked absolutely terrified.

Behind him, the dead man shuffled his feet and began walking toward the door.

"What are you doing?" he asked, looking back and forth between the dead man and the group outside.

"Shoot the girl with your gun," the dead man rasped between gritted teeth, slowly lumbering past him. "Kill her for me. Do it now."

Another wave of nausea overtook him, and he crumpled against the door frame. Yes, he had to kill the girl. It was the only way he'd get his wife back.

But a part of him fought against the thought, the part of him that knew shooting anyone, let alone an innocent little girl, was wrong. There was a line that he had yet to cross and he knew that, once he crossed it, there would be no going back.

He bit his tongue, using the adrenaline from the pain to fight the murderous impulse that was telling him to do it, to shoot her in the head, and not to question the Great Spirit's wishes.

Great Spirit? Where had that come from?

"Connor West," the little girl's monotone voice called out, "come to me now."

"Do it," West ordered, even as he followed the girl's orders.

He was out of the house now, walking down the sidewalk, lumbering like a three-day drunk. The dead man reminded Jeff of himself, of the numerous times he'd been too liquored up to even stand, and the memories shamed him.

The giant bent down and whispered something to the little girl.

"Tell your servant to drop his gun, and to follow you outside."

Servant? A spark of anger flared in his stomach. He was no one's servant, but when West turned to repeat the girl's words, to tell him to drop the gun and to follow him, he nevertheless felt compelled to obey. He felt the weapon slip from his fingers and fall to the tile floor with a loud clatter.

He followed the dead man out of the house and toward the little girl's voice. He ignored his every instinct, ignored the police sirens whistling in the distance, putting one foot in front of the other until he stood before West and his new masters.

Chapter 36

It was four in the morning, and Pete Snow was waiting for CSI to finish up before heading home in hopes of getting at least a couple of hours of sleep before starting the day all over again at seven. Everyone else was long gone, even Sandidge, and the cold cup of coffee he clutched in his hand was all that stood between him and falling asleep on his feet.

CSI had thus far come up empty, other than the thousand dollars—ten crisp one-hundred dollar bills—they'd found inside an unmarked white envelope stuffed in one of the dead security guard's pockets. Neither the envelope nor any of the bills offered them so much as even a partial fingerprint.

If only he could remember where he'd seen the guy. He checked the FBI database, but to no avail. Apparently, their victim had never seen the inside of a jail cell. He wasn't going to check with the Army. Tattoos were common among the rangers, and he wouldn't have added the skulls until after he was out of the military.

Wedesky planned to release the victim's photo to the local papers, but he doubted that would provide any leads. Most people didn't pay attention. Perhaps if they were to offer a reward, put up posters, then maybe…

Inspiration struck Snow and he ran out into the lobby, away from the crime scene, and booted up the laptop computer that he took with him wherever he went.

Maneuvering the unwieldy thumb pad that served as a mouse on this thing, Snow surfed to the FBI website and clicked on the FBI's Top Ten Most Wanted. The screen showed a terrorist, a man wanted for a triple homicide, and several others, but none of them was his John Doe.

Damn it, he'd been so sure. He was about to shut the laptop when he thought of something else. In the sidebar, there was a link titled "seeking information." He clicked on the link and there he was, staring at him through the screen.

His heart beating fast, Snow clicked on the blurry black-and-white photo of a man wearing a Cardinals baseball cap and read the information linked to the picture. His John Doe was wanted for questioning in the murder of Columbian drug lord Juan Rodriguez Escobar, a crime that had been committed in Florida just two months ago.

Escobar had been shot at long range, sniper-style, and canvassing had turned up a single spent cartridge wedged behind an air conditioning unit on the roof of an empty building several hundred yards away.

The building had long since been abandoned, but, luckily, the bodega across the street was still very much in business. A security camera, installed just days earlier by the owner, had caught a fleeting glimpse of the man slipping through the front door of the ramshackle building on the other side of the road.

Plagued by late-night robberies whose perpetrators seemed to vanish into thin air and cops that weren't willing to check out the building without a warrant, Pablo Melendez, the market's owner, had twisted the camera to face not his store but the old building in which he had been convinced the robbers were hiding.

Melendez's camera had failed to catch any of the robbers but had instead captured the suspected sniper on tape.

The ink made sense now. If the dead man was a former Army Ranger, there was every reason to suspect he'd been trained as a sniper.

The skulls decorating the back of his neck, probably counting kills, leant credence to the theory.

Snow was staring at the screen, sipping his coffee and trying to decide what all this meant when his cell rang, startling him so much than he nearly spilled the coffee on the keyboard. Jesus, he was more tired than he realized.

Slipping the phone out of his jacket pocket, he looked at Caller ID and saw it was from the station. He pushed the on button and answered.

"Hey, Pete, this is Ed Squillace," said the voice on the other end. He'd gone through the academy with Ed, and their friendship, unlike his with Sandidge, had managed to survive Snow's promotion. "Hey, listen Buddy, I'm on desk tonight, and we just got a 911 about your ex's house."

"I'm listening," Snow said, instantly awake. If anything happened to Elisabeth...

"A neighbor reported hearing multiple gunshots. We're sending a couple of units over there now, but I thought you'd want the heads up."

Snow's hand gripped the Styrofoam cup so hard that it collapsed in on itself, spraying coffee all over his shoes.

Heaven help anyone who hurt Elisabeth. They might not be married anymore, but he was still in love with her and probably always would be. He'd die before he let anyone lay a finger on her.

Snapping the phone closed and shoving the laptop in its case, he sprinted out the door and into the early morning, ready to do whatever he had to in order to keep her safe.

Chapter 37

Nadine shivered at the sight of the dead man standing in front of her, biting back a scream. Mr. Kingfisher's giant hand squeezed her shoulder as if to reassure her that everything would be all right, but it had the opposite effect. All of this felt like a surreal nightmare from which she might never wake.

Police sirens whined in the distance, coming closer. *Please hurry*, she thought, though she wasn't sure why it mattered. She'd already lost her parents, and had no real place to go. Her only living relative in the United States, an aunt, had been estranged from her mother for years. Would she take her in, or would Nadine wind up in a foster home somewhere, where the families only wanted her in order to pad their income?

She shifted her legs against the pervasive rain and wind and felt the glass shard hidden in her jeans pocket press against her thigh. It had worked its way partly through the material to pierce her skin, drawing blood. Her eyes began to water and she released a small gasp as she shifted her legs again, feeling the glass slip away from her skin. They mustn't know she had the weapon, for they would surely kill her.

"I am not Connor West," said the corpse, bits of blood and gray matter visible through part of his skull.

The dark-haired man standing behind him looked surprised by this revelation. He gritted his teeth, biting down hard, and she wondered again who he was, what he was doing here, and why he had shot at their car.

"Who are you?" she asked the man, her voice giving life to her question.

Mr. Kingfisher shook his head disapprovingly and she immediately regretted speaking without waiting for instructions, but the dead man mistook the question as directed at him and said a name in a language she couldn't understand, couldn't even repeat. It sounded something like "Tusk-hi-ya-hen-inny," though she wasn't sure she even got that much right.

"It's an ancient Creek dialect," said Mr. Quarry, surprising her. The man rarely spoke and, when he did, it was usually only a few words. "Roughly translated, it means head warrior. Ask him how he took possession of West's body, and tell him to speak English." He was speaking to her, but looking at Mr. Kingfisher.

Trembling, she turned her attention away from the dark-haired stranger and repeated Mr. Quarry's instructions.

"I simply jumped."

Mr. Quarry sighed. "All right, Ms. Pahari, ask him why he took possession of West's body."

The corpse answered, not waiting for her to repeat the question. "It was a mistake. I was inside of the dog and I lost control, and when the dog was killed I had nowhere else to go."

"Go on," said Mr. Quarry, looking annoyed. "Ask him the question."

"But he already answered," she started to say, but Mr. Kingfisher cut her off.

"Please do as Mr. Quarry says," he barked.

"O-okay," she stuttered, reeling from the man's sharp retort. "Why did you take possession of West's body?"

"I needed his abilities to become fully alive again."

"Then why didn't you use them?" Mr. Quarry asked, Nadine repeating the question.

"They aren't here."

"Where are they?"

"Connor West has them."

"And where is Connor West."

"Right here," the dead man thumped himself in the chest, a smile flickering across his face.

"Ms. Pahari," said Mr. Quarry, baring his sharp teeth in a half-smile, "ask our guest where Connor West's *soul* is."

She did as instructed, repeating his question word for word, having to shout to be heard over the sirens.

"Inside another body."

"Who's body is Connor West's ghost hiding inside?"

"This man's wife," he said, turned to indicate the man behind him. The corpse was clearly enjoying the game.

"And what is her name?"

"Claire."

The dark-haired man's eyes grew wide, but he remained silent.

"What is her full name?"

"Claire Marie Fleming Summers."

"And where is she?"

"I have no idea."

"You there," shouted a voice from the road, and Nadine turned to see that, thank God, it was a policemen. "I'm Officer Ryan, with the Rogers police department. There were reports of shots being fired. I want your hands where I can see them. Now."

Another officer got out of the police car just as a second cruiser pulled in behind the first. Two more cops joined the one that had climbed out of Ryan's car, approaching with weapons drawn.

"Mr. Quarry," Kingfisher said, putting a hand on his partner's shoulder, "can you keep an eye on things while I deal with this interruption?"

"Certainly, Mr. Kingfisher, certainly," he replied, giving his partner a half-bow.

Kingfisher handed over Nadine's chain to his partner and then turned and began walking toward the group of policemen.

"You," shouted Ryan, pointing his gun at Kingfisher, "get your hands in the air, and I mean now!"

The giant kept on walking, didn't stop even when Ryan pointed and fired his pistol. Only it didn't fire. Instead the gun just clicked, clicked over and over again, as the astonished policeman continued to pull the trigger.

Kingfisher reached out and wrapped his hand around Ryan's skull, crushing it as easily as someone might pop a water balloon. Skin and bone imploded beneath the giant's fingers, spraying across his jacket and the wet grass. The policeman's body spasmed once before falling to the ground, and then twitched no more.

The rest of the cops fired their weapons directly at Kingfisher's chest, with identical results. None of their guns worked. The triggers pulled, the hammers snapped, but the bullets wouldn't fire.

One of the officers, a young kid maybe nine or ten years older than Nadine, abandoned his pistol to swing a nightstick at the giant's knee. Kingfisher caught the baton before it could connect, twisting the weapon from the cop's hand. He drove one end of the nightstick straight into the man's chest, ribs and breastbone cracking beneath the blow. Stunned and broken, the cop stumbled backward, crashing into the two remaining policeman, and all three tumbled to the ground.

With a grace that belied his size, Kingfisher was on them in an instant. He brought a huge foot down upon one's neck, crushing his windpipe. The last officer, the only one still breathing, tried to get away, alternately screaming a litany of curses and prayers, but he was stopped short by the giant's hand on his shoulder.

Kingfisher spun the man around like a toy, crushing the cop's shoulder blade beneath his massive fingers. The injured officer screamed something unintelligible, and, to his credit, threw a kick at Kingfisher's leg, but it was too late. The giant shrugged off the attack as though the man were nothing more than a mosquito before ripping his arm from his socket and throwing it over his shoulder like so much garbage.

The police officer crumbled to the ground, face ashen white and whimpering gibberish into the night. Kingfisher stepped on his neck and twisted his foot. Finally, mercifully, the cop fell silent.

Nadine stood transfixed, her mind barely able to comprehend the carnage that surrounded her. The dark haired man, still standing beside the walking corpse, looked stunned as well, his jaw hanging open as he stared at the macabre scene that had just unfolded before them.

"Mr. Quarry, it's nearing dawn and this place is no longer safe for us," Kingfisher called out, brushing the blood and bits of bone and brain from his jacket and pants. "We'll finish this where it started."

Mr. Kingfisher withdrew a paper straw from his jacket, the same thing he had done after Mr. Quarry had killed her mother. She watched as he carefully tucked the paper wrapper into his pocket, and then began walking around the yard in seemingly random patterns. He stopped four times, at each pause sucking deeply through the straw.

"Ms. Pahari," ordered Mr. Quarry, "please tell our guests to follow us into the car."

She turned away from Mr. Kingfisher and repeated the order, only then realizing she had been crying. If Mr. Kingfisher could crush a grown man's head with his hands and his partner could not only eat a grown woman whole in a matter of minutes but also raise and control the dead, of what possible use was the sharp shard of glass she had naively hidden in her jeans?

It was at that moment that she began to think of other ways she might use her hidden weapon to turn the situation to her advantage.

✳ ✳ ✳

Pete Snow crouched behind a rose bush at the edge of his ex-wife's house. He'd arrived at the scene just minutes ago, parking half a block away. He hadn't wanted to risk alienating the boys even further by sticking his nose in a routine disturbance call, but needed to make sure Elisabeth was safe.

Normally he would have made his presence known and joined his co-workers as they were walking up the sidewalk, but the stupid altercation with Sandidge at the morgue had bothered him more than he wanted to admit. Danny's grudge had made him conscious about not stepping on their toes, and probably saved his life. If he got out of this alive, he'd have to remember to buy the man a beer and try to patch up whatever remained of their friendship.

Snow was surprised to see Claire Summers' blue Prius parked in the driveway, but even more so to see it nose-to-nose with an old-fashioned, black Chrysler station wagon. Did she have another fight with Jeff? As far as he knew, Claire's husband didn't own anything like that black monstrosity that had hit the Prius, but he couldn't be sure.

One thought led to another and he found himself considering the possibility that, drunk or stoned, Jeff might have followed Claire to Elisabeth's house and been responsible for the gun shots. If Jeff had hurt either one of them, legal system or no, he'd waste no time putting a bullet between the man's eyes. But something else seemed to be going on here.

The garage door was open and Elisabeth's Escalade was nowhere to be seen. The absence of the SUV gave him hope that the women had escaped, but he wouldn't know for certain until he explored the house.

He risked a look over the top of the bush, fully conscious that it had already lost most of its leaves in preparation for winter and offered very little concealment.

Was that Jeff Summers with them? Maybe he had been right, after all. He was almost positive it was Jeff, who, along with a young girl, a short, balding man with curly brown hair, and the giant, stood in the middle of his ex-wife's yard. And there was someone else with them as well, a fourth man who looked like he shouldn't be walking let alone breathing.

Snow shook his head. No way. No fucking way. It was hard to see through the drizzle, but the man sure as hell looked like their John Doe. He was completely naked and missing half his skull. From what he could remember from the crime scene photos, the cuts and bruises on the man's face and body matched up, and it looked like he had a tattoo. But Doe was dead. None of this made any sense.

He tried to push it away. Sandidge had once told him that when something didn't seem to make sense to concentrate on what did and the rest would eventually fall into place. It had been good advice, but in order to make it work you had to have something that actually *made sense*. The trouble was, very little about what he had just witnessed qualified.

Four good cops had been murdered here tonight, and God only knew what had happened to Elisabeth. He needed to get into the house to see if she was still alive, but also needed to call for backup. In his rush to check on his ex-wife he'd left his radio in the car, but at least he still had his cell phone. He couldn't just let these bastards get away with murdering four cops.

And what about Summers? He didn't like the man, didn't like how he treated Claire, but couldn't imagine he'd be involved with anything like this. The way he just stood there staring at his feet unnerved him. If he and the little girl were here against their will, there was no way he could leave them behind.

The small man with the shock of curly hair said something to the little girl, who in turn repeated the words to John Doe. Doe nodded, and the giant who had killed the police officers removed a set of keys from his pocket and passed them to Summers, who dropped them into the grass.

Summers stooped to retrieve the keys and for a moment their eyes met, and Snow stopped breathing. If he said anything, Snow was a dead man. Instead, Summers picked up the keys, almost-imperceptibly shaking his head, and then stood up like nothing had happened.

The small man said something to Summers, who turned to stare at the vintage Chrysler. He hadn't noticed it earlier, but the front driver's side tire was flat. He strained to read the license plate, but couldn't quite make it out in the darkness.

He had a choice to make, and if he chose wrong he might never again see Elisabeth. Did he follow them and risk Elisabeth bleeding out in the house, or choose the house and hope they didn't have her trapped in the trunk of the car?

Snow went flat as the group of men and the little girl tromped toward the station wagon. The giant pulled something out of the trunk. It was a tire, to change the flat. Snow tried to get a look into the trunk but couldn't see anything.

The big man handed the tire and a wrench to Summers, and then, after Summers had loosened the lug nuts, lifted the front end of the car into the air. Summers removed the ruined tire and replaced it with the spare, and the behemoth lowered the car back to the ground. Jeff climbed into the driver's seat of the vehicle, the others following suit. The engine turned over and they backed away from the Prius and headed out of the development.

Scrambling to his feet, Snow called in the incident in hopes that highway patrol would take them to ground as he ran at break-neck pace for the front door. He withdrew his weapon, a Kimber .45 caliber pistol, and pushed himself against the wall beside what remained of the front door.

"Police," he shouted, gun pointed down in front of him, "come out with your hands up."

He waited fifteen seconds before crossing through the doorway and pressing his back against the inner wall. Nothing. The house appeared deserted, and if Elisabeth and Claire were here they were more than likely injured, hiding, or dead.

The living room, kitchen, and dining room were all clear, as was the den and the laundry room. The garage, too, was empty, though the smell of burning rubber hung heavy in the air. Good. Maybe that meant they had escaped. He said a silent player, hoping it was true.

Back in the house, Snow started up the stairs. His heart caught in his chest as he noticed a long smear of blood on the banister. Sweet Jesus. Forgetting protocol, he sprinted up the steps to the bedroom he had long ago shared with his ex-wife. Empty, and no sign of a struggle.

Her purse was still in the bedroom, lying atop the same antique oak dresser he'd seen her throw it on a thousand times before. Whatever else this was, it wasn't a robbery.

He heard a muted thump in the closet and nearly discharged his weapon. He flattened himself against the wall and forced his lungs to take a deep breath. Someone was scratching at the closet door.

"Elisabeth," he whispered, "is that you?"

A pitiful meow echoed through the door in response.

Snow slowly slid the door open, and a huge white cat skittered out into the room and began rubbing itself against his ankles. He felt himself relax. It was Claire's cat Corduroy. But what was he doing here?

"Good kitty," he whispered, stroking the cat's long, white fur. "Hey, buddy, can you tell me where Elisabeth and Claire are?"

Corduroy, of course, didn't answer, but instead sauntered across the bedroom floor and disappeared into the hallway. Snow followed, watching as the cat led him into the guest bedroom that had once served as his office. Corduroy jumped onto the unmade bed, peering out the open window.

Though Elisabeth had redecorated much of the house in the seven years since he had lived here, the guestroom had changed the most. Gone were the bookshelves that had once held his small 1970's Mego World's Greatest Super Heroes action figure collection, replaced by a small antique writing desk and a sturdy maple chest of drawers over which hung a huge silver mirror. A double-sized bed occupied the middle of the room, flanked on either side by delicate pine nightstands. The walls, once white, were now painted a soft pink, and flowery curtains flapped in the cool morning breeze from the open window.

Snow walked over to the window. The branches of the big silver maple swayed lazily in the wind, and he was certain that someone had used the tree as a means of escape. Branches were bent or broken in a pattern that didn't quite look random, and he could almost visualize Elisabeth or Claire using the tree as a makeshift ladder.

A small, red purse setting atop the edge of one of the nightstands caught Snow's attention. He slipped on one of the pairs of latex gloves that he always carried with him and carefully picked it up, dumping the contents onto the bed. A matching red wallet fell out, and the driver's license inside identified it as belonging to Claire.

The rest of the contents—a tube of Revlon "Love That Red" lipstick, seven Ben Franklin half-dollars, two quarters, a nickel, a dry cleaning ticket stub, and a bill for *Lucky* magazine—held little clue as to what Claire was doing here or what happened to cause them to run away. The half-dollars were interesting in that they were all pre-1963 and made from pure silver, and he wondered if Claire had started collecting old coins.

Scooping Claire's things back into her purse, he noticed a crumpled ball of paper caught in the corner. He removed the paper and unfolded it, disappointed that it was just an ancient newspaper story about a man visiting from Chicago who'd died of a heart attack. The date, nearly forty years in the past, was circled in black ink, as were the names of the man's wife and twin daughters.

He stared at the story, which had been downloaded from the *Arkansas Democrat-Gazette* website, and sensed there was something he was missing, but couldn't quite put his finger on it.

Corduroy suddenly stood up, his hackles rising. He batted a paw through the air, hissing at some unseen phantom or imagined prey.

Snow stared at the empty space in front of the cat, expecting to see a fly or some other bug, but couldn't see a thing. The cat tensed, swiped at the air again, growling at nothing.

What happened next would haunt him for the rest of his life. The bedroom, already cold because of the open window, seemed to drop a good ten degrees in an instant. Corduroy felt it too, mewing plaintively as he paced back and forth on the bed. He suddenly stopped short, staring at the chest of drawers.

Snow felt a trembling shiver trail down his spine as he turned to follow the cat's gaze. His pulse racing and his mind reeling, he watched in bewildered awe as the mirror frosted over and words slowly began to form in the condensation.

Chapter 38

Jimmy Cross stood alone in the park, watching the rain slow to a drizzle, thinking about life and death. Unlike all of the previous nights, nights he'd spent thinking he'd soon be reunited with his wife and daughters, tonight was different. He knew what he was, knew his wife was probably long dead and his daughters grown and married with children of their own, knew that they were never coming back for him. He knew he was alone.

Claire had awoken something in him, and he still wasn't sure if that was a good thing or a bad thing, but it was something. It was different and, after all the time spent wandering this park in a stupor, he was grateful for even the smallest of changes. He was *aware*. It tore him up inside to know that he'd never again hold Dot or have the chance to watch Sheila and Sarah with their own children, but he had to accept it. Anything less would be a one-way descent into madness.

It was what it was. Life had dealt him a rotten handful of cards, and he'd stubbornly clung to those aces and eights until the very end. If he had waited out the heat or even stopped for directions, he might not have died that day. There were countless things that, if he had the chance to do over, he'd change in a heartbeat. But he couldn't. As much as he wished differently, there were no do-overs.

It was what it was.

Jimmy sighed, once again walking the perimeter of the park. With this new self-awareness came a sense of boredom and frustration. He'd been trapped here for as long as he could remember, and he wished fervently that he could step beyond its boundaries.

His thoughts turned to the mason jar of change that Claire had dug up from the base of the old maple tree. He didn't understand what was going on then, but he remembered now, remembered watching as Sheila and Sarah had sealed the money in the old jar and buried it beside the sapling that the city had let Dot plant in his memory, in the spot where he'd died.

The day the twins were born, the hospital cafeteria had been out of ones and Jimmy had received two half-dollars in change. Considering it a good omen, he saved them in an old sock in his drawer and added another pair of half-dollars, one for each twin, every birthday thereafter.

He'd brought the money along on the trip, intending to give the stash—twenty-six in total, thirteen each—to the girls on their thirteenth birthday. He had another pair of half-dollars in his pocket the day he died, intending to add them to the pot, but he'd never gotten the chance.

Dot must have told them about the half-dollars. Why they buried them there would forever remain a mystery, though he thought it might have something to do with him always saying that money didn't grow on trees. Or maybe they felt the money would always remind them of their father and just couldn't bear to keep it.

The more he thought about the half-dollars, the more he thought about Claire, and the more agitated he became. He had the strangest feeling that something was wrong. He wished he could go to her, check up on her, and maybe even talk for a while.

He walked over to the tree—his tree—marveling at how big it had grown since first it was planted. Where once a mere sapling grew now stood a huge, towering maple. He realized that it symbolized his life, in a way, only in reverse. Where he had died it had grown, and where he ended it had begun.

Jimmy thought again about the coins, and a dully-glowing doorway opened in front of him. Amazed and a little frightened, he reached out to touch it and felt himself being sucked in, pulled through the door. He fought against it, but it was no use. His hand disappeared, and then his arm, his shoulder, one of his legs, and then he was somewhere else.

He blinked, looking around. It was dark, but he could see just fine. He was standing beside an open window, in the middle of a bedroom. The bed was unmade, and a pair of nightstands, an old chest of drawers, and a large mirror hung on the wall, filling out the rest of the space.

Moving to the window, he watched as a woman in a bath robe shimmied precariously down a tree. Her robe snagged on a branch, causing her to teeter and nearly slip, but finally she made it to the ground.

And then Claire, dressed in red pajamas, was running *through* him, diving out through the open window. He watched as she caught a branch on the way down, spun in the air, and landed in a crouch on the wet grass.

The woman in the robe dropped to the ground and then they were off, running around to the other side of the house.

Jimmy tried to climb out the window, but something wouldn't let him. He could lean out, but the moment he tried to jump he found himself standing in front of the window again. Frustrated, he swung a fist at the wall, surprised when his knuckles dented the sheetrock.

Two men, one alive and the other dead, burst into the room. The dead man looked straight at him, and for an instant he thought he could see him, but then his eyes leapt to the window and he was walking toward it, looking out. The other man, the one who was alive, stared after him, his face contorted in rage. His eyes, however, were glazed over, as though held in thrall by some unseen siren.

The dead man shuffled away from the window and walked out of the room, his partner following close behind. Jimmy followed them downstairs, but couldn't make it past the open front door. Just like with the park, it was as though an invisible fence surrounded the house.

He watched in dismay as Claire's pursuers caught up to her and tried to wrestle her to the ground, but the girl had moves that would make Bruce Lee proud. She fought off both men and even managed to make one shoot the other, giving the girl in the bath robe time to run to her vehicle, crank the engine, and tear down the driveway. At the last possible second, Claire threw herself through the truck window and into the vehicle, and together they peeled off into the night.

Jimmy wanted to cheer. He had no idea what was going on, but at least Claire was safe. He turned to walk up the stairs, to try to find a route back to the park, when he heard another gunshot followed by a squeal of tires and the sound of metal hitting metal from outside the house.

Racing back to the front door, he felt like he was watching an episode of *The Twilight Zone* as the dead man ran straight through him and into the depths of the house. The dark-haired man, the one who was still alive, ran through the door and hid behind the door frame, looking out into the night. He seemed to struggle with some decision, eyes darting frantically back and forth between whatever was approaching from outside and the back of the house.

The dead man appeared again, ordering his companion to follow him to the back entrance of the home, but it was too late. A little girl's voice called to him, ordering him out of the house, and like a marionette dangling from the strings of some unseen puppeteer, the walking corpse obeyed and the other man followed after him.

Jimmy watched from the door, taking in everything that was said. For a reason that he couldn't begin to fathom, the girl, herself the prisoner of a huge man named Kingfisher and a smaller man named Quarry, possessed the ability to control the dead man and the dead man, in turn, controlled the dark-haired man he now learned was Claire's husband. It was like a line of supernatural dominos, each taking its cue from the one before it.

From what he could gather from the overheard conversation, the key to everything was a man named Connor West, whose spirit had somehow managed to take residence inside Claire Summers' body. That didn't make much sense to Jimmy, but then again nothing that had happened since the day he died made much sense.

The police showed up just then, two white kids, a Hispanic, and a Negro, but Kingfisher dispatched them all without even breaking a sweat. All four of the police officers were dead before they even hit the ground. The first one, a young kid named Ryan, had fired his weapon point-blank into the giant's chest, but the gun wouldn't discharge.

One by one, Jimmy saw their spirits emerge from their twisted and broken bodies. They looked shocked and bewildered, unable to comprehend their deaths. They didn't have much time to get used to the idea before Kingfisher was upon them again, sucking at them with a plastic straw.

The first one, Officer Ryan, tried to run, but it was of no use. Arms flailing and legs kicking, he flew backward, his disembodied spirit dispersing in the wind like so much smoke as it was sucked into Kingfisher's straw.

The Hispanic kid was next, followed by the Negro and, finally, the other white cop. Each swirled and flowed through the air, growing smaller as they entered the straw, ceasing to exist altogether as Kingfisher took them into his lungs.

Jimmy wondered if the same thing could happen to him, and where he'd wind up if it did. Were the souls of the policemen now in some eternal hell, or, like a peanut butter sandwich or a Hershey bar, were they simply digested by the giant?

Whatever happened, he knew he didn't want to find out.

Then they were leaving, walking toward a big, black station wagon, Claire's husband forced to drive. He watched as they all clambered into the vehicle, the little girl, Nadine, walking with a limp.

Jimmy was about to head up the stairs when he saw a blond man in a leather jacket burst from the bushes and run straight toward him. He stopped just outside the door, identified himself as Detective Snow with the Rogers police department, and then walked through the door. He flinched, but of course the detective barreled straight through him.

Elisabeth.

So strong were the man's emotions that in their brief moment of contact they had touched souls, and Jimmy was left with the impression of a woman's name. Elisabeth. He could see her in his mind, and immediately identified her as the raven-haired woman in the bathrobe who had escaped down the tree. Snow was in love with Elisabeth and would do anything for her, would go to any lengths to save her, and, by extension, to save Claire. Jimmy had to find a way to communicate with the detective.

He followed the man from room to room, wishing he could tell the detective what he'd just seen unfold. Claire and Elisabeth had escaped, but their pursuers weren't all that far behind. If Kingfisher and Quarry caught up to Claire, she and Elisabeth would be lucky to survive the night.

Snow finally headed upstairs, Jimmy close behind. He followed the detective into the master bedroom, where he rescued a mewling cat from the closet. The cat, a white tom named Corduroy, seemed to be able to see Jimmy, which gave him an idea.

"Here kitty, kitty, kitty," called Jimmy, walking backwards into the hallway.

If he could lead the cat into the bedroom with the open window, maybe Snow would follow and eventually realize that the two women had escaped. He wasn't sure how much good that would do, but at least it would give the detective a lead.

"Come on, Corduroy, that's a good kitty," Snow called, as the cat followed him through the hallway and into the bedroom.

Still walking backwards, Jimmy's legs met no resistance and he padded straight through the bed. Corduroy looked suspicious but immediately launched himself into the air, landing with a thump in the middle of the tangle of sheet and covers. He slapped at Jimmy, paws slashing harmlessly through his incorporeal fingers.

Jimmy pumped his fist triumphantly into the air. The cat had followed him into the room, and Snow had followed the cat. More dominos, every action leading to another action as the pieces finally fell into place. Now if he could only figure out a way to communicate with Snow.

We'll finish this where it started. That's what Kingfisher had said right before they left. He didn't know where that was, but perhaps Snow did. He tried screaming it in his ear, walking through him again, bellowing at the top of his phantom lungs, but nothing seemed to work.

Snow sat down on the bed and began to go through Claire's purse, taking out her wallet, some papers, a tube of lipstick, and seven of the half-dollars from the park. Jimmy cocked his head. Were the half-dollars the reason he was finally able to leave the park? He reached out to touch the silver but his fingers passed right through.

Once at the park, Jimmy had been so upset that he'd punched the wall and managed to chip off some of the paint. If he could do that, why couldn't he touch the half-dollars? Looking around for a means to communicate, something that Snow might understand, his eyes fell on the mirror. The cold from the outside intermingling with the heater had caused condensation to appear on the mirror.

He concentrated and tried writing on the mirror, but it just wouldn't work. The mirror wasn't frosty enough, and he was barely able to make a squiggle before it evaporated. It was something, but it wouldn't be enough. He watched as Snow started shoving the half-dollars and everything else back into Claire's purse. He was leaving.

Jimmy swung a fist through Snow's shoulder, and then another, cursing under his breath as his blows failed to connect. Damn it, there had to be a way! The cat was staring at him, looking puzzled. If the cat could see him, why couldn't Snow?

"Come on, kitty," he yelled, waving his hand in front of Corduroy's nose, "make some noise, God damn it, do something!"

The white tabby hissed, swatting through his hand. His hackles raised, the cat looked ready for a fight. But it was no use. Snow couldn't see him, and probably thought the cat was nuts.

He felt an incredible surge of anger rising up in his chest, and he screamed at the top of his lungs, yelled for someone, anyone, to help him, to make Pete Snow understand. And as the rage consumed him, as his anger grew darker, the room seemed to follow suit. Winds swirled outside, and the mirror frosted over in an instant.

Channeling the anger, using the frustration and the feeling of help-lessness, he concentrated all of his energy into the tip of his index fin-ger, and began to write on the mirror:

Go start take silver

His hands trembling with exhaustion, he stumbled through the mir-ror, past the wall, and into the master bedroom. He was so weak that he could barely stand, couldn't even think straight.

Jimmy collapsed into the floor, floating like a feather through the ceiling below to finally settle in the kitchen. Was he dying again? He'd used all the energy he had simply writing the message, and now there was nothing left. He felt himself falling to sleep as everything around him faded to black, and he hoped the message he'd written on the mir-ror would be enough to save Claire and Elisabeth.

Chapter 39

The temperature continued to drop but the rain, mercifully, was finally starting to slow by the time they pulled the Escalade into Claire's driveway. Despite the heater in the SUV, Claire shivered in her wet pajamas. She wasn't sure she'd ever be warm again.

Leesie's chattering teeth echoed in her ears, and Claire wished with all of her heart that they were back at the house, warm and safe, huddled together under the covers. But that wouldn't happen until they figured out what was going on.

Hell, if she were honest with herself, she knew it might never happen. If, despite all the evidence to the contrary, she wasn't Claire Summers and was instead some imposter, an alien doppelganger, she doubted Leesie would want to be in the same room with her, let alone the same bed.

The front door, thankfully, was unlocked, though she was certain she could have picked the lock if necessary.

She seemed to possess a lot of skills not usually found in a small-town girl turned children's lit illustrator, skills that proved strangely useful when trying to escape a vengeful husband and his zombie friend.

Leesie closed and locked the door the moment they were inside, collapsing into her arms. They held each other like that for a while, not talking, not daring to move, until finally Claire broke the spell.

"I'm sorry for all this," she whispered into Leesie's drenched hair, gently brushing it back from her face, "and I know you want answers, but first we need to make sure we're safe."

"You have to let me call Pete," Leesie said, taking her hands. "I know you don't remember him, but he's your friend. He cares about you, and he can help us."

"He'll arrest me," she said.

"No, he won't. Whatever you did to Jeff, you were just defending yourself. You have nothing to fear from Pete, though I won't say the same for Jeff."

"You really love him, don't you?"

"Of course I do, silly. Just because I'm a lesbian doesn't mean I didn't love Pete. We just…we should have stayed friends, that's all. Once I realized what I was, who I was, it broke his heart. I'll never forgive myself for that. But stop trying to change the subject. I mean, good God, Claire, they could show up any minute."

"You're right," Claire admitted, walking down the hall.

"Where are you going?" asked Leesie, following her into Jeff's office.

"This," she answered, gesturing toward Jeff's open gun case.

It was practically an armory in there. Claire dismissed the semi-automatic hunting rifle, paused at a small caliber Smith and Wesson handgun, and finally picked a 500a Mossberg shotgun.

"Put the gun back, Claire. We don't need it."

"You think?" Claire asked, pushing the shotgun into Leesie's hands. "I think we do. Have you ever fired one of these before?"

"Me? Sure, but I don't think…"

"With one of these, you don't have to."

"Claire, I don't want a gun."

"Jeff has one, and he tried to kill you with it. Remember?"

"Which is exactly why we need to call the police," said Leesie, pointing the rifle toward the ground. "They can handle this. We can't."

Claire picked up the Smith and Wesson, saying nothing. She liked how it felt in her hand, but something made her decide against it. Sliding the gun back into the case, she instead settled on something else—an old World War I German Luger pistol Jeff had displayed on a shelf above the case. The little plaque affixed to the shelf claimed the gun was a genuine Luger P08 9mm Parabellum, circa 1915, and she hoped he hadn't been duped.

Checking the magazine, she was pleased to find it was loaded. Only two bullets remained in a magazine designed to hold eight, but it would have to be enough.

Satisfied with the Luger, she dropped to her knees and opened the drawer at the bottom of the gun cabinet. Bingo. The drawer was filled with ammunition. She quickly selected a box of shotgun shells, handing them off to Leesie, as well as another cartridge with more modern bullets that she thought should fit the German pistol.

"This is just ridiculous," Leesie said, staring down at the bullets in her palm.

"Just humor me. Now, come on. We've got to get out of these clothes."

She grabbed Leesie by the hand, pulling her into the master bedroom. Claire had been in here before, yesterday, when she'd changed for her meeting with Jimmy Cross, but it still unnerved her.

This was the room where she had made love with her husband, where their baby had probably been conceived. She'd spent God only knows how many hours in here, sleeping and fucking, but couldn't remember any of it. If she were really Claire Summers, why couldn't she remember anything?

Leesie was already going through the closet, pulling out a pair of Levis and a black sweater.

"Do you mind?" she asked, and Claire nodded.

It's not like they were her clothes, and the real Claire, wherever she might be, was in no position to argue.

She watched as Leesie discarded the wet terrycloth robe, found a pair of black panties in the big chest of drawers beside the closet, and slid them on over her legs. Her pulse quickened at the woman's movements, her eyes drinking in her full breasts, her curvy hips, and full, luscious lips.

What was the matter with her? They were running for their lives, and she was getting off on watching Leesie get dressed? Snatching a pair of underwear from the chest of drawers, she turned her back on her best friend, slipped them on, and began to rummage through the closet.

"They're a little tight," Leesie admitted, "but they'll do."

Claire pulled another pair of jeans down from the hangers, added a black wool sweater to the ensemble, and put them on. They looked like a couple of frustrated housewives preparing to knock over an all-night liquor store. All they needed to really nail the look was some black ski masks.

"Look what I found," Leesie said, picking up a brown leather wallet from one of the bedside tables.

She tossed it to Claire, who caught it with one hand.

Claire opened it, and Jeff's driver's license picture stared back at her. She flipped through the wallet, counting nearly four hundred dollars in cash, not to mention a good half an inch of credit and gas cards. At least they were no longer broke.

Putting back the cash, she noticed a business card tucked into the fold. Jack Bethel, owner and CEO of Bethel Transportation. The name sounded strangely familiar, but she couldn't remember where she'd heard it before.

"Okay, so what now?" Leesie asked, pulling on a leather jacket she'd found in the closet.

"Now we talk," Claire answered, pushing the card behind one of the Visas before pocketing the wallet.

* * *

The lights in the house were off, save for a small lamp in the bedroom, and the Escalade was parked securely in the garage. If anyone were to come upon them, they would have the advantage. Claire didn't plan to stay long, but she had promised Leesie an explanation and she didn't intend to go back on her word.

"In the car, you asked me who I was," said Claire, sitting on the bed beside her friend.

"I'm sorry," Leesie said, her hand finding Claire's in the darkness, "it was a stupid, horrible thing to say. I was just surprised by some of the things you said, that's all."

"I'm not sure I'm Claire Summers," she admitted, the words coming out in a rush. "I've started to remember some things, and they just don't jibe with what you've told me about Claire. I was almost sure of it, before I read some things on my...on her laptop."

"First of all, your identity is not in dispute. You *are* Claire. Honey, I've known you half my life, and I'd recognize you anywhere."

"My memories...I remember bits and pieces. A birthday party when I was a little girl, the night of my high school prom, my father's funeral, and none of those events coincide with anything you've told me."

She didn't mention Louisiana or being captured by the Penn and Teller look-a-likes. She couldn't, because that would be admitting that she was a killer, and she wasn't ready to do that yet.

"Memories aren't always real," Leesie whispered, squeezing her hand. "Post-traumatic stress can do weird things to the brain. These events you're describing, maybe you saw them in a movie or read them in a book, and, because you're so desperate to fill in the blanks, you're conflating those scenes as your own."

"What about the healing, and the ghosts? Could the Claire you knew see dead people?"

"Well, no, she couldn't, but 'there are stranger things in this world than in all your philosophies, Horatio,'" she said, quoting Shakespeare, "so who's to say that whatever happened to you to bring about this amnesia didn't also trigger these abilities?"

Claire sighed. She was going to have to bring out the big guns, after all.

"Connor West," she finally said, hating herself for it.

She didn't want this, didn't want any part of West's life, and would give anything to make it not true. But the memories—the cemetery, her father's funeral, and certainly the hit she had been about to perform in Louisiana—those weren't her memories. Correction, those weren't Claire Summers' memories. They were Connor West's.

"Who?" Leesie said, clearly confused.

"Connor West," she repeated. "If I'm not Claire, I think my name is Connor West."

"Wasn't that the name of the guy with Jeff?"

She thought so, too, at the time, but now wasn't so sure.

"So you're a man now?" Leesie continued. "Hon, especially after last night, I can testify to the fact that you are definitely not a man."

She thought about what she'd read on the laptop, and the memories the words had inspired. Her memory matched up to the diary pretty well, but she couldn't have it both ways. Either she was Claire Summers or Connor West. She wondered if there could be another explanation for what she remembered.

"Occam's Razor," Leesie said.

"Occam's what?"

"Occam's Razor. It's an old adage that says, essentially, whatever seems to be the simplest solution to a problem is probably the correct one. It's a hell of a lot easier to accept that you have amnesia because of something Jeff did or because you were worried about your baby than because you're a man."

"Maybe…"

"So what exactly did you read to cast these theories into doubt?"

"Did I go to Florida recently," she asked, ignoring the question and instead answering it with one of her own, "for some sort of convention?"

"Sure you did, a couple of months ago. For the forty-first Annual Authors and Illustrators of America convention, or something like that. In Miami. Why? Are you remembering something?"

"What did I tell you about the trip?" Claire asked, ignoring the question.

"Not a whole lot, but you seemed…different, when you came back. Happy and excited, but also…I don't know, kind of melancholy, and yet more sure of yourself. More confident, if that makes sense."

"Leesie, I remembered something else, but it doesn't make sense. I remember Florida. But if I was really there, then what about all these other memories I've been having?"

"'Our memories are like a house', Dr. Sturdivant likes to say. 'We lay the foundation and build upon it, paving over the old stuff to make way for the new.' Maybe these memories you think you're having come from the basement, half-forgotten things that your mind is embellishing to help make sense of what's happening to you now."

Claire flashed on another memory, and the dry, stale smell of mildew and dust washed over her.

She was shackled with chains to a wooden chair in the middle of a basement, a dog collar around her neck attached to an old radiator behind her, the only light coming from a single 45-watt light bulb hanging from the ceiling. She watched with barely-restrained fury as a man with short brown hair and black glasses removed a shiny pair of jumper cables from their plastic prison, unkinking the cords to fall around his feet.

The smell of the new rubber and metal assailed her senses, a welcome respite from the basement she'd awoken in just a few hours ago. She took in the smell, reveling in the distraction, at the same time steeling herself for what she knew must come next.

"Tell them what they want to know," he said, letting the plastic drop to the cement floor, "and we can stop this."

"Tell them what they want to know," she answered, parroting him, "and I'm as dead as you're going to be the moment I get out of this chair, *Mister* Fuller."

"Fair enough," Fuller said with a shrug, stepping away from her, "but don't say I didn't give you a chance."

He attached one end of the cables to each of her hands, clamping them tightly between her thumbs and index fingers. It already hurt like hell, but she wouldn't give him the satisfaction of admitting it.

Fuller walked across the room, his navy blue suit swishing in the silence with his every step. He switched on a small, old-fashioned radio that sat on the windowsill of one of the blacked-out window that surrounded the basement, and the room was filled with the cacophonous sound of jazz.

"I thought big-and-ugly said no music?" she mocked.

"A little music never hurt anyone," Fuller said, padding across the cement to the car battery that sat in the middle of the room. "Besides, the maestro needs his inspiration, and what Mr. Kingfisher doesn't know won't hurt him. Now, do you have any last words before I turn this bad boy on?"

"Fuck you," she said, gritting her teeth against the pain she knew was about to come.

They'd been at this all morning. Even if she wanted to tell them what she knew, she couldn't because she didn't really know anything.

She didn't know how she did what she did, and certainly didn't know how to give the gift to someone else. And she couldn't heal anyone, no matter how many times they told her otherwise. Whatever she was, she wasn't her father.

Fuller attached the other end of the jumper cables to the battery and electricity began to crackle, flooding her body with pain. She started to scream and was still screaming fifteen seconds later when he finally broken the connection.

"Are we ready to have that conversation yet?" Fuller asked, the leads of the cables hanging casually in his hand.

She mumbled something, and drool slid down her chin to pool where her neck met her chest. Fuller leaned in close and she spit in his face, a great gob of phlegm hitting him between the eyes.

"Cute," he said, removing the horn-rimmed glasses that framed his face to clean them with the corner of his shirt.

He backhanded her hard across the cheek and one of her teeth, already loose from the previous beatings, skittered across the floor, lost forever in the darkness that surrounded them. Feeling the coppery taste of blood flooding her mouth, she spat again in his face, hitting his chin.

Fuller sighed dramatically and shook his head. Wiping his chin with the sleeve of his shirt, he once again connected the cables to the battery, this time letting it go on well past the earlier fifteen seconds. Mercifully, she passed out sometime soon after thirty.

"Claire," Leesie said, bringing her back to the present, "I know I'm starting to sound like a broken record, but can't we just call Pete? I promise you, all of this can only get better."

"If I can prove it to you," she said, shaking off the memory, "will you believe me?"

"But it's impossible."

"I said, if I prove it to you," Claire repeated, "will you believe me?"

"None of this is real, Claire. But, sure, if you can prove it to me, I'll believe you."

"Then let's go," she stood up and left the bedroom.

"Where are we going?" Leesie asked, following her.

"To the house where they tortured me," she said, the pieces finally falling together, "and into the basement where I finally made good on my promise to kill Mr. Fuller."

Chapter 40

Farris's feet ached and his legs felt like spaghetti. Zombie legs weren't supposed to get tired, were they? Or maybe that's where the phrase "dead tired" came from.

It was almost six in the morning. The sky was a hazy shade of purple and red, the sun still somewhere over the horizon. They were about a mile outside of Joplin and, if they could somehow get a car once they hit the city, just an hour from the Arkansas state line.

Gabriel seemed sure that his son was in Rogers, which was maybe twenty minutes away once you crossed into "The Natural State." There were a lot of "ifs" and "somehows" involved but, if everything went right, they should be in town by 7:00 a.m.

He looked over at the dead man, still putting one foot in front of the other as they marched down the highway. They'd been walking all night, and, despite Sabrina's repeated requests, her father had refused to stop longer than for a few minutes. He said they didn't have time.

In the six hours since the accident with the semi, they'd been intermittingly attacked by everything from crows and grackles to wolves and coyotes, all having recently (or, in the case of the skeletal crow that had pecked at Gabriel's shoes, not so recently) joined the ranks of the dead.

Their first attacker, a mangy squirrel, had taken them by surprise just fifteen minutes after they fled the scene of the accident. It had leapt at them from the branch of an overhanging evergreen, landing on Farris's shoulder. The zombie rodent bit his arm and left several scratches on his neck before he was able to grab it, throw it to the ground, and stomp it into oblivion.

They'd been more cautious after that, edging away from the surrounding forests and back toward the highway.

The final attack came from a huge coyote missing half its head. The thing was half-rotted and crawling with maggots but it had given them a run for their money, running in, nipping at their heels, growling at them before circling around to do it all over again.

Farris had finally managed to nail it with the water pistol, and it had dropped dead almost instantly. It took him three shots, leaving the reservoir less than half-full. Dead or not, the coyote was fast, and the melee cost them precious time.

Gabriel said the creatures were more revenants than zombies, demons infusing the corpses with life rather than inhabiting them, but Farris wasn't sure it mattered. The creatures were hell-bent on delaying them and, so far, were doing a bang-up job.

"Have you ever heard of Mike the headless chicken?" Gabriel asked, seemingly out of the blue.

"Umm, no, not that I recall," Farris answered, shaking his head at the mental image the words brought forth, "and I'm not sure I want to."

"Well," he said, "on September 10, 1945, Patrick Finnegan—he was my great-grandmother's brother, and everyone called him Patty—was driving his brand new truck through a little town in Colorado, when the tire blew out. No warning, nothing, he was driving over the Fruita Bridge and the tire just blew. He tried to control the pickup, but couldn't. Crashed through the railing and went straight into the Colorado River.

"Now thank goodness his wife was with him, because Audrey had been a swimming instructor at the YWCA and Patty couldn't swim. My great uncle drowned that day, was dead for just about a minute before

Audrey could pull him out of the water and resuscitate his pale Irish ass."

"But what's that have to do with a headless chicken?" Farris interrupted.

"I'm getting there. Okay, so Patty was out of it for less than a minute, but during that time, a farmer in Fruita, a man by the name of Lloyd Olsen, was preparing dinner. Using his best axe, he lopped off the head of one of his chickens, but the chicken wouldn't die.

"The thing went on to live for eighteen months. Olsen took it on tour to sideshows and fairs across the country, by some accounts raking in nearly a quarter of a million dollars before the thing finally choked to death in a hotel room in Arizona."

"So what's your point?" Farris finally asked. He was tired and his feet hurt, and he wasn't really in the mood for any more of the old man's stories.

"The *point*," Gabriel said, "is that, sixty some odd years ago, someone died who wasn't supposed to die, and a living, breathing, headless chicken was the result. Patrick Finnegan was dead for under a minute. If his death, however brief, brought a headless chicken back to life, can you imagine what sort of turmoil the world must be in now to allow the aberrations of nature we've seen today?"

"Are you serious?"

"As a heart attack," said Gabriel.

It was a sobering thought. They didn't talk again for the next few miles, trudging on in silence. There were few cars on the road and those that did pass didn't even slow down. It was Mount Vernon all over again, only without a Ray to come along and offer them a lift. He almost wished they'd stayed at the accident site and taken their chances with the authorities.

"Daddy, are we there yet?" Sabrina finally broke the silence, sounding punch-drunk and exhausted.

She'd been asking the question periodically for the last three hours, and, much like Abbot and Costello's "Who's on first" routine, he now knew both their lines by heart.

"Soon, princess," Gabriel answered, "we'll be there before you know it."

Ten minutes later, Gabriel's promise actually came true.

Cold and tired, they stumbled into Joplin. A huge billboard advertised a Fletcher Chevrolet dealership just a half mile ahead, and if they could slip in and steal a car they might make it to Rogers after all.

They walked down the exit ramp, so wary for dead animals that they failed to notice the small funeral home just before the car lot.

"You should still be dead, Gabriel Locke," warbled a voice behind them, like a sudden gust of wind whistling through the trees.

Farris spun on his heels, staring straight into the eyes of a dead woman standing on the steps of the Busbee and Sons Funeral Home, beneath a sign that proudly proclaimed the business had been "serving compassionately with dignity and respect since 1982." Dressed in a long, black dress and high heels, she walked calmly down the steps toward them, her eyes shifting from Locke to Farris and back again.

This was no mere revenant.

Two men, one dressed in a gray pinstriped suit and the other adorned in somber blue, walked down the steps behind her. The second man, probably no older than sixty, carried a long axe smeared with blood along the blade and down the handle.

"Get behind me," Locke whispered to Farris and his daughter, "I'm not sure this one's going down so easily."

"The gun was clever," she said, in that high-pitched voice, "but it won't work twice."

Her face, covered in makeup two shades too bright, seemed fixed into a permanent smile, and Farris was sure she was wearing a wig. The woman looked maybe forty years old, and from her too-skinny frame he wondered if she'd been a cancer patient before succumbing to the awful disease. Whoever she'd been, he knew that the creature that currently rode her body wasn't that person.

The two men joined her at the bottom of the stairs, flanking her on either side. These, Farris suspected, were being controlled by whatever monstrosity currently inhabited the dead woman. Neither man spoke, and their eyes looked as dull and lifeless as Ray's had after they killed him. But that didn't make them any less dangerous, as whoever had been on the receiving end of that axe could probably attest.

"Who are you?" asked Gabriel.

"It doesn't matter," she snarled. "What matters is that you walk no further. This fight does not concern you. Leave this alone, Gabriel Locke, and you may yet survive the morning."

"He's my son," spat Locke, hands curled into fists at his side, "and I'm not going to let you destroy him."

"His fate is no more my concern than yours is, old man. The gate has been opened, and will not so easily be closed again."

Farris tightened his grip on the water pistol. If they were going to go down, they were at least going to go down fighting. They hadn't come this far to be turned away by some undead bitch in high heels and a wig.

"And you, Farris Hale," she pointed at him. "You, too, have benefited from the crack in the gateway. If things were now as they were before, you'd be lying in a shallow grave and would never have received this glorious second chance at life. Are you so anxious to give it up for someone you don't even know?"

Farris grew rigid, and he jumped as Sabrina's hand found his in the pale morning light. How did this witch know so much about them? And, more importantly, what if she were right?

Sabrina, stepping out from behind her father, finally spoke. "We're not going to let Connor die. We'll go through you if we have to, but we're not going to lose him."

She was right, and at once he felt ashamed. He loved Sabrina, would do anything for her. But, more than that, if they could save her brother, if they could seal this rift that had somehow been opened, this rift that he himself still didn't truly understand, they had to do it, and he had to help them. Not just because he was in love with Sabrina, but because it was the right thing to do.

Both Gabriel and Sabrina, in their own ways, had given him this second chance, and he wasn't about to let them down.

"Child," the corpse laughed, a bitter falsetto that echoed through the yard, "your brother is already dead, and all that's left to be decided is who will pick clean the remains."

Chapter 41

Sabrina's face turned ashen, and she gripped Farris's fingers so hard that his knuckles turned white. Tears rolled down her cheeks, and she seemed to struggle to catch her breath.

Connor Locke was dead? If that were true, then this whole thing—traveling across the country, Ray's death, all of it—was for nothing. But that didn't make sense. If Connor were really dead, and if there were nothing they could do to set things right again, then why would they have bothered with the attack on the semi?

And more importantly, why was she wasting time talking to them now?

"She's lying," Farris said, hoping it was true. His other hand tightened around the water pistol and he pushed Sabrina behind him, for the first time in his life ready to fight for something he believed in. "They're just trying to waste our time, to delay us."

"Careful, boy," warned the dead woman. "Once this battle has started, it will not so easily end. You have the chance to leave here unharmed. What happens next is entirely up to you."

The two dead men flanked her, and the one with the axe locked eyes with Farris. He thought he saw a glimmer of intelligence in the man's gaze, but it was quickly replaced with a dull-witted stare like the one his companion wore.

"Farris is right," said Locke, ignoring everyone else and looking directly at his daughter. "If Connor were dead, I'd know it. Hell, you'd know it. You know you would. He's your blood. He's in trouble, serious trouble, but he's not dead. Not yet."

"He's not dead," Sabrina said, a steely determination in her voice and her jaw set in a way that Farris had never seen before, "but we will be if we stay here much longer."

"You are wise, child," the woman whispered, like the rasp of fingernails across a blackboard, "but your wisdom comes too late, and with a price."

A dead man with a full head of gray hair, still dressed in his pajamas, stumbled out the open door of the funeral home. His chest had been cleaved nearly in half, and blood still sloshed from the wound as he shambled toward them. It was Mr. Busbee, Farris imagined, the owner of the funeral home, murdered in his sleep by the woman or one of her revenants.

He was followed a moment later by a woman in her late fifties or early sixties, dressed in a flowered flannel nightgown that reached down to her feet. Her skull was shattered, bits of brain matter and bone tangled in her curly gray hair, and she carried a long, wood-handled butcher knife stained red with blood.

Behind them stood a blond-haired little boy maybe six or seven years old, and he looked enough like the man and woman to be their grandson. A long, red gash that resembled a ghoulish smile had been carved into his neck. The old woman had slit his throat with the butcher knife, drafting him as the youngest soldier in her undead army.

The boy, too, was in sleepwear, a bright yellow pair of SpongeBob Squarepants pajamas turned crimson with blood. Farris could only imagine the mind-numbing terror and confusion the little boy must have felt upon awakening to find his grandmother looming over him with a knife.

"Oh my God," Farris croaked, staring at the little boy, trying not to think of his own little brother safely at home in Carthage. "Why?"

The trio of corpses shambled down the stairs to the sidewalk, closing in on them, forming a wall. There was nowhere to go but through.

Farris squirted a long stream of water at the grandmother, hitting her cheek. Skin puckered and blistered but she did not fall, and that was the last of the water. He threw the gun at her face and it caught in the jagged bones that remained of her skull. It stuck there like a piece of twine or a plastic tie used in a bird's nest to guard against the winter.

Locke reached out to touch the woman, but whatever magic he possessed, the female zombie who controlled the grandmother was stronger. The old woman shuffled her feet, seemingly unsure of her actions, but then without warning slashed out with the knife, burying it to the handle in Gabriel Locke's chest.

"Dad!" Sabrina screamed, yanking him away from the murderous woman and her undead family.

Locke stumbled back, the knife still stuck between his ribs. Arms wind-milling, off balance, he fell against Sabrina, knocking her to the ground. He tried to scramble back to his feet, but by then it was too late, and he was overwhelmed by the dead grandfather and his wife.

The zombies rushed in, kicking, pinching, and biting, swarming over them like piranhas in one of those old adventure movies Farris had loved so much as a kid. The little boy leapt at him, sinking his teeth into Farris's forearm, ripping away a wet chunk of quarter-sized flesh before spitting his prize to the ground and biting again.

His arm screaming in pain, Farris bought his knee up into the boy's chin, snapping the zombie's head back. His heart broke every time he hit the kid, but he knew that the child that had once been inside this shell was gone, replaced by a mindless automaton intent on nothing less than murder.

He thought they might have a chance until the two dead men that had been flanking their attacker joined the fray, the one with the axe leading. Six against three wasn't very good odds.

Sabrina lashed out with a foot, kicking Busbee hard in the knee. The dead man stumbled but seemed invulnerable to pain. Instead of collapsing to the ground with a shattered kneecap, he used the opportunity to snake a hand around Sabrina's ankle. She struggled for a moment, like a dance move gone horribly wrong, but finally went down when Busbee twisted her foot sharply to the left. She careened into her father, who was still locked in battle against the old woman who had stabbed him. Locke collapsed to the ground again and the old woman was on him in an instant, scratching and ripping at his face.

Farris wrapped his arms around the little boy and hoisted him kicking and screaming into the air. Like his grandfather, the boy might not feel pain, but Farris was still bigger and stronger. He launched the kid into the air, throwing him at the old woman wrestling with Locke. They smashed heads and rolled off Locke in a tangle of limbs, hopefully giving Sabrina's father the chance to regain his bearings.

The empty water gun, dislodged from the old woman's shattered skull in the collision, lay useless in the middle of the yard.

Free of the boy, Farris moved to help Sabrina but was intercepted by the man in the pinstriped suit. The revenant wrapped his cold hands around Farris's neck, fingers digging at his windpipe. He struggled against the zombie's grip, punching him so hard in the side of the head that his knuckles hurt, but the man wouldn't let go.

The other dead man took a step toward Farris, the bloody axe he carried held high in the air. Farris kicked and clawed at his attacker, but couldn't break the man's death grip. The axe swooshed down, just missing his face as it severed the man's arm at his elbow.

Farris threw himself backward and the amputated arm came with him, still clutched around his throat. He slapped at the arm, threw it aside. Flat on his back, he watched in muted disbelief as the axe wielder used the weapon against the man in the pinstriped suit. This time he swung the weapon low, chopping at the other man as though he were a tree. The first chop took half his stomach, and the second finished what the first had started. The zombie clawed at his belly, trying to keep himself together, the top half finally toppling away from the bottom, cleaved in half by the axe.

"What are you doing?" screamed the woman standing atop the stairs.

"Farris," Locke yelled from across the lawn, "you and Sabrina go, get to Arkansas and find my son."

He looked again at the man with the axe and noticed his eyes gleamed with an intelligence that the rest of the zombies didn't seem to possess. And then he understood. In an effort to overwhelm them, the woman had been forced to control five bodies, stretching herself almost to the point of breaking. Locke had used his abilities to wrest away control of the axe wielder, the element of surprise in his favor. But the respite wouldn't last long. Even now the grandmother and the little boy were scrambling to their feet, eyes locked on Locke.

Farris launched himself into the air, tackling the old man just as he reared back to throw a punch at Sabrina's face. They rolled off her and the dead man wound up on top of Farris, but he only had the advantage for an instant. The Locke-controlled Zombie's aim was true, and his axe quickly relieved the grandfather of his head. Still, the body fought on, but Sabrina grabbed it by the armpits, hauling it off.

"Dad, we're not leaving you," she said, sprinting toward her father.

Farris caught her by the arm, spun her around. "No. you go. Call the police, do something. I'll stay here and help your father."

The man with the axe stumbled haltingly toward the grandmother, but Locke's control appeared to be weakening. With two less bodies to control—both fallen zombies now lay lifeless on the ground—the woman reaffirmed her control over the monsters she had created. Their axe-wielding savior was caught in the middle, and he lurched back and forth, one step toward the woman, another toward Locke, like a wind-up toy with a broken gear box.

Locke finally pulled the knife from his chest, using it to ward off the boy and his grandmother. He slashed the knife in a long arc in front of them and they danced away, darting back in just as he reversed the arc.

He was holding them off for the moment, but the impasse wouldn't last long. Once Locke lost control of the dead man with the axe, it would all be over.

"Get out of here, both of you," screamed Locke, waving the knife in front of him like a dancer from West Side Story. "I promise I'll be fine. Connor needs you more than I do!"

Locke's knife finally scored a glancing blow against the old woman's shoulder, but the attack left him open. They were upon him in an instant, the little boy running at his legs, knocking him off balance, the old woman working to wrest the knife from his bleeding fingers.

The axe-wielder's eyes grew dim once more, and Farris knew that Locke had lost the battle for control. The dead man stomped across the lawn, coming straight for him and Sabrina.

"Farris, we can't leave him here," Sabrina pleaded, struggling against his grip. "If we do, he's dead."

"And if we don't," he said, pointing at the man with the axe, "we are, too. Come on, there might be another way."

He whispered something in her ear, and together they ran past the zombie with the axe, ducking under his swing, and up the steps. Farris threw himself at the woman controlling the monster, knocking her to the ground, while Sabrina ran straight into the funeral home.

"Does your life mean so little to you," the woman screeched, struggling against Farris's weight, "that you'll so readily throw it away?"

He straddled her hips, pinning her arms to her side. He rattled numbers off in his head, counting the steps it would take the axe wielder to reach them. And there it was. He rolled away just in time, the axe burying itself in the woman's abdomen.

She was already dead, but maybe the wound would distract her enough to give Locke the advantage in their battle over the zombie and buy Sabrina a little more time.

The dead woman struggled to get to her feet, but the axe had gone through her middle, pinning her to the wooden porch. Farris kicked at the now-weaponless zombie, catching his shin, sending him teetering backward, tumbling down the stairs.

The woman, the zombie mistress as he was starting to think of her, reached down and with great effort wrenched the axe from her stomach. She rolled over and swung it at Farris, narrowly missing his thigh.

"You don't understand what you're doing," she trilled, almost pleadingly. "We've waited so long, and have done so much. The gateway cannot be closed again."

"It was never meant to be opened," yelled Locke, still holding off the grandmother.

The little boy, however, stood stock still, the same hint of intelligence that had once been in the other zombie's eyes now shining through his. He tangled his fingers in his grandmother's hair and yanked back hard, pulling her away from Locke.

Abandoning the axe, the zombie mistress struggled to her feet as Farris did the same. Just then he heard a rumble from the other side of the house. It was the sound of a car engine turning over, and he prayed that his plan worked.

A gleaming black Cadillac hearse roared down the driveway, swerving into the yard. Sabrina was leaning out the window, the water pistol Farris had rescued from the ground in the palm of her outstretched hand.

"Farris, catch," she yelled, hurling the little yellow toy through the air.

Always the last kid picked, he had never been good as sports. He got creamed in dodge ball, and he couldn't catch a baseball to save his life. He watched as the pistol arced through the air, the rising sun reflected in its handle. His hand shot up, reaching, reaching for the gun, falling just a few inches short. He stared in horror as the gun spun through the air and landed in the outstretched hand of the dead woman behind him.

A look of triumph flashed through her eyes, followed by a scream. The pistol broke in her hand, sending the salt water mixture Sabrina had prepared in the house streaming down her arm. Her flesh puckered and melted, pulling away to reveal the bones beneath her skin.

Sabrina gunned the hearse's engine, hurtling the car straight toward Locke and the old woman he still fought. Her father rolled away just in time, and the grandmother hit the hood and flew over the roof.

"Get in!" Sabrina screamed, leaning across the front seat to push open the passenger door.

The zombie mistress clawed at Locke's arm, screaming a litany of curses in a language Farris didn't understand. The stream of nonsense words ended abruptly, and she stood completely still, shook for a moment, before finally collapsing to the ground.

"This isn't over," said another voice, coming from the little boy. "You can't stop it. No one can, and no one can control it. They think they can, but they're wrong. In the end, he'll die, and this time nothing or no one will be able to put him back together again."

Farris scrambled into the car, Locke just a few steps behind him. He took shotgun position while Locke folded himself into the back seat.

He surveyed the yard; it looked like a battlefield. There were corpses everywhere. Countless people had died today, both here and on the road, just so this...this alien *thing* could deliver her message. Anger burned deep in his chest, and he wanted nothing more than to slam this damned gateway shut, even if it meant that he might die in the process. Some things were worth more than life, and keeping the world free of atrocities like the one they had just witnessed was one of them.

"Do you hear me, Gabriel Locke?" screamed the little boy, looking so out of place amidst the sea of bodies scattered around him. "You've already lost, and there's nothing you can do about it. Do you hear me? We are coming, and you've already lost!"

"Maybe," said Locke from the backseat, putting one hand on Farris's shoulder and the other on his daughter's, "but I think we still have a shot."

They pulled out onto the highway, away from the screaming dead boy in the Spongebob pajamas, and Farris prayed with all his heart that Locke was right.

Chapter 42

Claire was tired of sleeping. She felt herself being turned over, her unseen captors rolling her onto her stomach. She thought she heard something, a muted thump, but it was followed only by silence. She still had no idea where she was or who had taken her, but she was starting to remember.

She had been in Elisabeth's office, getting an ultrasound. The visit wasn't scheduled, the result of a frantic call to her best friend early that morning. But what had been so urgent that she couldn't just wait for an appointment?

Jeff. The flash of a memory, her husband slapping her across the face, Corduroy caught underfoot, tripping over him, falling, falling. She skidded across the tile, landing on her back. Immediately, Jeff was at her side, saying how sorry he was, asking after the baby. She thought that everything was okay.

Two days later, after she'd gotten up to pee, there'd been blood in her stool. Jeff was gone, had been gone since the morning after he hit her. A business conference in St. Louis. If everything went well, he said, the trip might lead to a promotion. Maybe then he'd get over the funk he'd been ever since they lost their first baby. Maybe then he'd stop hitting her.

She immediately called Elisabeth on her cell phone, who urged Claire to get to the hospital. Her best friend had wanted to call an ambulance for her, but they compromised by agreeing to meet at the clinic. She was closer to the clinic than she was to the hospital, so it would take less time to get there.

Things were still muddled and her body betrayed her, wanting nothing more than to go to sleep, but she fought the lethargy, determined to remember what had brought her to this point.

Claire watched the monitor, waiting for the tell-tale sign of the baby's heartbeat.

"Just wait for it," Elisabeth said, moving the probe across her stomach. "Babies don't always cooperate, and it can take a while to find."

Five minutes later, she was still looking.

Oh, God. She remembered crying, tears coursing down her face, trying to catch her breath, unable to breathe.

"I'm going to get someone else to take a look," Elisabeth said, her face white as a sheet.

"Please don't leave me," she pleaded, the world growing dark around her.

"Claire, this happens all the time."

"I can't lose another baby."

"You won't. Now, let me get Dr. Bartlett. I promise you, we'll find the heartbeat."

A tremor of cramps hit her, wracking her stomach with a pain so great that she thought she was dying.

Jesus fucking Christ, she couldn't lose the baby! The baby—Jeffrey Alexander Jr., the name she and Jeff had finally decided upon for a boy, if it were a boy—was all she had left. Her marriage was in shambles, and would probably be over for good if she lost another child. She needed something to hold on to, and that's what this baby had been.

She couldn't lose the baby, especially after what she had done to get pregnant...

"Elisabeth, I can't lose him. If I lose him, I don't want to live. I just can't." She was babbling now, but she couldn't stop. This wasn't happening. This was not fucking happening.

Dear God, she screamed in her head, *if I'm going to lose this baby, just take me, too. Don't you dare leave me here with Jeff, all alone with a man who stopped loving me the moment I lost his first child. Don't you dare. I don't want to live without my baby. I can't live without my baby, my sweet, innocent little boy, who didn't deserve any of this. I just can't. I'd rather be dead.*

That was the last thing she remembered. Everything had gone dark after that, just broken shadows in a half-lived life.

Had she really lost the baby? Maybe she was in purgatory, doomed to repeat over and over that single, defining moment of her life, the day that hubris and a bastard of a husband had caused her to lose the thing she loved and needed most in this world.

There was a sense of someone or something else with her now, hovering just outside her field of vision. She couldn't see anything, couldn't hear, couldn't taste, couldn't smell or even feel, but yet she somehow knew that they were there. She couldn't explain it, she just knew.

Maybe whoever was there was looking for her, would help her. She just had to do figure out how to make contact.

She'd already given up on her life once, and on her baby's life, and she wasn't about to do it again.

Chapter 43

Claire and Leesie pulled into the clinic parking lot just a little past six in the morning. The sun was already starting to rise, yellow rays of light straining to break through the storm clouds that hung over the city.

The rain had slowed to a steady drizzle. It was getting warmer, and the rising temperature combined with the dampness to create a low-level fog that seemed to cloak the building.

Claire stared at the spot across the street where she'd been hit by the car. She was starting to remember everything now.

"Are you okay?" Leesie asked, taking her arm.

She shrugged it off, climbing out of the car. She shoved the Luger into her waistband, took a deep breath, and shut the door.

"You're not going anywhere without me." Leesie climbed out of the car, keeping the shotgun close.

Claire steeled herself for the walk across the street. Despite the storm, the spot where she'd been hit was still stained with blood. Everything inside her said to get back in the car and drive as far away as possible, but she needed answers.

"I'll be fine once we're inside the house."

"You don't have to do this, you know," Leesie whispered, hurrying after her.

"You don't, but I do." She closed her eyes, trying to visualize her escape from the basement into the road. "If you want to go back, I understand."

"But what if someone's in there?"

"Then we'll leave, but I don't think that's going to be the case." She was almost positive that had been Kingfisher she'd seen driving the black station wagon heading toward Leesie's house.

Claire stared across the street. She'd been disoriented and half out of her mind with fear when she escaped the house, but she was pretty sure she could retrace her steps. A wave of dizziness had struck her seconds after bursting from the basement door, and it had been all that she could do just to run.

She'd been trained by the army, trained to be a ranger, had tracked terrorists across the deserts of Afghanistan. Picking up a two-day-old trail through a middle-class neighborhood should be easy by comparison.

"If we don't find anything, you'll let me call Pete?"

"I will," she said, knowing it was a promise she wouldn't have to keep.

She remembered only bits and pieces of her frantic escape. Allowing her body to retrace the steps, she walked between the giant pair of oaks, the memory of the first time she'd crossed the two ancient trees flooding her mind. Closing her eyes, she allowed her thoughts to drift back and let the memory swallow her whole.

How much longer would they torture her? The truth of the matter was that she didn't know how she spoke to the dead or brought them back to life again, and she sure as hell couldn't heal the living.

Her father could heal the sick and the wounded, but she couldn't. She'd never been able to do it, not for lack of trying, and the talent had never manifested itself even after he died. Whoever these people were, they not only wanted to know about all of the things she could do but apparently wanted her to transfer those powers to them.

"I told you," she said, ribs aching and her head on fire, "that it doesn't work that way. Hell, I don't know how it works."

"That's not what Mr. Lazarus says," said Fuller, popping his knuckles.

Fuller had been interrogating her for hours. She held back nothing, answering all of his questions, because it didn't matter. There was no way that she could give them what they were asking for.

She was the gateway between life and death, just as her father had been before her, and his father before him. None of them had known how or why, and no one had asked for this double-edged sword. It was just the way it was, the way it had been for as long as anyone could remember.

However, not everyone in the family inherited the gift. It was only passed on from first born to first born, and even then the blessed (some might say cursed) son or daughter would only come fully into their powers once the gateway before them had passed.

If the gateway died before producing an heir, the power would jump to someone else in the family. As long as one of them existed, the line between life and death could occasionally be bent but never crossed. The dead, with certain exceptions, stayed dead, only arising when called forth by her or one of her ancestors.

No one knew what might be unleashed on the world if she were to die without leaving someone behind to inherit the mantle. She'd tried to tell them that, warn them against killing her, but they wouldn't listen.

In Ireland, many generations past, Annette O'Shea had died from complications during childbirth. Her father had passed on the previous year, leaving her as the only living gateway. The child, thank God, had been born alive, but for the handful of seconds between her death and his birth there was chaos.

Three-legged frogs fell from the sky, dead men burst from their graves, and a great plague swept forth over most of England, wreaking havoc that spread throughout the world. Once unleashed, these disruptions could not so easily be put to rest. The only surviving gateway was a mere child, and would not come into his abilities for years. There was no one to control the damage, nobody to stuff the djinn back into the bottle.

Thousands upon thousands of people died, and many of the living were forever changed in unimaginable and horrific ways, all because of the precious few seconds when there was no gateway. The secret of what they were had nearly been lost altogether save for Annette's younger brother Paul, who dedicated the rest of his life to caring for and mentoring the child.

While Paul had not inherited his father's gift, he had freely taken on its mantle of responsibility, one which Claire herself had always looked upon with disdain. It was a burden, one which she would gladly rid herself of if given half the chance. But such an option didn't exist. She was the gateway, the only surviving door between life and death, and she owed it to Sabrina, to her damned father, and to all that had come before them to do anything necessary to stay alive.

If she were going to die, it wouldn't be at the hands of Mr. Fuller.

"So who the fuck is this Lazarus?" she finally asked, summoning up what little bravado he had not beaten out of her.

"Our employer, though obviously that's not his real name."

"Obviously."

"He wants what you have, and it's my job to find out how to take it from you," Fuller said.

"I've told you over and over, it's not something I can give."

"And I've told you over and over, they don't believe you."

"Then I guess we've come to an impasse. Why don't you just let me go and call it a day?"

"Look, Mr. West, this can only get worse. I can hurt you in a thousand different ways that will leave you a crippled, blithering idiot, but one that's still very much alive."

"You know that eventually I'm going to kill you, don't you? I will get out of these chains and, when I do, you're a dead man."

Fuller slapped her hard across the face, adding another welt to a host of many.

"If you were your father, I'd be dead already."

"I can't do what he could do!" she screamed, looking him in the eyes.

"At this point, I think that's fairly obvious."

The response baffled her. "So why are you doing this?"

"I might believe you," he said, looking almost sad, "but they don't." He gestured toward the stairs. "And until they get back and tell me otherwise, we're going to continue our little experiments."

So Kingfisher and Quarry weren't in the house. If she were going to escape, this was probably her only chance.

"So you're Mr. Kingfisher's lap dog?" she taunted him, knowing full well that his partnership in the trio was limited at best. "Do you suck his cock, too, or is that what the short guy's for?"

Anger flashing over his face, he reared back and hit her in the face, splintering her nose. But she knew the punch was coming. She rolled with it, took the punch and went slack, eyes rolling back in her head, blood dripping down her chin.

"Aw, fuck," said Fuller through the fog that threatened to engulf her brain, "why'd you go and make me do that?"

He turned around and walked over to the radio that he kept on the windowsill, clicking it on and spinning the dial. He moved past a top ten station and a station devoted to classic rock before finally settling on adult contemporary, snapping his fingers in time to the jazzy beat of Wynton Marsalis.

Claire's hands were handcuffed behind her back and her feet were
in chains, shackled to the old kitchen chair she'd been sitting in for the
last two days. But she'd been busy these last forty-eight hours, slowly
working the leg irons against the legs of the chair, moving metal against
wood, weakening the joints that held the chair together.

She ducked her head forward, at the same time pushing hard
against the cement floor with her feet, rocking the chair.

Violently thrusting her legs out in front of her, as far as the short
length of chain would allow, she threw herself backward into the radiator, smashing the chair into the wall. Joints weakened, the chair shattered, exploding in a crash of screws and pre-fabricated lengths of
lacquered wood.

"Hey!" Fuller turned around, surprised.

She scrambled to her feet. Leaping straight up into the air, she
swung her handcuffed hands beneath her legs and out to the front of
her body. Spinning around, she grabbed the chain that connected the
dog collar around her neck to the radiator and pulled hard, feeling the
radiator crack under the strain, the pipe that secured the chain finally
wrenching loose.

Fuller was moving, but, injured as she was and legs shackled together, she was still faster. He reached the old wooden table that he'd
used to spread out his tools of torture, his hand closing around a long
serrated knife just as she barreled into him, knocking him to the
ground. She was on him in a second, driving her elbow down into his
nose, bringing a knee up into his groin, knocking the knife out of his
hands with her fists.

He tried to dance away from her, but the moment he gave her his
back he was already dead. She tightened the length of chain between
the handcuffs around his throat, pulling back hard. He struggled, tried
to scream, but he wasn't going anywhere. In the end she crushed his
windpipe and then snapped his neck, mercifully ending his life before

the lack of oxygen to his brain would have caused his body to shut down.

The room spinning, she took a huge, greedy gulp of air before pushing him off of her and going through his pockets in search of the keys. She located the key to the manacles that bound her feet, but the handcuff key was nowhere to be found.

She removed the dog collar, and then, after dislocating her thumbs, finally managed to slip out of the handcuffs. Her hands hurt like hell and were near-useless now, but she was finally free. Stumbling to her feet, she stopped in her tracks as she heard noises filtering down from the floor above.

Panic seized her and she splintered the cellar door with one kick, bolting from the basement, bursting out onto a lawn of dying grass. So long had she been shackled in the basement that the sunlight seared her eyes, making it hard to see.

She ran on blindly, never once looking back. With her body bleeding and screaming with pain, she sprinted between two giant oaks, past a mailbox and onto the road, straight into the path of the silver BMW that killed her.

"Okay, we're here," Leesie said, bringing her back to the present, "so now what?"

Claire blinked, focusing. They stood before a large brick house that was set back from the road. A weather-worn American flag hung from the shaft beside the front door, and a ten-speed bicycle leaned against one of the three pillars that stood guard before the entrance. The side of the house sported a two-car garage, and a sidewalk connected the driveway to the front of the house.

This was where they had held her?

She circled around the side of the house, Leesie reluctantly follow-ing, and there she found the basement door she had fled through just two days ago. It had been replaced, and was also locked.

"What are you doing?" Leesie whispered, casting furtive glances toward the road. "We can't just go snooping around somebody's house."

Ignoring Leesie's protests, she pulled two long wires she had scav-enged from the Prius from her jeans pocket and inserted them into the lock. A few seconds later they were inside.

The basement was just as she remembered. The remains of the shattered chair were scattered across the basement floor, and blood splatters from Fuller's exuberant experiments still stained the walls. There was the car battery, cables still attached. Everything was here, just as she remembered.

But Kingfisher and Quarry had added something new to the room: a perfectly-preserved skeleton, every strip of flesh cleaned thoroughly from the bones. Thirteen burned-out candles and a broken ring of salt surrounded the remains.

Someone had used a piece of chalk to draw squiggles and other ar-cane symbols at various points between the candles, some of which she recognized from the walking corpse at Leesie's house.

"My God," whispered Leesie, eyes gone wide, "who was that?"

"I think that's Mr. Fuller."

"And you…you were here?"

"This is where they tortured me," she said quietly. "Do you believe me now?"

"I don't know what to believe."

"Stay behind me." She withdrew the pistol, holding it close to her body.

The steps creaked as she took the stairs, unfinished wood settling against the frame. Not bothering with stealth, she bumped the door to the kitchen open with her shoulder, ready to shoot anything that moved.

The room was empty, save for another skeleton just as well-preserved as the one they'd found in the basement. Everything else about the kitchen looked normal, other than the broken cordless telephone sitting on one counter, directly opposite an old, black rotary model someone had plugged into the wall in its place.

Leesie's face had gone white. She stared at the skeleton, tears silently rolling down her cheeks. This was all too much for her. Claire hooked an arm around her waist, pulling her past the nightmares in the kitchen and into the dining room.

She hadn't seen this part of the house before. A huge oak table with seating for six filled most of the available floor space, and an antique side table stood against one wall, overloaded with fine porcelain tea cups, plates, bowls, and saucers. The floor here was a light stained wood, which contrasted perfectly with the white stucco walls.

It felt strange that something as horrific as had happened to her could take place in such a normal dwelling.

She took Leesie's face in her hands and looked deep into her beautiful brown eyes. "This'll all be over soon," she promised, "and then your life will be back to how it was before."

"But what about you? What about us? I mean, if all this is true…"

"Let me worry about me, and you just worry about keeping it together long enough for me to get you away from all of this."

It was a mistake bringing her here; Claire saw that now. In a selfish and desperate act to prove to Leesie and herself that she wasn't insane, she'd exposed the woman she loved to a mindless evil. After last night's attack, and the skeletons this morning, she wasn't sure how much more Leesie could take.

But Leesie surprised her.

"Jeff and that monster, they attacked me, too. They came into my home. And you Claire, I've loved you for as long as I can remember. I think I started loving you the first day we met, did you know that?"

She didn't know that, but kept her silence.

"Of course I didn't realize it then," she continued, "and certainly didn't know that I'd end up liking girls instead of boys, or that we'd ever be together like this, but…but if all of this is true, and if you're not really Claire, then I don't know you at all, do I?"

"I don't know who I am."

"But you're not really Claire, are you?"

"No, I'm not really Claire."

Leesie slapped her hard across the face, and Claire reeled back in shock. She felt an intense anger well up inside her, an irrational rage that far outweighed the attack, but she pushed it down, quashing it.

"We made love last night. You seduced me, you used me, you almost got me killed, and you're not even Claire. My Claire, the real Claire, could never walk past those skeletons without as much as a sideways glance. You're every bit as much of a monster as that thing that tried to kill us!"

Her words hurt more than the slap ever could. "Maybe I am Claire," she began to ramble, grasping at straws. "You said it yourself; if I have her body, her fingerprints, then I must be Claire. Who else could I be?"

"You're not Claire."

"I might be. If I'm not Claire, how could I remember what happened in Florida?"

"I don't know, but you're not Claire," Leesie repeated, grabbing her shoulders. She looked into Claire's eyes. "You're not Claire, and you never were."

"I want to be Claire," she whispered, looking away, "I do. But what I want more than anything in this world is for you to love me."

"You're not Claire," she said softly, the steely look in her eyes finally melting, "and, damn it, I think I already do."

She felt herself being pulled into Leesie's arms, and then she was sobbing, the emotions and fears of the last several days catching up to her in a rush. She melted into the embrace, wanting nothing more than to forget the horrors of the last few days and just lose herself in Leesie's arms.

"I'm sorry I slapped you, and I'm sorry for the awful things I said," she whispered into Claire's ear after a while, stroking her short, blonde hair. "We'll figure all this out, I promise."

She hiccuped into Leesie's shoulder, the tears finally abating. "I thought I was the one making the promises here."

Leesie laughed, a throaty chuckle that reverberated against her cheek, and she thought it was the most beautiful sound she had ever heard.

"It goes both ways, silly. Now, come on, let's see what else we can learn from this house, and then we're definitely calling Pete."

"All right," she said, though the thought of putting her fate in the hands of the police still terrified her, "we'll call Pete."

A sudden harsh trilling set her heart to thudding, and only after the third ring did she realize that the sound was coming from the antique telephone they'd passed in the kitchen.

Chapter 44

Claire checked her Mickey Mouse watch. Though it had taken a beating during her fight with Jeff and the zombie, it still seemed to be working. It was six forty-five in the morning.

"Should we answer it?" Leesie asked, after the fourth ring.

They were standing in the kitchen, across from the skeleton and next to the 1950's-style rotary telephone. She removed the handset from the cradle on the sixth ring and held it to her ear.

"Hello?" said a man's voice on the other end. "Have you found him yet?" He sounded agitated, almost desperate.

Found who? She wanted to ask but said nothing, remaining silent, hoping the man would speak again.

"Kingfisher, God damn it, answer me!"

"Not yet," she said in a low voice, muffling the phone.

"Who is this?" he asked, instantly alert.

"Not Mr. Kingfisher."

"Then where's Kingfisher? And who're you?"

"Mr. Kingfisher's new partner," she lied. "And you must be Mr. Lazarus."

"Well, is he there?"

"He and Mr. Quarry are out taking care of business. Mr. Fuller was killed two days ago, and I've been hired to take his place."

"Fuller's dead? I'm sorry, but I don't feel comfortable talking to anyone about this but Kingfisher."

"Then you'll have to call back later." She stopped talking, hoping he would think she was about to hang up the phone.

"No, no, wait, God damn it! When will Kingfisher be back?"

"As soon as the job is done."

Mr. Lazarus grew quiet on the line, but finally said, "And what is this job?"

Lazarus was obviously the one who had ordered her kidnapping, but how much did he know of what had happened since her escape?

"To track down the girl," she said, instantly realizing her mistake.

"What girl? What in the hell are you talking about?"

She was remembering more and more, finally putting the pieces of the puzzle together. In an instant, the handful of memories she had re-covered shifted. She no longer saw herself as the blonde-haired woman she was now, but instead as the red-headed dead man she first encoun-tered outside the clinic. Everything she remembered was colored by that revelation, and she finally understood the dream about the prom.

Theresa Kirk. That had been her date's name. It was an insignifi-cant piece of trivia, but it hammered home the realization that she was not the person she had believed herself to be for the last two days.

"Claire, what's he saying?" Leesie whispered, and she realized the phone was still in her hand.

Her father's funeral. That hadn't been Mel sitting beside her. She'd never even met Mel Fleming. The girl's name was Sabrina, and she was her—no, his—sister.

"God damn it, I don't have time for these games," blared the voice at the other end of the line. "Who are you?"

"Mr. Lazarus, I'm not certain how this happened, but I think my name is Connor West," she finally whispered into the phone, griping the handset so tight that her knuckles turned white, "but I can promise you this: when I find you, I'm going to kill you."

She ripped the phone from the wall and threw it across the room, shattering it against the kitchen cabinets, showering the skeleton in a rain of cracked black plastic and metal.

"Claire, who was that?" Leesie asked, her voice shaking.

"My name's not Claire," she said, feeling the world spinning out of control around her, "it's Connor West, and that was the man who murdered me."

✳ ✳ ✳

The hairs on his arms stood at attention as Snow stared into the mirror. *Go start take silver.* That's what the writing said, plain as day. He shook his head, blinked, watching in fascination as the words slowly faded from view and the temperature in the room returned to normal.

He looked behind the mirror, but there was nothing there. Where had the words come from? He didn't believe in ghosts, but with what he had seen tonight, he was starting to accept that anything was possible.

Assuming for the moment that the message was real, what did it mean?

Go start take silver.

Was it some sort of ransom note? Was he supposed to go somewhere and bring something made of silver in order to bargain for Elisabeth's life? But that didn't make any sense. If they wanted something from him, they'd just call or send a letter. No, whoever was responsible for the message in the mirror was trying to help.

He heard sirens in the distance: at least four squad cars, a fire truck, and an ambulance. He hated to leave the scene, but if he didn't he'd be stuck here for hours while God only knew what was happening to Elisabeth and Claire. No, he had to get out of here. He needed time to think, to decipher the riddle.

"Corduroy, you're coming with me," he said, pulling the long-haired tom into his arms.

The cat clawed at the bed, not wanting to be picked up, and its paw caught on one of the straps of Claire's purse. The purse turned upside down, dispersing the contents all over the bed. The tube of lipstick rolled off the bed, and the half-dollars clinked together and mixed with the rest of the change as they fell on the comforter.

The half-dollars. They were Ben Franklin halves, made of pure silver. *Take silver.* The message wasn't meant to be taken as a whole but rather as two separate directives. Whoever had written it wanted him to take the half-dollars with him.

He scooped up the money and shoved it all, quarters included, into his pocket.

Go start.

Go to the start. To the start of what? Where had all of this started? If Jeff was involved, it could mean the church where he and Claire were married. Or maybe it had something to do with Elisabeth or the little girl. His ex-wife's friendship with Claire had started when they met in grade school. He didn't know who the Indian girl was, so had no clue where she fit into all of this.

And then it hit him: Thirteenth Street, on the road outside of Elisabeth's clinic. That's where John Doe had been killed, the very same John Doe he'd seen walking around mere minutes ago. That's where everything had started going crazy.

The sirens were much closer now, and he knew he had to go.

"Sorry, Corduroy, but you'll just have to take care of yourself."

Running out of the room, Snow scrambled down the stairs, through the back door, and out into the back yard just as the squad cars and emergency vehicles pulled to the front of the house. He remembered how he had wanted a privacy fence but Elisabeth had talked him out of it, and he was thankful for that now.

Skirting the perimeter of the house, he slipped through the neighboring yard that backed up to Elisabeth's and circled the block, finally coming to his unmarked cruiser.

The street was lit up like a fireworks display, and the clamor of the engines masked the start of his own vehicle as he slipped into the seat and turned over the engine. He backed slowly down the street, not daring to hit the lights until he maneuvered the car around the corner and toward the highway.

He pointed the car in the direction of Thirteenth and Walnut, the nearest cross street to Elisabeth's clinic and the accident, and wondered not for the first time just what in the hell he was getting himself into.

The car turned a corner and he heard the silver jingle in his pocket, somehow comforted by its weight.

Go start take silver.

He just hoped that whoever or whatever had given him the message would be on hand to tell him what to do once he got there, because he didn't have a clue.

Chapter 45

The air in the kitchen was stultifying and Claire felt the walls beginning to close around her as she tried to work out their next move. She was starting to remember more of her life as Connor West, and the memories terrified her. She remembered every one of the nine kills she'd made, but couldn't seem to recall ever going to school or learning to ride a bicycle.

"So let me get this straight," said Leesie, staring at the remains of the broken phone, "you really are a man, after all? C'mon, that doesn't make any sense."

She remembered her father's funeral six weeks ago, remembered her frustration at not having made peace with the man before he died, but couldn't remember what drove them apart. West was her mother's maiden name; that much she knew. But why had she chosen to abandon the name Locke? What argument had led her down that road, past the point of no return? Was it a specific event or simply the culmination of a lifetime of missed birthdays and sporting events that she was just starting to remember?

Her memory was like Swiss cheese, filled with a scattershot of random holes that blocked out important parts of her past while leaving other, seemingly insignificant events intact.

"West is my mother's maiden name. I'm not sure why I changed it. I think my real name is Connor Locke."

"Hello?"

Claire went still. "Did you hear that?"

"Hear what?" Leesie whispered, her eyes frantically scanning the room. "Are they back? Let's get out of here."

"No," Claire put a hand on her wrist, "it was something else."

"Please, you've got to help me."

"There it is again."

"Okay, Claire, you're really scaring me here."

"I'm trapped and I can't see anything! Please, call the police. Call my husband."

The voice rattled off a phone number, which Claire repeated aloud.

"That's your phone number," Leesie said. "Why are you telling me your phone number?"

"I didn't," she said, feeling a shiver, "it was the voice."

"What voice?"

"The voice inside my head."

"Okay, we're getting you back to the hospital right now." Leesie pulled her toward the door, but Claire shook her off.

"Please, can anyone hear me?" pleaded the voice. *"I know someone's out there, I can hear you talking. You've got to get me out of here!"*

"It's her," Claire said, starting to understand.

"Who? What are you talking about?"

"It's her, it's Claire Summers."

"But where? Inside your head. That doesn't—"

Claire waved her hand in the air, cutting Leesie off.

"I know. Just be quiet, all right? Just for a minute."

Hands on her hips, staring ahead, Leesie looked like she wanted to say something more but instead fell silent.

"Claire Summers?" Claire spoke inside her head. *"Where are you?"*

"Oh, thank God! You've got to get me out of here. I'm pregnant, and I'm worried about my baby."

"I'm sorry to tell you this, but there's nowhere to help you escape from."

"What're you talking about? Look, the last thing I remember is being at the clinic. Dr. Elisabeth Greenwald, you can check with her."

"Leesie…I mean Elisabeth was examining you, and you were worried about your baby. And then nothing, right? That's the last thing you remember."

"Exactly. But how did you know? Are you one of the men who kidnapped me?"

"Nobody kidnapped you, Claire. My name is Connor Locke, and I'm you. I mean, I'm inside your body. I don't know exactly where you are."

"Inside my body? Am I possessed? Are…are you…a demon?"

Claire laughed out loud. No, she wasn't a demon. At least she didn't think she was. If she was anything, she was a ghost.

"What's so funny?" Leesie asked, breaking her silence.

"The real Claire asked me if she was possessed."

"Well, if any of this is true, isn't she?"

That thought sobered her. Claire supposed she was.

"Hello? Are you still there?"

"I'm still here, I was just talking to Leesie."

"Leesie?"

"Elisabeth Greenwald. Your doctor. Your best friend."

"Elisabeth's there? Is she possessed, too?"

"No, and you're not, either. I mean, maybe you are, but I'm not a demon, and it wasn't my fault."

"You stole my body and it wasn't your fault?"

"I died, and my soul had to have somewhere to go. Believe me, I don't understand it any more than you do."

As she thought the words, she realized that wasn't quite true. The world needed her, or someone like her. Nature abhorred a vacuum, and, having nowhere else to go, his spirit was shuffled off into the closest available body.

But it wasn't exactly available. Why this body? Why not Leesie or someone else in the clinic, or even someone at the scene of the accident? And then another thought occurred to her.

"Do you remember what happened right before you blacked out? I mean, exactly."

"Sure I do. Elisabeth was having a hard time finding the baby's heartbeat. I remember thinking that if my baby didn't live, then I didn't want to either. And then I woke up here."

That must be it. The real Claire Summers had wished her life away, and Connor Locke's spirit just happened to be on hand to make sure her wish was granted. It was a big coincidence, to be sure, but maybe nature or fate or some other force beyond their understanding or control had manipulated events in just such a way as to enable the Locke family line to go on living.

Or maybe it was just dumb luck.

She felt like she was missing something important, but couldn't put her finger on whatever it was.

"Leesie," she said, speaking aloud, "when you were examining me…I mean Claire, what happened?"

"I couldn't find the baby's heartbeat. I was afraid we'd lost him when suddenly there it was. I was about to go and get Dr. Bartlett, another doctor in the practice, one who has a lot more experience than I do, when I finally found it."

"What happened right before that?"

"I'm not sure what you're asking."

"I mean, what did Claire say? What did she do?"

"I don't remember. You…she, I mean, she seemed really freaked out. She kept saying over and over that she couldn't lose the baby and that she didn't want to live without him."

"Maybe that explains it."

"Explains what?"

She told Leesie everything, carefully repeating the words in her head so the real Claire could hear them as well. She kept only one thing from the voice inside her head, making certain it was just Leesie who heard lest the real Claire freak out.

When she was done, she searched Leesie's eyes for acceptance but saw only confusion and doubt. She saw something else there as well: fear.

"If you're a gateway between life and death," said the voice in her head, *"can't you just take over another body and give mine back?"*

"I wish it were that simple. This is new for me, too. I've never been dead before. I don't know how any of this works."

"But what about my baby? Is he okay?"

She chose her words carefully. *"The baby is still alive."*

"What do you mean 'still'? Is he in danger?"

"Don't worry, everything will be all right."

"No, I want my body back!"

"It's not my choice."

"I won't let you hurt my baby!"

A sudden and fierce pain rocked Claire to her knees. She closed her eyes and leaned against the counter for support, feeling herself slip away.

"I'd never hurt your baby," she said aloud, before realizing her error and repeating the sentence inside her head.

"She thinks you're trying to hurt the baby?" asked Leesie.

"Do you hear me? I won't let you hurt my baby!"

Damn it, not now. If the real Claire Summers were to retake possession of her body it might mean disaster for all of them. She had to hold on for just a little bit longer. Once she figured everything out and dealt with it, she would happily "go gently into that good night," but she'd be damned if she'd leave Leesie and Sabrina and everyone else she cared about behind to deal with a world without death.

"Please," she thought, pushing hard against the voice, *"I would never hurt you or my baby. Your baby, I mean. I just need—"*

She never got to finish her sentence.

"Claire, open your eyes," Leesie was screaming in her face, "for God's sake, open your eyes. They're here. They're here!"

I just need…what? What was she going to say?

She felt herself slipping away, falling from her body and into somewhere else.

Chapter 46

Connor Locke stood in a field of corn, rows stretching as far as the eye could see. A bright, blistering sun hung overhead, and the soil felt warm as it squished between his bare toes.

He was on his grandfather's farm, just outside of Carthage. The farm, long since gone, looked just like this the summer he turned thirteen, the summer he'd spent helping Grandpa Bill harvest the corn.

"Connor," called a voice from behind him, a voice he recognized but never thought he'd hear again in this lifetime.

A chill went through him. He hadn't cried for years, not even for his father's funeral, but he felt hot tears fill his eyes. He shook his head, trying to dispel the voice, knowing it just wasn't possible.

Holding his breath, he turned around.

"Come on, boy," said Bill West, stretching out a beefy hand towards his grandson, "the corn won't harvest itself."

Grandpa Bill was a bear of a man, standing well over six feet tall and tipping the scales at a good two-fifty. He looked healthy and full of life, a far cry from the way he'd been just a couple of years later, when the cancer had taken hold of him and squeezed every last ounce of vigor from his body.

But this was Bill West before the chemo, before the radiation, before he'd given up hope of hanging on long enough to see his grandson graduate high school.

This Bill West had a full head of thick, gray hair, and a beard and moustache to match. His piercing blue eyes weren't filled with the pain and anguish of trying to fight a disease that wouldn't be extinguished, and of the anger of a life cut far too short. He wore a huge smile that nearly touched his ears, and he had a spring in his step that belied the fact that, at age fifty-five, he still turned fourteen-hour days and could do twice the amount of work in half the amount of time of anyone else who worked the farm.

Though long since divorced, Gabriel Locke had remained friends with his father-in-law and no doubt would have moved heaven and earth to help Bill West if only they'd been able to find him. But Locke had been on one of his walkabouts, unreachable by telephone, while the most important man in his son's life lay dying.

He left the country two weeks before Bill West was diagnosed with terminal cancer, and arrived home too late, just three days after West died. Connor had never forgiven him for that. The missed baseball games and birthdays paled in comparison to the loss of his grandfather.

"Grandpa Bill, is this really you?" he said, half-expecting the man to disappear into the corn field if he spoke.

"It's me, all right," he said. "I've missed you."

"I've missed you, too."

They worked for a while, pulling the corn from the stalks, shucking it, loading it into baskets. It was hot and the work was tiring, but at the same time it felt good to be moving, to be doing something physical.

"You should forgive him, you know," Grandpa Bill finally said, as they filled their fifth basket.

"Who?" he asked, knowing full well Grandpa Bill was talking about Connor's father.

Grandpa Bill ignored the question. "The man has a lot of love in his heart, but his timing was always off. Can you hate a man for the rest of your life just because he has bad timing?"

"Had, you mean."

"Beg pardon?"

"You said 'has,' but it's 'had.' Gabriel is dead."

"Since when has that meant anything in your family?"

Was it his imagination, or was the sun getting brighter? The corn was awash in a fiery glow of yellow and orange that hurt his eyes just to look at it.

"I talked to him," he admitted, shading his eyes from the glare, "right after his funeral. He told me he loved me."

"And you didn't believe him?"

"Doesn't matter what I believe. He was never there for me. Hell, he wasn't there for you when you needed him most."

"He didn't know."

"Well, he should have known," he shouted, anger at his father bubbling to the surface. "You were the most important person to me in the world, did you know that? If I couldn't have a real father, couldn't he at least have helped me keep you around for a little while longer?"

"I loved you, Connor, and I know you loved me, but a father and a son…that's a special bond, and your father was a damned fool for taking that for granted."

"Damned fool is right."

"But you were every bit as much the fool for not giving him another chance."

"How many chances did he need? How many chances did he deserve? He screwed up long before he disappeared. Your dying was just the final straw."

"Connor, if you love someone, and they love you, there are no final straws. Besides, it goes deeper than that."

"What do you mean?"

"Your mother, my daughter, she's a wonderful soul, but your father…there was no way he could ever stay any one place for too long, and I think, deep down, she knew that."

The light was growing brighter, and his eyes began to water. Was this the Light he'd always read about? But that didn't make any sense. He'd seen enough ghosts to know that they didn't go anywhere. At least, not most of them.

"Life doesn't always make sense," Grandpa Bill said, reading his mind. "And, yes, that's the Light, with a capital 'L,' and you're dying, but it doesn't have to be this way."

"I'm dying?" he asked, already knowing it was true.

He remembered now. Claire Summers. Their minds—their souls?—had briefly touched, circling around each other like two dogs in a fight. For a brief moment they shared control of her body, inhabiting the same space. In that moment he knew her and she knew him, and he finally remembered exactly what happened in Florida.

He thought they might come to an understanding, but instead she recoiled, rallied against him, pushing him out of her body, and now his spirit had nowhere else to go. Of course he was dying, and he was strangely okay with that. He was tired of fighting.

"I said it doesn't have to be this way." His grandfather laid a hand on his shoulder. "Whether you live or die is up to you now, but I can tell you this: you hold on to your grudge against your father and Sabrina and this isn't going to turn out well for anyone."

Sabrina? He loved his little sister, but, as much as he hated to admit it, he knew it was true. His father had returned to Carthage from his year and a half in Australia with a new wife and a beautiful baby girl that shared Connor's green eyes if not his red Irish hair. He loved her, but also resented her.

Connor was nearly sixteen when he met his little sister, and he hated her because she was a symbol of everything he had lost. But that hate quickly turned to acceptance and, eventually, to love, though he'd always known that some of that resentment remained, like a grain of sand in an oyster, agitating the bond between them. But from that grain of sand had grown a pearl, and, flawed though it was, he cherished it all the same. But, yes, the resentment was still there, at least in part.

He'd all but forgiven Sabrina for supplanting him in his father's life, but he could never forgive his father for abandoning him when he needed him most.

"But don't you see?" Grandpa Bill said, squeezing his shoulder, "she didn't replace you. She never could. He loved you the best he knew how, and if anything Sabrina was his second chance to do right by you."

"I don't understand."

"He knew he screwed up with you, screwed up bad. He wanted to make things better, but didn't know how. So he started over. That's just human nature. It doesn't mean he loved you any less, just that he was human, and sometimes it's easier to go back to the beginning than to fix what's already broken. He couldn't see his hubris any more than you could see yours. You both made a lot of mistakes, and, like your father, you're just as pigheaded about owning up to them."

"What could I have done differently?"

"Any number of things. You could have been more receptive to Gabe's overtures, and you didn't have to run away. That would have been a good start."

"I didn't run away."

"You dropped out of college and joined the Army, and then when that went bad, you let yourself be dishonorably discharged instead of sticking around and defending yourself. You've spent your entire life running. Do you think any of that made your father happy?"

"I didn't give a damn whether or not I made him happy, and I still don't."

"The thing is, boy, you do. You did those things to hurt him, but in doing so you also hurt yourself."

Connor thought about that for a moment. "Okay, even if that's true, what can I do about it now?"

"Gabriel Locke once again walks the Earth, and he's about to need your help in a very big way."

"But how?"

"Your death changed a lot of things, son, but your resurrection changed things even more. The gateway…your gateway…is caught in a flux, halfway-open and halfway-closed. Some things have gotten through that were never meant to walk the Earth, but some good has come from it as well. Gabe is mobile, and he's recruited your sister and a boy named Farris to help you. They're on their way to you now, only it's not going to work out quite the way they envisioned."

"Sabrina? That son-of-a-bitch brought Sabrina with him?"

"Watch your language, Connor," the old man smiled sternly, "I may be dead, but I can still take a switch to your backside if I put my mind to it."

"Sorry." He actually blushed. "But Sabrina? Why would he bring her?"

"She's stubborn, and she loves you. Do I have to say anything more?"

Connor smiled. When Sabrina set her mind to something, heaven help anything or anyone who got in her way.

"So how do I help them?" He looked around, gesturing at the expanse of corn. "I'm not really in a position to help anyone."

"You go back. You settle into the baby's body, where Claire Summers has been for the last three days, and you fight like hell to take control again. Getting control of that body is the only way you're going to be able to help anyone."

"So it was the baby. It…died, and that's how…"

"That's how your spirit was able to take possession of Claire's body," Grandpa Bill finished for him. "Claire was so connected to her baby that, when you came calling, she gladly fled, taking up residence in the shell of her dead baby."

"Which is where you want me to go."

"Precisely."

"I'm just so tired, Grandpa, and I've missed you so much. Let Claire have her body. She deserves it a hell of a lot more than I do. Grandpa, the things I've done…"

"And, with this one act, you can make amends for all of it. Wipe the slate clean. All will be forgiven, if you'll only forgive yourself first.

"But if you don't…Claire, Leesie, Sabrina, Farris, Gabe, and more…they'll all die, and nothing will be able to set any of this right ever again. The world as you know it will be forever changed.

"You've been given a great gift, son, and some mighty scary people are trying to take it away from you. Don't let them."

He had tried to heal his grandfather, even though he knew it wasn't supposed to work that way. For whatever reason, the gateway had never been able to heal anyone they were related to by blood. His powers didn't function the same way after that. Something had broken in him, and he'd lost the ability to heal.

But that wasn't right. He healed both Corduroy and Leesie, though he hadn't known what he was doing at the time. Had he been able to heal all along and simply forgotten how? Could it really be that simple?

"When you put it that way," he finally answered, "I guess I don't really have much choice. Okay, what do I need to do?"

"You see that trail?"

Grandpa Bill pointed over his shoulder, in the opposite direction of the Light, and he turned to follow. Where only corn had been before, now a winding path presented itself, weaving and turning through the endless rows of green stalks.

"Take that trail, and don't turn back. Don't even look back. If you do that, if you just keep walking, your feet will lead you where you need to go."

Grandpa Bill's strong arms and calloused hands pulled him into an embrace, and it was as if the last seventeen years simply vanished. His clothes were dusty and his skin smelled faintly of Hai Karate cologne, just the way Connor remembered.

"Now go!" He pushed Connor toward the path.

Putting one foot in front of the other, he turned away from the light and began walking. He was perhaps a dozen yards away when he heard the old man call out.

"I almost forgot," he yelled, "watch out for the little girl. She's important, too."

Little girl? He wondered who his grandfather meant. He almost turned around to ask but caught himself and instead continued down the trail.

Chapter 47

Claire didn't know where she was, and everything was happening in a blur. Elisabeth was there, clutching her arm, pulling her through a house she didn't recognize.

"Slow down," she said, resisting Elisabeth's pull.

They stood in a living area awash in reds and browns, surrounded by a leather couch and two metal and glass end tables on one side and a fluffy recliner on the other. A brick fireplace was set into the far wall, and a huge television occupied the opposite side of the room.

Behind the couch, up against one wall, stood a huge fish tank filled with all kinds of exotic saltwater fish—four-stripe damsels, dragon goby, angel fish, clown fish and half a dozen others she didn't recognize. Except for a handful of hardy survivors, they were all dead. The fish floated near the top of the aquarium, the water having long turned a sickly shade of green.

"We have to go!" Elisabeth said, pulling at her.

The sound of a door opening echoed through the house, and she let herself be dragged along behind Elisabeth. They reached the sliding glass door at the back of the house just as someone stepped in front of it from the outside.

The man was huge, more than a foot taller than she was, and was dressed in a dark business suit with his long, black hair pulled back in a tight ponytail. He pushed the door open with hands the size of catcher's mitts, ducking his head as he crossed the threshold into the house.

"This way," said Elisabeth, turning on her heels.

Suddenly Jeff was there, blocking their exit, his left arm hanging limply at his side. He stood next to a little girl who was attached via a chain around her wrist to a short, balding man, and someone she knew instinctively to be Connor Locke. Only it wasn't him; if anything, it was a caricature of the man she saw so clearly in her mind's eye. Part of his skull was missing, and he looked as though he shouldn't even be breathing, much less standing.

"Jeff?" she asked, turning her attention back to her husband. "What are you doing here?"

"He's with them," Elisabeth replied, fingers tightening around Claire's hand. "He tried to kill us."

And then the giant was upon them, hooking his arms around her chest, lifting her high into the air. His arms were like pythons, and for a moment she struggled to breathe. Claire looked to Jeff for rescue but saw only desperation and fear reflected in his eyes.

"Let her go," screamed Elisabeth, punching and kicking the giant. She swung the shotgun toward his face, pulled the trigger, but nothing happened.

The bald man whispered something to the young girl who in turn whispered something to Connor Locke, who launched himself at Elisabeth and knocked her to the ground, sending the shotgun skittering against the television.

He wrapped his broken and bloody hands around her throat, squeezing so hard that her eyes rolled back in her head.

"No, don't hurt her," Claire shouted, "I'll do whatever you want, just don't hurt her."

The bald man once again whispered something to the girl, and she ordered Locke to stop. Elisabeth wasn't moving, but her chest rose and fell so at least she was still alive.

"You know what we want," said the giant, loosening his grip just enough to allow her to breathe. "Give it to us, and she can leave here unharmed. You have my word."

"We have maybe ten thousand in the bank, and I have another twenty in a private account," she saw Jeff's eyes widen, "and some CDs and stocks I could probably liquidate within twenty-four hours. I have jewelry, my car…"

A sudden pain rocked her, and she thought her spine would snap. The giant's arms were like twin vises, squeezing so tight that her vision blurred and she almost blacked out.

"No more games," said the balding man, moving closer. "Mr. West, you've made things quite difficult for us, but I'm afraid it's time for all of this to come to an end."

"I don't…" she gasped, concentrating on getting the words out. "I don't understand…"

"It's not him anymore," Elisabeth said from the floor, her voice weak.

The corpse glowered at her, eyes flickering back and forth between the bald man and the girl, but remained still.

"Explain," said the giant, hot breath in Claire's ear, "and quickly."

"Connor's gone," Leesie said, rising shakily to her feet, "maybe gone for good. Claire took her body back."

"Claire, honey?" said Jeff from across the room, his eyes searching hers for recognition. "Is that really you?"

The man who inhabited her body had walked two days in her shoes, and in the brief moment their minds touched she caught glimpses and shadows of the last 48 hours. It wasn't pretty.

What Jeff had done to her, almost raping her, trying to kill her, she could never forgive. She'd forgiven him for far too much already, and she felt ashamed that it had taken losing control of her body for her to finally see that.

"I know what you did to me, you son of a bitch," she whispered, perversely enjoying the recoil she saw in his eyes, "and you can go to hell."

The short man ignored the exchange, dropping the girl's chain and then producing a dangerous-looking dagger from the folds of his suit. He popped something into his mouth—it looked for all the world like the tip of a finger dangling from a string—and quickly strode over to Claire, grabbed her arm by the wrist, held her hand palm up, and pricked her thumb with the knife.

"Ouch!" she cried, involuntarily jerking her hand back. "What are you doing?"

He said nothing, but withdrew the finger from his mouth and pressed it against her newly-created wound. Smearing it with blood, he cupped it in his hand, held his fist up to his mouth, and whispered something.

He let the little bit of finger dangle from the string, and at first it did nothing, but then it started to spin. The finger moved in ever-widening arcs, slowly at first but growing faster with every revolution. Finally the string drew taut and it stopped spinning, hovering motionless in the air, pointing at her.

The bald man shook his head. "Mr. West is lying."

She started to protest, but the giant's words cut her off.

"Mr. West, it isn't polite to lie. And what did this charade gain you? The outcome will still be the same."

"I'm not lying," she shouted, the words tumbling from her mouth. "I'm me, I'm Claire Summers. Connor's gone."

"Claire?" A voice echoed in her head, and she knew it was Connor.

"Where did you go?" she thought back at him, amazed at the relief she felt upon hearing his voice. *"They're going to kill us."*

"Let me back in," he demanded. She could feel his urgency, like a white-hot scalpel cutting through her mind. *"If you don't, we're both dead."*

"Mr. Quarry, I'm going to take our guest back down to the basement," the giant said, shifting her to his shoulder. "Would you be so kind as to dispose of his friend?"

"Oh God, no," she begged, "Please, I'm not lying!"

"It's not him," Elisabeth screamed, launching herself at the giant.

Quarry was on her in an instant, one arm wrapped around her throat, pulling her toward the ground. His jaw seemed to dislocate before her eyes, and the gaping black maw where his mouth should have been showed only row upon row of razor-sharp teeth.

"They're killing her," Claire screamed into the silence of her thoughts.

"Think about Leesie, and about your baby," Connor's words flooded her mind, *"and, for the love of God, let me in!"*

Her heart beat wildly in her ears and she resisted him, pushed him down. She couldn't go back to that dark room with the false promises of safety and security, she just couldn't.

But she knew she had to.

She closed her eyes, blocking out Elisabeth's screams, blocking out everything except for the image of her baby and Connor Locke's voice.

"Do it!" she screamed, unsure whether she had just thought the words or actually said them aloud, and then everything changed.

✳ ✳ ✳

Claire grabbed the frame of the door leading to the basement and yanked back, throwing Kingfisher off balance. She twisted out of his grasp and slithered down his back. Tucking her head, she landed hard on her shoulder. Rolling to a crouch, she grabbed his ankles and pulled, sweeping his legs out from under him.

The startled giant careened into the wall, knocking plaster loose, scrabbling for purchase before falling into the stairwell. Kingfisher crashed down the steps, snapping the safety railing in two in a vain attempt to gain purchase before finally landing flat on his back at the bottom of the wooden stairs.

She slammed the basement door, locking it before sprinting to the dining room. The door wouldn't stop the giant, but a few extra seconds might mean the difference between life and death.

A shrill scream echoed through the hallway. Leesie!

Pulling the Luger from her waistband, holding it pointed at the floor, she burst into the living room. Her old body, the shell that had once held Connor Locke, stood rigid against the wall, beside a frightened Indian girl. Jeff stood beside her, mouth hung open, staring across the room.

"Oh God, please, no," pleaded Leesie, Mr. Quarry straddling her hips, her hand caught in his mouth like a fishing hook in a large-mouthed bass.

She yanked her arm away, blood splattering in an arc against the fish tank and spraying the wall. The last two fingers from her right hand were gone, little ragged stumps the only evidence of what had once been flesh and bone, the hand of a doctor rendered useless by a monster's insatiable appetite.

Claire stood in the entrance to the living room, feet apart, and aimed the pistol at Quarry's head. Before she could pull the trigger, the sliding glass doors exploded in a rain of glass. She threw herself flat to the floor as a gunshot echoed through the house.

A bullet whizzed past Quarry's head, hitting the fish tank, burrowing itself into the heavy glass. A second shot sounded, this one grazing the small man's cheek and drawing blood before embedding itself three inches from the first.

A tiny trickle of water dripped from the hole, a slow crack arcing from it to the impression the other bullet had made into the glass, and then the tank was exploding outward, salt water and fish raining down on Jeff and the dead man, just missing the little girl, who threw herself into a ball against the base of the tank.

The monster's skin began to smoke, huge welts puckering across his skin as the salt water seemingly ate at his wounds and the symbols drawn in blood upon his chest. He howled once, a blood curdling gasp of pain, and then Claire saw a third bullet, spaced slightly apart from the first two, zip past Quarry to bury itself into the dead man's stomach. He jerked back, falling into the tank, water and glass and dead fish cascading over him like a waterfall.

Jeff shook his head, looking like he's just snapped out of a three-day drunk. He grabbed the girl, kicking and screaming, and pulled her away from the tank. She struggled in his arms until finally he threw her over his shoulders in a Fireman's carry and scuttled toward the dining room. And then he was shuffling backward, his gait awkward and unsteady.

Kingfisher, already back up the stairs, had met him in the doorway. In one quick motion he covered Jeff's head with his hand, crushing his skull with the merest flex of his wrist, squeezing bone and blood and gray matter between his fingers, sluicing down Jeff's neck.

The girl sobbed hysterically as Jeff's body slumped against her, pushing her to the floor. Kingfisher picked up the body and quickly threw it aside, scooping her up into his arms, charging into the living room.

The corpse's chest was a mass of angry, blistering sores, hissing and popping as the water from the fish tank rolled over him to soak and pool into the carpet at his feet. The symbols were burning away, little wisps of smoke coming off his chest. Screaming at the top of his lungs, he beat at his chest, clawing, ripping away skin, leaving a gray mass of flesh that resembled rotten hamburger meat.

And then the screaming turned to laughter.

Quarry threw himself on top of Leesie when the shooting began, but now he rolled off of her, eyes quickly moving from Kingfisher and the little girl to the laughing corpse. Leesie cradled her ruined hand to her chest, crawling across the room toward Claire. Quarry didn't try to stop her.

"Mr. Kingfisher," the little man said, shooting glances toward the back of the house, "I think we have a situation. The binding has come undone."

Claire swiveled the gun back and forth between Kingfisher and Quarry, knowing she might never have another chance to act, but finally tucked it back into her jeans and dragged Leesie to her feet. Getting Leesie out of here was more important. Not sure if whoever had fired the shot were friend or foe, she angled away from the shattered glass doors.

Leesie's hand was a mess; there was blood everywhere, and little bits of bone poked out from the holes where two fingers used to be.

A wild-eyed man with sandy-blond hair suddenly burst through the ruined outside doorway, handgun drawn and pointed at the ground. She withdrew her own pistol, but let it fall to her side as Leesie tightened her good hand around her wrist.

"It's Pete," Leesie whispered, her face pale. She was losing a lot blood, probably going into shock. "Please don't hurt him."

"Claire?" he said, moving slowly toward them, raising his revolver, wavering between Quarry and the quivering dead man. "My God, Claire, what's happened to her? What's happened to *you?*"

"Move away from the aquarium," the Indian girl said to the corpse, no longer struggling in Kingfisher's arms, "and destroy the man with the gun."

The dead man pushed away from the aquarium and brushed himself off, picking out little shards and slivers of glass from his hands and forearms, dead fish and small bits of rock and gravel flopping to the carpet all around him.

"I'm no longer yours to control," he said, a lopsided smile covering his dead face, "and you are of no interest to me. Command me no further, and you may live."

"What the fuck?" whispered Pete, putting his body between Claire and Leesie and the rest of the room. "C'mon, we have to get out of here. Now!"

"Take Leesie," Claire whispered back, surprising herself. "This needs to end here. And that girl…we can't leave her."

Watch out for the little girl. Surely this is what her grandfather meant.

"I'm not leaving you here, Claire. I don't know who these men are, but they were at Elisabeth's house with Jeff, and—"

"Jeff's dead," she cut him off, "and Leesie will be, too, if you don't get her out of here."

"Jeff's dead? But…how? When?"

She ignored the question, instead pushing Leesie into his arms. He looked like he might protest but instead lifted her into a fireman's carry, ignoring her delirious objections.

"I'll be back for you," Pete called over his shoulder.

"You won't have to. I can take care of myself. Leesie's car is by the clinic, it's unlocked and the keys are over the visor. Take her there and wait. Keep her safe, bind the wound, and I can fix her. I'll be right behind you, I promise."

"Fix her? She needs a hospital, Claire."

"Damn it, just trust me!" She said, moving away from Pete and Leesie and edging closer to Kingfisher and the girl.

Kingfisher lowered the girl to the ground, but kept his massive hand encircled around her wrist. "Mr. West," he said, staring directly at Claire, "this has gone on long enough. Well played. But I need you to submit to us now, before it's too late."

"She's mine," the corpse said, moving closer. "I need her."

Quarry drew something from his black bag—a handful of chalky white powder—and blew it at the dead man, but whatever inhabited Connor Locke's former body was quicker. He clapped his hands and yelled something in a guttural language, and the air inside the house began to stir, spinning fast, forming a cyclone between him and Quarry, blowing the powder back into the small man's face.

Mr. Quarry bent over at the waist, coughing and blinking back tears. He held a small object that looked like the decayed foot of a chicken in his hand, but never had the chance to use it. The cyclone roared straight into him, sending him flying over the coffee table. The talisman was ripped from his hand, falling somewhere behind the couch.

The dead man began to chant, a keening, high-pitched wail, like the song of a dolphin gone horribly wrong. For the first time, Claire saw real fear in Kingfisher's eyes. He took a half-step toward Quarry, who was now on his knees, eyes moving between him and the Indian girl.

The walls began to shake as the cyclone grew bigger, ricocheting back and forth from one side of the room to another. The television vibrated off its base, crashing to the floor. Books and knick-knacks cascaded off shelves, flying this way and that, adding to the wild wind that whipped through the house.

Quarry struggled against the wind, but it flattened him to the ground, his arms and legs spread-eagle. His bag skittered away from him, the miniature gale pushing it beyond his reach. The more he struggled the stronger the winds became, holding him fast.

As the winds buffeted the walls the pressure inside the house began to drop, and Claire felt her ears pop. Her eyes began to water, and it was hard to breathe. She reached out a shaky hand to brace herself against the wall, little black dots floating before her eyes. Her stomach gurgled, and she fought the urge to throw up.

Ignoring the pain in her ears, she turned to Kingfisher.

"Give me...the girl," she panted, struggling to be heard above the wind, "and let me get her to safety. Do that, and I'll stop running, and we can finally settle this."

Indecision passed over Kingfisher's face, but finally he nodded.

"Take her," the giant yelled, removing the chain from around the girl's wrist and pushing her toward Claire. "I will hold you to your word."

"I wouldn't have it any other way," Claire said between gritted teeth, taking the sobbing girl into her arms and half-pulling, half-carrying her toward the door.

The dead man leapt for them, but was met by Kingfisher, and they went down in a tangle of limbs. Like a pair of grotesque grapplers they wrestled for control, rolling into furniture, knocking over an end table.

The cyclone continued to grow, bouncing from wall to wall like a metal ball in a pinball machine, punching beach-ball sized holes in the sheetrock. The walls started to shake, long, jagged cracks moving upwards from the foundation to the ceiling as the load-bearing studs could no longer contain the force of the winds.

The house began to collapse in on itself, and that's when all hell broke loose.

Chapter 48

The sun was rising and the rain had finally let up as Jimmy Cross materialized in the middle of the road. A light fog covering the city was all that remained of the previous night's downpour, and the early morning rays were already starting to burn through. He imagined the morning air was at once both cool and humid, though of course he really couldn't feel anything.

The last thing he remembered was falling through the wall at Leesie's house. It took every ounce of strength he had to communicate with Pete Snow, and he feared that whatever supernatural energy kept him bound to this mortal plane had finally worn out and he was gone for real.

And yet here he was, still walking among the non-living. Before Claire came into his life—or his afterlife, he supposed—he thought he was alive, was convinced he could feel the world around him. Had he been better off with the illusion? In the end, it didn't really matter. Claire was in trouble, and he had to help her.

He appeared to be in a residential neighborhood, with dozens of houses on the north side of the road and a scattering of businesses to the south. Parked in front of some sort of clinic stood a large, silver and black monstrosity that looked like a cross between a van and a pick-up truck, and beside it a white sedan.

He watched unseen as Pete appeared from around the side of one of the houses that dotted the opposite side of the street, carrying a wounded and bleeding Leesie over his shoulder. Pete had the silver dollars, and Jimmy was connected to them. He knew that now. Wherever they went, he could follow.

His words had gotten through to Pete, and he had managed to arrive in time to rescue Leesie. But where was Claire?

Pete gently lowered his ex-wife to the ground, just a few feet from where Jimmy stood, doing his best to ignore her grunts of pain as he removed his jacket and used it to bind her ruined hand.

Leesie had lost a lot of blood. Her eyes stared off at some distant point and she wouldn't answer Pete, couldn't even focus on him. She needed a doctor, fast. There was nothing more that Jimmy could do for either of them.

A thunderous boom broke the early morning silence, sending Pete sprawling to the ground. The house the cop had just come from began to collapse in on itself, wood creaking, support beams snapping, as if being sucked into the depths of hell. The windows shattered and then the walls went, buckling inward, and the entire structure imploded, showering the ground with nails and roofing tile and other bits and pieces of debris.

"Claire!" Pete rasped, his eyes moving back and forth between Leesie and the ruined house.

Jimmy began to walk toward them, but stopped short. What could he do? If Claire had been in that house…

"C'mon, Elisabeth, c'mon, c'mon, c'mon," Pete whispered, his gaze finally settling on the woman in his arms. "I need you to stay with me here. You're gonna be okay, God damn it! I am not gonna lose you again!"

The shrill honk of a horn and the screech of rubber on pavement startled Jimmy into movement. He spun on his heels, watching in horror as a long, black hearse swerved away from him and barreled straight toward Pete and Leesie.

Cat-like reflexes had Pete up and moving, scooping Leesie into his arms, rolling out of the way just as the car slammed into a pair of trees.

Vehicle met nature in a cacophony of exploding metal and glass, mixing with screams and shouts from inside the hearse. The trees buckled but did not bend. Almost as if in defiance, they showered the car with what few red and brown leaves fall had not taken from them, mixing with the steam that poured from the vehicle's radiator.

The driver's side door of the hearse swung open and out climbed an old man in a crumpled suit, followed by a brown-haired boy and a girl with long, dark hair and porcelain pale skin.

"Jesus, dad," screamed the girl, rubbing her shoulder. "What the hell?"

"It...he...I almost hit him," said the old man, staring straight at Jimmy. "I thought...I thought he was real. It's getting harder for me to tell."

"Who?" the girl asked, scanning the road. "I don't see anybody there."

"Police!" screamed Pete, stance wide, service revolver drawn. "What the hell do you think you're doing?"

"Who are you?" asked the driver of the hearse, ignoring Pete, staring at Jimmy. "You're tied to my son. I can feel it. Do you know where he is?"

"You can see me?" asked Jimmy. "My name's Cross. Jimmy Cross. Who're you?"

"Of course I can see you," the old man said. His face was pale and he looked like he hadn't slept in a week. "My name is Gabriel, and this is my daughter Sabrina and her friend Farris. Do you know my son?"

"Spread your legs and put your hands against the vehicle," the detective ordered, walking through Jimmy.

The ghost could feel the fear and anger rolling off the cop in waves. He meant to get Leesie to the hospital, and nothing or no one was going to stand in his way.

"It was an accident," said the girl, voice shaking as she followed Pete's orders. "We're trying to find my brother."

"I said against the car, you son of a bitch," Pete yelled, grabbing the old man by the shirt and pushing him violently against the side of the ruined hearse. "My wife is hurt, maybe dying, and you just tried to kill us. If you're working with them, I swear to God I'll blow your fucking brains out."

The teenage boy lunged for the gun, but Pete was ready for him. He sidestepped Farris's attack, raising a brutal knee into the boy's diaphragm. Farris crumpled to the ground in a wheezing, coughing heap.

"We don't have time for this," the old man said, stepping between Pete and the boy. He touched the detective's wrist.

In an instant Pete's blond hair turned dull silver, and the light in his eyes faded. His hands and face wrinkled and turned a mottled brown, aging twenty or thirty years in a matter of seconds.

Pete stumbled against the old man, gasping for air. His revolver fell limply from his grasp, skittering across the pavement.

"Stop it, you're killing him," yelled Jimmy, punching at the old man with phantom fists. "He's trying to help Claire."

"We have to find Connor," Gabriel pleaded. He held tight to Pete's wrist as the detective's knees buckled and he collapsed to the road. "We have to find my son."

"We will, Dad," Sabrina said, pulling at her father's arm. "Just let him go. He can't hurt us anymore."

"I'm sorry," he finally said, releasing Pete's wrist. "I'm just…I should still be in the ground. The longer this goes on, the worse it'll get."

"What...what the hell did you do to me?" Pete stuttered, looking up at the old man through rheumy eyes. "What *are* you?"

"He's my father," said Claire, dragging a young Indian girl with her and away from the collapsed house. "And that's my sister, Sabrina. Jimmy Cross is here, too, though I'm not sure how."

"It's the silver dollars," Jimmy said. "It seems that I can go wherever they go, and right now they're with Detective Snow."

"Connor, is that really you?" asked Sabrina, walking straight through Jimmy. "How? They said you were dead."

"I kind of was, but that doesn't matter right now," Claire said, pushing the girl toward Sabrina. "Keep her safe. I've got to fix this."

Claire dropped to her knees beside Leesie, taking the woman's hand in her own. She closed her eyes, a look of concentration crossing her features.

Leesie's hand began to heal. The fingers were still gone, but Jimmy stared in amazement as the wound instantly scabbed over. A few seconds later, the scabs flaked off, revealing bright, pink skin underneath.

"Attagirl, Claire!" Jimmy cheered, pumping a fist into the air. He would never have believed it if he hadn't seen it with his own ghostly eyes.

"How in the hell?" wheezed Pete, leaning against the hearse.

"Claire?" Leesie looked up, eyes fluttering. "What happened? And...oh, Pete! What's wrong with Pete?"

Claire didn't answer, but immediately rose and walked over to the detective. Pete pushed himself to his knees and she helped him to his feet, then put her hands on his shoulders.

"Leesie loves you, you know," she said, looking into his eyes, "and for some crazy reason she trusts me, and if that means anything to you, you're going to have to trust me, too. Okay?"

Pete nodded, and closed his eyes.

✳ ✳ ✳

Claire's memory was still shaky, but it was all coming back in bits and pieces. Gabriel had leeched the life from the detective, something she had never learned to do, but just because she didn't know how to cause the damage didn't mean that she might not be able to reverse it.

She bowed her head and started to work. Pete began to change, his eyes clearing up, the age spots disappearing from his skin, but it wasn't enough. Claire's hands were shaking, and she dug her fingertips into the cop's shoulder. She leaned heavy against him, closing her eyes, her knees so weak that she felt like she might collapse.

"Let me help," said Gabriel, moving to her side. He peeled one of her hands from Pete's shoulder, clasping it tight, and then placed his other hand on Pete's other shoulder. "Together, we can do this."

And together they did. Pete's hair color changed from silver back to blond. The bow his back had developed straightened, wrinkles on his face disappeared, and he once again looked like the man Claire had first seen earlier tonight.

"Thanks, Dad," Claire said, then took a deep breath. She felt dizzy and leaned against her father for support. "About time we worked together, huh? I'm just sorry it took us both being dead to finally get to this point."

"Me too, kid," said Gabriel, hooking an arm around her shoulder, "more than you know."

Sabrina walked over to them, staring at Claire. "Is that really you in there, big brother?"

"It's really me," Claire said, "though I'm not sure how much longer I'll be able to stay."

"What happened to you?"

"Two men by the names of Kingfisher and Quarry, some sort of magical bounty hunters as far as I can tell. They were in the house, and if we're lucky, they're dead. Someone hired them to torture me until I gave them my abilities, which of course..."

"Which of course you couldn't do," Gabriel interrupted.

"I escaped them and then got hit by a car. I…died, and somehow my consciousness went into this body, into Claire Summers."

"I'm not sure we have time for this right now," said Pete. "Look."

Claire looked. Her former body, the body of Connor West, was climbing out of the debris of the ruined house, and she was certain that Kingfisher and Quarry couldn't be far behind. She'd promised Kingfisher that she'd stop running and finally, once and for all, deal with him and his partner, but she hadn't specified where the confrontation might take place.

"Connor, it's…you," whispered Sabrina, clutching his hand.

"In the spirit, if not the flesh," Claire said, then turned to Pete. "Do you have the keys to the Escalade?"

"Never got that far," he said. "They're still over the visor. Escape plan?"

"Something like that. Leesie, are any of Claire's relatives buried around here?"

"Sure. Her grandparents, I think, and maybe a cousin or two, at Rosewood. Why?"

She ignored the question. "Do you know where that is?"

"Sure, down Olive and into Bentonville, just past J Street. But how is that going to help us?"

"You're just going to have trust me one last time," she said. "Come on, everyone, into the Escalade across the street. If we've got a chance, it's going to be in that cemetery."

"We don't have a chance with that after us," Gabriel said, pointing at his dead son's body lumbering toward them. "I'll hold him off, you do what you have to do. I'll get there when I can."

"Dad!" shouted Sabrina, the teenaged Indian girl standing silent beside her, "we're not leaving you here alone."

"He won't be alone," said Pete. "I'm staying, too." Leesie opened her mouth to object, but he silenced her with a look. "Don't worry, we won't be stupid. We'll hold him off as long as we can, and then get the hell out of here. Now go!"

"Stay safe," Claire said, and then: "Pete, you have my half-dollars?"

"I do. Do you want them?" He reached into his pocket and pulled out a handful of silver.

Claire took them, shoving all but two into the pocket of her jeans. "You hang on to one of these," she said, flipping one back to Pete. "Trust me. You, too, Dad." Claire handed the other coin to Locke.

"I love you, Connor," said Gabriel, pocketing the coin. "Be careful."

"I love you, too, Dad. And one last thing. If two men that look like Penn and Teller make it out of there, tell them we're at the Rosewood Cemetery. They're not going to give up, and at least this way the fight will be on my turf."

Claire, Leesie, Sabrina, Farris, and the young girl they'd rescued from Kingfisher all climbed into the Escalade, with Claire driving and Leesie giving directions. Claire watched in the rearview mirror as whatever possessed her former body made its made toward Pete and her father, and she hoped with all her heart that she'd see them again.

Chapter 49

Everything was falling apart. Jack Bethel thought himself insane when the Voices first started, a part of his sickness, but soon enough they'd proven him wrong. They told him what to do, what steps to take to make this happen, and for a while everything went exactly as planned.

A sacrifice was needed on his part, the Voices told him. Sure, it hurt to kill Gabriel Locke—hurt like hell, actually—but it really shouldn't have. He'd known where the old man's loyalty lay, after all, and it wasn't with him. It had never been with him.

Once Locke was in the ground, he'd thought the plan a *fait accompli* and began to rush things. That had been hubris on his part, though no one could blame him for wanting to hurry. He was dying, and would be dead within six months if this didn't work.

Everything they'd told him to do, he'd done without question. After Locke, he'd murdered six people he didn't even know and used their blood to perform rituals that made him shudder. He'd fasted beneath the full moon and painted himself in symbols the Voices showed him in his dreams, all in an effort to ready his body to become the vessel, the gateway between life and death.

Bethel knew that even after he obtained Connor's powers, he wouldn't be able to heal himself. That wasn't how it worked, no matter what he'd told Mr. Kingfisher and Mr. Quarry. The Voices had insisted that they'd never go along with the real plan, so he'd been forced to tell them that Connor could willingly choose to transfer his powers to a blood relative. That was how he'd gotten them to torture Connor. Bethel was certain that if the men ever found out he'd lied, they'd kill him.

Once he obtained the powers and gave himself over to the Voices, however, he'd be untouchable. Beyond life and death. Immortal. More than that, even. He'd be a god in a world where the dead ruled the living.

He was still convinced that hiring Kingfisher and Quarry was a good decision, though the Voices didn't agree. He had used them once before, for another job, and wanted to use them again, while the Voices wanted him to do everything himself. That was his one act of defiance in all of this. His real mistake, however, had been in not doing enough research, in not preparing for every single contingency.

Connor Locke wasn't supposed to die the way he had. The plan was to weaken him as much as possible, to bring him to the brink of death, and then Bethel himself would deal the *coup de grâce*, the death blow, in person. Instead, he'd acted on instinct when he'd witnessed Connor escaping the house and run him over.

The markings, the rituals, the sacrifices, all of it, were supposed to serve as a sort of psychic magnet, transferring Connor's powers to Bethel at the moment of Connor's death, provided he was sufficiently broken. Only that hadn't happened. Even though he wasn't physically touching Connor, Bethel was a hell of a lot closer to him than Sabrina was, and by all rights the power should be his. Of course, the powers hadn't gone to Sabrina, either.

He'd never, not even for a moment, imagined that things could go as sideways as they'd ended up going. Connor's spirit had apparently taken up residence inside of some random woman, and his abilities with it. Not even the Voices had foreseen that possibility.

Bethel looked down at the syringe he was holding. The Voices had given him the recipe, and he'd had to travel to Carthage to obtain dirt from Gabriel's grave. The rest of the ingredients hadn't been as hard to obtain, but they had been expensive. If the concoction worked, however, it would be more than worth it.

Chapter 50

Gabriel wiped away tears with the back of his hand, surprised to find that there weren't any. He'd dealt with the dead for years, but he still wasn't used to being a card-carrying member of their ranks. He no longer needed to eat or breathe, and he certainly couldn't cry. Dead or not, however, he hoped he would get the chance to see Connor one last time before all of this was over.

"You are a gateway, too, but not nearly as strong as Connor West," said the dead man, limping toward Gabe and Snow. The corpse's left arm was crushed and his neck was bent at an angle that it was never meant to go.

"I'm strong enough to stop you from hurting anyone else," Gabe said, standing his ground.

He wasn't sure whether or not it was true, but if he could just buy his son a few extra minutes, whatever happened to him was of no consequence. He was on borrowed time as it was.

Detective Pete Snow stood beside him, weapon draw, pointed at the dead man. Snow fired two shots straight into Connor Locke's former body's chest, but the walking corpse just kept advancing.

"You are of no concern to me," said the dead man, pushing past the detective.

"How do we stop this thing?" asked Snow, staring at Gabe.

Gabe stepped in front of the body, planting a hand against its chest. Because it was no longer Connor, he could affect it. In an instant he drained the life from the corpse, leaving nothing but a decrepit husk that collapsed to the ground at his feet.

He watched as a dark cloud of energy arose from the dead body, growing larger as it circled into the sky.

"You have just done me a favor," the spirit whispered into the wind, *"and, for that, I will let you both live."*

"Oh shit," Gabe mumbled, as he watched the spirit zoom off in the direction the others had driven just minutes earlier.

"What in the name of God was that?" asked Snow, staring after the disappearing cloud of energy. "And if bullets can't stop it, and your powers can't stop it, what can?"

"I can," said a giant of a man, pushing out of the rubble, "now that you've freed it from that body." A smaller man limped behind him. Both were battered and bruised, and the larger of the two had an angry gash across his cheek.

"These were the guys at Elisabeth's house," said Snow, turning his gun to point at the pair. "They killed four cops."

"We haven't been properly introduced," said the giant, "My name is Mr. Kingfisher, and this is my partner, Mr. Quarry. We have no intention of harming either one of you unless provoked. Our quarrel is with Connor West."

"Then you also have a quarrel with me," Gabe said, balling his hands into fists. "You murdered my son. He can't give you his powers, even if he wanted to. You killed him for nothing."

"He told us that as well," said Kingfisher, glancing at Quarry. "Perhaps we were unwise not to believe him, regardless of what our employer claimed. Alas, a contract was signed, and we're bound by honor to see this through."

"Honor is very important to us," added Quarry.

"I didn't see much honor when you killed those police officers," Pete said, gun still pointed at the pair. "Or when you bit my wife's fucking hand off."

Kingfisher ignored him, instead settling his gaze on Gabe. "Your son promised me that we'd end this, but he isn't here. Where is he?"

"Fuck you," said Gabe. Connor wanted him to tell the two men where he was, but the least he could do was buy his son a little time.

"It doesn't matter, Mr. Kingfisher," Quarry said, "I still have this. It will show us the way." He opened his hand to reveal something hanging from a string. It looked to Gabe like the tip of a finger smeared with blood.

Gabe lunged for the string, but was met with an open-handed slap to the chest from Kingfisher that sent him pedaling backward into the hearse. He thumped hard against the metal, seeing stars.

Snow swiveled his gun to point straight at Kingfisher's face, pulled the trigger, but nothing happened. He pulled it again, and again, with the same result.

"Technology and I have never really gotten along," said the giant, smiling. He snatched the gun from Snow, bent it in half, and tossed it over his shoulder.

Not missing a beat, the detective feigned a punch at the man's jaw, allowed the strike to be blocked, then sent a spinning back kick straight into his gut. Kingfisher caught Snow's foot, tossing him into Gabe. The two went down in a heap, arms and legs akimbo.

Gabe watched helplessly as the pair climbed into their vintage station wagon and drove away. He and Snow had only bought Claire two or three minutes, at most.

Snow scrambled to his feet, and then offered his hand to Gabe. Gabe took the hand and stood up, swaying on shaky legs. A sudden pain flared through his head and he reached around the back of his skull. His head was caved in where he'd slammed into the hearse.

His already-dead body was failing him, and there wasn't a damned thing he could do to help his son and daughter.

Chapter 51

Claire had just called forth her third ghost from the cemetery, the great-great-grandfather of the woman whose body she currently possessed, when the hairs on the back of her neck stood up.

They'd made it to Rosewood Cemetery easily enough. The graveyard was small, run down, and didn't look to have had any new interments in years. They were the only ones there, which suited Claire just fine. In fact, she didn't want anyone here but herself.

"None of you need to stay for this," she said, looking in turn at Leesie, Sabrina, Farris, and the girl who called herself Nadine Pahari. "You can go somewhere, anywhere, and wait this out. The same goes for you, Jimmy. Go back to the park. You've done enough already."

"I'm not going anywhere," Jimmy said, looking resolute. "Before you found me, I'd wandered that damn park for almost forty years. You gave me a gift when you took away my ignorance, and I'm not about to abandon you now."

"I'm not leaving," Leesie said, unknowingly echoing Jimmy. "You've got Claire in there with you, and I love you both."

"I'm staying, too," added Sabrina. "Sorry, big brother, you're stuck with us."

Farris nodded in agreement, his hand finding Sabrina's in the morning light.

Nadine shrugged, making no move to leave.

"All right, then, but we have to be smart about this. That…thing inhabiting my body isn't going to give up easily, and neither are Kingfisher and Quarry. I don't want any of you getting hurt. If I go down, run. No playing hero, and no arguments. Got it?"

"Got it," Sabrina said, though she looked more than a little unsure.

Claire's heart ached for her, the little sister that, until recently, she'd forgotten she even had. Sabrina kept sneaking glances at Claire, probably trying to come to terms with the loss of her brother's body if not his spirit.

She pulled Sabrina into a sudden, fierce hug, the younger girl at first growing stiff, but finally returning the hug with just as much fervor, sobbing into Claire's shoulder.

"It's okay," whispered Claire, feeling tears push at her eyes. "I love you, Sabrina, and I'm so sorry for all the time we missed. But it really is me in here, and I'll stay as long as I'm able."

"I love you, too, big brother," Sabrina said, finally pulling from the embrace. "Now get to work. I have a feeling trouble is coming, and sooner than later."

Farris took Sabrina's hand and the pair walked over to Leesie and Nadine, leaving Claire to begin the work that she'd explained to them in the Escalade. The threat, of course, was two-fold. Even if they dealt with whatever had possessed her old body, there was still Kingfisher and Quarry.

Nadine stared at her from Leesie's side. Claire wondered not for the first time just what exactly her story was, and how she'd come to be in the custody of Kingfisher and Quarry. Leesie had tried to broach the question in the brief ride to the cemetery, but the girl had clammed up. All she'd tell them was her name and that the ruined house on Thirteenth Street had once belonged to her parents.

Nadine's story didn't matter, though, at least not at the moment. Claire cleared her mind, kneeled in the dirt between two gravestones, and began to work. She placed both hands in the dirt, feeling the soil against her palms as she attempted to wake the ghosts that slept beneath.

The first one came easily enough, called to her by blood. The ghost of Claire's great aunt Gertrude rose through the ground, sleep in her eyes, dressed in an old-fashioned black dress, looking confused.

Claire explained to the woman as best she could what was going on and what she needed from her, and then went on to the next ghost, and then the next, and that's when the malevolent spirit that had until recently inhabited her old body arrived. Claire hoped they'd have more time, and feared for the safety of Pete and her father.

"Connor West," said a jet black cloud of energy, its voice echoing inside her mind, *"I have searched long and hard for you these past two days. Submit now, and I will let your friends live."*

Apparently they could all hear it, because everyone as one turned to stare at the dark cloud descending upon them. Jimmy bum rushed the cloud and was summarily shunted aside, his body wracked in ghostly pain.

"None of you can hurt me, least of all a shade," said the spirit.

Claire had severely miscalculated. She assumed the spirit would still be inhabiting her original body and had planned to ask the ghosts in the cemetery to overwhelm it, to seek to possess the body and push the evil spirit out, not realizing that the being would be even stronger not confined to a human form.

Whatever this thing was, it wouldn't be easily defeated.

"What do we do?" asked Sabrina, staring into the black cloud.

A bolt of lightning shot out from the floating wisps of air, crackling into the ground at Sabrina's feet. Her hair stood up for an instant before she threw herself back, tumbling into Farris.

Claire moved between the cloud and her sister, planting her feet on the ground, concentrating on the three old ghosts she'd just called up. As one they ran at the cloud, seeking to disrupt it, but they stumbled back in shock and pain, suffering the same fate as Jimmy.

The cloud rushed at Claire, engulfing her in its mists. She screamed, taken by surprise, as the spirit began to force itself inside through her nostrils and throat. It was using the same tactic that Claire had planned to use against it.

Claire stumbled backward, swatting at the cloud, unable to breathe. She could feel its invisible tendrils probing her body, working its way inside her, pushing at her mind. Claire could feel the other soul inside her, the real Claire, screaming, and soon she was screaming, too, both of them finally connecting in a dance of pain and anguish as the spirit pushed deeper.

Chapter 52

The light of a new day shone down on the ruined house, illuminating the cracked foundation and shattered frame that had once provided someone a home. Though it was no longer raining, the morning air still hung heavy with moisture and not for the first time Gabe shivered despite no longer being alive.

"Come on," Snow said, his eyes meeting Gabe's. "We've got to go after them. Maybe I can run those two off the road, at least delay them a little."

A loud crack echoed through the neighborhood, like a cannon firing. Snow bucked forward, a gaping hole appearing in his forehead as a bullet tore though, embedding itself into Gabe's shoulder. The detective slumped forward, collapsing into the former gatekeeper's arms. Blood rushed out of his ruined face, soaking both men in red.

"No!" Gabe screamed, already trying to heal Snow, but it was too late. The detective was already dead, and, after helping Connor to undo the damage he had done to Snow earlier, Gabe wasn't sure he had the strength to bring him back from the other side.

"Hello, Gabriel," said a voice, and he looked up to find a gray-haired man holding a cane in one hand and a smoking 10mm Glock handgun in the other. Something about him…

"Why?" Gabe cried out, still holding Snow in his arms. "Who are you?"

"You don't recognize me?"

Gabe stared at him. The set of his eyes, his nose, looked familiar, and then it hit him. "Johnny Bethel?"

"The one and only," said the man, giving Gabe a half bow. "Though I go by Jack these days. You might even know me as Mr. Lazarus, if you've talked to Mr. Kingfisher and Mr. Quarry."

"What are you doing here? And why for the love of Jesus did you kill Pete?"

"So many questions, and I have all the answers," Bethel said. "Pity you're not going to live long enough to hear them."

"You think you're going to kill me, too, Johnny? Just in case you haven't noticed, I'm already dead."

"You think I don't know that?" Bethel snapped. "I'm the one who put you in the ground in the first place, as much as it pained me to do so. But it had to be done."

"What are you talking about? I died from lung cancer."

"Actually, you were going into remission. I'm a wealthy man, Gabriel, far more so than you could ever imagine. It wasn't difficult to hire someone to infiltrate your house and replace your pills, and then to bribe your doctor into saying that the cancer had come back. So, yes, I killed you, so that I could live."

"You killed me? But why?"

"I'm dying, Gabriel. Terminal bone cancer, and I'm just not ready to go yet. Nothing personal."

"Johnny, I didn't even know you were sick," said Gabe, his mind reeling. "I haven't seen you since you and your family moved out of Carthage when you were, what, fourteen? If I'd known, I'd have—"

"You'd what?" Bethel yelled. "Heal me? We both know you can't do that, and we both know why."

Gabe felt like someone punched him in the gut. "You know? How? You were never supposed to know."

"Again with the questions," Bethel said, smiling. "I've known since I was little. Mother was never discrete, and dear old Dad was blind. But I'm done with your questions. Once again, I'm going to kill you, and then I'm going to kill your precious son, and there's not a damned thing you can do about it."

"I can stop you," said Gabe, moving toward Bethel. "I might not be able to touch you with my abilities, but that doesn't mean I can't kick your ass. I'm not going to let you hurt Connor any more than you already have."

Bethel smiled, reached into his pocket, and pulled out a small syringe filled with liquid.

"What," Gabe said, laughing, "you're going to infect me with Small Pox?"

"Oh, nothing so crude. There is power here, old man. It cost me a small fortune and a trip to—"

Gabe punched him hard in the jaw, sending the younger man reeling backward. Johnny's legs flew out from under him and he landed flat on his back.

"Keep talking, you son of a bitch."

He reached down, picked Johnny up by his throat, and yanked him to his feet. He didn't want to kill him, couldn't stomach the thought. He'd already taken so much from the boy already—no, he reminded himself: Johnny Bethel was a man now, responsible for his own actions, and, regardless of the sins of the past, Gabe would do whatever he had to in order to keep his family safe.

Both hands tightened around Bethel's throat, and he began to squeeze. The younger man's arms flailed, and the syringe poked through Gabe's shirt and into his arm.

And then Gabe was falling backward, his arms and legs like jelly. He couldn't move, couldn't even talk. He landed in the grass, immobile, staring straight up into the morning sky.

"This serum temporarily paralyzes the undead," Bethel said, rubbing his jaw. "It disrupts the connection between the body and the soul, but just for two or three minutes. Not a lot of time, but it's more than enough for what I have to do.

"When I said earlier that I was going to kill you, I lied. You're right, I can't do that. But what I have in mind for you, Gabriel Locke, is far worse."

Gabe stared into the eyes of the man he'd wronged so many years ago. He tried to scream, but couldn't make a sound. Johnny disappeared from view, and for a moment Gabe thought he might be gone, but then he was there again, bending over Gabe, holding a satchel close to his chest.

"This," he said, lying the satchel in the grass beside Gabe, "cost me considerably less than the ingredients for that little concoction did, but using it on you is going to be a whole lot more fun."

Chapter 53

Jimmy appeared amidst a cacophony of chaos. Flashing lights and the blaring of sirens filled the early morning, people all around him shouting over the noise. Yellow police tape attached to orange road cones cordoned off the area. The neighborhood was filled with police cars and ambulance, cops and emergency medical technicians, all gathered around something in the grass. Jimmy was almost scared to see what it was, but nevertheless edged closer.

"What the fuck happened here?" said one, a female police officer who looked like she was about to lose it, her pretty blue eyes filling with tears.

"He and I were partners for years," said another, a short, overweight cop with graying hair, "and I was such a shit to him when he made detective."

"Edwin Grackle, with homicide," a tall, plump detective with red hair and a beard to match said to one of the EMTs. "I'm officially declaring this a crime scene."

"Look at this one," said one of the EMTs, a young man probably no older than thirty, ignoring Grackle. "Aside from the obvious cause of death, this body looks like it's been dead for weeks. What the hell is going on in this town?"

Walking through the female cop, ignoring the rage of emotions emanating within her, Jimmy stared down at the scene before him. Detective Pete Snow lay face-first in the wet, brown grass, a bloody hole the size of an egg in the back of his head.

Another body lay beside Pete's, presumably Claire's father, but Jimmy couldn't get a good look because at that moment the EMT spread a yellow tarp over it.

Shit. He'd come here for help, because Claire was losing the battle against the spirit. Both Pete and Gabriel were dead, which meant that things were about to get even uglier at the cemetery. Jimmy concentrated on the half-dollar in Claire's pocket, willing himself to her, and felt himself begin to vanish just as he noticed Pete standing outside the police tape.

He thought about the coin in Pete's pocket, and stopped fading. Hurrying over to Pete, he hoped he could learn something that might help Claire and Leesie.

"Pete," he said, "I'm so sorry, man. What happened?"

"Sir, this is a crime scene," mumbled Pete, eyes glassy, "and I need you to stay behind the yellow tape."

Pete didn't know he was dead.

"My name is Jimmy Cross, I helped you at Leesie's house. I'm sorry to have to tell you this, but you're dead."

"Dead?" Pete asked, craning his neck to peer over Jimmy's shoulder. "Hey, Danny, get a load of this guy. He thinks I'm dead. Danny? Hey, Danny, over here."

Jimmy turned to look at the overweight cop, who of course couldn't hear either of them.

"Hey, Pete," said Jimmy, "watch this." He walked through Danny, turned around, and stared at Pete.

"How…how did you do that?"

"I'm a ghost, just like you. I know you don't want to hear that, but we don't have time. Now, what happened to you?"

"Who did you say you were again?"

"I'm Jimmy Cross, damn it! Claire and Leesie are in danger."

"Elisabeth," Pete said, his eyes taking on focus for the first time, "is she okay?"

This was going nowhere fast. He hated to abandon Pete, but he needed to let Claire know that Kingfisher and Quarry were on their way.

"She will be," Jimmy finally answered, hoping it was true. "I'm sorry, buddy, but I have to go. I'll come back and explain things if I can."

"But where are you—"

Jimmy concentrated on Claire and the silver half-dollars she carried. The last thing he saw before fading from view was Pete's astonished face.

Chapter 54

Jimmy appeared back in the cemetery just as a black Town and Country Woodie barreled through the cemetery gates, the very same vehicle he'd seen parked outside Leesie's house last night.

The car barely rolled to a stop before Mr. Quarry leapt out of the passenger's side, a large piece of cardboard in his hands, running toward the center of the cemetery.

Quarry placed the cardboard on the ground, weighing it down with a rock in each corner. Something was sketched with black Sharpie onto the surface of the material, but Jimmy wasn't close enough to see what it was.

The dark cloud of energy had engulfed Claire, using a field of wind and lightning to keep the others at bay. Farris sat on the ground rubbing his head, no doubt struck down by the cloud, while Leesie and Sabrina tended to him. The girl who had last night commanded the spirit stood by herself beside a tree, staring at Quarry.

"Submit to me, Connor West," roared the spirit, *"this doesn't have to be painful."*

Mr. Kingfisher stepped out of the car and walked toward Claire and the spirit. He blew a silver cloud of dust from his hand into the spirit cloud, and the spirit screamed in agony as it separated from Claire, who dropped unconscious to the damp graveyard ground.

"You dare?" asked the spirit, hovering over Claire.

Kingfisher quickly backed away from the cloud, moving to Quarry's side.

"*Tusk-hi-ya-hen-inny,*" chanted Quarry, "*Tusk-hi-ya-hen-inny, Tusk-hi-ya-hen-inny.* By the power of three, I summon you."

"*You can no longer bind me,*" screamed the spirit in all of their minds. "*I will destroy you and feast on your soul.*"

"Not if I feast on yours first," said Kingfisher.

"*Tusk-hi-ya-hen-inny,*" Quarry repeated, "*Tusk-hi-ya-hen-inny, Tusk-hi-ya-hen-inny.* By the power of three, I summon you."

"*You can't do this!*"

"*Tusk-hi-ya-hen-inny,*" chanted Quarry for a third time, "*Tusk-hi-ya-hen-inny, Tusk-hi-ya-hen-inny.* By the power of three, I summon you."

The cloud slowly moved toward the flat piece of cardboard, drawn by Quarry's chants and whatever he'd inscribed upon its surface. Just as it was almost there, Kingfisher pulled something from his jacket pocket and stepped onto the cardboard.

"*I will rip you into tiny pieces and scatter them to the winds!*" yelled the cloud, growing darker, as it met Kingfisher on the makeshift altar. "*I will...I will...what are you doing?*"

Raising a drinking straw to his lips, Kingfisher tilted his head into the cloud and began to suck. The cloud fought against the current, but it was no use. More and more of the spirit disappeared through the plastic straw and into the giant's lungs, until finally it was gone.

Kingfisher's skin began to smoke and crackle with energy, almost as if the power he now contained was too much for him. He stood stock still for a second, swallowed, and the electricity and smoke dancing over his body began to dissipate and finally disappeared. The man was full to bursting, but apparently strong enough to contain and digest the cloud.

"And now, Mr. West, I believe we have some unfinished business," Kingfisher said, walking toward Claire.

Chapter 55

Claire groaned, rubbing her head. She felt like she'd been run over by a bus. Leesie was staring down at her. The sunlight framed Leesie's head like a halo, making her look almost angelic.

"What happened?" Claire asked. She had a splitting headache.

"That cloud almost killed you," Leesie answered, "but then the big guy showed up and ate it."

Everything came back to her in a rush. The Great Spirit, as it thought of itself, infiltrating first her body and then her mind, seeking to wrest control of the vessel away from her and the woman she shared her body with. It had pushed her down, suffocating her, and then she'd blacked out.

"And now, Mr. West, I believe we have some unfinished business," Kingfisher's booming voice intoned from the other side of the cemetery. "Stand up, please."

She was on her feet in a second, putting herself between the giant and Leesie. She surveyed the grounds. Sabrina and Farris were safe, as was Nadine Pahari, and there was Jimmy, just a few yards away from Mr. Quarry.

"Claire," said Jimmy, meeting her eyes. "Your dad and Pete…they're both dead. I'm so sorry."

Claire felt like someone had plunged a knife into her chest. "You killed my father? You killed Pete?"

"Pete's dead," Leesie said flatly.

The giant looked confused. "We left him and the policeman unharmed. This is between us."

"Liar!" Claire pulled out the Luger, aiming it at Kingfisher's face. She pulled the trigger. Nothing. Damn it all to hell. She thought this might work. One bullet left. She turned the gun, aimed it at Quarry, and once again pulled the trigger just as Kingfisher stepped between her and his partner.

The gun blazed, a huge pop echoing through the deserted graveyard as the bullet tore into Kingfisher's shoulder, spinning him around. He looked surprised, but then began to laugh.

"Oh, Mr. West, you are so full of surprises," he said, touching his wounded shoulder. "That's an antique, right? With original ammunition? What year?"

"1915," she answered automatically, wishing the gun had more bullets. She'd brought along a clip of modern ammunition, but doubted it would work.

"Well played. Unfortunately for you, it wasn't a fatal shot. Now come along and let me get you to Mr. Lazarus."

She had sensed the man was somehow able to affect technology, and that newer tech was more easily disrupted. The vintage car they drove, the ancient telephone in the house where Claire had been held prisoner, the old radio in the basement, it all began to add up. It wasn't that the giant necessarily preferred those things, but rather it was because, for whatever reason, newer technology failed around him.

Claire flung the gun at the giant's head, but he batted it away with a flick of his monstrous hand. He snaked his other hand out, faster even than she remembered him, and encircled her wrist with his fingers.

She punched Kingfisher in the chin with her free hand, instantly breaking half her knuckles. The blow didn't even phase him, and the spot she'd struck crackled and buzzed with energy. By absorbing the Great Spirit, the giant had become even stronger.

"Leave her alone, you bastard!" shouted Leesie, running toward them, but Quarry was quicker.

The small man tackled Leesie, took her to the ground, and held her struggling form face first against the cold, wet ground.

"We will take our leave of you now," Kingfisher said, looking to his partner as Quarry wrapped his arm around Leesie's throat, "and if any of you try to stop us, Mr. Quarry will snap her neck. We need Mr. West alive, but this one? Hardly."

"Stay back," Claire warned Sabrina and Farris, both of whom had already begun to move. "I can handle myself. Just take care of Leesie and Nadine. You'll leave Leesie alone if I go with you, right?"

"No!" yelled Leesie. "They killed Pete."

Claire moved her eyes around the cemetery, but Nadine had vanished. Good. That was one less potential victim to worry about. Hopefully, she'd run away to safety.

"Yes, we will. You have my word," said Kingfisher, his hands crackling with electricity as he squeezed her wrist tighter, almost to the point of snapping. "Now, come. We have work to do."

"I'm not going to lose you again," Sabrina said, tears coursing down her face. "I can't."

"You won't, I promise. Just trust me."

"Can't you leave them alone?" Jimmy pleaded, standing in front of the three ghosts Claire had raised earlier. "She already told you, she can't give you what you need."

Kingfisher laughed. "If I wasn't already so full, ghost, you'd be my desert. With your newfound abilities to move from place to place, I suspect you'd be quite piquant."

"Arthur," said Jimmy, turning to look at the ghost behind him, "Gertie, William, now!"

As one, all three of the ghosts, Claire's great grandfather, her great aunt, and a cousin that died nearly eighty years ago, rushed at Kingfisher, surprising him. He released Claire's wrist as he batted his hands through their bodies, but still they kept coming.

Claire was moving in an instant, running, kicking Quarry in the side of the head, watching as he fell away from Leesie and rolled onto his back. She yanked Leesie to her feet, pushed her toward Sabrina and Farris, and then kicked down at Quarry, catching him square in the forehead. His body went limp, and he passed out, or worse, tongue lolling out of the side of his mouth.

She turned just in time to see great-great-grandfather Arthur claw his way into Kingfisher's mouth, while Gertie flew up his nose. William, her cousin, followed Arthur, and quickly disappeared down the giant's throat.

The huge man stumbled backward, the electricity on his skin licking the sky. His eyes were wide, but he was smiling. He threw back his head and roared, a fiery orange aura now glowing over his entire body.

"You're just making me stronger," Kingfisher said, laughing. "Maybe I will have dessert, after all."

"Here it comes, you son of a bitch," screamed Jimmy, hurling himself through the air at Kingfisher.

The giant swallowed him in an instant, not even needing the straw.

"No!" Claire screamed, falling to her knees. And then she felt something buzzing in her pocket.

Startled, she looked down and saw a phantom hand sticking out from her leg. Jimmy! And beside her, Leesie had part of a foot protruding from her pocket, where she'd earlier stored the silver half-dollar Claire had given her.

Kingfisher's laughter turned to screams. Jimmy was appearing everywhere at once. With the corpses of her father and Pete, with Leesie and Claire, and, she imagined, at the Casey's General Store where she'd spent almost half the money she'd found three days ago, or with the clerk that had more than likely purchased the half-dollars and taken them home.

Kingfisher was shaking, violently convulsing as spirit after spirit spewed from his mouth. Claire saw her great-great-grandfather, a brown-haired toddler, an old woman, and more, shooting off in different directions, disappearing almost as soon as they left the giant's body.

The black cloud of energy that had been the Great Spirit was next, but somehow it looked different, not as dark, and almost translucent. Whatever had been holding it together was gone, and it was coming undone.

"I am...I am..." it said inside Claire's mind, before breaking apart into wisps of wind and fading into nothingness.

Jimmy came out last, his body whole again, racing from Kingfisher's throat faster than a bullet. He headed straight at Claire, and then through her. She turned around, but he wasn't there. Gone also was the hand that had been attached to the old Ben Franklin half-dollar she held in her pocket, as well as the ghostly leg that has earlier been attached to Leesie.

Kingfisher, looking gaunt, struggled to his feet, the aura gone but his skin still crackling with electricity. He convulsed one last time as a gigantic explosion of energy left his body, pushing Claire into Leesie, knocking them both to the ground. The energy Kingfisher had absorbed from the Great Spirit was gone, as well as the vitality he'd stolen from who knew how many ghosts, leaving him more vulnerable than he'd most likely been in a very long time.

Almost before she knew what she doing, Claire was on her feet. Running at full speed toward Kingfisher, she leapt into the air and dropkicked him in the chest. He stumbled backward, careening into a hundred-year-old headstone, crushing it beneath his bulk. She hoisted part of the stone into the air, bringing it crashing down just as he rolled out of the way.

Kingfisher lunged out at her with massive legs, but Claire was faster. Dancing away, she kicked the giant so hard in the face that for a moment she thought she'd broken her foot. He rolled backward, stunned, and then she was on him, raining down blows, feeling his nose crunch beneath the palm of her hand in an explosion of blood, and still she kept hitting.

Something sharp pierced her back, and she cried out. She turned away from the bloody and beaten giant to stare into the eyes of Nadine Pahari. The young girl, tears in her eyes, held a jagged piece of glass in her hand. She stabbed Claire again and again, first in the shoulder, then in the stomach. Nadine was still thrusting the bloody piece of glass into Claire when Leesie pulled her off.

Watch out for the girl, Grandpa Bill had told her.

Claire felt her eyes roll back in her head. She shuddered once, and then knew no more.

Chapter 56

Connor Locke was falling through darkness, his hands scrambling for some kind of purchase, for anything, but finding nothing. Jimmy sacrificed himself to save Connor, and it had worked, but now Connor was going to die. It couldn't end this way, it just couldn't. Jimmy's sacrifice had to mean something.

"What happened to us?" asked a female voice with the hint of a Southern accent.

He opened his eyes. Connor was lying in a bright yellow field of corn, the sun shining down from far overhead. It was the same field he'd visited earlier with his grandfather, but the old man was nowhere to be seen. Instead, a pretty young woman in a blue flower-print dress knelt over him, golden circles of hair falling down around her face. She had the most beautiful green eyes.

"Claire?" he asked, reaching up to touch her cheek. She flinched away, and he let his hand drop.

"Yeah, it's me. Are we…dead?"

"I don't know yet. I knew I'd wind up here eventually, but I never wanted you to go with me."

"Can't you heal us?"

"Doesn't work that way," he said, with a shrug. "We share your body now, and as long as I'm in it, it's partly mine, and I can't heal myself."

"Why are you staring at me like that?"

"I finally remembered where I know you from."

"What do you mean?"

"Florida."

"Huh?"

"Florida," he repeated, "about two months ago."

She stared back at him. "Oh!"

"I don't want to die, Claire."

"Neither do I. So let's not, okay?"

"I'm not sure we have any choice in the matter."

"Didn't your Grandpa Bill tell you that there's always a choice? I've been fighting you ever since you took over, and maybe I shouldn't have. By ourselves, we're goners. But maybe together…" Claire let the words trail off.

He reached out to touch her face again, and this time she didn't pull away. Instead, she kissed the palm of his hand.

"I remember Florida. I remember everything. Let's do this," she said.

"Are you sure?" asked Connor, not sure himself.

"We've got to try," said Claire, reaching down to press her lips against his. "Besides, you're awfully cute."

He was four years old, sitting on his Daddy's lap in the den, listening to the vinyl soundtrack from Disney's *Robin Hood* on an old record player.

She was four years old, on a playdate with her cousin Theresa. They were in a park, swinging, stretching their toes to touch the sky.

He was riding his bike through Carthage. His parents had just had another fight. He couldn't stand listening to them bicker anymore. Just get a divorce, already, and leave me alone.

She was in school, in English class, and Doug Matthews, who'd sat behind her all year, kept snapping her bra. She'd complained to Mr. Kennedy at least a dozen times, but the old bastard just told her to ignore it. Well, no more. She turned around and punched him in the nose.

He was in the graveyard, talking with Margaret and her friend, also a ghost, named Jacob.

She was in the kitchen, baking cookies with her mother.

He was driving through the rain, his dishonorable discharge lying crumpled in the seat beside him.

She was graduating college, her parents and Mel proudly sitting in the first row.

He was sitting in a dingy apartment, drunk, wishing Sabrina would stop calling him.

She was getting married, her best friend Elisabeth her maid of honor. She wasn't sure about Jeff, but she'd already said yes.

He was on top of a roof, a rifle in his hands, ready to make his first civilian kill. His hands were shaking.

She was in a small comic book store in Miami, looking for the latest *Go Girl* graphic novel, when a handsome man with red hair caught her attention. She slipped off her wedding ring as he approached. They made small talk, and she could tell he was interested. Yes, this was the one, and it was the right time of the month, too. She had butterflies in her stomach, and knew that she was finally going to do it. If her husband couldn't get her pregnant, then she and this stranger would make a beautiful baby together, marriage vows be damned.

He noticed her just as he was about to check out, then doubled back to pretend to leaf through more comics. She was gorgeous, and even better she had good taste in comics according to that issue of *Morning Glories* she had in her hand. She seemed interested in him, too.

He didn't have to set up the kill until tomorrow, so decided to strike up a conversation and see where it might lead.

They were eating dinner at the Captain's Tavern, an expensive sea-food restaurant on South Dixie that she'd always wanted to try but never had. They shared a delicious stone crab appetizer and killed half a bottle of *Marnier-Lapostolle Chateau de Sancerre* before dinner came. He had curried shrimp and scallops, while she had Dijon roasted snapper. The food was wonderful, but the company was even better.

They flirted over dinner, and Connor couldn't stop staring at her sparkling green eyes. She had an easy laugh and used it often, but there was also something sad about her, a fragility that broke his heart. It probably had something to do with the pale spot on her left hand where her wedding ring used to be. He could easily see himself falling for this girl, even though that would be insane. Hell, she might still be married. He didn't need that. After tonight, in all likelihood, they'd never see each other again. Besides, he had someone to kill tomorrow.

They were in her hotel room, and he was undressing her. His hands on her body, on her breasts, felt amazing, and he kissed her with a passion that she rarely if ever felt from Jeff anymore.

Jeff. She felt a sudden, intense guilt for betraying him, though if it wasn't for her husband, she wouldn't even be here. Jeff couldn't get her pregnant, and having a baby was the only way she could save their marriage. Besides, she needed this, needed to be with a man who, at least for one night, didn't hate her, didn't want to hurt her, and didn't want to punish her for something that wasn't even her fault.

The smell of her skin (jasmine?) as he trailed little kisses down her neck was intoxicating. She grabbed his face, pulled his mouth to hers, and they were kissing hungrily, lost in each other's embrace. They were making love, moving together, everything around them falling away, the condom he'd offered to use lying unopened on the nightstand.

He was inside her, she was enveloping him, losing themselves in each other. She no longer existed, and he ceased to exist as well, and it was only them as they melted together, one body with two minds, and they saw each other completely, warts and all, and knew each other as no two people had ever known each other before.

Two became one.

Chapter 57

Leesie stood in the early morning light of the Rosewood cemetery, staring down at the body of her best friend, the shell that had until recently held Connor Locke's soul. Hot tears clouded her eyes. Claire was dead, and, with her, Connor.

"Why?" she asked Nadine Pahari, who was now standing by the giant.

"They're all I have left now," said the thirteen-year-old girl, voice trembling, "I couldn't lose anyone else. I just couldn't."

"I'll kill you!" Sabrina screamed, launching herself at Nadine.

Kingfisher was between them in an instant, pushing Sabrina back into Farris, who caught her in his arms. She struggled against him until, finally, she collapsed, cursing and sobbing into his arms.

Leesie knelt beside Claire, cradling her head. She stared at Nadine with a white hot intensity, but said nothing. Her chest ached with loss, not only for Claire and Connor, but also for Pete. She'd loved Pete, even if she hadn't been *in* love with him, and he'd died because of his love for her, because he'd wanted to protect her.

"She saved you from those monsters, Nadine," said Farris. "How could you do this?"

"What's done is done," Mr. Quarry interjected, rubbing his bruised forehead. "Our employer won't be happy, but we'll deal with that."

Leesie stared down at Claire's body, and what she saw took her breath away. Claire was healing. The ragged lacerations left by the shard of glass were stitching themselves up, skin kneading together. The wounds quickly scabbed over, and then the scabs fell away, revealing fresh, pink skin beneath. Her chest, still just seconds before, began to rise and fall. She took one shallow breath and then another, deeper one, sucking in a mouthful of oxygen.

"Umm, guys?" Leesie said, eyes filling with tears. "Something's happening here."

Sabrina tore herself away from Farris, dropped to her knees beside Leesie. The girl gasped and took Leesie's hand, gripping it tight.

Claire opened her eyes.

Chapter 58

Claire pushed herself up from the ground, but she wasn't Claire any more, nor was she Connor. She was…something different, someone different. She wasn't either one of them, she was both, but she was also something more, something better. Just a few moments ago, she lay dying, but now she felt more alive than ever. Her skin was vibrating, her senses fully awake for possibly the first time in her life. In both her lives.

"Connor?" asked Sabrina, a few steps from her.

"I'm still here, baby sister, but I'm also Claire now," Claire said. "We needed to accept each other in order to heal, to break the limitations that being the gateway placed upon us. We needed to become one person, one mind, and so we did."

Kingfisher stared at her, his mouth hanging open. She'd never seen the man confused or unsure before, and she almost laughed. Then her eyes moved to Nadine Pahari, the girl that almost killed her but had instead set her free. Tears ran freely down her cheeks.

She wanted to hug the girl, to tell Nadine that she forgave her, but instead walked over to Kingfisher, touched his ruined face and shoulder, and healed him in an instant.

"Mr. Kingfisher," she said, staring into his eyes, "you're free to go, you and your partner, but if I ever see either of you again, I'll kill you."

"It's partners, now," Kingfisher said, taking Nadine's hand. "And thank you, but I'm afraid we can't do that just yet. There's still the small matter of our employer, and what he paid us to do."

A silver BMW with a huge dent in the bumper pulled up outside the cemetery, and Claire knew in an instant that was the car that had hit her outside Nadine's house. A gray-haired man holding a satchel got out of the car. He walked with a cane, limping toward them. Something about him looked familiar. She hadn't seen the driver of the car that killed her, so it had to be from somewhere else, but from which of her lives she didn't have a clue.

"Mr. Kingfisher, kill Connor's sister, and then Connor," shouted the man. "Go on, do it. Do it now."

Kingfisher turned to the approaching figure. "Killing Connor West was never part of our arrangement, nor was murdering his sister."

"Mr. Lazarus, I'm beginning to think that you haven't been entirely honest with us regarding your intentions," said Quarry.

"Do what I say, goddammit. I'll pay you double what we agreed upon. No, triple."

"Johnny?" Claire asked, finally recognizing her childhood friend. "Johnny Bethel?"

Bethel ignored her, instead focusing his attention on the giant. "If you don't do what I say, Kingfisher, so help me…"

"Johnny?" asked Claire again, reaching out to take his wrist. "You're Mr. Lazarus? Why?"

Claire's mind was reeling. This didn't make any sense. She hadn't seen Johnny in over fifteen years, and, as far as she knew, he had no reason to want her dead.

"So, you're the bitch that saved Connor's soul," Bethel said, shrugging his arm away from Claire as he turned to face her. "It shouldn't have happened the way it did, you know. I should have gotten your abilities when you died. The Voices promised."

Voices? "What're you talking about?"

"I killed you. I'd planned to anyway, of course, but you escaped my employees just as I was pulling up, and I saw a perfect opportunity. It should have worked."

"What should have worked?"

"I killed Gabriel—twice!—for your powers," he said, as if he hadn't heard Claire's words, "and I deserved them, but instead—"

"You killed my father?" Claire interrupted.

"*Our* father, you dolt," said Bethel.

He sat down his satchel and began to unlatch it.

"You're…my brother? How?"

"I was one of Gabe's little secrets. He couldn't keep his dick in his pants. My mother was pregnant with me while yours was pregnant with you. You were born two weeks premature, a week before me. It's your fault that I'm dying from bone cancer. Your fault!" He pulled up his right pants leg to reveal a prosthetic. "I lost my leg because of you, and I'll be damned if I'm going to die because of you."

Claire's mind was reeling. She had indeed been born first, and, if Johnny was telling the truth, he would have been the gateway had she not been a preemie.

"I couldn't heal myself, and neither could Gabriel," she said quietly. "Blood can't heal blood, at least that's the way it's always been. Surely you know that. If you were the gateway, you'd still be dying."

"I do know that, but once I have your magic, I can trade it for immortality."

What was he talking about?

Bethel reached into the satchel and pulled something out. For a moment Claire just saw blood and hair and didn't understand what it was, and then it hit her. It was a human head.

It was Gabriel Locke's head.

Her father.

Gabriel's lips moved, but nothing came out.

Sabrina screamed.

"Johnny," Claire whispered, "what did you do?"

"I couldn't kill him," said Bethel, holding the head aloft by its gray, scraggly hair, "so I did the next best thing."

Claire hit him in the stomach with a lightning fast spin kick, sending him tumbling to the ground. The head flew from his hand, rolling across the cemetery and through the cold, wet grass before finally coming to a stop against an old gravestone.

"No!" Bethel yelled, holding his stomach. "I need that."

"What did you do to my father?"

"I need it, to draw your abilities to me after you and your sister are dead. They said it would work."

He flipped open the satchel, revealing a bloody hacksaw and a pistol. Bethel withdrew the pistol, a 10 mm Glock, levelling it at Sabrina, pulling the trigger.

"No!" Claire yelled, throwing herself between the bullet and Sabrina.

The bullet struck her in the chest, but she healed herself and expunged the projectile before she even hit the ground. It still hurt, though, hurt like a son of a bitch, and she grimaced as she climbed up from where she'd fallen.

"How?" Bethel asked, eyes wide.

Kingfisher, who had stood silently throughout most of their confrontation, reached out and took the gun from Bethel's trembling hand.

"You lied to us, Mr. Bethel. Our contract is now null and void, and you have forfeited your payment. Moreover, if Mr. West doesn't kill you, I think that we might."

"I don't need you or anyone else," spat Bethel, whirling on Kingfisher, "as long as I have them."

Claire followed Bethel's eyes to the back of the cemetery, where there stood a group of three dark, nearly black creatures, each at least ten feet tall and wearing tattered shrouds. If they'd been there before she'd have seen them, unless they had the ability to hide from her.

"It's too late," said one of the amorphous beings, blinking into and out of existence. "The gateway is once again secure."

"More secure than ever," added the next.

"Too late? What do you mean too late? I killed people for you. I poisoned and murdered my own father for you!"

"There was a window," said the third, "but you waited too long. The gateway cannot be closed now."

"We told you to work quickly," said the first again, "but you didn't listen."

"I listened! I did everything you asked. I even brought the head. Wait! Don't go. Stay!" Bethel was sobbing now, grasping at the air in front of him. "Please. We can still do this. Please!"

The shades faded out of existence, and Bethel crumpled to the ground, defeated.

Sabrina ran up, threw her arms around Claire, and they stayed that way, embracing, for a long time.

"Mr. West," Kingfisher finally said, holding Bethel by the shoulder. "Do you claim this one, or should we?"

"It's Locke, now. Claire Locke. But hold on," she said, pulling away from Sabrina. "This'll only take a second."

She took Johnny Bethel's face in her hands, closing her eyes. Concentrating, sensing the cancer throughout his body, she eradicated it in an instant. The sickness had spread to his brain, so maybe he wasn't completely responsible for his actions, but that didn't excuse him from all he had done.

Opening her eyes, she released her brother and took a step back.

"Thank you," Bethel said, tears rolling down his cheeks.

"He's all yours," she said to Kingfisher and Quarry, turning away from the man who had once, long ago, been her best friend, but who had also murdered her father and sought to destroy her.

Taking Leesie and Sabrina by the hands, with Farris trailing behind, Claire turned and walked away, leading their little group out of the cemetery. She didn't look back.

Bethel screamed once, and then fell silent.

It was over.

Chapter 59

It had been almost a week since the events in the cemetery, and Claire was still having nightmares. Had she done the right thing, healing Johnny only to let Kingfisher kill him? She wasn't sure she'd ever truly know the answer to that question, but it felt like poetic justice at the time.

"Tell her that none of this is her fault," said Pete's ghost, standing near the debris of the ruined house on Thirteenth Street, "and that I'll always love her."

"She already knows both of those things, Pete, but I'll tell her."

Through Leesie, Claire had already made arrangements to buy the plot of land where Pete now stood. It would be months before all the legal issues were worked out, but a few bribes here and there assured them that the property would soon be theirs. They'd build a nice house here, one that Sabrina and Farris, or Mel, could use whenever they were in town, and where Pete and her dad would be free to roam.

The thought of Gabe made her smile. They'd buried his head here, beneath one of the maple trees that surrounded the remains of the house, and then she'd separated his spirit from what was left of his flesh. Gabe and Pete could keep each other company, at least until one or the other decided to let go and move on to whatever came next.

"So what did he say?" asked Leesie, standing beside Claire.

Claire repeated Pete's message word for word.

"Tell him I love him, too, and that I miss him so much."

She reminded Leesie that her ex-husband could hear her and that she could speak to him directly, even if she couldn't hear his responses. It took someone a while to get used to the rules of spirit communication, but she was confident that Leesie would soon catch on.

Gabe phased into view, along with the phantom dog they'd found wandering the property last night. Her father rubbed the coon dog behind the ears, and Claire wondered for not the first time how ghosts could touch.

"He told me his name is Butchie," Gabe said, with an easy smile. "He sure is a good dog."

Claire almost asked how Butchie could tell anyone anything, but let it go. Perhaps some things should remain a mystery. In life, her father had been allergic to dogs, but in death he really seemed to have taken a liking to this one. She was happy for both of them.

Butchie licked Claire's fingers, but of course she couldn't feel anything. She called him a good boy, and pretended to ruffle his fur. That seemed to satisfy him, and he took off running after a bird he could never catch.

Earlier today, courtesy of Claire's Prius, Sabrina and Farris finally drove back to Carthage. The plan was to tell everyone that Susie Parker, the girl responsible for the plot to murder Farris, had killed Brian Blackford and threatened to do the same to them if they said anything, and, in fear for their lives, they'd run away. She'd transferred the title of the Prius to Farris, payment for the car he'd lost on their mad dash to Rogers. He seemed happy with the trade.

Farris was surprised but relieved when Gabe finally admitted that the teenager wasn't a zombie, after all. He'd healed him in plenty of time. Gabe lied because they needed his car, and wasn't sure if Farris would help if he thought he could easily go back to his life pre-Susie Parker. The way Farris looked at Sabrina, however, and hung on her every word, made Claire think that he probably wasn't all that upset over the deception.

Claire put her hand on her stomach, marveling at the life growing inside of her. He or she had been through so much already, had even been dead at one point. She still hadn't figured that one out, but decided that when she'd merged and learned to heal herself that she'd somehow healed the baby as well. It was as good a theory as any.

Pete and Leesie exchanged a few more words through Claire, Claire said goodbye to her father and Butchie, and then it was time to go.

Dying, it turned out, had been the best thing that had ever happened to her, in either of her lives. Looking forward to cuddling with Corduroy and then falling asleep next to the woman she loved, Claire took Leesie's hand and whispered, "Let's go home."

Epilogue

Ten months later

They walked together through Graceland cemetery in Chicago, Leesie using a map of the extensive grounds to navigate while Claire pushed the baby's stroller. It was hard to believe that little Jimmy was already three months old, and she thanked whoever might be listening that he had been born alive and healthy.

"Almost there," Leesie said, "at least if I'm reading this correctly."

"No rush," said Claire, glancing at her Mickey Mouse watch. "We're still a little early."

The grounds were beautiful, and Claire could easily have spent all day walking around and studying the architecture and the landscaping, something she hadn't really enjoyed in either of her previous lives. It was a little hard to accept sometimes, but she really was a different person now. She was still Connor, and still Claire, but she was also something more than just the sum of her parts. She was a whole new person.

Some things, however, hadn't changed one bit. She was still deeply in love with Leesie, and, thank the stars above, Leesie returned those feelings, in spades. They'd gotten married in Massachusetts, just two months before the baby was born, and honeymooned in Martha's Vineyard. It had been the best week of Claire's life, and she looked forward to going back again sometime soon.

Almost before they realized it, they'd reached the grave of James Montgomery Cross. The small grave marker declared him to have been a beloved father and husband, and Claire had no doubt it was true.

Jimmy's wife, Dorothy Janine Cross, died eleven years ago, and had been laid to rest beside him. She'd never remarried, and had apparently found peace with her life and moved on, for her ghost was nowhere to be found.

Two near-identical African-American women who looked to be in their early fifties sat on a small, iron bench, waiting for them. Sheila Pringle and Sara Cross, Jimmy's twin daughters. Both were dressed differently and one's hair was short while the other's was long, but other than that Claire would have a hard time telling them apart.

"Mrs. Pringle and Ms. Cross," Claire greeted them, "I'm Claire Locke, and this is my wife Elisabeth Greenwald."

"It's so nice to finally meet you," said the short haired woman, giving Claire a quick hug. "I'm Sara, and this is my sister Sheila."

Claire tracked them down through the Internet a few weeks after Jimmy's sacrifice, and they'd spoken on the phone several times since then. She'd made contact with Sara first, making up a story about her grandfather having been friends with Jimmy, but the woman didn't buy it and had almost hung up on her before Claire came clean.

She didn't tell Sara the whole story, but admitted she was blessed with the ability to see ghosts and that Jimmy had directed her to dig up the half-dollars and return them to his daughters. They'd become quick friends after that, and Claire had enjoyed hearing stories about the twin's lives growing up.

Claire now possessed all twenty-six half-dollars the twins had originally buried in the park, after returning to Casey's General Store and paying the clerk more than double their worth. She'd even replaced the Mason jar with a near-identical one she'd found on eBay. The hardest part had been retrieving the two that her father and Pete had on them when they were murdered, but Pete's still-active key code for the police station evidence locker and Claire's stealth had solved that problem.

Claire bent over and retrieved a red gift bag from the storage space beneath Jimmy's stroller. "This is for you," she said, handing the bag to Sara.

With a smile on her face, Sara reached into the gift bag and pulled out the Mason jar filled with half-dollars. "Thank you so much. Did you know there were originally twenty-eight half-dollars? I mean, before we buried them."

That was news to her.

"Didn't you ever wonder why we believed you?" Sheila asked.

"Yes, actually, more than once," Claire admitted.

"Our dad had two half-dollars in his pocket the day he died. When we buried the half-dollars," Sara said, "we each kept one of the ones he'd had with him. As a keepsake or something, I don't know. Last October, I was awakened early in the morning by the strangest noise. Took me a moment to realize it was coming from my nightstand. That's where I kept the half-dollar, you see, in a wooden box along with some other things that are important to me. I opened the box, and the half-dollar was literally vibrating."

"I keep mine in a cloth pouch, in my dresser," said Sheila, "and the same thing happened to me. So I opened up the pouch and took out the coin, and the moment I touched it…Daddy was there with me, just for an instant."

Sara unscrewed the Mason jar, took out a Ben Franklin half-dollar, and kissed it.

"He was there with us both, at the same time, in two different places," Sara said, her voice catching. "When I touched the half-dollar I felt his spirit, and I heard him whisper that he loved me. Can you believe it?"

Claire could believe it. Jimmy had loved his daughters with all his heart, and he'd found a part of himself there, with them, when he'd split himself into parts to stop Mr. Kingfisher. Of course he would tell his daughters that he loved them one last time. Claire wiped her eyes with the back of her hand.

Little Jimmy started crying just then, and Leesie pulled him out of his stroller to hold him. He wriggled in her arms, reaching toward Sara.

"What a beautiful baby," Sheila said, "and it touches us so much that you named him after Dad."

Leesie bounced Jimmy on her shoulder, but he wouldn't stop crying. Claire had breastfed him in the rental car on the way to Graceland, so he wasn't hungry.

"Can I try?" asked Sara, reaching out to take Jimmy.

The baby stopped complaining the moment Sara took him into her arms, staring in fascination at the silver coin that the daughter of the man he was named after held in her hand. He reached out for the coin, and Sara let him touch it.

Gooseflesh prickled the back of Claire's neck as she thought back to the final showdown in the cemetery all those months ago, and Jimmy flying through her right before he vanished.

She smiled.

Coming fall of 2015…

Sundown Rising & Other Stories

Joe DeRouen's upcoming short story and novella collection.

Please turn the page for a sneak preview of the Merryland novella from the collection

Coming fall 2015

Zara Boone was asleep when she got the call. She had been suffering from a nasty cold for the last three days and finally decided to call in sick that Friday morning, to hopefully give her body time to recuperate so she could enjoy the weekend with her husband and daughter.

"I understand," she sniffed into the telephone, her nose stopped up and tears starting to blind her deep green eyes. "She just seemed so healthy, so full of life, the last time I saw her."

Zara realized guiltily that had been almost a year ago. She'd been too busy with her family and job in Arkansas to visit the woman who had taken her in when both her parents had died in a car crash, the woman who had nurtured and raised her from just before the age of six.

"I'm sorry for your loss, ma'am," the deep voice that had identified itself as belonging to Hancock County Sheriff Lyle Brady said for the third time in as many minutes.

Lucille Brennan, her 75-year-old grandmother, had apparently died in her sleep. One of her neighbors found her when she missed a breakfast date and immediately called 911, but the paramedics had been unable to revive her. She was pronounced dead at 8:15 this morning.

"Thank you, Sheriff," she heard herself say, almost by rote. "I'll catch a flight out as soon as I can, and hopefully be there tonight or tomorrow morning."

"The body... your grandmother's body, I mean, will be held at Wiseman's Funeral Home on Locust Street in Carthage. If you can tell me where you'll be staying, I can give you directions."

"I grew up in Carthage. I know where it is."

She knew exactly where it was. The Wiseman's had handled her parents' funeral when she was just a little girl. And the big funeral home, two stories' worth, was just down the street from where her grandmother lived. At least she wouldn't have far to travel.

"Well, Miss Boone, if you have any questions, please don't hesitate to give me a call." He rattled off a number that Zara dutifully copied down. "And, again, I'm so sorry for your loss."

"Have a nice day," she said, folding the paper and tucking it into her purse.

She hung up, staring at the telephone. Have a nice day? Had she really just said that? She shook her head. He had just called to tell her that her grandmother had died, why the hell should she care what kind of day he had?

Zara's grandmother had drilled into her the need to be polite even in the face of tragedy, and she supposed such niceties would always stick with her. Like so many of the woman's lessons, and her stories.

Oh, the stories she had told! Stories about her life growing up in Ireland, about coming to America with her family when she was just thirteen, tales about her two husbands, but mostly stories about a fantasy land called Merryland.

Merryland, her grandmother had said, wasn't always merry, but even when troubles came to the fantastical place, everything always turned out happy in the end.

The stories began the night of Zachary and Sara Boone's death. Grandma Lucy had held her all night, doing her best to comfort her crying, weaving tall tales about majestic knights and great wizards in this wonderful, terrible, beautiful land called Merryland.

Grandma Lucy had promised her that, one day, when she was older and stronger and ready to go on an adventure, she would show her the secret path to Merryland, and they would go together, but of course that day never came. By the time she was twelve or thirteen she had grown tired of the tales, and eventually her grandmother had stopped sharing them.

It had been years since they spoke of Merryland, and she had no idea why she was even thinking about it now. It was part of her past, she supposed, part of the rich tapestry of memories she shared with Grandma Lucy, and would never really go away. She'd give anything to sit on her grandmother's lap one last time and lose herself in those wonderful stories of magic and bravery.

Zara tied her long brown hair into a pony tail and then, with no little effort, pushed herself up from the couch. Her stomach was grumbling, and she had the start of a headache tickling the edges of her forehead. She desperately needed breakfast, hopefully something that would help clear her sinuses.

She moved with a sigh from the living room couch where she'd been napping toward the kitchen. This weekend was supposed to be special. Tomorrow was Tildie's fifth birthday, and she and Matt had a fun weekend lined up for her, starting with a Build-a-Bear birthday party for Tildie and two of her friends, and then a trip to the American Girl store, finally ending with a party at home.

She absolutely hated to be apart from her daughter on her birthday, but hated even more the thought of dragging her along to Carthage to prepare for her great-grandmother's funeral. She knew — or at least hoped — that Matt would understand, but five-year-olds weren't nearly as understanding as twenty-nine-year-old medical sales reps.

Speak of the devil, she thought, as her cell phone rang. It was Matt, calling from his office phone. She leaned against the fridge and answered the phone.

For more news about Sundown Rising and Other Stories, and Joe's other novels, including the Small Things trilogy, be sure to visit www.JoeDeRouen.com.

You can also connect with Joe on Facebook at www.facebook.com/jderouenwriter or Twitter via @jderouen